Praise for Jaine Fenn:

'A beautifully paced quest, a novel that doles out its revelations slowly yet confidently. The characters are well-drawn and believable. There's more than enough here to suggest that British SF has a major new talent in its midst'   *SFX*

'The mutually dependent relationship between Kerin and the stranger is sensitively drawn, as is the depiction of a society kept in ignorance by a religious elite'   *Guardian*

'A potential star in the making'   *SF Crowsnest*

'[Consorts of Heaven] ... Takes the best of SF and blends it with a touch of fantasy'   *Falcata Times*

'I look forward very much to journeying once again into Fenn's universe'   *Bookgeeks*

GUARDIANS
OF PARADISE

JAINE FENN

The right of Jaine Fenn to be identified as the author
of this work has been asserted by her in accordance with
the Copyright, Designs and Patents Act 1988.

First published in Great Britain in 2010 by
Gollancz
An imprint of the Orion Publishing Group
Orion House, 5 Upper St Martin's Lane, London WC2H 9EA
An Hachette UK Company

This edition published in Great Britain in 2011 by Gollancz

1 3 5 7 9 10 8 6 4 2

A CIP catalogue record for this book
is available from the British Library

ISBN 978 0 575 08327 1

Typeset by Deltatype Ltd, Birkenhead, Merseyside

Printed in Great Britain by
CPI Mackays, Chatham, Kent

The Orion Publishing Group's policy is to use papers
that are natural, renewable and recyclable products and
made from wood grown in sustainable forests. The logging
and manufacturing processes are expected to conform to
the environmental regulations of the country of origin.

www.jainefenn.com
www.orionbooks.co.uk

James: this one's for you. For past and future friendship and for years of technical advice, some of which I've even listened to.

'Strike dear mistress
And cure his heart'

'Venus in Furs', The Velvet Underground

'We are no monsters, we're moral people
And yet we have the strength to do this
This is the splendour of our achievement
Call in the airstrike with a poison kiss'

'Nemesis', Shriekback

PROLOGUE:
NERVES SHEATHED IN SILVER

Above, golden sunlight sparkles off an azure sea. Down here, white light shines on clean, cold surfaces. The green-and-orange robes of the woman walking between the sealed tanks, monitoring stations and interface consoles are a splash of colour in the otherwise antiseptic lab. The hem of her robe has a subtle batik pattern on it picked out in white and midnight blue: a breaking wave against a starfield.

The same design appears as a logo on the breast pocket of the older man who walks beside her, though he's dressed in a white shirt and grey slacks. His skin is several shades lighter than hers, and has an unhealthy pallor due in part to spending too much time under artificial light. She has listened to what he has to say, and now she responds, 'So this last one is definitely viable?'

He nods. 'The transference is almost complete; I'll be starting the first test runs today. We have a ninety-seven-point-five per cent chance of a completely successful encoding.'

'Good. That'll give us twenty-eight from the original thirty-five.' She smiles mirthlessly. 'Five fewer than last time; good job it's a seller's market.'

'Will the buyers want to come down here? Last time, one of them did.' He shivers at the memory, decades-old but still enough to thrill and chill him in equal parts.

'So Mother said. Frankly, I have no idea. It's not like we can tell them what to do.'

'How about the new batch? Any word yet?'

'No.' Her reply doesn't invite further conversation and he draws back, expecting her to leave. Then she says, 'I've seen your latest test results.'

'Which tests?' he asks warily.

'Yours. Not the project's.'

'Oh.'

'You should have told me yourself.'

'Yes, I ... I probably should.'

'I'm sorry,' she says, and makes to put a hand out to him, withdrawing it when he flinches away.

'I need to get on,' he says, not looking at her. 'If that's all right.'

'Of course.' She walks back towards the elevator, leaving him alone in the lab.

He returns to his workstation, the only one active. He spreads his hands over the console's tactile interfaces, then blinks to coordinate his optical displays with the tank readouts. He feels a momentary disorientation as his consciousness enters a limited unity with the machinery and what is held within – a state few human minds can achieve. The sensation passes and his view of the featureless black oblong in its nest of wires and cables is overlaid with a familiar pattern in glowing silver: a central column emerging from a rough-edged oval, and a tracery of fine lines branching out from the column. The dark patches in the cortex are in the usual areas: memory, sensation, emotion, all functions now surplus to requirements.

His hands dance over the controls, programming the test. After forty years' experience he can almost do this in his sleep, but he still barely catches a nutrient-feed imbalance which, left unchecked, could disrupt the final transition.

The irony that his own brain is degenerating beyond science's ability to heal is not lost on him. He is determined to complete this last encoding before he succumbs, just as he has said he would.

Finally the parameters for the current test are set. He applies the stimulus slowly, with an instinctive feel for how much is required when. How much *what*, he is careful not to consider. Not only because this is where science shades into more arcane disciplines, but because then he would have to think about the reactions he is producing in human terms, and that would mean using words like *distress* and *pain*.

He makes the final adjustments.

The tank shimmers, as though straining at the edge of reality, then flickers out of existence. Almost before his dual sight registers the disappearance, the tank is back in the real world. By the time he's dealt with the brief backwash of nausea, his overlays are back online too.

He calls up the results. The test was flawless. He was being pessimistic when he said ninety-seven-plus per cent: it will be more like ninety-nine-plus.

He smiles, though with his own mortality catching up on him, he finds himself briefly thinking about what he's doing, and who he is doing it to.

As he has hundreds of times before, he reminds himself to take the long view. In effect, they are already dead before they arrive at his lab.

And what he does here, though unseen and uncelebrated, is essential to the human race. It is vital work.

Holy work.

CHAPTER ONE

Taro was watching clouds. He loved the way they shifted and evolved, like they were alive, and he still couldn't get over the sheer scale of these great floating masses of water vapour.

Nual had suggested, with a rare burst of dry humour, that it was a good job he liked clouds, given that Khathryn's sky was usually covered in them. Apparently, sunny days were few and far between here. That was fine with Taro. He'd spent all his life, up to a couple of weeks ago, in an artificial environment less than twenty klicks across. He was still getting used to the idea of an infinite universe. Looking up into an empty sky made his balls twitch.

Right now, standing in scrubby grass on the cliff-top near the house that had belonged to Nual's one-time guardian, he was giving the clouds more attention than they deserved. He could've stayed inside: it was cold and damp out here, and Nual hadn't asked him to follow her. But she hadn't forbidden him either, and he wanted to be there for her if she needed him.

Even though he knew this was a moment he couldn't share, his eyes kept straying to the lone figure at the edge of the cliff. Nual had been standing there for a while now, looking out over the heaving grey sea, her body held rigid, her mind locked tight. When she raised her arms, Taro's resolve not to intrude on her grief wavered. He watched as she opened the urn, though he was too far away to see the ashes fly off on the wind.

He'd met Elarn Reen briefly, when they'd both been scared and on the run. He'd tried to help her. He'd failed.

Nual had once told him that Elarn was the last person she'd trusted, seven years before she met – and chose to trust – Taro himself. Given the unpleasant end Medame Reen had come to, that wasn't a very reassuring thought. It was one of many worries Taro didn't allow himself to dwell on. Over the last few weeks he'd experienced changes he could never have imagined back in Khesh City: big, scary changes. At least he no longer had to worry about where the next meal was coming from, and, as far as he knew, no one wanted him dead – both major improvements on the recent past.

At the cliff edge Nual lowered her arms, then turned and started back towards the house. Taro went to meet her, but when she looked up and saw him, the surprise on her face jolted him; she must have been so wrapped up in her mourning that she hadn't even sensed him. Tears glistened on her cheeks. For a moment he felt an odd mental jostling, his desire to get close warring with her half-apologetic exclusion. Though the sensation was familiar, this time she'd have to be way more forceful if she wanted him to back off. He half expected she would, but she stopped and waited, letting him come up and put his arms around her. He pulled her to his chest, her head tucking in under his chin.

Taro felt a surge of emotions: sorrow for her pain, helplessness at not being able to do more to help her, joy that she'd let him in this far, and that familiar dash of lust.

They stood there in silence while the mist turned to rain. Taro felt the heavy drops hit his head, soaking his hair, dripping off the ends and under the collar of his coat. He didn't care. He'd stay there until he drowned if she needed him to.

Nual pulled back, but kept hold of his hand as they walked back to the sprawling house perched on the cliff-top. The nearest door opened for them as they approached, and lights came on in the glass-roofed room full of plants – most of them dead or dying – that Nual had called the conservatory.

The house still amazed him: so many rooms, so much *stuff*, all for one person. And now, even more amazingly, it belonged to Nual. The old cove she'd visited when they'd first arrived on

Khathryn had told Nual that Elarn Reen had never changed her will – so everything that had been hers was now Nual's. Taro was still hazy on exactly what the relationship between the two women had been. He'd asked Nual, and she'd said Elarn had been a lonely person who'd projected her needs onto those around her. That hadn't exactly cleared things up.

They walked from the conservatory into the lushly carpeted hall that ran through the centre of the house to find the wallscreen at the far end flashing and chiming to itself. Taro felt a tinge of fear as Nual went over to read the display.

'It's all right,' she said. 'It's just the autopilot on the aircar.'

'Right.' Taro exhaled. 'What's it saying?' Dealing with machines was one of many new skills Nual was teaching him.

'Apparently the rental agreement will be invalidated if we attempt to fly after dark in this weather,' said Nual. 'I suspect the autopilot won't even let us take off. And neither of us actually knows how to fly an aircar manually.'

'Does that mean we're staying here tonight after all?' Nothing would make him happier than the two of them spending some time here alone, but the Sidhe knew about Nual and Elarn, and once they realised she'd left Vellern this would be one of the first places they'd look for their renegade. Although their enemies' reach was limited by their need for secrecy, Nual was paranoid enough that she hadn't linked her personal coms device into the local network – and the com wasn't even registered in a name the Sidhe knew. Now she'd laid Elarn Reen to rest, they'd be stupid to hang around here for long.

'We don't have much choice. We might as well make ourselves comfortable.'

Taro allowed himself to hope that her idea of getting comfortable might finally match up to his. Though their impressively believable IDs claimed they were brother and sister, and they'd had separate cabins on the starliners, that was just their cover, and Taro had noticed that the late Medame Reen's house had several large, comfortable-looking bedrooms.

But Nual actually meant they should get something to eat. She led him into a spotless kitchen full of wooden cupboards and shiny tech. Taro knew two ways to cook food: you put it in a pot on a fire-box, or you cut it up and put it inside the firebox. He didn't want to risk breaking or burning anything, so he sat at the central table and left Nual to it. Elarn must've changed her kitchen round after Nual left, and it took her a while to find stuff. She didn't like him watching her, so he stared at the rain streaming down the outside of the window. She didn't want to talk either, so he kept quiet.

The house had a room just for eating in, but the kitchen table was way big enough for the two of them. 'It's curried mince and noodles,' said Nual as they tucked into the steaming food. 'An odd combination, but there wasn't much choice.'

'Tastes great,' he said through a mouthful of noodles. And it did, especially compared to a lot of things he'd eaten. He remembered how Nual had bought him a meal when they'd first met, though back then he'd been in no position to appreciate it. Hard to believe that was only four weeks ago.

He stopped short of licking the plate, now he knew that wasn't acceptable behaviour in polite society. Nual ate her food more slowly, and left some noodles, which she offered to him. Taro was pretty full, but a lifetime of borderline starvation had left him with a lot of catching up to do. Once he'd finished, he thought about offering to clear up, though he was feeling a bit bloated.

Before he could say anything Nual leaned forward on her elbows, not quite looking at him. 'I'm sorry,' she said.

'Fer— For what?' He was trying hard to stop using Undertow patois; what was cool as fuck in Khesh City got him funny looks everywhere else. Even Nual had started to say 'yes' instead of 'aye' sometimes.

'For excluding you. Stopping you getting close – no, Taro, not just in that way. Since we arrived on Khathryn I've been project-ing misery, making myself unapproachable – forcing you away. I mustn't do that.'

'By forcing me away, d'you mean using your evil alien mind-powers on me?' He tried to make a joke of it, but it sounded feeble.

'Maybe I am,' said Nual miserably. 'I'm not sure. Half the time I don't even know I'm doing it.'

'If you can't help it, then it ain't your fault, right?' He wasn't scared of her. Perhaps he should be, but he wasn't.

'It's not that simple.'

''Course it is. So you're Sidhe, and you can fuck with people's heads. Most of the time you don't, 'cause you keep all that stuff bottled up. But with me ...' He paused. Now they were getting to the heart of it, sidling up to the conversation she'd been avoiding ever since they left Khesh. 'With me it's different, ain't it? 'Cause we've been ...' He searched for a way to describe the strange bond they shared.

Nual whispered, 'In unity. We've been in unity.'

'Aye— I mean, yeah. So it's all right. I know you won't screw with my head on purpose. But sometimes you can't help influencing me a bit, even when you don't know you're doing it. I don't mind. Really, I don't.'

'I know,' she whispered. Then she looked up, meeting his eyes. 'If I ever hurt you, I'll never forgive myself.'

Even as her words set off a warm glow in his chest, his hormones cut in and he found himself saying, 'Then let's go to bed! 'Cause it does hurt me, us both feeling like this but not doing anything about it!'

She looked away and said quietly, 'I won't sleep with you, because if I did, then I *would* hurt you. Or worse.'

He couldn't – *wouldn't* – believe that. 'Is that what happened with Elarn? Was her and you ... was it more than her just looking after you?'

Nual nodded. 'She found herself attracted to me, though such emotions went against her sexuality and her religious upbringing. I was young and scared and desperately lonely, so I responded. But before things went too far she realised what I was, and she threw me out. I was surprised she left her will unchanged; I imagine she had planned to alter it as soon as the right man came along. Poor Elarn: it says a lot about how lonely she was that that never happened.'

'But that was, what, seven years ago, weren't it? You was a lot younger.' Seventeen: the same age Taro was now, though he wasn't going to mention that. 'You got more control now.' He paused, then decided this wasn't the time for subtlety. 'And Medame Reen, she seemed nice enough, and we should be grateful she left you her stuff an' all, but you said it yourself: her and you, that was a mistake. She was hardly hot for it, was she? Now me, I know what I'm doing when it comes to the grind.'

Nual smiled. 'So you are saying that your previous profession and experience would make you more ... shall we say *resilient* to sex with a Sidhe?' She sounded amused, but Taro was deadly serious.

'Yeah, I am.' She wanted him; it didn't take scary mind-powers to work that out. He just needed to persuade her that she wouldn't end up sucking his brain out through his cock.

Nual took a sudden intense interest in the pattern of the stone floor. 'I have no way of knowing what would happen – how far I might end up going.'

'You mean you've never—? Oh! Shit, I didn't ... I mean, I assumed you'd ... But I s'pose you wouldn't've. Right.'

She managed to get her gaze up as far as Taro's hands, lying flat on the table. 'No, I haven't. I see you find that all but incomprehensible. And you may be right; my fears may be unjustified.'

Taro said gently, 'Then how 'bout we start with a kiss? And if my head falls off, we'll leave it at that.'

For a while she said nothing, then she looked at him and smiled. 'I could use some comfort at the moment,' she said, 'but just a kiss, for now.'

It was better than nothing. When she didn't move, Taro eased his chair back and walked round to her side of the table. Nual turned to him, but she stayed sitting, as though that would stop her getting carried away. Taro crouched in front of her. Being so tall, he could look her in the eyes; he still had no name for that colour: somewhere between violet and the darkness of space. She looked worried, almost shy, an expression he'd not seen on her before.

9

'We'll take it slow,' he said. He put a hand on her knee and leaned forward.

She began to bend towards him. He could feel the heat of her. He closed his eyes.

'Can you hear something?' she whispered.

All he could hear was the sound of the rain and his thudding heart ... or was that a faint, insistent chime? 'Don't think so,' he murmured.

More loudly, Nual said, 'It's the alarm on the house com.'

Taro scooted out of the way as she stood up. If that was the air-car saying the storm was blowing over and it would be happy to take them back to Kendall's Wharf now, then he'd find something heavy and blunt and seriously *invalidate the rental* on the fucking thing.

He followed Nual out into the hall. 'What's up? More bad weather?'

Nual looked up from the screen. 'No, visitors.'

'Who?' Taro wiped suddenly sweaty palms on his thighs. 'Does it say?'

'We're picking them up because of Elarn's paranoia. After I left she installed *very* good security, because she knew my sisters would come looking for me one day – as indeed they did. Whoever this is, they are being stealthy, and they aren't transmitting a greeting.'

'But they're definitely headed for the house?'

'There's nothing else out here.'

Taro took a deep breath, and found he didn't feel as scared as he expected to. 'I'll get the gun,' he said.

CHAPTER TWO

It occurred to Jarek as he drove at well over the local speed limit through weather bad even by Khathryn standards that even if he did catch up with the aircar flying half a klick in front of him, there wasn't a hell of a lot he could do. His current resources consisted of this aircar – souped up by the less-than-reputable yard he'd hired it from, but hardly a performance vehicle – and his dartgun, loaded – as usual – with tranq.

He'd think of something. He couldn't just turn around and return to Kendall's Wharf now: the car ahead had crossed the Ornsay Strait and was still heading south. There was only one place it could be going. He thought about calling the house again, but he'd been trying on and off ever since he'd arrived in-system two days ago. Initially he'd assumed Elarn was in – it wasn't like she ever went anywhere – but, stubborn as ever, was refusing to take his calls. This afternoon he'd resorted to calling her agent, who'd frostily told him that she'd taken a trip out-of-system some weeks ago and was due back any day. *Elarn leaving Khathryn?* He wasn't sure he believed that.

He kept his distance over the sparse woodlands, flying low in case the larger vehicle in front was checking for a tail. He couldn't think of any good reason for an unmarked private aircar to be coming out this way, so when his contact in traffic control had called him to report a vehicle making a sudden and unscheduled trip due south – just as he'd been bribed to do – Jarek had decided to follow up the lead. His suspicions were heightened when he discovered they weren't broadcasting a hail … then again, neither was he.

The other car slowed and landed in a clearing in the woods, fifty metres short of the bot-maintained rough parkland surrounding the house. It put down just outside the range of the house's surveillance – or at least, just outside the range of the security package Elarn had had the last time he'd visited her, seven years ago.

Jarek found a tree-free spot invisible from the car's landing site. As soon as his vehicle had settled he popped the hatch, pulled up the hood on his rain-cape and leapt to the ground. His face and hands were soaked before he'd gone a dozen steps – as if he hadn't spent quite enough time exposed to the elements over the last few months, he thought grumpily. At least now he was wearing hi-tech wet-weather gear that actually kept the rain out. He jogged through the woods, alternately watching the uneven ground and checking for activity ahead. The other aircar was a low hump amongst the trees. Figures were heading towards the open ground, running semi-crouched. The light was fading, but he reckoned there had to be at least half a dozen of them.

He wished he had some idea who these unexpected visitors were, and, more importantly, why they were sneaking up on what might well be an empty house. He'd intended getting up to speed with what had been happening around here before he ventured out to face Elarn, but as usual, his master plan had lasted just long enough for him to regret not following it later.

He passed as close to the other aircar as he dared. It wasn't parked, just hovering, which probably meant they'd left someone on board. Looked like they expected to leave in a hurry. One thing was for sure: they were up to no good.

As he skirted the edge of the woods the house came into view, a vague dark shape a couple of hundred metres off to his left. He stayed under cover until the trees petered out, keeping low as he neared the cliff-edge.

The rain had melted back into salt-tinged mist and twilight was coming on fast now. He'd lost sight of all but one of the intruders in the murk. They were probably trying to surround the house, or at least cover the exits. He wasn't sure how good their informa-tion was, but he'd spent much of his childhood here and they were unlikely to know the layout of the place better than he did. The person nearest him – definitely a man, from the way he moved – was staying close to the cliff, possibly heading for the door to the conservatory, a small extension on the back of the house. Jarek thought he might be able to catch up with him there, out of sight of his friends, maybe take him by surprise and get some answers. He patted his gun, almost subconsciously.

Now he had a plan. He followed at a distance, ducking between the ornamental shrubs, passing the occasional sculpture. The land-scaped features ended about seventy metres from the house and he stopped, wary about venturing into the open. His target had already closed half the distance to the conservatory when he sud-denly fell to the ground, dropping in an instant and folding in on himself.

Shit! Jarek hunched down behind a quartzite monstrosity sup-posedly portraying a dolphin and a child – not one of Elarn's most tasteful purchases, but excellent cover. From what, though, he wondered? Even if Elarn had upgraded the security, anything that incapacitated unwanted visitors had to be preceded by a broadcast warning. Of course, if whatever had downed the intruder wasn't lethal, then it might give Jarek the opportunity for a quick inter-rogation – assuming it wasn't going to go off again as soon as *he* got in range.

The sound of a dull concussion from the front of the house made his mind up for him. He sprinted out from behind the stat-ue, heading for the cliff, thankful for the repeated false alarms caused by landing skeppies during the spring migration that had made them recalibrate the house security to stop two metres back from the edge. He scurried along the cliff-top, careful not to look at the lethal drop to his right. Even after all these years, and in spite of the circumstances, he found himself tuning in to the puls-ing rhythm of the waves; the long smooth rumbles meant the tide was out.

As he drew level with the intruder he heard another *crump!*

13

from the far side of the house. Before he could talk himself out of it he cut inland, running flat-out to reach the fallen man, and threw himself down to use the body as cover—

—or rather, the *upper* body. Something had sliced the man clean in half just below the ribcage. The legs must have kept going for a fraction of a second, as they lay a little further on. Whatever had hit him had almost cauterised the wound, and Jarek's nostrils were filled with the reek of charred flesh. He swallowed hard and looked away from the ooze of parboiled guts to the man's face. His eyes were open in understandable surprise, but the rest was hidden under a half-face mask. Pressing his tongue to the roof of his mouth to stop himself retching, Jarek pulled the mask off, wondering if he'd recognise the man, but he was a stranger, hard-faced under the slackness of death. He looked like typical muscle-for-hire.

Jarek looked around, trying to spot what had taken the intruder down, but the house was dark and he could see no movement. Perhaps he'd be safest staying put, seeing how things panned out … except he'd be no use to Elarn out here.

He heard a tinny squawking coming from his hand and realised that the mask was actually a rebreather, with a built-in com unit. He held it to his ear and heard a strident female voice saying, '—peat: Seven is down. Eight, prep for retrieval or cleansing. Six, cover Seven's exit. Two and Five hold station.'

If unlucky number Seven was the severed torso next to him then someone else would be heading this way soon. Well, that made his decision easier.

He scrambled to his feet and ran for the conservatory door, zigging and zagging, half expecting to be cut down at any moment. He reached the door safely – to find it shut tight. Given the house was either empty and locked up, or Elarn had activated the security and locked everything down, this wasn't much of a surprise. He slipped the mask over his head in time to hear, '—ith me. We're going in.'

Which was exactly what he needed to do. If Elarn *was* in there, she was in trouble. The conservatory wall was toughened glass and impossible to climb, but a bushy vine covered the wall of the main house at the back here. When he was ten he'd got into enormous trouble for climbing that vine, and after that little escapade his parents had cut it back, but Elarn had let it grow again. It looked strong enough to support an adult now, and if it held, he could get up onto the optimistically named sun-terrace above the conservatory. Unless Elarn had upgraded it, the forceshield that protected the terrace from inclement weather wouldn't stop a person forcing their way through. It would leave him numb and tingling, though – something else he'd discovered when he was a boy.

So there: he still had a plan, of sorts. He grabbed one of the thick, hairy stems and started to climb. Though he couldn't really see what he was doing through the glossy leaves, the gnarled main trunk formed a sturdy, if irregular, ladder. There were twinges of discomfort from the ribs he'd bruised a couple of weeks back, which didn't help, but he tried to ignore the pain and concentrated on moving slowly and carefully.

The com squawked, 'Target sighted – don't approach her.'

Jarek started, nearly losing his grip, as the female team leader concluded, 'Let the gas do our work for us.'

Gas? Oh shit! So that was what the rebreather was for.

He began to climb faster, feeling for his footholds when the trunk narrowed and divided. He should be coming up to the terrace soon. He leant out slightly and looked up and across.

He didn't remember the weather-shield being *that* transparent; surely there should be a faint shimmering? It was almost as though it wasn't there any more.

His left foot began to slip and he tightened his grip just as part of the vine tore away from the wall. He pressed himself into the leaves, his foot flailing.

Almost as though echoing his own panic, a voice he hadn't heard before came over the com, asking, 'Control? Do you read? Where are you?'

He found a new foothold, but now the whole damn vine was beginning to pull away from the building. He had to get his weight off it, fast. He leaned across to the right, blindly reaching for the edge of the terrace.

Over the com a male voice muttered, 'Holy fuck!'

His hand found a solid surface and he braced himself for the bite of the weather-shield – but there was nothing. He walked his fingers in until he found a post, part of the fence his parents had installed when they found the shield wasn't an adequate deterrent for a small boy with an insatiable curiosity and little sense of personal danger.

He gripped the post and pulled himself up until he could peer over the lip of the terrace. The ornate legs of the white wickerwork table were beaded with water from the misty rain; the shield was definitely off. He reached further up the fencepost and took a firm hold. With a degree of uncomfortable contortion, and after a couple of dodgy moments, he managed to get his right leg onto the lip and from there he hauled himself up onto the narrow ledge outside the fence.

As he stood upright it occurred to him that whatever had killed the intruder could have come from up here, but other than a new lounger, the terrace was exactly as he remembered it.

As he put his foot onto the lower cross-rail of the fence the com started up again. 'Control's down! Control's down!' The man on the com sounded like he was about to lose it. *Good.* Jarek wondered what could have taken their leader out, not to mention the one he'd got the mask from. Just what had Elarn done to the house security while he'd been away?

As he braced himself on the post and swung a leg over the fence, the door from the house slid open and a figure ran out onto the sun-terrace: someone unfeasibly tall, and yet hard to focus on; he must be wearing a mirror-tech cloak. Another figure followed on his heels: smaller, female. Her cloak was thrown back, revealing indoor clothes, as well as a slender, efficient-looking black rifle slung over her shoulder. Both of them bent over and started coughing hard.

As the door closed behind them and the woman caught sight of Jarek straddling the fence she tensed, then straightened and stared straight at him. Though her eyes were red and streaming, they were also, suddenly, the only thing in the universe. He knew those eyes – even as he felt her presence slip into his mind, starting to freeze him in place, he used the last of his will to rip the rebreather mask off and shout, 'Nual! It's me! S— Jarek!'

He felt her momentary surprise and as the pressure let up his gaze was drawn to the long, silver blade that had suddenly appeared in her companion's hand. Nual murmured something and the blade disappeared, faster than Jarek's eyes could follow.

The boy – and he was a boy, Jarek saw now, no more than late teens, and irritatingly pretty in a fey, scrawny way – gave Jarek a look of naked suspicion and said, 'Who the fuck're you, then?' His voice was hoarse.

So was Nual's, presumably a side-effect of the gas, when she said, 'Jarek is Elarn's brother.'

'Oh.' Something about the way the boy's expression changed instantly from hostile to wary and apologetic made Jarek's blood run cold.

Before he could say anything, a voice came over the com still hanging from his ear. 'Abort, abort: cleansing imminent. Repeat, cleansing imminent.'

'Shit,' said Jarek, 'I think they just called in the air support.'

'Who are they?' asked the boy.

'No idea. People who don't like leaving loose ends, I'd guess. We need to get out of here.' He looked at the door. 'Do you reckon you could hold your breath long enough to get out through the house?'

Nual shook her head. 'The gas has filled the entire ground floor.'

'It's fierce stuff,' agreed the boy.

'Then we'll have to climb down the way I came up.' Assuming they had time. Assuming the vine would hold them.

'No,' said Nual, 'they might see us running away. We need them to believe we're dead.'

She swung the gun off her shoulder and pointed it at the fence on the seaward side of the terrace, then traced a broad arc through the air with the tip of the weapon.

A section of fence about three meters long collapsed. Jarek heard the crash and tinkle of breaking glass as the handrail fell through the conservatory roof. 'What're you doing?' he yelled.

'Making an exit.'

'We'll land in the conservatory – that's just as big a drop as jumping off the side, with added furniture and broken glass.'

'Which is why we need to get a good run-up.' She slid the gun back onto her shoulder and took a step back.

'No, Nual, wait,' said Jarek. 'Even if we jump out far enough to miss the conservatory – and I don't think we can – it's only a few metres to the edge of the cliff. If we cock up the landing, that's sixty metres down to a rock shelf. You might want them to believe we're dead, but if we go with your plan then we will be!' Over the hysteria in his voice he thought he heard a distant whine, the sound of an approaching engine.

'We will be fine. I need you to grasp your elbows. Like this—' She demonstrated, looking for all the world as though she was about to perform some sort of ethnic dance, arms clasped in front of her.

'Nual, I have no idea what you think you're—'

< *Trust me!*>

And he did. Without thinking he stepped back and made a tight circle of his arms. Somewhere in the depths of his head he was furious – Nual had once promised never to steal his will – and terrified – because they were about to jump off a cliff, for fuck's sake – but his body appeared to be going along with this crazy plan without any input from his brain.

Nual linked arms with him on one side; the boy moved to the other side and did the same.

The aircar engines were louder now. Jarek wondered, in a vague, disinterested way, whether he'd be killed by the fall or by the explosion.

Then they were running towards the edge.

CHAPTER THREE

It would have been nice, thought Taro as he watched Nual trash the fence so they could jump off the roof, if she'd maybe mentioned that Elarn had a brother. Except she obviously hadn't expected him to turn up at the house. And this Jarek cove didn't know his sister was dead, not given how careful they'd been about who they'd told.

Worry about that later. Now: survival.

Following Nual's wordless direction he linked arms with Jarek. He began to run, moving in perfect step with Nual, while Jarek stumbled between them.

As he kicked off the edge Taro felt gravity pulling Jarek down, trying to tear him free. The effort of holding onto him tugged at Taro's shoulder, and for a moment he considered letting go. *Why were they saving this cove anyway?* Because he might be an ally, and they needed all the allies they could get. Taro tightened his grip, ignoring the other man's amazed gasp, and the three of them flew above the shattered glass roof of Elarn's conservatory, barely losing any height.

Then they were over the cliff, and a lifetime's terror of falling kicked Taro in the guts for a brief moment, before the fear receded. It was as though the emotion belonged to someone else. He'd felt the same during the attack, when he'd watched impassively as Nual shot one of the intruders, then ambushed and skewered the gang-leader inside the house. As they began to drift down in front of the cliff-face, Taro wondered if being so chill when your arse was on the line was another part of the package, along with the blades, and the implants that stopped his body breaking under normal gravity – and allowed him and Nual to fly, not fall, if they happened to jump off a cliff.

Light erupted above them with a loud bang. Taro looked up to see red-lit smoke billowing over the edge of the cliff and he dropped his head quickly as debris rained down on them. Jarek had gone rigid in their grasp and Taro could hear his harsh, rapid breaths even over the aftermath of the explosion and the pounding of the water below them.

<I will go back once we have got Jarek safely down.>

After a moment's disorientation, Taro thought back *<Why?>*

<I have to find out who sent them.>

Though Nual wasn't turning on the compulsion, Taro knew better than to argue.

The whoosh of the sea grew to a roar. Taro had looked over the cliff when they'd first arrived and he hadn't seen anywhere safe to land, just dark waves smashing into the rock, throwing up plumes of white. Jarek had mentioned something about a shelf, though it was dark now and even Taro's excellent night-vision couldn't make out much more than white froth below. He soon saw that the foam wasn't directly below them, and as they sank lower, he was able to separate the sound of the sea from the noise reflecting off the cliff. It looked like there was ten metres or so of dry land to play with.

When they touched down and his boot landed in a pool of chilly water, he decided that 'dry' might have been a bit of an exaggeration. He let go of Jarek and stepped onto a drier spot. Nual pulled her cloak tight around herself, instantly disappearing into the darkness.

Jarek, raising his voice to be heard above the sea, called out to her uncertainly, 'What are you doing?'

A moment later Taro sensed Nual springing back into the air. 'She's going to see who the men who attacked us were,' he told the stranger.

For the first time, Jarek looked at him. 'I still don't know who *you* are.'

'Taro sanMalia,' he said.

Jarek continued to stare at him, and, as the adrenalin began to fade, Taro felt exposed in a way that went beyond being outside in the cold and dark. Finally Jarek said, 'And what are you doing here?'

Taro's first instinct was to say he was with Nual, but she was gone for now, and if this was Elarn's brother, he needed to know the truth. 'We're here because of your sister,' he said.

'What about her?' asked Jarek, a little uncertainly.

'I'm sorry: she's dead.'

'What?'

'I— I tried to help her, give her a chance to get away—'

'Away from what? How did she die?'

'Away from the bastard who shot her. He's dead too.' A lot of people were dead now.

'This wasn't on Khathryn, was it?'

'On …? Oh, no. It were in Khesh City. On Vellern.'

'Vellern? Of course. Shit – you two are Angels! Hence the flying.' Jarek snorted, a harsh laugh. 'God, I might have known Nual would end up in that line of work.'

'That's right,' said Taro, unable to keep the pride out of his voice, 'we're Angels.' Jarek didn't need to know that while Nual had been one of the most revered of the Khesh City assassins, Taro had had his implants for only a few weeks, and had yet to use his blades in anger.

'But what the hell was *Elarn* doing on *Vellern*?'

'Looking for Nual.' Jarek looked confused, so Taro added helpfully, 'she didn't wanna be there. She— She didn't've much choice.' He wondered how much he should say.

'I'll bet she didn't,' said Jarek, his voice tight.

'So … d'you know about – about *them*?'

'If you mean do I know that the Sidhe aren't long-dead like most people think but are alive and well and still fucking over humanity, then yes, Taro sanMalia, I know that very well indeed. And I'm not surprised those bitches sent Elarn to her death.'

'Like I said, I'm sorry she's dead.' Taro shivered. 'They fucked me over too.'

'That's something we've got in common, then.' Jarek's voice was loaded with bitterness.

They lapsed into uneasy silence. It started to rain again. The novelty of weather had definitely begun to wear off.

There was a slight disturbance above them and a moment later Taro made out a figure outlined against the red glow of the burning house. Nual dropped quickly, slowing at the last moment to land gently on the damp rock. When she shrugged the cloak back Taro saw that she'd managed to rescue the gun case and the overnight bag from the aircar. He relaxed a little; without the case to recharge it their gun would soon stop working, and the overnight bag contained the one memento of his old life he'd hate to lose.

She gave Taro a brief nod and turned to Jarek. 'I am sorry,' she said.

'You mean about Elarn?' said Jarek. 'Your companion here already told me she's dead.'

Nual looked slightly taken aback. 'No,' she said, 'though I am sorry for that too. I meant, I'm sorry I broke my promise. I would not have overridden your will if it had not been necessary for our survival.'

So Jarek Reen knew that Nual was Sidhe? What else did he know about her?

'It's all right,' said Jarek, 'I was pretty pissed off, but you're right, you had your reasons. God, Nual, it's good to see you – even with … *everything*.'

He opened his arms and she hugged him in return.

Jealousy wasn't an emotion Taro had much experience of, but seeing the two of them embracing sent something searing through him. When they broke apart, he asked Nual, his voice a little too loud, 'So d'you find out who those lags were, then?'

Nual replied, 'The aircar had already picked the survivors up. They were professionals, but as for who hired them, I do not know.'

Taro turned to Jarek. 'How about you? Any idea?'

'Not a clue,' said Jarek.

'So nothing to do with you, then? Just coincidence, you showing up at the same time?' Taro knew he was being unreasonable, but it hurt to see how much Nual cared for this cove she hadn't even bothered to mention before.

Jarek didn't reply.

Nual said, 'Taro, I trust Jarek with my life. We are old friends.'

'I can see that.'

'I think we've all got some explaining to do,' said Jarek, 'but I don't think this is the time or the place. The tide comes in pretty fast around here. Can I suggest we go somewhere a little more comfortable to talk?'

No one could object to that, so they flew slowly back up the cliff, taking a diagonal course that brought them out some way along from the house. When they landed Jarek looked back at the burning building. 'The authorities will arrive to investigate soon, so we need to get out of here. My aircar's parked in the woods.'

As Jarek turned to lead the way Taro noticed his eyes were glistening in the light from the flames. He felt sorry for the cove, losing his home and his sister in one day. But he had to know how things stood with him and Nual, so when Jarek led them into the trees he hung back with her, and thought *<Why didn't you tell me about him?>*

Nual's gaze was fixed on her feet. *<I should have. I am not used to trusting.>*

<But you trust him. How far?>

<He is my friend. He understands me as few people ever have.>

<How come? Why's he so special?>

<Because Jarek is the first human I ever met.>

'Were you staying at the house?'

Taro jumped at the sound of the question spoken out loud, but Nual answered, 'No, we have rooms in a hotel in Kendall's Wharf. I do not think we should return to them.'

'Reckon you're right. The hitmen were talking about using gas to take out a female target. They must have meant you. Elarn—

Well, they could just have come in with guns and Elarn would've surrendered. Who knows you're here?'

'Your family lawyer is the only person I have identified myself to. Taro and I have been using Vellern IDs.'

'If it's still the same firm then he wouldn't sell you out by choice. Did you read him?'

'I detected no sign of Sidhe influence when we met. The Sidhe can leave traps in the heads of their agents; I delved only deep enough to check he wasn't lying.'

'If you're not sure, you'd be wise to play dead. It might be better if you stayed with me for now.'

Nual didn't object to his offer. It looked like this stranger was automatically their friend.

After a while Nual said, 'Jarek, how did the Sidhe find out I was on Vellern? Was it from you?'

'Yeah, it was. But I didn't tell them willingly. And at the moment, they probably think I'm dead.' He ducked under a low branch. 'The aircar's just through here.'

Jarek's vehicle was smaller and more battered than the one they'd left parked outside the burning cliff-house. The back seat was tiny, so Nual offered Taro the roomier seat up front, next to Jarek.

Though Taro was glad to be somewhere warm and dry, as the lid came down he had a moment of panic. Nual trusted Jarek, but she'd not seen him for years, and she hadn't expected to see him now. 'What you said about us coming to stay with you,' he asked, 'what d'you mean?'

'On my ship.' From the way Jarek handled the controls, he obviously knew how to actually fly an aircar, not just rely on the autopilot like they had.

They took off, and Taro had a brief snapshot of tree branches caught in the lights before the view settled into rainy darkness. 'Ship? Like at the port at Kendall's Wharf?'

'Not that kind of ship,' said Jarek. 'A shiftship. For travelling between the stars.'

Taro was confused. The two starliners he'd travelled on had been huge and luxurious, and just getting from Vellern to Khathryn had used up nearly half their credit. Someone who owned one of those surely wouldn't be driving around in a car that looked like it was hardly worth jacking.

From the back, Nual said, 'Jarek is a freetrader.'

Before Taro could ask what a freetrader was, Jarek, his voice all comradely-like, said, 'I used my inheritance to buy myself into a partnership running a small tradebird, and when my partner retired I bought him out. I've been travelling the shipping lanes ever since.'

Taro had been staggered to discover that there were hundreds of different places beyond the small, closed world of Khesh City, and he'd already resolved to see as many of them as he could – in Nual's company, of course. 'Right,' he said.

CHAPTER FOUR

Elarn was dead. Jarek had expected to find her still pissed off with him, or shit-scared after a visit from the Sidhe. Not dead. And though the Sidhe had sent her to her death, ultimately it was his fault.

Was that why he'd offered to help Nual and her companion, despite having problems of his own? That old sense of responsibility getting him in trouble again.

As the silence stretched, Jarek stole a look at the boy sitting next to him. His extreme height must be a result of being born in a low-g environment, but the rest of his look – tight leggings, loose shirt, oversized dark jacket and scruffy collar-length hair with one longer strand plaited with red and black – was all artful contrivance. Taro's reaction to finding himself in the company of a man Nual cared for told Jarek all he needed to know about their relationship: this was a lad well under Sidhe glamour. But he was also an Angel, a member of Vellern's élite assassin caste – as was Nual. That was somehow fitting. He felt something not entirely unlike fatherly pride for a moment before catching himself; now she was a murderer, for God's sake, on top of being a Sidhe.

But none of that changed the fact that he'd been delighted to see her. Sometimes he wondered if he was as free from her influence as he thought he was.

He had a brief urge, borne of stress, to ask how the two of them met, as though they were just a pair of young lovers he was giving a lift to on a rainy night. But right now he had more important questions. Turning his head to make it obvious he was speaking to Nual he asked, 'What brought you back here now?'

He saw Taro's lips thin at being excluded. *Grow up, kid*, he thought, even as he noted how the sour expression leant an interesting touch of hardness to the boy's exotic looks.

Nual said, 'I wanted to bring Elarn home – her ashes, at least. I owed her that much.'

'Oh.' He was surprised and a little dismayed at how quickly he was adjusting to the idea that his sister was dead. Though in some ways she'd been lost to him years ago, in his heart of hearts he'd always hoped they might eventually be reconciled. 'You mentioned her lawyer. Does that mean she never changed her will?'

'No, so in theory I am rich. However, if I claim my inheritance now it will become known that I survived the attack on the house.'

'The authorities will realise that when they don't find a body inside.' Then Jarek remembered the panic over the com: *Control's down!* 'Except they *will* find one, won't they?'

'Yes,' said Nual, 'they will. And I intend to be far from Khathryn by the time they realise that it's not mine.'

'You sound like you've got a plan.'

'Not really, beyond trying to discover what the Sidhe are up to and finding a way to curb their influence.'

You and me both, thought Jarek.

'We got licences,' said Taro, 'so we can get ourselves hired by any law enforcement agency authorised to use external agents deploying lethal force.'

Jarek suppressed a smile. The boy was obviously quoting that from somewhere. 'I didn't think – what's the phrase? *Agents of the Concord?* – ever got to leave Vellern.'

'Normally they don't. The Minister owed us, big time.'

Taro's tone of voice was begging Jarek to ask more, but he didn't feel inclined to indulge the kid's ego just now. 'I can't help noticing you've only got one gun between you. I thought Angels had one each.'

Taro's expression implied he'd rather not discuss that.

Nual said, 'We share the laser. The Minister is somewhat jealous of his technology.'

Another awkward silence. This time, somewhat to Jarek's surprise, Nual broke it. 'You know why I came back. Why are you here? Were you hoping enough time had passed for Elarn to forgive you?'

Jarek grimaced. 'Yes – but that's not why I came. I wanted to warn her. I tried to contact you too, but I wasn't really surprised my message bounced; after all, you did go to Vellern to hide. When Elarn didn't reply either I assumed she was still angry with me, so I came in person. I had to make her listen – even if she wasn't interested in my crusade against the Sidhe, you'd lived here with her for a while, and she had to know that they'd want to talk to her about that. Looks like I was right.' He sighed. 'Just too late. And—' He stopped, trying to restore his equilibrium. He wondered if he'd ever get used to this sinking feeling in the pit of his stomach when he thought about Elarn being dead.

'And?' prompted Nual gently. 'Was there another reason?'

'Yeah. I found something out about the Sidhe, something big.'

'What sort of something?' Nual leaned forward between the seats.

Jarek realised that she probably knew as little about her own people as the average human, who was happy to believe the Sidhe'd died out a millennium ago.

'I found half a conspiracy. The kind of thing put about by those unreasoning paranoids who believe the Sidhe lived on after the Protectorate just because they have to believe in something. Except I've only got part of the story.'

'Explain, please.'

He stared out into the darkness. They had plenty of time; he'd programmed an indirect course back to Kendall's Wharf to avoid running into anyone coming out to investigate the incident at the cliff-house. He just wasn't sure he was ready to discuss his recent experiences. But he'd invited these two on board, and maybe talking it through with others might help him work it out in his own head.

Still not looking at his passengers he began, 'After I left you on Vellern all those years ago, I tried to find out more about the Sidhe. I made discreet enquiries and collected what data I could. I hoped I might find allies, but most people were the kind of nuts I mentioned earlier: never mind finding evidence or coming up with reasons, let's just blame everything on unseen monsters. The Sidhe must love people like that: there's nothing like an endorsement from a kook to make the truth seem kooky.

'Anyway, I kept my eyes and ears open, but freetrading's a marginal living at best and I couldn't afford to go off chasing rumours all the time. Then, a few months back, I made a killer deal – the kind that doesn't come along often in my line of work – and that gave me a bit of freedom to poke around, follow some stuff up. To be honest, the lead I was investigating wasn't directly related to the Sidhe; I'd heard about this freetrader outfit who left the shipping lanes every twenty-five years or so and I thought they might be using an unregistered beacon.'

'Unregistered beacon?' interrupted Taro. 'So what's one of them?'

'You know what a beacon is?'

''Course I do,' Taro said. 'You need beacons to transmit beevee communications and to allow ships to make transits between star systems.'

That was memorised too. The boy must've led a *very* sheltered life. Jarek went on, 'Well, in some ways a beacon is more like a door between reality and shiftspace, one that's been left ajar. You've been through shiftspace to get here, so you know what a fun place that is.'

'We spent the transits between Vellern and Khathryn in stasis,' Nual broke in.

I'll bet you did, thought Jarek, *and now I know why*. 'Given how chaotic things were after the fall of the Sidhe Protectorate, there're plenty of rumours about beacons – whole systems, even – whose locations have been lost. Finding just one would open up new shipping lanes and beevee capacity, not to mention new resources and markets, and for a freetrader that's real treasure! This ship I'd heard about only took its little trip every couple of decades, which sounded a bit odd if it was exploiting an untouched system, but I decided it was worth looking into. So I lurked around in the system they made their transit from, and a few weeks later the *Setting Sun* – that's the name of the ship – turned up. When it went into the shift, I slipstreamed it.' He'd only found out how big a risk he'd taken later. 'I was right, sort of. It did go to a lost system – except it wasn't exactly lost, more like deliberately hidden.'

'By the Sidhe?' asked Nual.

'By the Sidhe. There's an inhabited planet there, really lo-tech, and with no idea the rest of the universe exists. Unfortunately, before I could investigate further the *Setting Sun* tricked me into docking with them, and I was captured by the Sidhe on board. They—' Jarek stopped and coughed, trying to clear his suddenly tight throat. 'They found out everything I knew, eventually, even about you. I guess they passed that on to their sisters elsewhere, and decided to use Elarn to draw you out. Was that how it was?'

'Aye,' said Nual in a small voice. 'That was how it was.'

No one said anything for a few moments. Then Taro asked, 'How'd you escape?'

'The ship had a human crew. Mostly mutes – conditioned slaves. One of them managed to break her conditioning, and she freed me.' He addressed Nual over his shoulder, 'That's something I've been thinking about: given how much control a Sidhe can exert, I was surprised a mute could do something like that.'

'So am I. Did you give her a reason to disobey her mistresses?'

'I guess I showed her kindness when she would've expected abuse. The urge to fight back must've already been there though.'

'My sisters tend towards arrogance. Perhaps they assumed her obedience was total, and so failed to spot the signs of rebellion.'

'What happened to her?' Taro interrupted.

'They must have caught her, so I imagine she's dead now, poor cow. When she let me out of my cell I was half-crazy. All I could think of was getting away. I took a solo evac-pod to Serenein – that's the name of the planet.'

'Did the Sidhe come after you?' asked Taro.

'No. They'd got what they wanted; after that I was more trouble than I was worth. They'd have freaked the locals. And—' Jarek hesitated, unsure how to summarise the strangest three months of his life. 'It took me a while to get over what they did to me. They'd messed up my memory. And then I had to find a way to get back up into orbit. I finally managed that, thanks to some local help, and we took out the Sidhe.'

'You killed them?' Nual sounded understandably surprised.

'Like I said, I had help.'

'And this lost world is the big secret you wanted to tell Elarn?' Taro's tone of voice implied he wasn't sure why a recluse like Elarn would care about such a place.

'There's more to it than that. The reason the Sidhe kept Serenein isolated was that they were manipulating the genetics of the population to produce certain ... *talented* individuals. Then they shipped them out – that's what the *Setting Sun* was there for, to pick up these boys, who'd been put into stasis for easy transport. They've got the whole culture geared up for it—'

He broke off: a blinking light was indicating an incoming message from local traffic control. He hesitated, then hit Receive; not answering would only make him look suspicious.

Before he could say anything a man's voice said, 'Good job you're on your way back.' After a moment he recognised the chatty evening-shift operator who'd been happy to accept Jarek's incentive to keep him informed of anything interesting on his watch.

'Really?' he said with forced casualness, 'so why's that?'

'Well, I've just cleared a whole load of vehicles heading out to your last known co-ordinates: police, fire-tenders, ambulances, press and all the other chasers, quite a party. And I notice that you're taking a roundabout route back. You know, if I'd had any idea how much interest that neck of the woods would be receiving tonight ...' He let his voice trail off.

... you'd have asked for more money up front, Jarek thought, and said, with all the sincerity he could muster, 'Given how helpful you've been, I'm truly sorry to have put you to any additional inconvenience.'

'How sorry?' asked the other man bluntly.

'I'm not sure we should be discussing this right now—'

'Don't worry, our com system's been a bit flaky recently. The call-logs don't always record cleanly ... . So, I ask again: how sorry?'

Jarek weighed up his options. Finally he said, 'About another twenty per cent.'

The traffic controller grunted, then said, 'Forty.'

Which was robbery by any other name. With Nual on board he couldn't take any risks, so, 'Done,' he said, knowing he had been. 'Though of course it'll be a case of as and when.'

'Meaning?' The man's previously friendly voice had an edge to it now.

'Meaning that as soon as I'm safely up in orbit, that's when you get your bonus.'

Silence. Eventually the traffic controller said, 'All right. But nothing gets deleted until we're straight, understand?'

'Got you.' Jarek cut the connection.

He felt oddly unclean. For the last few months he'd been living a very different life. Not that there wasn't corruption and deception on Serenein, there was, and sometimes on a breathtaking scale. But he was finding something petty-minded and rather grubby about the necessary small lies and greasing of palms that came with the freetrader lifestyle.

'Right,' he said to his passengers, 'I need to focus on getting us away safely. We'll talk again later.'

CHAPTER FIVE

One of the first lessons Taro had learnt when he left Vellern was that he had no chance of faking it out in the real world. If he didn't know something – and there was shitloads he didn't know – he'd save himself a lot of grief if he just asked. Ideally he'd ask Nual, but if she didn't know, or wasn't around, he'd bother anyone who might give him a useful answer.

He soon found that people – at least the kind of people he met on starliners – assumed that not knowing something everyone else knew meant he was stupid. So, just because he had no idea what terceball was (one of the most popular sports in human-space, apparently), or why the cap-index influenced how much stuff his credit would buy (because even though cap just meant the capacity of beacons to transmit data, it was the universal currency that all local currencies were rated against), they assumed he was some kind of idiot. At first he'd been insulted, then he'd tried to prove the fuckers wrong; finally he'd decided he didn't much care what those rich dicks travelling between the stars for fun thought of him.

Now he wanted to ask if Jarek would carry on from where he'd left off before the com-call, but before he could open his mouth Nual stopped him.

<Jarek has suffered a lot recently, and now he finds his sister is dead. Let him decide when to tell us the rest.>

With his friendly, slightly lopsided smile and expression suggesting that while he was giving you all his attention, he was not intruding, Jarek was, Taro reluctantly admitted, a personable-looking sort of cove. He was also a good ten years older than Nual, and Taro had no doubt he knew what was what in the world. But Nual was right; for all that self-confidence he oozed, there was an underlying uneasiness about him, like he was putting on a brave face. Hardly surprising given he'd just lost his only relative – Taro knew that feeling all too well. Looked like they were going to be hanging round with Jarek for a while; they could catch up fully later.

For the rest of the journey to the starport the three of them sat wrapped in their own thoughts. Jarek occasionally checked his console, and he made another couple of com-calls, all routine-sounding stuff to do with getting off-planet.

As Taro had discovered when they first arrived on Khathryn, *starport* was a generous term for what was basically a patch of flat ground with a few basic buildings off to one side. Compared to Vellern, this world was a backwater. Tourist liners only stopped at Khathryn so the punters could see something called the Rainbow Falls. Taro wouldn't have minded seeing them himself, but he and Nual had parted company with the tourists as soon as the two shuttles had touched down. The rest of the passengers had been whisked off to the hospitality – such as it was – of Kendall's Wharf. Taro hadn't been sorry to say goodbye to their recent travelling companions.

Their starliner must have moved on: its shuttles were gone and the starport looked deserted, except for a small round craft parked away from the buildings. The flattened disc tapered slightly towards the edges, and there was something Taro immediately labelled a tit on the top. The ship had probably been white, once.

Jarek landed the aircar neatly next to it and they got out into the cold night air. At least it'd stopped raining. The darkness beyond the perimeter lights was total. Jarek went up to a door set in the rim of the disc and looked into a blinking green light on one side. He stepped back, the door slid open and a short ladder folded out.

They followed Jarek up the ladder and crowded into a tiny room, like a cheap version of the elevators on the starliner. The outside door closed, then another door opposite opened to reveal a short corridor leading into a large, semi-circular room, twice the size of the common room in Taro's old homespace. There was a thick column bulging out of the middle of the shorter inside wall, with a ladder in front of it leading upwards. There were a couple of closed doors on either side of the column.

Jarek cleared his throat and said, 'Welcome to the *Judas Kiss*.'

Taro had spent a little time in other people's personal space – most often in hotel rooms, and he'd been there on business – but he'd never been anywhere quite as *lived in*.

The smell wasn't strong, but it was distinctive: a mixture of food, drink, laundry and human male. An open galley area curved along the wall on the left; plates, mugs, drinks-bulbs and food containers covered most of the surfaces. On the right was an impressive set of entertainment units – looked like they included holo, flatscreen, gaming, audio, the works. A couple of large plush couches were perfectly positioned to watch, play or listen from; it was obvious which seat Jarek usually used, as only one was free of debris. Beside the couches was a multi-function fitness station, like those some of the passengers had used on the starliner; Taro hadn't bothered to try one himself; the ability to run for a long time seemed a bit pointless when you could fly.

Taro was discreetly trying to work out what was draped over the fitness station's handlebar when Jarek said, sounding at once irritated and embarrassed, 'I wasn't expecting visitors.' He headed across the room as he added, 'I need to get us off-planet before the authorities decide they want to talk to us.' He gestured vaguely around. 'Make yourselves at home.'

'I'll find out what the newsnets have to say about the cliff-house,' said Nual.

'Good idea. I'll be on the bridge.' He started up the ladder.

The bridge must be in the tit on top, Taro thought, looking around again.

Nual wandered over to the lounge area and fired up the holo. Over her shoulder she said, 'If you are tired, you can rest in the spare cabin. I'm sure Jarek won't mind.'

Taro felt anything but tired. 'So you've been on this ship before, then?' he asked.

'Yes, although it was some time ago.' She straightened and pointed to one of the doors. 'The spare cabin is through there.'

Taro felt like he was being sent to his room ... except she wasn't *sending* him, was she? She was just *asking* him. If she really wanted him to go away, he wouldn't be given any choice in the matter. He decided to risk it. 'Actually I thought I'd look around. If Jarek won't object.'

Nual looked up at him and smiled. 'I'm sure he won't.' After a moment she added, 'I am sorry I did not tell you about Jarek. I never expected to meet him again, so I didn't see the need. He is a good man, Taro.'

Her apology threw him. 'Yeah, I know: he didn't have to help us.' In fact Taro suspected he was already regretting his offer. 'I was wondering, though, about him and Elarn.'

'What about them?'

'You said something about her forgiving him, and he wasn't in her will, even though he's her brother. Whatever they fell out over, it must've been pretty major.'

Nual looked away. 'It was,' she said.

'D'you know what it was then?'

'Aye,' she said, 'I do. It was me.' She turned her attention back to the tech, and Taro took the hint. He felt horribly confused: annoyed at Nual and Jarek for leaving him out, and at himself for being annoyed, and for reminding Nual about bad stuff in her past.

After a few moments he decided to follow his first plan and explore the ship. He found the spare cabin, and Jarek's – it was obvious which was which from the differing levels of mess – and he found where to wash and where to shit and where a whole load of stuff was stored. The only door that didn't open when he approached was the one halfway down the corridor between the main room and what he now realised was the airlock.

He went back to Nual, who told him it was the cargo-hold. He didn't really need to see it, but Nual added, 'I will ask Jarek to put you on the ship's security system. Wait there, I'll see if he can do it now.'

She stood up, stretched, and flew up the ladder, disappearing into the bridge. After a moment she called back down, 'Taro, go up to the iris scanner on the cargo-hold door and look into it for a minute. It's the little green light.'

Taro did as she said. 'Nothing's happening,' he muttered to himself, then, 'Oh wait—' as the door opened.

The emptiness of the hold was quite a contrast to the rest of the ship, and the air was cold enough that his breath steamed. As the door closed behind him he turned in panic, until he spotted the iris-scanner on this side and proved he could open it again. Then he had a look around.

From the shelving around the sides, the hooks welded to the floor and ceiling, and the straps, Taro guessed Jarek usually carried a fair amount of stuff, though he couldn't actually see anything that looked like cargo. Further round he found a much bigger door on the outside wall, next to which were the only two items being transported. One was a stasis chamber, or comabox, as the tourists they'd met had called it. The ones they'd used on the starliners had been smaller and smarter than this, more like sealed-in techno-beds. They'd had to sign waivers, due to the tiny risk that they might wake up with brain damage, or even not at all, but Nual had assured him that stasis was a better option than being conscious in shiftspace. Looked like Jarek only had the one; he wondered what would happen when the time came to make a transit.

The other item was a box about a metre square. The screen on the side sprang to life when Taro touched it, displaying some sort of listing. He sat cross-legged in front of the box and traced the words with one finger. Several were repeated: they weren't ones he knew, but they weren't that long either, so with a bit of time he should be able to work them out—

'You can take a look if you like.'

Taro jumped, banging his knee on the box. He thought briefly about standing up as normal, then flexed his legs *just so* to activate his flight implants, uncurled and rose to float a little above the floor. He looked down at Jarek, trying to pretend he hadn't been startled. 'I thought you were getting us out of here.'

'We're on our way to the beacon. It'll be a few hours yet, so I thought I'd come and see how you were settling in. You'll probably want to get some sleep soon, given it's after midnight local time.'

Taro had expected to feel the ship take off, though when he thought about it that didn't make sense. 'Won't they be suspicious, what with you cutting and running like this?'

'Possibly. I'm relying on being gone before anyone I haven't bribed works out we were at the cliff-house.'

'Gone where?'

'Initially, to the nearest hubpoint. That'll make us harder to follow.'

'Fair enough.' He knew what a hubpoint was, at least – they'd changed starliners at one of these artificial environments in deep space; it was where the main shipping lanes met. From their brief stopover Taro got the impression that hubpoints were bustling, busy places, but not exactly glamorous or that interesting. He'd had a moment of paranoia there when he reckoned one of the officials had paid them rather too much attention. Nual hadn't picked up anything from the man, so he'd probably imagined it. Whatever, when it came down to it, Taro was up for anything that made them more difficult to trace. He nodded towards the cargo box, settling back to the floor as he did so – being able to fly was never gonna stale. 'You said I could have a look?'

'Sure, if you like.' Jarek thumbed the lock to open the box. Inside were several packages, wrapped in cushioning material. He got one out and unwrapped it carefully. 'It won't open, for obvious reasons,' he said as he passed it to Taro.

The box had a transparent window in the lid, with a screen next to it. The item was displayed on a dark-coloured cloth, lit by a light built into the box. It was a pendant, a cross like some

Salvatines wore, though this one had arms all the same length, and was made out of thick twists of wire that looked like they needed a good clean. An uncut yellowish stone, like a blob of snot, sat in the centre.

'The authentication's excellent; that's as sure as anything you'll ever see,' Jarek said, a little proudly.

Taro thought it was as much like tat as anything he'd ever see. Without thinking, he said, 'Sure of what?'

'You read the list? It's got the provenance on the box …'

For several heartbeats the two men stared at each other. Jarek opened his mouth again, but before he could speak, Taro said in his best *Wanna make something of it?* voice, 'That's right, I can't read.' Nual was teaching him, but until he'd met her he'd never had to do more than recognise the names of bars.

Jarek closed his mouth and nodded. 'Ah. Sorry, I didn't realise.' He looked awkward, then continued, 'It's antique jewellery – a speculative cargo, but low-weight and non-perishable, so I thought it was a worthwhile investment. It's from Old Earth.'

Taro had heard of Old Earth: an exclusive tour destination, according to one of the tourists on the starliner, who'd called it *an absolute must for history buffs*. 'That's where we came from, ain't it, long ago? Humans, I mean.'

'Yeah,' said Jarek, 'that's right.'

Taro was working out what to ask next when Nual joined them.

Jarek turned to her. 'Are we headline news then?'

'Not as far as I could see. We're almost out of range of Khathryn's comnet.' She frowned at the comabox. 'Is there—? Is that occupied?'

'Ah, yes,' Jarek said. 'I meant to tell you about him when I got a moment.'

'There's someone in there already?' Now Taro was confused.

'Oh yes.'

'Who?' asked Nual.

'I don't actually know his name.'

39

'Then what's he doing in your comabox?' asked Taro.

'Well, you remember that Sidhe ship I told you about, the *Setting Sun*?' Jarek drew a deep breath. 'He's the pilot.'

CHAPTER SIX

Taro said, 'I thought the Sidhe got trashed? Or is he one of the slaves you told us about?'

'The pilot's a normal human,' replied Jarek. 'Bastard worked with them willingly.' He caught Nual's look of confusion. 'I'll explain, but not here. I need to keep an eye on what's happening in-system. Unless you'd rather get some sleep first?'

'I want to know the whole situation before I rest,' said Nual, and Taro nodded his agreement.

'All right. We'll talk on the bridge, if you two don't mind sitting on the floor. Don't worry, it's a lot tidier than the rec-room.'

Jarek had left the shutters open a little, so the section of the dome immediately opposite the ladder showed the starfield ahead. Taro stared with rapt fascination.

'Here,' said Jarek, 'I'll open us up fully.' He touched a button on the main console and the bridge lights dimmed further as the shutters round the rest of the hemispherical dome retracted, leaving them surrounded by the magnificence of space. Khathryn itself loomed behind them, a great circular vortex of blue and white.

Taro turned. 'Whoa,' he said, putting a hand up to his eyes.

'I think the view may be a little too much,' said Nual.

Jarek nodded, and dialled the shutters back to half. Typical tourist, he thought wryly, only used to seeing space in small, pretty doses. He plonked himself into his couch and spun round to face the others. 'The floor's clean, have a seat.'

Nual knelt and Taro sat cross-legged. Though Nual was in her mid-twenties now, he still saw in her the child he'd once known,

41

and the boy probably wasn't legally an adult on most worlds. He felt like a parent, about to give a stern lecture. He shook off the feeling.

'I'm not going to tell you everything that happened on Serenein. Most of it isn't relevant. But I want to help those people. They've been screwed over by the Sidhe, kept deliberately isolated, and they live short, shitty lives. That's got to come to an end.' He'd failed to save his sister, but now he had a whole world to save. And his months on Serenein felt more real to him than all his years as a freetrader. 'It won't be easy. The only organisations that operate throughout human-space are the Treaty Commission, the Salvatine Church and the Freetraders' Alliance.

'The Commission's job is to stop disputes between systems getting out of hand – which isn't that hard, given how few shiftships there are. And it makes sure interstellar trade runs smoothly. The Commission doesn't have the experience – or the clout – to administer a whole new world. The Salvatines would send a mission to convert them before you can say 'cultural genocide', and given almost everyone on Serenein believes their world is flat and unique in the universe, not to mention ruled by goddesses who are in fact the Sidhe, this would be a disaster.

'That leaves the Freetraders. They're hardly altruists, but you can't trade with a broken culture, and I'm one of theirs, so they're my best bet.

'However, right now all of this is hypothetical because there's no beacon in the Serenein system.'

'Wait,' said Taro, 'don't you need a beacon to get anywhere? You said you slipstreamed this Sidhe ship to get to Serenein, but if you trashed the ship, how'd you get back out again?'

'I went back to the system the *Setting Sun* had transited in from. You only need a beacon to leave shiftspace, not enter it; you have to program your transit-kernel with the pattern of the exit beacon—'

'"Pattern of the beacon"? What's that mean?' asked Taro.

'It's hard to explain. Shiftspace isn't really a place, it's more a *state*.'

'Right. I'll take your word for that. So if you don't need a beacon to go *into* shiftspace, just to get out again, does that mean you can start a transit from anywhere?'

'In theory, yes – provided, you've, *ahem*, disabled the relevant safeties.'

'Like you have, you mean.'

'Quite.'

'So why ain't we gone already? Why're we hanging round here waiting for trouble when we could just go straight to this hub-point?'

'Because that kind of thing is seriously frowned upon. For a start, transiting near habitation – and that includes other ships – can seriously fuck them up. And I do mean seriously; slipstreaming is the least of it. Secondly, if two ships tried to use the same exit beacon at the same time then that would be very bad – as in *major rift in spacetime* bad. Beacons are powerful objects: that's why there's only one per system, and they're at stable points in trailing orbits, a long way behind whichever world they serve.

'What you're *meant* to do is decelerate as you approach your local beacon. Once you're close enough to avoid signal-lag – and we're talking *big* distances here, tens of light-seconds – then you query it, and the exit beacon, to make sure you've got a clear run. When the beacons schedule you a window you can shift out from anywhere within the safe transit radius of that beacon.'

'That sounds like a shitload of hassle.'

'It is – but this way not only can local traffic control avoid accidents, they can keep tabs on everyone who shifts in and out of their system – and, of course, they charge extra for anyone who breaks the rules. Freetraders do make unscheduled transits if the cargo they're running makes it worth the risk, but you're looking at a hefty fine – not to mention all the unwelcome attention you'd attract. So right now we're making our way out to Khathryn's beacon as fast as we can get away with, and when we're in range we'll request a transit-window and leave in an orderly and entirely non-suspicious fashion.'

'Makes sense,' said Taro, 'but what I don't understand is how the Sidhe got to Serenein to start with if there ain't no beacon there.'

'Nor do I,' Jarek admitted. 'I did wonder if maybe there is a beacon, only it's hidden, so when I scanned for it I didn't pick it up. Either that, or the Sidhe have some other method of making transits.' He'd suspected for some time they must have, and now he looked at Nual. 'Any thoughts?'

She looked pensive. 'To enter the void we – my sisters and I on the ship where I lived – we would go into unity. I believed we did this to protect ourselves from the agony of such travel, but for all I know it may have been the means to initiate it as well.'

Jarek didn't bother asking if she knew more about shiftspace transits now she'd experienced a few outside 'unity' – they'd get to that whole dark mess soon enough. Implying she might not be sharing everything she knew wasn't very constructive. 'That's what I thought. Well, a mere human like me certainly won't get very far without beacons, but what I do have is lots of juicy files from the *Setting Sun*'s computer, though most of the damn stuff's encrypt- ed. And I've got the ship's pilot. He's wounded, but I picked up some medical supplies in Kendall's Wharf. Which brings us back to our guest.' Jarek had a sudden thought. 'Actually, Nual, maybe you could take a look at him? See if there's anything you can do to heal him – assuming all the stuff about Sidhe healing people is true.'

Nual and Taro exchanged a look – quite possibly more than a look – and then Nual said tightly, 'I would prefer not to do that.'

What was all that *about?* 'Fair enough. How about helping me question him? He's unlikely to want to tell me much, but you've got other means at your disposal.'

Silence for a while, then, 'Perhaps I could do that,' said Nual. 'What information would you wish to extract from him?'

Jarek didn't like the signals he was getting. He sighed. 'Listen, I'm not going to drag you – either of you – along with me if you don't want to come. I can just drop you off somewhere, and we can go our separate ways.' That would be the simplest solution; he wouldn't have to change his solitary lifestyle to accommodate other people. But it would also mean casting loose his only allies in the cause he had committed himself to.

'Are you asking,' said Nual, 'whether I am willing to join your crusade against the race of my birth?'

'Yeah, I guess that's exactly what I'm asking.'

'I have turned my back on my people. They are my enemies now. They were willing to destroy an entire city just to kill me.'

'No shit!' said Jarek. 'Which city?'

'Mine,' said Taro, his voice low. 'Khesh City.'

'I'm guessing they failed, or I'd have heard about it.'

'Yeah,' said Taro, 'we stopped them.' He gave Nual a look that held such solid belief, such love, that Jarek felt his cynical old heart soften for a moment.

'How did Elarn fit into this?' he asked.

'Khesh City is built on a floating disc,' said Nual. 'The Sidhe hid something in your sister's head, a sort of ... mindbomb, that could be activated in a number of ways, including by her death. The mindbomb was able to disrupt the operations of the City and bring the disc down. In the end, we managed to limit the damage, but it was too late for Elarn.'

'The fuckers,' breathed Jarek. 'Did she have any idea what they'd done to her?'

'Not until it was too late, and then she tried to stop it. But the Sidhe had allies in the City, and one of them killed her.'

Jarek cleared his throat against the lump that had lodged there. 'So,' he said, 'now you two are on for a noble but possibly doomed fight against impossible odds?' He smiled to show he half meant it as a joke, but it felt more like a grimace.

The two of them nodded, not quite in unison.

'Then I'll get our guest out of stasis. I'll keep him sedated and let the med-bay get to work on him. When he's a bit stronger we'll see what we can find out between us. He may know some of the passwords for the files I got from the Sidhe ship; even if he hasn't got the access codes, he's been with the Sidhe a while, so he'll know the kind of things his little cell got up to. But first, I think it's time you two got some rest.' Jarek stood, and the others

45

followed suit. He decided to take the direct approach. 'How many beds do I need to find?'

Taro opened his mouth, closed it, then looked at Nual.

'Two,' she said, firmly.

'Well, one of you gets the spare cabin. The other one can either use mine, or a couch in the rec-room. Your choice.'

'What about you?' asked Taro.

'I'll just doze up here.' In a quiet system like this, he'd normally slave the bridge alarms to his com and use the run out to the beacon to get some rest in preparation for the shift, but he doubted his paranoia would let him sleep right now.

In the end Taro insisted Nual take the spare cabin. The boy seemed half-inclined to use Jarek's bed, then said he'd sleep in the rec-room 'for the moment', rather implying, Jarek thought, that he expected to be sharing Nual's bed sooner rather than later. Jarek swept some hardcopy, a hand-weight and an empty beer-bulb from the larger of the two couches, flicked the dirty sock off the fitness station when Taro wasn't looking, then rigged up a makeshift curtain for some privacy.

He considered taking some stim, but decided against it; he'd just be fully awake to experience every nervous twitch, and bored shitless if nothing happened. What he really wanted to do was to get roaring drunk whilst listening to some of Elarn's recordings, maybe have a good long, ranting cry. Unfortunately, he couldn't afford that kind of self-indulgence.

CHAPTER SEVEN

Though he didn't expect to, Taro dropped off to sleep easily, but quickly found himself in a nightmare of being chased through the nets and mazeways of the Undertow. Part of him knew he was dreaming, yet insisted he had to stay asleep, to see how the dream ended. The other part, the sane part, fought this crazed logic until he finally allowed himself to awaken. He came to sweating, grabbing the sides of his hammock – except he wasn't in the hammock slung in his old homespace, even if it was dim as downside in here. He was on a couch in Jarek Reen's ship, with the lights set low for sleeping.

When the last of the nightmare had trickled away he got out his flute. He ran his hands over the familiar smooth lines, then put it to his lips and played one of his favourite tunes, 'Ania's Jig'. He had no idea who Ania was; he'd learnt the tune from his line-mother, back when his hands were too small to reach all the holes. At the end he found himself overcome for a moment with a stupid, pointless desire to cry. He felt homesick, for fuck's sake! But there was nothing for him in Khesh; the only person he cared about was here.

'Nice tune.'

He looked up to see Jarek peering through the half-open curtain. 'Sorry, Taro, I shouldn't have disturbed you. I just came down to use the head and I heard music.'

'It's all right.' Jarek was making the effort to be nice; he should too. He uncurled and stood up.

Jarek's gaze lingered on the flute. 'That's an interesting looking instrument,' he said. 'May I see it?'

Taro handed Jarek the flute and watched as he turned it over in his hands, frowning. 'This looks like bone.'

'It is,' said Taro. 'The arm bone of my birth-mother. That's how we honour our dead, by keeping a part of them. She died when I were a baby. Her sister brought me up. She's dead as well.'

'You've had a pretty shitty life, haven't you?'

'Sometimes. I've had some pure blade moments too.'

Jarek took the hint. 'I'll let you get back to sleep.'

Sleep took a while to return. When it did, it was mercifully free of dreams.

Taro woke up to an enticing aroma, something rich and sharp: caf? Nual had introduced him to the drink; it was still a prime treat. The room no longer looked like a crime scene; Jarek must have tidied up during the night. Nual and Jarek were sitting opposite each other at the galley table.

And there was someone else in the room.

What had been a blank wall had been pulled down to form another couch. An unconscious cove about Jarek's age was lying on it, attached to a number of machines. After a moment of sleepy confusion Taro realised who he was looking at.

'That the pilot, then?' he said, with as much cool as he could muster. He hoped Jarek's tech would do the trick on their prisoner; he knew what Sidhe healing did to your mind, the link it created. No way was he sharing Nual's affections with this scumbag Sidhe collaborator.

'That's him,' said Jarek. 'He'll be out of it for a while yet. And good morning to you too.'

'Er, yeah, good morning,' muttered Taro.

'If you want to eat you should do it soon,' said Nual. 'We'll be making the transit in a couple of hours.'

'Oh. Right. Did I oversleep?'

'You looked so peaceful, I didn't want to disturb you.'

Taro couldn't work out whether Jarek was joking, so he said nothing. He made full use of the ship's facilities – he had years of hot showers to catch up – though he had to put his dirty clothes back on, as they'd abandoned most of their possessions on Khathryn. He decided against food. His stomach was doing a kind of low-level flutter, like it knew he should be nervous, but wasn't sure why.

When he got back to the galley, Nual said, 'I may as well go under now.'

'Under what?' asked Taro.

'Nual's going to use the comabox during the transit,' said Jarek. 'I'm afraid you'll have to manage without one.'

So *that* was what he should be worrying about: Nual, going into stasis without him; he enduring his first transit out of stasis without her. He swallowed. 'You ain't got a spare 'box hidden away somewhere then?'

'I didn't have one at all until I took on our guest over there. Everything has to be locked down before entering shiftspace, so I need to stay conscious during transit, ready to restart the ship's systems the moment we come out of the shift.'

'Have you not transported passengers before?' asked Nual.

'Not often enough to justify buying a comabox, which takes up valuable cargo space. And the kind of people who travel with freetraders don't tend to be overly concerned with comfort. Right, let's get you safely asleep.'

Taro trailed after them as they walked to the cargo-hold. Nual let him hold her hand as she lay down in the comabox. She closed her eyes as soon as her head touched the pillow. If he'd believed in a god, then he'd have been praying he'd see her open them again, safe and well, the other side of the shift.

Back the rec-room Jarek told him, 'I need to prepare for the transit from the bridge. I'll be back down in half an hour or so. Make yourself comfortable, and try to relax.'.

Taro found that easier said than done. He wandered over to the ents unit in search of distraction. He'd just selected a simple, non-immersion splat-the-alien-menace game when he heard a loud oath from above. After a moment's hesitation he kicked off and flew up the stairwell.

Jarek was bent over his console. He turned as Taro landed

behind him. From his expression he didn't appreciate the interruption.

'What's up?' asked Taro.

'We've just been pinged.'

'Is that bad?'

'Maybe. The ship that's pinged us arrived in the last few minutes. They must've picked us up on long-range sensors, but noticed we're not transponding. They're probably just checking we're all right.'

'So why don't we tell them we're fine?'

'Because any message I send will carry our ship ID.'

'And that's bad, is it?' Taro knew he was being dense, but he was still getting his head around how this wide world outside Khesh City worked.

'I haven't been able to decipher much data from the *Setting Sun,* but I did read the engine-log. They transited out from Serenein soon after I escaped from them; that must be when they put the word out about Nual. The chances are they also told the other Sidhe about the *Judas Kiss.*'

'Oh shit. Is that a Sidhe ship out there then?' Taro wondered how scared he needed to be for the Angel reflexes to cut in.

'Not necessarily. It's transponding as a tradebird; but so did the *Setting Sun.* And someone hired that team back on Khathryn, presumably to snatch Nual. The Sidhe might be here to pick her up, or at least to find out what's happening. But even if that's not a Sidhe ship, I'd prefer not to broadcast my presence.'

'So what're you gonna do?'

'I'm going to request a flash-transit.'

'That's not the same as one of them unscheduled transits, then?'

'No, it just means we can shift out as soon as we're at the beacon's safe radius, and keep the transponder turned off.'

'Won't that be suspicious?'

'Yes, and expensive, but all the other ship – whoever they are – is going to know for sure is that someone who didn't want to be ID'd left in a hurry.'

'They won't know where we've gone, then?'

'Only if they fly all the way to Khathryn, then physically go into the traffic control offices there and persuade the authorities to let them have a look at the beacon logs. Which, if they *are* Sidhe, I wouldn't put past them. But we'll be long gone by then.'

'What if they come after us instead? Could they catch us?' Taro could feel his unfocused panic damping down, his mind clearing. He was able to see possibilities without being scared by them.

'They can't intercept us: we're going too fast, and space is big. But if they're willing to take the risk, they could change course and get close enough to slipstream us into the shift – which is another reason we need a flash-transit. Which I need to sort now.'

'Sure. Sorry. I'll wait downstairs.'

The minutes crawled by. Taro felt himself ease down from Angel fight-readiness and back into gnawing nerves. He started to pace, listening for noises from the bridge.

Finally Jarek half-climbed, half-jumped down the ladder. 'Ten minutes to transit,' he said. 'We need to get ourselves ready.'

'Uh, sure, what do I do?'

'Well, have you done many drugs?'

'Not today. Why, you think I should?'

Jarek smiled. 'Possibly, but I meant in general. Shiftspace is an altered state, so previous experience sometimes makes it easier to deal with.'

'I've been around,' said Taro warily.

'Good. Remember that when it gets weird. I need to make sure our passenger's stable so I'll sort something to ease us into the transit while I'm at it.'

Taro sat on the couch, hands between his knees, his shoulders tensing, while Jarek checked on the unconscious pilot in his cocoon of machines. He made some adjustments, then came over to sit next to Taro. He had an inhaler in his hand.

'It's a sedative,' he said, 'to relax you.' He took a small hit himself, then handed it across.

Taro breathed deep. He didn't recognise the drug, but the heavy warmth spreading through his body felt good. Even so, he experienced another small spike of panic when the lights dimmed.

'It's all right,' said Jarek, 'just the ship's systems shutting down. Basic life-support and gravity are hardwired, so there's nothing to worry about there.'

Taro nodded to show he understood, even though he didn't. After a while he said, 'Is there a countdown or something?'

'Nope. You'll know when it happens.'

Taro tried to relax.

The change wasn't violent, but it was sudden. One moment he was sitting next to Jarek, a little apprehensive despite the drugs, with all sorts of stuff going through his head.

The next he was somewhere else. Or rather *here* was somewhere else. His eyes still registered the now-familiar room, but it didn't mean anything. Or perhaps it meant everything. Perhaps the way that thing-he-had-no-name-for lay across that other thing-he-had-no-name-for was the true meaning of life, the key to himself. To … who? Who was this, doing all this thinking? And what was going on?

Wait, he knew the answer to this one. *Wrecked*, that was it. *Off his face.* Been here before. He lifted a hand, feeling the weird, complex pull of flesh and muscle. He focused on his palm. It appeared to be further away than the walls were. Now that *was* odd.

Somebody giggled.

Was there someone here? Where was *here* anyway?

He dropped his arm as a new sensation washed through him. He'd cast himself loose, cut himself off from everything he knew, everyone who'd been part of his life. That had been bad enough, but now he'd taken an even bigger step. This one took him out of the universe.

There wasn't anyone out here. No one at all. Not even himself.

He'd lost his grip and fallen off the edge of reality.

CHAPTER EIGHT

Jarek could hear singing. He knew, in the bit of his mind still operating rationally, that it was only a shiftspace hallucination, but it sounded just like Elarn practising her scales. He listened for a while, because sometimes the best way to deal with shiftspace was to just let the weirdness wash over you.

The scales resolved into a tune, one he thought he knew, and suddenly he found he was crying. He didn't fight the tears. His sister was lost to him for ever, and she'd died without forgiving him.

As he raised his hands to rub his eyes he remembered there was someone else here; he was spending this transit in the rec-room, not the bridge, because he had company. He blinked until his vision cleared and looked around. The room still swam and sparkled, but that was a common shiftspace effect. At first he couldn't see anyone else. Then he looked down.

Taro was lying on the floor, curled into a tight foetal ball.

Jarek hesitated. He was accustomed to the altered states experienced during transit, but he wasn't used to dealing with other people while he was in the shift. He would always remember Nual's violent reaction the first time she'd gone into transit with him.

Taro, on the other hand, appeared to have gone catatonic.

Jarek knew better than to bend down. Bodies got unpredictable in the shift, and moving your centre of balance too far or too fast was unwise. He slid off the sofa, momentarily seeing himself as an avalanche of flesh, before firmly shutting out that particular illusion. He landed next to Taro. The boy didn't move and for a moment Jarek thought he might be dead. He reached out a careful hand to touch his back. The flesh felt warm, alive, but Taro didn't react to his touch.

He kept his hand where it was and called Taro's name. His voice sounded muted, with a faint buzz to it – another shiftspace special – but Taro gave no sign of having heard him. Jarek hesitated, then put both arms around him. Though he had a good natural immunity to the effects of shiftspace – pretty much a prerequisite in his line of work – everyone knew of people who lost themselves completely in the shift, emerging irrevocably insane. He held Taro, saying his name all the while.

At some point he felt a change go through the boy's body and he realised Taro was saying something, over and over. It sounded like 'They're all dead, they're all dead, they're all dead.' Then he raised his head and stared blankly at Jarek with no recognition in his eyes. He started to cry, the deep, unselfconscious sobbing of a much younger child. Jarek wondered if he should talk to him, but he had no idea what to say, so he just kept holding him while he cried.

Even when the tears ran out Jarek didn't move, though he could feel his legs going numb.

Finally, normality returned.

Taro gasped and pulled back, looking confused and embarrassed.

'It's all right,' said Jarek, secretly relieved at how ordinary he sounded, how boring the world looked; he'd weathered another transit. 'We're out of the shift and everything's fine.'

'Is it ... over?' Taro croaked.

'It's over. I need to get up to the bridge now, but I won't be long. I suggest you lie down because you probably won't be good for much for the next few hours.' He stood, and exhaustion, magnified by the usual shiftspace hangover, hit him so hard he almost fell. *What a way to make a living*, he thought, and hauled himself up the ladder.

The core systems restarted without a hitch. As soon as coms

were up and running he paid the additional tariff for making a flash-transit and informed traffic control that he was just passing through. Then he slaved his com to the main comp, instructing it to inform him if any other ships arrived in-system, setting the alarm loud enough to wake the dead.

Taro had managed to get himself onto the couch and was dozing. He opened his eyes when Jarek approached. 'I remember ...' he slurred, then tried again, 'Was I ...?'

'Don't worry. That kind of shit happens in shiftspace.'

Taro's eyes were already closing again.

Jarek lurched off to his own cabin. He allowed himself six hours' sleep, though he'd have liked twice that long. The alarm awoke him from a dream of trudging through mud in ill-fitting boots. He'd spent a lot of time doing that on Serenein.

When he got up Taro was sitting at the galley table drinking caf. 'You're looking a lot better,' Jarek said.

'I feel it. Shiftspace is well freaky. Thanks for looking after me.' He nodded to indicate his drink. 'You want one?'

'Yes. Thanks.' Jarek had been uncomfortable at the thought of having his haven invaded, but so far he was finding his guests surprisingly easy to get on with. Perhaps he'd been alone for too long; maybe the time had come to risk relationships that went beyond commerce or sex. He watched Taro tuck his long braid behind his ear, then bend down to get Jarek a mug. *And talking of sex ...* whatever else, having the boy around gave him something interesting to look at – even if the little sod was a little too aware of how pretty he was.

Taro managed to stay quiet while they finished their drinks, but as soon as Jarek pushed his mug away he asked, 'Can we wake Nual up now?'

'I'll make sure she's all right, but I wasn't going to wake her yet.'

'Why not?'

'Because I'll only have to put her out again in a couple of hours. I'm afraid we're going to make another transit as soon as the transit-kernel has ... recharged.' Jarek hoped Taro wouldn't pick up on his hesitation. 'I don't know if the ship that shifted into the Khathryn system was Sidhe, but I've got a list of suspicious ships, and that one was on it. I'd like to put a few more transits between us and them.'

'What about the time we spent in shiftspace? It felt like we were in there for hours.'

'As far as anyone has been able to tell, no time passes in real-space during a transit. From the point of view of someone outside shiftspace, it's instantaneous. Possibly no time passes in the shift, our brains just try and make some to keep us sane.'

'That's pretty gappy.' Taro put his head on one side. 'Any chance of something stronger to deal with the smoky shit this time?'

'The first transit is usually the worst, but I'll see what I can find.'

Taro insisted on accompanying Jarek to the hold. Nual was stable, all life-signs normal.

Back in the rec-room Taro said, 'Can I ask you something? About Nual.'

'Sure,' said Jarek carefully.

'How'd you find her?' Taro added more uncertainly, 'I could ask her but she don't like talking about the past.'

'Yes, I've noticed.' Jarek should have seen that question coming. He gestured for Taro to sit again and tried to order his thoughts. 'So, what *do* you know?'

'You met seven years ago, and she trusts you. That's about it.'

'Well, we met by accident. I was taking a rarely used transit-path, trying to make up lost time after an incident with some un-reasonable customs officials. When the *Judas Kiss* came out of tran-sit, I realised I wasn't at a registered beacon. I was deep in inter-stellar space, nowhere near any known paths or inhabited systems. But there was a ship there. I didn't spot it at first because it had no running-lights and it wasn't transponding. I tried pinging it, but got no answer. I went in closer. It looked like a huge bronze egg. I wondered if it could be an alien artefact – that would be a *real* find – but the design looked human; when I got up close I could see it had normal-looking airlocks and standard sensor apparatus. It reminded me of the old colony-ships, early Protectorate stuff, but they're all long gone, except for the ones that got stripped down and incorporated into hub stations. The ship was dead in space, though I couldn't see any damage.' Jarek laughed at himself. 'I started thinking of claiming salvage rights, but first I needed to check there was no one alive on board.

'It turned out there was, sort of. It was a Sidhe ship, and there must have been hundreds of them on board, maybe thousands of people including their mutes. Only ... something had happened. They'd gone mad, turned on each other. It must have happened a few days before I got there because by the time I arrived most of them were already dead and the rest – well, they just ignored me. A lot of them had mutilated themselves. Or each other ...'

Jarek swallowed hard. He wasn't likely to ever forget the things he'd seen on the derelict ship. 'Nual hadn't been affected because she'd been isolated from the rest of them. Later she told me she'd rebelled, questioning the authority on the ship, and they'd put her in a cell. When the madness started, she barricaded herself in.'

'How did she know you weren't one of these crazy Sidhe when you turned up?'

'Because she called me to her. Somehow she pulled me out of shiftspace.'

'That sounds pretty heavy.'

'It is. I've no idea how she did it. She didn't know herself. I doubt she's done anything like it since, but she was desperate, scared out of her wits and half dead from thirst and hunger.' He remembered that most clearly, his pity when he first saw her, filthy and naked – pity which, she later admitted, she'd amplified to make sure he helped her. Even now it was futile to try and work out how many of the choices he'd made that day had been truly his own. 'When I found her, she couldn't even speak.'

'Had they ... tortured her?'

'Maybe; I didn't ask. What I meant was that she didn't know *how* to speak. The Sidhe on her ship hardly used verbal communication, unless occasionally to reinforce what they were "saying"

– the way we use body language. They'd use certain sounds to add extra emphasis.'

'So how did she talk to you?'

'At first it was pure emotion: terror, pity, then when she realised I used spoken language, she read how to do that from me.'

'How long did that take?'

'About ten minutes, for the basics.'

'Shit! That's fast—'

'Yeah, I know. Once we'd established communication, I helped her out of the cell and we set off through the ship. There were bodies everywhere, and some live crazies, but they hardly seemed to notice us. Then we bumped into a Sidhe who wasn't mad, or at least, not totally psychotic. There was something different about her. Something ... focused, I guess. By this time Nual was flagging and I was supporting her; this other Sidhe came up behind us, shoved me forward, and pulled Nual out of my arms. I stumbled and fell, but once she'd got Nual she lost interest in me and by the time I'd got to my feet she'd pinned Nual down on the floor and was staring into her eyes. There was some sort of silent battle going on, and Nual was losing. The Sidhe had her back to me, so I shot her. Then we ran.

'We got back to my ship and I transited out to the beacon I'd originally been heading for. Nual said the transit-kernel in her ship was damaged, but even if it had been working I don't think the Sidhe were in any state to come after us.

'I took Nual to Khathryn. I don't know if she told you, but she reacts very badly to transits, so she could hardly stay with me – I travel all the time. I didn't have a comabox then – I could've bought one for her, but I wasn't comfortable with the idea of trolling around the spaceways with a Sidhe in tow. Elarn and I had our differences but I thought – stupidly – that the two of them might help each other. Elarn has – *had* – a sort of misplaced mothering instinct, and Nual was completely alone in the world, with no clue about the wider universe. Anyway, it was a *really* bad idea. They got too close, and then Elarn realised I'd brought a Sidhe into her home. She threw us both out and said she never wanted to see me again. I took Nual to Vellern in the Tri-Confed system because I thought it was a good place for her to hide, being so busy and anarchic. I was right, because they didn't find out she was there until they captured me at Serenein and ... interrogated me.'

They sat in silence for a while. Then Taro said, 'I reckon she hates herself sometimes. For what she is, the stuff she can do.'

'Yeah,' said Jarek, 'you may be right.'

Though neither of them had any more than the usual human level of empathy, Jarek thought they were both thinking along the same lines: their shared transit experience had given them the beginnings of a bond, and with Nual unconscious, they were as independent of her influence as they'd ever be. Yet they still loved her, both of them, in their different ways. He had no idea if that observation came from true objectivity or was just a comforting illusion.

CHAPTER NINE

Jarek was right, thought Taro as he watched the formless blobs of nameless colour amble through his vision: shiftspace wasn't so bad when you got used to it. This was his third transit; according to Jarek, three back-to-back shifts should ensure they'd lose any possible tail from Khathryn.

He remembered – vaguely – that he'd gone well gappy during the first transit. Jarek didn't mention it afterwards, so Taro decided not to stress about it. Truth be told, he felt a little better for letting some of that shit out.

For the second transit he'd snorted a bit too much of the happy-dust, and all he recalled now was grinning till his face hurt, and some odd dreams about body parts dropping off. To his embarrassment he came out of it to discover he'd pissed himself. Jarek said that happened sometimes if you over-medicated and got a bit lost so Taro decided to ease back on the inhaler in future.

This time the transit wasn't much worse than a smoky trip. The coloured blobs smelled surprisingly nice, except for that last one, which was a bit like shit burning. Taro considered asking Jarek whether there was any shit on fire around here, but he found he'd lost the ability to speak. He'd best just assume there wasn't. After a while the smell went away and the blob morphed into a giant floating head which expanded until the features were stretched absurdly tight, then burst in a shower of petals.

The trick with transits was to remember that this head-fuck was something that would pass, like bad drugs, or a nightmare: it was weird shit, maybe even nasty, but it wasn't dangerous. Even so, he was relieved when it was over. He resisted the urge to sleep off the after-effects, though three shifts in quick succession left him pretty trashed, because it was finally time to wake Nual up.

He waited by the comabox while Jarek sorted the controls and she came to. It took ages. She finally emerged groggy, but unharmed.

'You all right?' asked Taro. She looked a bit pale.

'I'm fine,' she said, 'and I remember nothing of being in shift-space. How did you cope?'

'Oh, it was a bit smoky at first. We made three transits while you were out, so I'm a veteran now.'

Back in the rec-room, Jarek fixed them some caf and food, or what passed for food now the ship had run out of fresh supplies and they were relying on recycled flavoured gloop or freeze-dried rations. Nual insisted on clearing up afterwards. Taro watched her from the table, glad she was awake and unharmed.

Jarek stood up and said, 'I need to get some sleep now, and then we'll wake our guest. He should be more or less healed by then, and able to answer a few questions.'

Taro had almost forgotten the pilot from the Sidhe ship, who was still lying, totally out of it, on the couch by the wall.

'You might want to get some rest too,' he said to Taro. Then, to Nual, 'I'm guessing you're not tired. Will you be all right by yourself?'

'Now that we won't be making any more transits for a while?'

'Yeah.'

Nual looked at him oddly. 'What is it, Jarek? What is it you need to say? I'm trying not to read you, but your mind is full of this *thing* whenever you talk about shiftspace.'

Jarek expelled a low breath and sat down again. 'I should've told you earlier, but the time wasn't right. Actually, it's probably better I didn't mention it before, for Taro's sake; it's not something you want to think about during your first transit. It's about Serenein. The big secret, the whole reason the Sidhe set the place up—' He looked at Nual, then Taro. 'They're selectively breeding boys with a certain ... unusual talent. They can enter shiftspace at will.'

'Why do they want these boys?' asked Nual warily.

Jarek cleared his throat. 'Actually, I wondered if you might have an idea about that, given what happened when you first went into shiftspace alone.'

'You think – you think this relates to the mind I sensed in the shift? The mind in your ship?'

'Am I missing something here?' asked Taro, looking between the two of them.

'Jarek is referring to my problem with shiftspace. Did he tell you about that?'

'Not really. He did tell me how he found you, on the ship where everyone'd gone gappy.'

'That would be one way of putting it. We used to enter the shift in unity; I would mesh my will with my sisters to create our own island of sanity amidst the chaos. On the *Judas Kiss* I had no such support, and once in shiftspace my mind instinctively searched for another of my kind to save me from the void. I couldn't help myself. And I found ... There *is* a mind here, within the drive-column of this ship, and it has been here for many centuries, imprisoned, warped; driven mad. I ...' She looked down at her hands. 'I knew then that broken creature was the force that powers your ship through shiftspace, but I did not say. Perhaps I should have.'

'So—' Taro looked at her. 'So you're saying there's a boy from Serenein hidden on board this ship, and that's what makes us go into shiftspace?'

'Not exactly,' said Jarek. 'Transit-kernels were invented by the Sidhe, and they're very hard to make – hence the rarity of shiftships. They're sealed black boxes hidden deep within the drive-column. Trained engineers can't do much more than check the interface between the kernel and the rest of the ship's systems, because if they fuck with the box then the kernel stops working – or worse, blows up spectacularly. They say one set off a chain-reaction with a beacon at a hubpoint once. Thousands of people died. That whole system was lost.'

'Where do these transit-kernels come from?' asked Taro.

'A handful of companies, operating under great secrecy, supply them to the shipyards. But now I believe the minds within them come from Serenein. The locals send the boys who make the grade up into orbit, thinking they're ascending to Heaven, but what actually happens is that the Sidhe pick them up. That's why the *Setting Sun* went to Serenein.'

'The sick fuckers,' said Taro angrily. 'So where do they take them?'

'I don't know. But the pilot will, and that's why we need to wake him up. But first, I have to get some rest. And so do you.'

Nual told them both she'd be fine; she just needed time to think, so Taro used the spare cabin. When he lay down he buried his head in the pillow, trying to catch her scent, but it just smelled musty. He slept badly, with more nasty dreams, this time of being slowly walled up inside a tiny room, paralysed and unable to do anything but watch as the last chinks of light disappeared and the air grew thick and hard to breathe.

Jarek was already up and about when he awoke. Over the meal that Taro decided to call breakfast he asked where they were now.

'Xantier. It's a hubpoint.'

'Is there much to see here? The last hub we visited was pretty boring.'

'Hub stations usually are when it comes to sightseeing, though Xantier's a hollow-earth, so it's a bit more interesting than most. They're where I do most of my business though.' He pulled a wry face. 'Thanks to the assorted bribes and fines I've had to pay recently, I need to sell those Old Earth artefacts quickly, so we're going to have to stay here a while, at least long enough for messages from potential buyers to catch up with me.'

'Is that safe?' asked Nual. 'Could the Sidhe pick up your beevee communication?'

'If the Sidhe have got good databreakers they could theoretically spot messages being routed to me, but they'd have to actively search through massive amounts of well-protected data, and that would attract attention. I'd prefer to assume they haven't got that much power.' He stood up. 'While we make our way to Xantier

Station we should talk to our guest.' He went over to the medical couch. 'It's probably best if you two stay back there, out of his line of sight. Nual, there's a good chance he won't co-operate, in which case, I might need to call on your talents. If that's all right.'

She must have sensed Taro's unease, for she spoke in his mind <*Reading someone is not like healing them. There will be no bond created.*>

Taro projected reluctant acceptance.

Out loud Nual said, 'I will help if you need me to.'

Jarek strapped the pilot firmly onto the couch, then made adjustments to the drips and monitors. When he was satisfied, he stood back and waited.

After a few minutes the pilot twitched, then groaned. He tried to move his arms, grunting in surprise when he found he couldn't. Taro didn't see him open his eyes but he saw the way he stopped struggling and focused on Jarek.

His voice hoarse, the pilot said, 'You—? You killed them, you bastard!'

'That's right,' Jarek said calmly. 'Your mistresses are dead. They've been dead more than three weeks, and we're far from Serenein. But you're still alive and back in good shape now, thanks to me.'

'I don't owe you shit.'

'I didn't really expect gratitude. And I'm guessing you don't particularly want to tell me about your life with the Sidhe.'

'Go fuck yourself.'

'That's pretty much what I thought you'd say.'

The pilot snorted. 'Is this the bit where you tell me there's an easy way and a hard way and I just picked the hard way?'

'Actually, no.' Jarek gestured towards Nual, who got up and began to walk across the room. 'This is the bit where I introduce you to my friend.' He stepped back. The pilot turned as far as his restraints allowed.

'What—?' he said, confused. Then his eyes widened. 'My God, you're—'

'Aye,' said Nual. 'I am.'

She stood close enough that he could have touched her if his hands had been free. They stayed like that for some time, silent, staring into each other's faces. The only thing that moved was the pilot's heaving chest.

Taro felt a flash of jealousy; this was the first time she'd shared head-space with anyone other than him. He pressed his hands together and tried to fight the feeling.

Finally Nual shook her head and took a step backwards.

The pilot closed his eyes and let go an explosive sigh.

An expression of dismay on her face, Nual said, <*We need to talk. On the bridge, away from him.*>

She must've been speaking in Jarek's head too, for he started moving at the same time as Taro.

They followed her up the ladder. On the bridge the viewing bubble was half open. A couple of the distant lights were moving, which seemed to Taro like an odd thing for stars to do. When he stared at them, Jarek said, 'Those are other ships. This is a busy place.' Then, to Nual, 'So, what was all that about?'

She folded her legs and sat down on the floor; Taro followed suit. Jarek took the couch.

'His mind is not like that of other humans,' she said. 'Though the Sidhe have conditioned him to worship them, his contact with them has also given him some ability to resist their powers. I cannot force him to co-operate with us.'

'Damn it,' said Jarek. 'How about just charging through? Never mind what he wants, go in there and get what we need to know. He had his chance to tell us freely and he turned it down. The gloves are off now.'

Nual shook her head. 'He has deep, strong shields, unlike anything a human could normally maintain. This was something the Sidhe did to him – similar to what I did to you, with your consent, to hide my whereabouts. I suspect it happened because he was lover to more than one of them, and each sister wanted a piece of his mind that was her own.'

'Shields like that can still be broken,' said Jarek bitterly. 'I should know.'

'They can, but it would take skill, and possibly more than one Sidhe acting in unity. I could maybe penetrate them by brute force, but in doing so I would probably break his mind, making him useless to us.'

'My original plan, before I met up with you, was to use drugs on him. Perhaps if we combined drugs with your powers we might get somewhere?'

'Perhaps,' she said. She didn't sound convinced.

'Do we have to get into his head at all?' asked Taro.

'We may never get a chance like this again,' said Jarek, 'so, yes, we have to try. Nual, what effect would be best? The med-bay's got a fair selection of drugs.'

'I am really not sure that would work. Drugging him might make it easier for me to break through, but it would also increase the chances of destroying the very knowledge we are trying to extract.'

'I guess that's a risk I'm willing to take,' said Jarek.

'There is another option.' Nual sounded hesitant. She rubbed her wrist, looking uneasy. 'He told me … This man's whole existence revolves around his intense love for the Sidhe. He has made it clear that he will allow me freely past his shields if I …' Her voice trailed off.

'Oh no,' said Jarek. 'He wants you to sleep with him, doesn't he? The *shit*.'

'It may be our only choice – if you think the information he has is worth it.'

'No way!' Taro stared at her, horrified. 'You can't – you're not serious!'

Ignoring him, Nual said to Jarek, 'Is his knowledge really that important?'

'I think it is. But I won't ask you to—'

'Fuck's sake, why're we even having this discussion?' said Taro, his voice rising.

Nual turned to him and he felt the full force of her will, subtle as mist, hard as rock. 'This is not about you, or about you and me, Taro. This is about the Sidhe and what they have done, and what they are still doing to humanity.'

Maybe she was right, but the pain, sharp as a kick in the balls, made him selfish. 'You said you'd never hurt me and now you're about to fuck some Sidhe stooge!'

'How many people have you slept with whom you did not love, Taro?'

'That's different. That was before. I'm with *you* now.'

'And this would be different. It is a ... necessary evil.'

'What if it's a trick? Like with Elarn: you get inside his head then it all goes to shit!'

'Such a trap would have sprung when I first read him. He has the resilience of one accustomed to close contact with the Sidhe, but I do not believe his head contains anything that can harm me. If we want the information he is hiding, this is the only way.'

Taro wanted to scream at her, but he knew it wouldn't do any good, so he turned away.

Behind him he heard Jarek say, 'You don't have to do this.'

And Nual replied, 'No, I don't. But I will.'

CHAPTER TEN

Jarek suspected the only reason Taro didn't storm off was that there was nowhere to storm off to.

Nual said, 'If it is to be done, I will do it straight away.'

Jarek got up and followed her. Taro didn't move.

The pilot opened his eyes as they approached and dismissed Jarek with barely a glance. He looked only at Nual. His ravenous adoration made Jarek want to shudder, even as he undid the restraints and stepped back.

The pilot sat up a little shakily. To prepare him for his interrogation, Jarek had administered drugs that would temporarily offset the effects of spending several weeks unconscious. That energy was going to be put to a rather different use now. Nual held out a hand. The pilot took it and eased himself off the couch, already looking more alert and comfortable. As she led him to the spare cabin, Jarek turned away. Disgust and guilt washed through him, but he told himself this was Nual's choice. He hoped he'd been right when he told her that it was a price worth paying.

He headed up to the bridge to check on Taro, who was sitting exactly where they'd left him, his head on his knees, hugging himself. When he raised his head, Jarek saw the raw pain on the boy's face. It stirred his confused emotions: pity tinged his annoyance at Taro's immaturity.

He had no idea what to say, but Taro saved him the trouble. 'How could she fucking do this to me?' he spat.

Irritation overcame sympathy. 'She's not doing it *to you*, Taro,' said Jarek. 'She's doing it because *she* chooses to. It's *her* choice; you don't get to make choices for her. That's not how love works.'

'How can you say that?' Taro was breathing hard. 'You have no fucking idea how much I fucking love her. There's nothing I wouldn't do to make her happy. *Nothing!* If she asked me, I'd fucking die for her.'

For a moment Jarek weighed up the wisdom of antagonising the boy, before deciding that getting him angry might be what he needed; it would at least spare him several hours watching Taro wallow in abject self-pity. 'Well, obviously you would,' he said. 'She's Sidhe. That's how they are; they make us love them.'

'No!'

Jarek took a step back at Taro's shout.

'It's not fucking like that with us!' He sprang up suddenly, moving with alarming speed as he swept both arms back and the blades appeared from nowhere.

Jarek jumped back, unable to stop staring at the long silver spikes, the Angels' trademarks, alongside the lasers and the flight.

Taro drew a sudden breath, as though he'd surprised himself, and brought his arms forward, staring at his hands. As the blades retracted he curled his fingers, pressing his nails into his palms to make tight fists. He sank to his knees, crying and swearing under his breath, '*Shit, shit, shit, shit, shit!*'

Afterwards, Jarek analysed all the possible reasons for what he did next: a reaction to thinking he was about to get his throat ripped out, then finding he wasn't; Taro's odd combination of world-weariness and vulnerability; his intriguing looks, and finally a sudden and totally unexpected flash of lust that came out of the blue but was most likely, he later realised, the mental backwash from the cabin below.

Now he acted without thinking, walking up to the boy and lifting his head in his hands – on his knees, the top of Taro's head came up to his chin – then bending down to kiss him hard on the lips.

He felt Taro tense and he pulled back as his mind caught up with what his body had just done.

Taro focused on him, swallowed hard, then leaned up and

returned the kiss with bruising force. He began to float to his feet, one arm creeping round to grasp Jarek's arse, the other hooking around his neck.

While Taro's tongue insinuated itself into his mouth Jarek tried to remember the last time he'd had sex – far too long ago. He'd just spent several months on a world where, even if he hadn't had other things on his mind, his sexuality could've got him into a lot of trouble. And Taro was a fine-looking creature, slender, youthful, sensuous ... and suddenly amazingly self-assured.

As Taro broke from the kiss he was moulding his body to Jarek's—

This was wrong: Taro was barely an adult, and he was deeply messed up. He was only coming on to Jarek because of what Nual was doing; to respond would be taking advantage ...

So why did Jarek feel like he was the one being seduced?

'What's the matter?' breathed Taro into his ear. 'Never fucked a whore before?' He moved his hand from Jarek's arse, trailing it round the side of his leg, 'Or didn't you know' – his hand came to rest on Jarek's groin, which appeared to be the only part of his body that was functioning normally – 'that's what I am?'

Jarek had occasionally paid for sex, in theocracies – like Khathryn, his homeworld – where homosexuality was illegal and the only safe alternative to celibacy was to use prostitutes. But he didn't much care for it, and he'd never paid to screw someone he actually knew. If he'd been thinking straight he'd have pushed the boy away ... but then Taro started to stroke him with just the right mixture of firmness and tenderness, and he began having trouble thinking at all.

Taro stopped, hand splayed across Jarek's crotch. 'You do want me,' he breathed, 'don't you?'

'God yes, I think that's pretty fucking obvious,' said Jarek, with some difficulty. Somewhere in the back of his mind, a vague justification was beginning to take shape: Taro needed this, to make him feel he was worth something in the terms he was used to – and that meant sex.

'So what's the problem?' Taro started to press: gently, firmly, expertly.

Before he lost the power of speech completely, Jarek murmured, 'No problem. Carry on.' He only hoped he had enough sense left to get himself out of his clothes without help.

How could humans have only one word for love? Because she did love Taro, she was sure of it. If she didn't, she would never put up with him, his sulks and tantrums. Yet here she was, *making love* with someone she did not know at all – not even his name. The pilot had defined himself entirely by the role he had held, and though he used names when dealing with humans, they weren't real; his birth name was buried too deep for her to unearth.

Only two humans had seen her naked before: Jarek, when he first found her, and Elarn. And though Elarn had touched her, their lovemaking had been cut short when she realised what Nual was. Nual's inexperience was making her a little nervous, and the pilot picked up on that. She let him take the lead, projecting an air of passivity that both baffled and excited him. He had anticipated dominance from her and this unexpected chance to display his skills flattered his ego.

Though she felt no threat from this man, she felt no attraction to him either. But she knew that the ability to give and receive pleasure existed independently of the physical actions of sex, so she let him fondle, lick and nibble, and tried to tie the sensations he caused with those she knew as pleasure. She began to touch him in return, edging into the surface of this mind in order to read how her efforts affected him, assimilating the knowledge of what he liked, then using it. Sometimes she misjudged him, because his ideas of pleasure were complex, tied up with concepts of power, pain and addiction.

<You're quite young, aren't you?>

His voice in her head made her freeze. After a moment she responded, *<Not so young as you think. And I suspect I have killed more people than you have slept with, human.>*

That shut him up. He concentrated on showing her how good

at this he was. She let him, and as she became accustomed to this strange new language of flesh and fluid, she started to take enjoyment as her right.

After a while his need began to eclipse everything else in his head. She let him guide himself into her. It hurt. She dulled the pain at once, but for a moment it drove out any idea that this was an act of pleasure. He ground into her, grunting like a beast, and she tried to latch onto the sensation, either to enjoy it or to use it, but he was lost to her, his mind a whirl of formless desire. He came quickly, with an undignified bellow. She would have liked to get deeper into his head while his guard was down, but the release was too sudden, too unexpected.

When he collapsed onto her she felt a moment of nausea, revolted by the idea of his seed inside her, although she knew he was clean and healthy – his Sidhe mistresses would not have tolerated anything else.

So far all the experience had done was increase her contempt for the man, but if she stopped now she would have achieved nothing; his deep shields remained as strong as ever.

Besides, the backwash of his climax had awakened something in her mind that was nothing to do with sex or pleasure. A shadow of unity.

Stifling her feelings of distaste she thought to him, *< That hardly met the terms of our agreement.>*

<No, I'm sorry. Please, give me a moment.>

He withdrew, leaving her feeling sticky, and a little cold. Though she did not relish the thought of continuing, now he had made himself vulnerable to her by letting himself go in orgasm, she felt more comfortable with this thing they did.

When they resumed she found that his shields had finally begun to relax. She took care broaching them. If he chose, he could still block her. She did her best to make sure he was distracted enough not to.

By the time he was ready to enter her again she was somewhat distracted herself. Even though the situation was unpalatable, there was no doubt his mixture of confidence and subservience was arousing her, helped by her imagining that the hands stroking and fondling belonged to Taro. She was also growing more confident herself; having maintained a parallel mental connection to their physical contact, she suspected she could, if she chose, control his pleasure purely by exerting her will over him. It was tempting, but as she had said herself, that was not the bargain they had made.

This time, she took the lead.

As she rocked up and down and he writhed under her, she felt their physical union strengthening their mental connection, a coming together of minds that fed off the coming together of bodies.

This wasn't unity, because unity had nothing to do with such mindless grinding and rubbing to stimulate physical pleasure. But it was what he craved, and perhaps what she needed.

Letting her body do what it wanted, she dived deeper into his head. The resistance was gone. In return, she felt her mind opening, just as her body did.

Opening to him.

He knew this sensation well; his life was built around such false unity. She was new to it, inexperienced and uncertain. He began to take control. She felt her resilience cracking, felt herself falling into desire, willingly becoming its slave. He knew how sex could affect the mind. Even as he gave himself to her, he was undermining her psyche.

But he was only human.

She was Sidhe.

She neither knew nor liked this man, but in some ways she understood him more completely than she did Jarek or Taro. He was a creature of the Sidhe, conditioned to their touch; his joy was to love and obey them.

To receive such adulation was her birthright.

First she reined back her own pleasure, dissociating herself from what her body was doing so she could focus. Then she clamped her will over his, deflecting his attempts to subvert her mind. At the same time she froze his pleasure, cutting his consciousness free of the cycle of arousal and fulfilment.

He gasped in shock.

She released him again, amplifying and enhancing the sensations he yearned to feel. He bucked beneath her, giving a wordless cry. Those parts of his mind not drowning in ecstasy were filled with remorse, a wordless pleading for her forgiveness for having dared to become the dominant partner.

She took him to the brink and left him there, not granting him the release of orgasm, pulling back even as he begged her to let him go.

Then she did it all over again.

This was almost too easy. He revelled in the exquisite torture, any ambition to fight her driven from his mind. And she had free access to his thoughts.

The wave of rising pleasure surprised her. The signals from her own body were interfering with her concentration, and for a moment she considered blocking the sensation, or else bringing herself to climax quickly, the better to free herself of such distractions.

But then, why should she not enjoy this to the full?

Maintaining her hold, forbidding him to orgasm, she forced him to work faster, slaving his will to her pleasure. As she came she heard herself cry out and wondered at the lack of dignity, even as she relished the mindless release.

After the last shudders had passed through her she pushed herself fully upright, focusing on her partner for the first time in some minutes. His skin was grey and filmed with sweat, his half-healed stomach wound livid. But he looked up at her as a worshipper looks upon a goddess.

She touched his forehead with a quivering finger, smiling as pleasure exploded through him and he shuddered beneath her. She let herself ride the sensation, all thoughts of reading him forgotten in the face of this wordless, animal communion.

She felt his physical climax riding hard on the mental one, and retained just enough self-control to block it.

Her eyes were still closed when he spoke in her head, his voice ragged with yearning. *<Please, like we agreed. Make it complete.>*

She opened her eyes, and looked straight into his.

As she began to move on him for the last time, she sensed the fear in him, the soul-deep realisation of what he had committed himself to.

A final wave of resistance passed through him.

She dispelled it effortlessly.

CHAPTER ELEVEN

Jarek woke slowly, wondering what the weight on his leg was. Of course: Taro. They'd ended up in his cabin eventually. The couch on the bridge wasn't built for sex, though that hadn't stopped Taro trying. Jarek smiled to himself, before remembering how the evening had started. Hot on the heels of that memory a new realisation swam up from the depths; another discovery he'd made at Serenein, one that hadn't seemed immediately relevant before last night.

He eased Taro's leg away and sat up, wincing at a twinge from his bruised ribs.

Taro opened his eyes, smiled up at Jarek, then frowned, no doubt also remembering why they'd ended up in bed together.

'Did you want to stay here for a while?' asked Jarek. He hoped he would. The extra complication that had just occurred to him was going to make things even worse for the boy.

'No,' said Taro, though he didn't look convinced. Jarek found some relatively clean clothes, and lent Taro a robe.

Nual sat alone at the table, nursing a steaming mug. From her still-wet hair Jarek guessed she'd just showered. 'Good morning,' he said with forced cheerfulness.

She looked around, surprised; she must've been so deep in thought that she hadn't sensed them there. Taro put his arms around Jarek's waist, with his head on his shoulder and one hand dangling just above Jarek's groin. Jarek resisted the urge to shake him off; pleasant though the contact was, Taro wasn't doing it for his benefit.

Nual said nothing, just looked at the two of them, her face un-readable.

Jarek decided there was no easy way to tell her what she needed to know. 'Listen, did you ... if you didn't, uh, take precautions you might want to get yourself checked out.'

He felt Taro tense.

Nual spoke slowly and carefully, as though each word was fragile, potentially dangerous. 'What do you mean?'

'Well, you know ...' He'd assumed she'd probably use contra-ception, until he thought about the kind of solitary life she must have led. 'Precautions, as in—'

'No,' she said, her voice as cold as space. 'I did not.' She stared at him for a moment, then flinched. 'Why did you not tell me this before?' she hissed.

'Tell her what?' Taro's voice was loud in Jarek's ear. 'What is it?' He pulled back.

Jarek wanted to go up to the bridge and pretend he was still alone on his ship. But even before these two had come into his life he'd already started thinking differently. His experiences on Serenein had changed him; he was no longer just a footloose trader, and his ship was no longer a lonely refuge from which to view the universe. He sighed and turned to Taro. 'It's something I forgot to say. I only worked this out recently. Everyone thinks the Sidhe are aliens, a different race to humans. They're not, at least not exactly. They're humans who've mutated – they've been changed genetically. We had a common ancestor, that's for sure, so it's possible—'

Nual cut across him. 'I will do as you suggest. Are there any other revelations you have kept back from us?'

'No,' said Jarek, 'and I didn't mean to hide anything, but the Sidhe screwed me up pretty badly. I'm still getting my life back. If I haven't been as up front as I could've been, then I'm sorry.' In passing, he wondered if Taro had noticed that she said *us*, not *me*.

If he did, he didn't say anything, and neither did Nual. Jarek was tempted to leave them to it, but it looked like restoring har-mony on his ship was down to him. 'So,' he said as casually as he could, 'is it just the three of us for breakfast?' He hoped it was. The atmosphere was bad enough already.

Nual pushed her chair back and stood up. She turned to face them. 'That is right. There will just be the three of us.'

Jarek wasn't sure whether it was intuition or Nual's failure to fully shield her emotions, but he knew something terrible had happened.

'What is it?' he asked. 'Where is he?'

'The pilot is dead.'

'*What?*'

'He is dead, Jarek. I killed him.'

Taro made a strangled noise. Jarek felt his knees buckle. 'I – where is he?' he asked stupidly.

'In the spare cabin.'

'Wait,' said Taro, his voice breaking, 'that can't be right. You— You can't … you didn't.'

'I did.' Her voice gentle, she said, 'It was his wish to die. I granted that wish.'

'You're saying you killed him, but didn't fuck him?' said Taro.

'I am saying that I gave him the death he craved.'

Taro rushed forward, then caught himself. 'No fucking way!'

'Shit, Nual,' said Jarek, as his imagination worked through what she'd just said.

'That was our deal,' said Nual. 'That he be allowed to die in the bliss he was addicted to; in return he let down his barriers and permitted me into his mind.'

Taro stared at her in disbelief.

Jarek said, 'Listen, when I said we needed to find out what he knew— Having sex with someone is one thing; taking their life is something else!'

'And what did you plan to do with him?' asked Nual.

'My plan? I was going to find out what I could – without killing or seriously hurting him – then drop him off somewhere so he could get over what'd happened to him and find a new life.'

'He would *never* be able to *get over it*!' Nual's voice was fierce. 'Do you not understand? He had been with the Sidhe since he was a boy – *they were his life* – and without them, he was already dead inside. All I did was complete the process.'

'Ah, right, so it was a mercy killing, was it?'

'It was, though if you choose not to see it that way then I will have to accept that. You know what I am.' She sounded upset, and Jarek's initial horror and anger began to give way to pity. *Was she doing that to him? Was she influencing his feelings, making him understand her actions, even though she'd just murdered a stranger?*

She shook her head. 'I keep my promises, Jarek. Even the difficult ones. Your feelings are your own.'

'So, was it worth it?' said Taro bitterly. ''Cos if you fucked him and killed him and you never got any secrets out of his head, well, that'd be a top prime joke, wouldn't it?' From Taro's tone of voice he thought it was anything but funny. But he had a point.

Nual closed her eyes and said, 'I have his life.'

Taro grunted and said, 'Enjoy it. I'm going back to bed.' He turned and walked back into Jarek's cabin.

Nual's gaze lingered on the door after it closed. Then she said, 'Did you wish me to ... deal with the pilot?'

Jarek was tempted to say yes; he'd cleared up enough of other people's messes back on the *Setting Sun*. But Nual barely looked capable of holding herself upright, let alone manhandling a dead body anywhere. And he had asked her to do this ...

Jarek hadn't wanted to look at the man's face as they covered it, but he did; he wondered what it would be like to go out in such a state of ecstasy. They carried the body to the airlock, wrapped in the sheet on which he'd died. Before they opened the outer door Jarek said the spacer's elegy, a utilitarian yet sentimental little prayer. He wasn't a Salvatine – and he doubted very much that the pilot had been – but he felt he had to say something to make their actions less like disposing of the evidence after a murder and more like the aftermath of an unavoidable accident.

In the rec-room, Nual started passing on everything she had taken from the man they'd just flushed into space. She spoke quickly and quietly, almost as though she was exorcising herself of him.

Perhaps she was: Jarek briefly wondered if she'd been in his mind at the moment of death. But whatever the means, they'd got the desired result. He asked if she minded him recording her recollections. After a moment's hesitation, she agreed.

The pilot's information was sketchy, of course. He knew of several corporations and worlds with Sidhe infiltrators, but though he might have been aware which companies harboured Sidhe agents, he'd had no idea of their names or positions. He'd heard of a dozen compromised freetrader ships like the *Setting Sun*, four of which were new to Jarek. And he had known where the real Sidhe power-base lay, even if he'd never seen it for himself: six Sidhe mother-ships hidden in the vastness of interstellar space.

Jarek asked, 'A mothership – was that what I found you on?'

Nual started, jogged out of the stolen memories. 'Yes,' she said slowly, 'mine was the seventh. The pilot knew it had been lost, but he had no idea how.' She smiled mirthlessly. 'We know rather more about that, of course.'

'And was he right about the motherships? Are they where things are run from?'

'I suppose that must be the case, though I saw almost nothing of the world outside our ship when I was growing up; until we come of age and adopt a role in the unity our lives are very insular. I knew only that our community was one amongst several, and that we sometimes met others like us.'

'And do they have labs on board?'

'Labs?'

'Laboratories. The Sidhe on Serenein used a tailored retrovirus to control the population. I wonder if they made it on a mother-ship.'

'Possibly. There were places I was forbidden to enter, one of which was the ... I suppose the concept would translate into words as "birthing area". That was where most of my sisters started their lives.'

'So the Sidhe really are clones?' That was the accepted wisdom: the Sidhe were all female, the males were long dead. Legend had it that the last few males had helped humanity to bring down the Protectorate, but they had paid for it with their lives.

'I believe most are clones, though as I never saw these places I cannot know for sure.'

'Most – but not *everyone*? Are you a clone?'

'No. Perhaps one in ten of us were ... the term would be "natural born", though we were all raised together.'

Jarek remembered the male mute he'd seen on the *Setting Sun*. So the Sidhe kept male slaves around for more than just heavy lifting. The mutes were believed to be humans, altered somehow by the Sidhe to make them more compliant, but with the close genetic relationship between human and Sidhe, interbreeding wouldn't necessarily be a problem. 'So they didn't distinguish between the clones and the "natural born"?'

'We were not meant to make such distinctions; but we did, as children do. We naturals thought we were superior, and in our mastery of our abilities, perhaps we were, though we also matured more slowly. And we were more prone to question the natural order.'

'Like you did. That's why you were in that cell, wasn't it? Because you questioned the way things were on the mothership?'

Nual nodded slowly.

She was obviously uncomfortable, but Jarek needed to know as much as she was willing to tell him. 'Can you explain?'

'I had always been fascinated by shiftspace. During one transit I reached out to the transit-kernel at the heart of our ship. I did not know what it was, merely that there was this sleeping ... other ... who awoke during transits. Because I did this from within the unity, I was shielded from the worst excesses of the twisted mind within the kernel – unlike when I made contact with your transit-kernel later. But I sensed enough to know that it was a living sentience, related to us in some way, but tortured beyond endurance. I was appalled, and, because I was in the unity, I could not hide what I'd found, or my feelings about it – I was even proud of myself for taking such a stand, fool that I was. Such disobedience is not to be tolerated. I was punished – isolated physically and mentally – and

I am sure my sisters expected a few weeks of such torture would cure me of my stubborn streak of morality.'

'But that's not how it worked out,' said Jarek carefully.

'No,' said Nual, and looked away.

Jarek wondered if that was the end of it. Between her own memories and the pilot's she'd given him plenty to think about.

Then she said, 'There is something else you need to know, though it is not something I know much about. There is an élite faction that rules the Sidhe. I had no name for them, merely the concept. The pilot knew them as the Court. They have representatives on all the motherships and, according to the pilot, out in the wider universe as well.'

Jarek said, 'Did the pilot ever meet any of this ruling class?' When she shook her head, he pressed her further, asking, 'How about you?'

The pain of recalling her past was beginning to tell; her voice sounded strained as she said, 'The members of the Court on my ship judged me and determined my punishment. Before that I had had little to do with them. There really is nothing more I can tell you about the Court.'

Jarek changed the subject. 'I don't suppose the pilot had the access codes for the computers on his ship?'

Nual's expression grew more distant as she rifled through memories that weren't her own. 'Only the functions he needed to do his job. The rest was gene-locked to the Sidhe.' Then her gaze sharpened. 'One thing he did know: the *Setting Sun* was heading to the place where the boys from Serenein are processed.'

'Now that I'd like to hear about,' said Jarek.

When Jarek went back to his room a little later, Taro was doing a bad job of pretending to be asleep. Jarek showered, went back to the galley and grabbed some food, then made his way to the bridge, where he sat and thought about what they should do next. The autopilot had put them in a wide parking orbit around Xantier Station; Jarek had yet to make a docking request.

When he came back down, Nual was sitting at the table. Taro

was playing a game over at the ents unit, kitted out in interface headset and gloves. The atmosphere in the room was painfully tense. Jarek overrode the game from his com then waited while Taro's arms dropped to his sides.

'Sorry about that,' he said when Taro took the headset off. He raised his voice to make it clear he was addressing them both. 'We need to decide where we go from here.'

'Yes,' said Nual. 'We do.'

Taro was looking anywhere but at Nual.

'I meant generally,' added Jarek, in case they expected him to sort out their relationship problems.

'As did I,' said Nual. 'What do you suggest?'

'I think we need to follow up on what happens to the boys from Serenein.' Jarek turned to Taro. 'We now know that they go to a world called Kama Nui. There's only one shipment every two or three decades – that's how often the Sidhe visit Serenein, because it takes that long to accumulate enough talented boys to make it worth their while. And this time the shipment won't be turning up.'

He looked back at Nual, including them both again. 'By now, the Sidhe's contacts on Kama Nui must be wondering where the *Setting Sun* has got to. The other Sidhe are probably concerned that it hasn't checked in too, so we need to act quickly, before they start acting on their suspicions. However, there're a few complications.

'The first is that if my ship *is* known to the Sidhe, then it would be unwise of me to start sniffing around one of their dirty little secrets. The second is this: I've got business I can only do at a hubpoint: if I don't sell my cargo and raise some credit soon then we won't have a ship with which to carry on the fight against the Sidhe. Also, I still need to get the files I took from the *Setting Sun* decrypted, and Kama Nui isn't the place for that.'

'So you want us to go to Kama Nui and follow up this lead?' Nual didn't sound averse to the idea.

'You don't have to – you're free agents – but that would be ideal. I can drop you there, and I'll only ever be a beevee call away.'

'I am willing to do this,' said Nual. She looked at Taro, who was still ignoring her.

'Taro?' prompted Jarek.

Taro shrugged. 'Maybe,' he said.

Jarek resisted the urge to go over and shake him; he'd probably been just as much of a jerk himself when he was seventeen. 'It'll take us a couple of days to get to Kama Nui: you've got that long to decide,' he said, then added, 'You might want to look the place up and see what you think. It's a top destination for rich holiday-makers, and it's meant to be very beautiful, though I've never got beyond the capital myself.'

'It sounds like an odd place for the Sidhe to be ... *altering* these boys,' said Nual.

'The last place anyone would look, perhaps. There've always been rumours about the place; I met a freetrader once who said she'd taken biotech supplies to Kama Nui in the same run as luxury foodstuffs – both legit, but an odd combination. Though I've not seen any direct evidence myself, I wouldn't be surprised if there's stuff going on there that never sees the light of day.'

The atmosphere aboard the ship remained tense. Taro appeared to be dealing with what Nual had done by pretending she didn't exist, while she was making a conspicuous effort to be considerate without crowding him.

Much as he'd enjoyed the boy's company in bed, Jarek had no intention of being part of his little love-war with Nual, and he suggested he return to sleeping in the rec-room. Taro didn't argue. He did ask if he could join Jarek on the bridge, and he reluctantly agreed. Though he suspected Taro was using it as an excuse to avoid Nual, he soon found that the boy had an insatiable – and refreshing – curiosity about everything from interstellar travel to Jarek's tastes in music.

They were on their final approach to the Kama Nui homeworld when Taro asked Jarek to show him how to download a selection of music tracks onto a dataspike.

'I take it you're going with her then,' said Jarek.

Taro nodded. 'I have to. I still love her, even with ... what happened.'

'Yeah, well, you haven't exactly been faithful to her.'

Taro looked at his hands. 'That's true.'

When the time came to say goodbye he hugged them both, and made sure they knew how to contact him. He could only hope he wasn't sending them into a situation they couldn't handle.

CHAPTER TWELVE

For most of his life Taro had viewed tourists with a mixture of awe and avarice: awe because they came from outside his City – his world – and avarice because of the wealth they brought. Yet now here he was, a tourist himself – well, sort of. Their remaining credit wasn't going to go far on Kama Nui if they went for the full luxury experience, so they took Jarek's advice and entered on youth visas. The permits would allow them to live and work here for a limited time; it was popular with a lot of rich kids who got their families to stump up the price of a ticket, no small expense in itself, and then were able to see the place on the cheap – relatively speaking.

Jarek had timed their arrival carefully, dropping them off just before a regular shuttle from a starliner. Though they looked out of place amongst all the designer finery, they would be able to move through customs with the ordinary tourists.

At least that was the theory.

Taro wasn't surprised when one of the uniformed officials took them aside and asked, politely enough, what a pair of registered assassins wanted to come to Kama Nui for.

'Nothing sinister,' said Nual. 'Just a holiday.'

'I see,' said the man. Taro wondered if he was after a bribe; that was how they'd got the gun past customs on Khathryn: a little bit of hush money. Nual would know. 'The thing is,' continued the official, 'we're a peaceful world. Weapons like yours are illegal here.'

'I understand,' Nual said calmly. 'I am aware that we will have

86

to leave the gun with you for the duration of our stay.'

Taro hadn't been aware of that at all – but he'd left the research to Nual, because he'd thought for a while he might be carrying on without her. Part of him still thought he should be.

'Your blades are a problem too,' continued the official apologetically. 'I'm afraid we'll have to peace-bond them.'

'Of course.'

Taro wondered why Nual didn't apply a bit of Sidhe coercion, rather than leave them completely defenceless, but the peace-bonding turned out to be no more than a token gesture: the official sprayed their wrists with a synth-skin compound which covered the slits the blades emerged from and had them sign waivers; they'd get fined if the covering was broken when they left. Taro hoped no one pissed him off, as his blades still weren't entirely under conscious control.

The pictures and holos of Kama Nui he'd called up on the *Judas Kiss* had looked almost unreal – all shining blues and greens and golds. Jarek had let him watch as they approached over an expanse of deep turquoise water. Taro could hardly believe the sea here was the same stuff as Khathryn's grey-green oceans.

The colourful impression was reinforced when they came out of customs into a reception area bright with flowers and tasteful adverts. The new arrivals were greeted by well fit dark-skinned young men and women who put garlands of pink and orange flowers around their shoulders. Taro had to bend down to receive his.

Beyond the starport, things were rather different. A clean but plain bus drove them the short distance to Stonetown, the capital, through a barren, dusty landscape of faded yellow under a bleached blue sky completely free of clouds. The sea shimmered on the horizon.

Taro found his first impression of Stonetown an odd mixture of the familiar and the alien. The blocky buildings reminded him of Khesh, though the roofs were sloping rather than flat, and the windows were larger. When he looked more closely he saw carved and painted stone decorations, eye-catching patterns with hints of plants or animals or faces, set over doorways and under eaves, running in bands to mark different floors. The streets were crowded, and everywhere he looked he could see familiar business going down: shopping, sightseeing, haggling – though he didn't spot any less respectable trade. Instead of riding in pedicabs, people who weren't walking got around on motorised bicycles or in groundcars or buses. Most of the people were brown-skinned and black-haired, and they were wearing less – though brighter – clothing than he was used to. They even moved differently: less purposefully, like they were walking this way because they felt like it, not because they actually needed to get anywhere.

When the bus doors opened to let them off in the main square, he discovered another difference between here and Khesh. The bus, like the spaceport, had had tinted windows and artificial cooling – *aircon* – but out in the open the burning sun sucked all the moisture from the air and replaced it with heat. Sweat broke out all down his back the instant he stepped into the square and he found himself squinting in the bright light despite the shade from the odd-looking tall trees dotted around the place.

They'd booked accommodation in a hostel, which turned out to be a communal living-space on the third floor of an office building. There were separate sleeping rooms for men and women, and a shared kitchen and common room at one end. And there was aircon too, though it was erratic.

He was half relieved, half annoyed to be forcibly separated from Nual by the sleeping arrangements. They still hadn't talked about what'd happened with the pilot. It hadn't felt right to have that discussion with Jarek around, and meanwhile, Nual continued to act all calm and distant, like there wasn't any problem.

After he'd staked his claim by leaving his few possessions on a bed he went to see how Nual was getting on. He found her looking out of the window in the women's room. The view was mainly rooftops, and the distant glitter of the ocean. Like him she'd stripped off her outer layers; he tried not to stare at the bits of her body her vest top revealed. He wondered if the time was right to bring up what she'd done. There was no one else around, and they had to have it out sometime. Maybe later today. Not now, when they were hot and tired. He nodded at the view and said, 'It don't look much like the brochure; good job we're not really here for the scenery.'

'Would you like to know some of Kama Nui's history?' she asked. She kept her tone neutral, like she was only asking because she knew he couldn't read well yet, not because he'd almost decided not to come with her and so hadn't bothered to research the place. 'It might be useful.'

Taro shrugged. 'If you like.'

'It is not a natural world,' she started. 'When the Sidhe first brought humans here, back in Protectorate times, there was no life on land.'

'Don't look like there's much now.'

Nual ignored the interruption. 'There are two large landmasses, both deserts, but Kama Nui is mainly a water-world. There are tens of thousands of islands. Its natural weather-cycles were always extremes: hot and dry and still for days or weeks or months, then suddenly everything would come together in a wave of cyclones – violent storms, far worse than anything you saw on Khathryn. Anything living in the sea was relatively safe, but life never had a chance to develop on land. What land creatures are here now are all imports, many of them from Old Earth.'

'Seems like an odd place for – what d'you call it? – a "holiday resort"? Odd place for one of those if there was fuck-all here.'

'It is believed the Sidhe carried out some terraforming. They also limited their settlements to areas out of the paths of the worst cyclones, and provided weather-shields for the major islands and the one city – there is still only the one city. The people the Sidhe took from Old Earth to settle Kama Nui were native to marine archipelagos there. They had been relocated when the seas inundated their original homes, so they were used to the idea of retaining their culture through change. Most now live a traditional island lifestyle – at least that's what the guidebooks claim.' She smiled quizzically. 'They also say that even during the Protectorate this place was exclusive, visited only by the lucky few – and of course in those days the lucky few would have been Sidhe.'

'So does that mean they've still got a lot of influence here?' Taro looked around, like he might catch Sidhe agents hiding under the bed. Paranoia was catching.

'No, there is no need to worry,' said Nual. 'The pilot did not consider this place to have any Sidhe presence. He knew only that one of the corporations here is responsible for producing transit-kernels.'

Taro tried to think only about the facts, not how she came to have them. 'I don't s'pose you know which one?'

'No, he'd never been here himself. The last drop-off of shift-minds occurred twenty-five years ago, before he came to live on the *Setting Sun*. He was looking forward to visiting Kama Nui—' Nual appeared to catch herself, then continued, 'There are five corporations large enough to hide such an operation. Once we've settled in we need to find out which one it is.'

'Right,' he said.

She pushed herself away from the window. 'But first we should go shopping: we need clothes and we need food.'

Taro followed her out in silence.

Halfway down the stairs they met a youth a little older than Taro coming up. He had pale skin and sandy hair and wore a brightly coloured shirt with a wrap in clashing colours tied around his waist. 'Kioruna!' he said brightly as he passed.

To Taro's surprise Nual responded, 'Kioruna!'

The boy stopped on the stairs, his gaze flicking between the two of them with open curiosity. 'Just arrived?' he said cheerfully.

'Yes, this afternoon,' said Nual.

'Well, if you're heading out for supplies, don't go to the harbour-side market. Never mind what the guides say, you'll pay through the nose for shopping by the sea and half of what's for sale is just for the tourists.'

'Aren't you a tourist?' asked Taro. He didn't like the way the boy was looking at Nual.

'Technically, yeah; you got me there. But I'm here for the year and I'm working to pay my way. Name's Thimo Lauren, for which you can blame my parents. Everyone calls me Mo.'

Despite his misgivings, Taro found the boy's open and friendly manner infectious. 'Taro sanMalia,' he said.

Mo turned to Nual. 'I'm Ela sanMalia,' she said.

Taro still found it odd to hear her use the name on her ID.

Mo looked between the two of them, 'So you two are ...?'

'Taro is my half-brother,' said Nual.

'We had different fathers,' said Taro, truthfully enough.

'The tall half of the family then. Where're you from?'

Before Taro could embellish further, Nual replied, 'Vellern, in the Tri-Confed system.' Other than Nual's name and their relationship, the IDs the Minister had provided were otherwise accurate; *a partial fiction is a lot easier to maintain than a downright lie*, the Minister had said.

'Vellern? Isn't that the world ruled by assassins?'

'Not exactly,' said Taro.

'Although we do have an odd system of government,' said Nual. 'And we also have areas with differing levels of gravity.'

'Aha, hence the height.' Mo shifted slightly. 'Listen, a few of us are going out this evening, to a local bar. Would you two like to tag along?'

'That would be good, thank you. Taro?'

'Guess we could.'

'See you later, then,' said Mo, and bounded away up the stairs

Nual had registered her com with the local network – it was in her new ID, so she reckoned it should be safe enough here – and now she looked up an alternative market. They ended up in an open-sided warehouse where the thick air was stirred by slowly beating ceiling fans. The place was loud and smelly and full of locals who greeted them with smiles and invitations to examine their wares, which consisted of piles, baskets, jars, boxes and bags of items in a bewildering variety of shapes and colours. This much fresh stuff would've cost a fortune in Khesh. If the occasional outbreaks of legs and eyes and fins were anything to go by, a lot of it used to be alive. From the movement in the tanks filled with murky water at the back of certain stalls, some of it still was.

They bought bread and various exotic fruits, two silver-scaled fish and a bunch of floppy green leaves that the stallholder assured them could be fried together to produce a tasty meal. With food sorted, they headed further in to explore the stalls hidden away down alleys formed by piles of half-empty boxes and stall-backs. One of these sold the brightly coloured wraps that everyone wore, and they bought a couple each, along with dark glasses to shade their eyes from the sun's glare. Behind a stall selling fist-sized hairy fruits that might well have been a local delicacy, but which Taro thought looked and smelled vile, they found a place doing cut-price tech. Some of the stuff on sale was the scavenged cast-offs Taro knew from life in the Undertow, but there was some good gear too. Nual bought him a com, to help him find his way around, and so he could stay in contact when they were apart. Taro wasn't sure whether to be upset she was assuming they wouldn't be hanging around together, or glad that she was buying him a gift. It was just a basic slap-com, worn on the back of the hand. He'd seen a few of the locals with implanted coms, like a lot of the Angels and other high-status types had in Khesh; he fancied the idea of getting one of those some time, though Nual had never bothered.

As they came out of the market a group of youths beckoned them over with friendly waves. The boys had set up a variation of a game Taro knew well, with three containers – in this case shells – and a small ball – in this case some sort of round red-brown seed. Only the most gullible tourists usually fell for this one, so Taro was stunned when Nual wandered up to the boys. He trailed after her while the main shyster started his patter.

'Guess which shell the ball's under, Medame! Double your money!'

Nual entered into the spirit of the game; perhaps she was thinking her talents would let her win? Taro didn't try to stop her; hell, it was her choice ... but he did watch her back, so when the smallest member of the gang edged up from behind with an eye on the bag slung over Nual's shoulder, he was ready. The light-fingered little fucker darted away when Taro turned on him, slinking off empty-handed. After that the gang exchanged wary glances with Taro, then let the frontman do the business.

Nual came out evens. As they walked away Taro said, 'You didn't honestly expect to make money out of them, did you?'

'No, but I wanted to read those boys to get a feel for the street-life here.'

Taro snorted a laugh. 'So you knew all about the littlest lag, the one creeping up behind you?'

Nual frowned. 'I was concentrating on the boys running the game. I sensed a stranger come close to me at one point, but I didn't pick up any desire to hurt me, so I ignored them. No one there meant us any harm.'

'Other than trying to lift my new com from where you'd left it in the top of your bag, you mean? Shit, Nual, you might be able take people's heads apart with a nasty look, but you know fuck-all about how things work on the street!'

He'd never spoken to her like that before and for a moment he wondered if she'd take offence, maybe even lose her temper. But she just nodded and said, 'I'm afraid you may be right.' Then she added, 'Thank you for watching my back.'

Taro half-wished she'd got angry with him so he'd finally have something to kick back against.

Neither of them said anything for the rest of the walk back to the hostel.

CHAPTER THIRTEEN

The place Mo took them to that night was rough and ready. Taro got the impression he was trying to impress them – or rather, Nual – with his local knowledge. The regulars treated them with amused tolerance. Though the bar sold beer, served so cold it was almost tasteless, Mo insisted they also tried the local liquor, *kava*, served in something Mo called a coco-nut shell. The drink looked and tasted like muddy water to Taro, but it gave a gentle buzz with a nice sense of chill underneath, and made his tongue go numb.

As they sat on wooden stools next to the well-worn bar, Mo told them about his family, who owned a shitload of land on a world Taro'd never heard of. One day he'd inherit some of that land and have to settle down, but until then he was seeing as much of human-space as he could. He wanted to know all about life on Vellern, and Taro shared enough to keep him happy while discouraging the more personal questions.

Taro talked ten words to every one of Nual's, and he was still up for staying out when she was ready to head back. 'Will you be all right by yourself?' he said, remembering the street-kids earlier.

'I will be careful.' Her tone said she appreciated his concern, but she didn't want his company.

It might've just been coincidence that she chose to leave while Mo was off having a piss, but he looked mildly annoyed when he found she'd left early.

Later, as they walked through the hot, dark streets back to the hostel, Mo said, 'Ela's quite something, isn't she?'

'She certainly is,' said Taro.

'I can't work her out, though,' continued Mo. 'I mean the signals she's giving off: I reckon she's paying attention to me, like she's interested, but then I'm not sure, and I think maybe she hasn't even noticed me. You know her better than me; d'you think she fancies me at all?'

'Unlikely,' said Taro, who'd just thought of a way to put Mo off.

'Why not?'

Just about managing to keep a straight face he said, 'You don't have breasts.'

'Oh, right. I didn't realise.'

When they rounded the next corner they found the street ahead cordoned off. People in dark brown uniforms were standing on this side of the grav-batons while others in lighter uniforms took measurements and holo-pix in the empty street beyond. One of the shop windows had been broken, and there were long impact marks on the road, along with some suspicious dark stains and some unidentified debris.

Taro's experience of the Khesh City militia made him inclined to turn around before anyone noticed him, but before he could leave Mo had sauntered up to one of the guards. 'Kioruna!' he said. 'What's up?'

The guard responded with a reassuring smile and said, 'We've just had to close this street for a while. Would you like alternative directions back to your hotel?'

'No, I'm sure we can find our way. Thank you.'

Once they were out of earshot Taro asked, 'What was all that about?'

'*Ngai* business, I reckon.'

'Ung-what?' said Taro.

'*Ngai*. You know, the big companies?' Despite the amount of *kava* they'd consumed, Mo didn't stumble over the odd word. 'Might be a botched dataswap, or possibly even personnel, though that's rarer. Or maybe someone was muscling in on a deal.'

'I've no idea what you're on about.'

Mo said conspiratorially, 'There's stuff goes on here that the brochures don't mention.'

Taro tried to will himself sober, or at least focused. This sounded important. 'What sort of stuff?'

'Well, the *ngai* all make a big thing about how traditional and primitive they are, but that's just on the surface. They don't want to mess up the tourist scene so everything goes on in the background, but they're always trading knowledge, prototypes, even staff. Sometimes it's amic—friendly, sometimes not. Often it's on neutral territory, here in Stonetown. Something like we saw back there, where there's obviously been trouble but the authorities are making like it's nothing, that's a sure sign at least one of the *ngai* was involved.'

'How d'you know all this?'

'Hang around long enough, you pick stuff up.'

Trouble in paradise. Just what they were looking for.

Jarek felt a certain guilty relief when he'd dropped Taro and Nual off. He'd gone straight from Serenein to warn Elarn, only to discover she was dead, and he was still in shock when he'd recruited his two unlooked-for allies. He hadn't thought it through. He needed breathing space, time to consider the course he was committing himself to. And he needed to try and reclaim his old life.

Although Xantier wasn't the closest hubpoint to Kama Nui, it was the best place in this sector to sell his current cargo. As well as trying to drum up interest in his box of antique artefacts, he hooked up with less formal contacts, spending time with the people who ran the local Alliance offices, and any passing traders. Over a drink or two those who knew him asked why he'd dropped out of sight for several months; he brushed off their curiosity with casual camaraderie and vague evasions. But the very ease with which he deflected their interest started to get to him. Though freetraders saw themselves as a breed apart, at the back of their minds they always knew that tonight's best buddy could be tomorrow's business rival. They asked because they wanted to know what his angle was; when it became obvious he wasn't going to let them in, they lost interest. Most of them didn't give a shit about his welfare; they just wanted to know whether he'd got himself into something lucrative that they might be able to get a piece of.

Arguably, by finding a lost world, he had – except that while he'd started on this mad errand to Serenein with the idea of making his fortune at the back of his mind, he now found that what had happened to him there had driven thoughts of personal profit right out of his head.

He and Elarn may have lost their Salvatine faith, but they had both been looking for something to replace it. His sister had filled her life with music while he'd gone off into the wide black yonder. He was dirtborn, and he'd had a lot to learn about the world outside of gravity wells. He might have dumped the Salvatine precepts, but his upbringing had left him with a stubbornly moral streak and a distrust of invasive technologies, both unhelpful traits in a freetrader. Even with these disadvantages, he'd quickly taken to the lifestyle, but freetrading didn't feed his soul. He'd joked about his support of a hopeless cause, and the Sidhe scared the crap out of him, but perhaps fighting to free humanity from their not-so-ex overlords was – though he winced at the word – his destiny.

He soon found himself not only turning down offers to meet up with acquaintances, but actually losing enthusiasm for securing the best deal for his cargo. Instead, he took to checking out agents, brokers and potential buyers against the pilot's list of Sidhe contacts; he didn't expect, or get, any matches, but paranoia was becoming second nature.

So much for getting back to his old life. Time to turn his attention to his mission.

Any Sidhe ships abroad in human-space had to be operating autonomously, and whilst that meant that an individual human working with them would only know what he (and it would usually be a he) needed to know, the Sidhe would need instant access to a lot more information, which they'd obviously store in their ship's comp. His initial attempts to access the memory-core from the *Setting Sun* had proved fruitless, but he was no expert. He decided to start with some off-the-shelf decryption routines, testing them on limited memory segments copied to discrete storage, which turned out to be a wise move, as the routines either had no effect, or else scrambled the data.

It was beginning to look like he needed to enlist a human data-breaker. The problem was, he didn't know what the files contained, and the kind of people who dealt in decryption tended to take an excessive interest in the data they were cracking. Information stolen from the Sidhe would be hot stuff. He might pay the extra premium for discretion, but such individuals operated in a legal grey area, so he'd never be sure they wouldn't take a peek. The one databreaker who was most likely to be able to decrypt the files, and who wouldn't be shocked at the data they contained – quite the contrary, in fact – came with their own complications.

He decided to try locally first, picking a Xantier-based operator who was listed in the Alliance's archives and personally recommended by some of his contacts. Even so, he provided only a subset of copied data.

He also made some tentative enquiries about false IDs, implying that this was for a third party, a practice not unknown amongst freetraders, who occasionally took large risks (and large fees) to run individuals who'd fallen foul of the law on their homeworld to a new system to start a new life. What he really needed was a new ship ID, but changing that was all but impossible. As soon as a ship came into service it was registered on the unhackable data-fortress that was ConTraD – the Consolidated Traffic Database – and there the ID stayed for the duration of the ship's life, inviolate and unalterable.

Nine days after arriving on Xantier, his finances went into the red. He devoted most of that day to trying to shift his cargo profitably, and took the decision to make use of the services his Alliance subs paid for by speaking to the financial reps about an extended line of credit, something he'd not had to resort to since he'd bought his old partner out.

He also wanted to use the Alliance's archive to do some research. There was one question he needed answered before he went any further; he'd spotted a potential problem with his idealistic decision to bring Serenein into the fold of human-space and he needed to confirm his suspicions.

Shiftships were rare: his ship's comp listed just over 700 free-trader outfits operating in human-space, and there were perhaps the same number again of other shiftships, mainly starliners, run by and for the super-rich. Each transit-kernel lasted between one and two thousand years before it became unstable. Every freetrader knew this, even if they rarely thought about it: a thousand years was a long time, as long as humanity had been free of the Sidhe. That meant that a lot of the transit-kernels had actually been created during the Protectorate. It took only very basic maths to realise that very few new ships were being produced. Jarek needed to confirm just how few.

That information proved surprisingly hard to track down; the handful of companies involved in commissioning new vessels were reticent about making their doings public – hardly surprising, considering what lay at the heart of every shiftship.

He ended up inferring the data by looking at the detailed histories of various freetrader ships. When he extrapolated that to include other types of ship, the conclusion was inescapable: only one or two new shiftships a year were commissioned – barely enough to replace those going out of service or lost in accidents.

In the twenty-five years since the Sidhe had last visited Serenein, thirty-seven – no, thirty-*eight* – boys had been found with the unique talent they required. Assuming not all of these young minds survived the transition into transit-kernels, that gave an average of just over one per year.

Serenein really was the only source for the minds that powered shiftships. If Jarek succeeded in his crusade to save that one world, he might ultimately bring about the end of human interstellar civilisation.

CHAPTER FOURTEEN

Finding out about hidden trouble on Kama Nui turned out to be easier said than done. Nual did most of the research using the public com services; Taro helped by scanning the newsnets. He also volunteered to listen out for rumours. It wasn't his fault if the best place to pick up loose talk was in bars.

The *ngai* Mo had referred to were a cross between big businesses and large family troupes. They were mainly run by women, and their leaders met in the House of *Ariki*, Kama Nui's equivalent of the Assembly back in Khesh. Though there was plenty of gossip about the inter-house rivalries, there was nothing firm to link them to the occasional unexplained unpleasant incidents – an executive poisoned by bad fish in a bar, an accountant robbed of his data but not his valuables, a kidnapping on a main street in the middle of the day with no apparent witnesses – and there wasn't a whiff of the *ngai* being into anything more hi-tech than making sure visitors to their islands had a good time. Nual's research suggested the tensions between the *ngai*s went in cycles, with incidents building to a head over a few years then dying off. Taro got the impression they were about to head into a hot phase.

Despite concerns over their mission and the continuing tension with Nual, Taro started to enjoy life in Stonetown; it was a large and interesting city, but chill and friendly too. Life happened at its own pace, and you didn't feel like you had to watch your back all the time.

Despite Mo's assurance that most people at the hostel were on working holidays, a lot of them spent their days down at the harbour doing nothing in particular. Mo was happy for Taro to join them, and he taught him to fish – or rather, to laze in the shade on the dockside dangling a line in the water. The sea was clear enough to see the brightly coloured creatures scuttling along the seabed or gliding around in shoals, but nothing down there showed much interest in being caught. When the day got too hot, they all stripped off and jumped into the water. Taro joined them cautiously, claiming he wasn't a good swimmer. He used his implants to keep himself afloat and copied the others' actions, managing to avoid anyone spotting that he was using gravitics while he learned to swim. He reckoned that was good; he didn't want any of them sussing that he was an Angel. It was way too hot to wear anything with sleeves, so he was glad of the peace-bonding job customs had done on his wrists. Right now his implants looked like faint matching scars and he wasn't sure anyone had even noticed them – certainly no one commented on them.

Nual generally stayed back at the hostel in the evenings, while Taro combined his rumour-gathering with drinking, dancing and flirting. He liked to dance, and soon picked up the local method of strutting your stuff, a combination of fast footwork, sexy hip and hand movements, and some frankly gappy face-pulling. After Mo went off with a hot native girl one night Taro wondered whether he should take up one of the offers that'd come his way. Though this culture wasn't into sleeping with your own sex, that still left half the population. But while his body kept distracting him, his head and heart said *no*. To go with someone now would only make things worse with Nual.

It did occur to him, during their second week, that his credit was going down fast and he might not have the choice soon. Nual had registered them with one of the agencies providing casual workers out on the resort islands, but there was competition for even the shittier jobs and it could be up to a month before anything came up for the two of them together. She said they should avoid being split up if possible, and he didn't argue. He'd seen plenty of people practising his old trade; Mo had told him it was all legit and well-regulated, with no pimps to fuck you over. But leaving aside the practical problem that he was underage here, he just didn't feel comfortable selling himself to strangers any more. Though he was still finding his place in the world, one thing he did know: he wasn't anyone's whore.

On the tenth day a girl called Kise arrived at the hostel. Mo made his customary attempt to get into her pants; she turned him down politely but firmly. Commiserating with Taro the next evening Mo said, 'I don't reckon she's after fun at all.'

'What else would anyone come here for?' asked Taro innocently.

'Career progression. And I don't mean waiting tables or cleaning bungalows. She's a qualified geneticist, you know, with a special interest in anagathics. Told me all about it by way of a put-down.'

Taro made a mental note to ask Nual what anagathics was, then said, 'But she's still entitled to a holiday, right?'

'No, I know that sort. Some of my father's people are like that; not born into privilege but determined to work themselves to the top.'

'So,' said Taro, 'you're saying she's here to get recruited by one of the *ngai*, to do this smoky stuff that's meant to be going on out of sight?'

'That's exactly what I'm saying.'

'So, which *ngai* does anagathics then?'

'No idea. I think she only told me about it to put me off.'

'But you think she might know?'

'Why else go to the effort and expense of coming here? She must reckon she's got a chance of getting in with these people.'

Anagathics was the science of extending life, Nual said – a tricky area, given a lot of the religious worlds had laws against it, and those treatments that were around were expensive and risky. It definitely qualified as the kind of thing that would be carried out on the quiet.

Taro chatted to Kise when Mo wasn't around and found that he'd been right: she was polite enough, but not particularly friendly. But he and Nual had more than one way to find out what they needed to know.

The next day was the Salvatine holyday, and a lot of the hostel's residents went to church. Taro was still getting his head around religion. He'd grown up with a vague but pervasive view that his City watched over its residents, only to find this was both literally true and ultimately false, and as a result he no longer felt inclined to believe in a higher power. Apparently a lot of people did though, and followed some variation of Salvationism, the belief in a mysterious creator God who saw all from a distance, and a Son who sacrificed himself so humans could get back in with their divine Father. The Salvatine religion came in a number of flavours. On Kama Nui, it involved the worship of the Lord of the Sea, and their version of the Manifest Son was a character called Tongaroa. Mo followed the Mithrai sect, but that was no problem as there were churches and temples to all the major Salvatine sects here for the tourist market.

Given her specialist area, Taro wasn't surprised to find Kise didn't attend church. They found her sitting alone in the common room, reading. Nual went over to her while Taro hung around in the kitchen area, keeping an eye out to make sure they weren't disturbed. The two women had a short conversation that looked harmless enough from where Taro was lurking, after which Kise put down her reader and fell asleep.

Nual got up and left; Taro followed her out to the men's dormitory, which was empty.

'Her family are small-time corporate,' Nual reported quietly, 'but they live on a theocracy, and their company is never going to be involved in the kind of cutting-edge work she's interested in. She knows that Kama Nui has a hidden hi-tech culture, though she doesn't know all the details. She's been putting forward a tame version of her résumé – she's also a qualified geriatrics nurse, and a lot of rich people retire here – with a hidden embedded file that a smart recruiter will spot, decrypt and open.'

'Good for her,' said Taro, trying not to think about Nual going into the girl's mind. 'Can't see how that helps us, though.'

'It narrows our search: she's only applying to three of the five big *ngai*, because the other two aren't biotech specialists. Whoever is taking these boys and turning them into transit-kernels would have to be with one of those three.'

'I guess so.' Taro thought that was the end of the conversation and turned to leave.

Nual said quietly, 'I'm sorry.'

He moved back and looked at her. She was backlit in the harsh light from the window and he couldn't make out her expression, but he felt a slight lessening of her shields, like a willingness to let him in a little. He tried not to react. She was the one in the wrong and he wasn't going to let her just melt his pain away. 'For what?' he said stonily, though he knew full well.

'I'm sorry for hurting you, Taro. That was never my intention.'

'So why'd you do it?'

'Because there was no other way to find out what we needed to know.'

After so long avoiding the subject Taro found himself suddenly furious. 'Don't give me that shit! Why didn't you just make him *think* you were fucking him? You can do that sort of thing, can't you?' The killing'd had to be done for real of course, but as far as Taro was concerned the pilot's death was no great loss, even if the way it'd happened still made him feel sick.

'Even if I had had sufficient knowledge to create a convincing illusion of sex – which I did not – the pilot knew the ways of the Sidhe well. He would have realised he was being deceived.'

Damn her and her logic. 'All right, so I s'pose that's all true.' Taro decided to take a different tack. 'But ever since you've been acting like nothing happened.'

'I thought – incorrectly, I now know – that given the pain my actions have caused you, it would be better if I did not draw attention to them.' He thought she was looking directly at him now, though her eyes were in shadow. 'Would you prefer that I had lied to you and said I had not had sex with him? I could have easily made you believe that.'

'I know you could! That's not—' He wouldn't let her honesty deflect his anger. 'I have to know one thing,' he said slowly. 'If you had the chance to go back, would you do it again, just the same?'

'We can never go back, Taro. And I have told you: I regret the pain I've caused you.'

'Meaning you *would* do it again!'

'If I had to, but—'

'You didn't *have to* this time! You—'

Taro stopped at the sound of a slamming door and voices in the corridor outside. He clenched and unclenched his fists, then turned and walked out of the dormitory, out of the hostel into the searing midday heat, and he kept walking and didn't stop until the anger had drained away. He ended up at the harbour, where he stood for some time, staring at the sea.

The next time they spoke, Nual was polite, distant, careful, just like she'd been before. He found himself remembering a comment she'd made when they first met, how most people would call her a monster. Well, she'd said she wouldn't sleep with him for fear of hurting him, and he hadn't wanted to believe her. Turned out she'd been right. Maybe she *was* a monster: if he could just make himself believe that, then perhaps the pain might go away.

The day after the aborted row, Mo burst into the kitchen. 'I've got a job! It hasn't gone to the agencies yet, but I know a man who knows a man. This is a big one, a wedding out at one of the top-notch resorts, some big dynastic thing between Tawhira-*ngai* and Ruanuku-*ngai*. It's gonna be hard work, but there's a chance to stay on for free afterwards. Are you two up for it?'

Nual looked up from the vegetables she was chopping. 'I certainly am.' Kise was interested in both Tawhira-*ngai* and Ruanuku-*ngai*. 'I am not sure about Taro though,' she said, looking over at him, sitting at a table practising his reading.

She was giving him the chance to go his own way, just like he'd decided he should do for himself.

As if it was that simple. ''Course I am,' he said.

CHAPTER FIFTEEN

'It's a fair offer, Sirrah Reen.'

Jarek had hoped for better, but he was in no position to be choosy. And the man sitting opposite him in the pleasant if unprepossessing restaurant was an agent he'd had extensive dealings with before. Falk Lukas had no reason to lie to his client, not when his commission depended on finding the best deal.

'All right, I accept.' At least the credit from selling the Old Earth artefacts as a job lot would clear his immediate debts, even if it was less than half what he'd hoped to make by splitting the shipment.

'Excellent. Shall we shake on it?' Lukas leaned across the landscape of empty dishes to present his hand.

Jarek shook it, then turned his own hand so Lukas could swipe his wrist-com – a charming whimsy, disguised as an antique chronometer – to seal the deal.

'And can I just say,' the agent added, with a look that was probably meant to be sympathetic but came out as lugubrious, 'how sorry I was to hear about the death of your sister. I have all her recordings.'

'Thanks. I ... I appreciate that.' That Elarn had died in an accident on Vellern had been public knowledge for more than a week now, and though he knew Lukas was a musical connoisseur his concern made Jarek uncomfortable. He glanced over the agent's shoulder at the disconcerting view out of the fifth-floor window: buildings sloping up and away on the curved cylinder of Xantier's inner surface. He looked back at Lukas. 'You said something about more work?' He'd been on Xantier for nearly two weeks, and though he'd accepted that he couldn't fully embrace his old lifestyle, he still had to make a living.

'Oh yes, I have just the thing.' Lukas's shoulders twitched, a habit Jarek always associated with him having come up with what he'd call *a peach of a job*. 'You know the Krishnan run you did a few years back for me? Lotus petals for their Festival of Lights? If I remember rightly you took a rather unorthodox route away from the main lanes and got there early, with every one of their little blooms still in its prime. I'm tendering on the run again this year, and naturally I thought of you. Are you interested? It's likely to be highly lucrative: we're looking at a six per cent increase over the previous fee, with a very generous ten per cent bonus on top if you can manage zero spoilage on the cargo again.'

Jarek hesitated. Krishna was in a different sector, down a spur. If he risked the rarely used route he'd taken last time he could cut down the number of transits to eight, but that would still leave him twelve transits from Kama Nui. Though Nual and Taro hadn't made much progress yet, if they needed to contact him quickly while he was in a backwater system like Krishna it would cost them a small fortune in beevee fees, and if they needed his help it would take him a week to reach them.

He sighed. 'Normally I'd be more than delighted to take this on, but I do have a number of other possibilities on the horizon—'

'I understand. Of course you do. And I would be willing to drop a full percentage point from my previous commission on that run, provided the zero-spoilage clause is fulfilled.'

Damn the man. Six months ago that would've been exactly what Jarek wanted to hear. He considered demanding the agent drop by five per cent, but that would be unreasonable greed, which could seriously damage his rep. And there was a risk Lukas might call his bluff, in which case not taking the run would be career suicide, at least on this hub.

If Lukas had come up with the job yesterday, Jarek might've taken it. He'd have told himself that Nual and Taro were probably having the time of their lives on Kama Nui and were unlikely to uncover anything of interest in the near future. But last night he'd dreamt about Serenein again: a jumble of mountain passes, lo-tech discomfort, homely people and haughty priests. But he'd also dreamt of Kerin, the ordinary woman who'd risen to an extra-ordinary challenge ... no, whose challenge was just beginning, after he'd abandoned her to it. He knew he'd treated her badly – not least by marrying her – but he couldn't change the past, and the only way he could ensure a secure, free future for her and her people was by exposing the Sidhe's secret hold over humanity and bringing them down. It might mean that one day humans lost their access to the stars, but that day was a long way off; the Sidhe were exerting their vile influence now, and had been doing so un-opposed for centuries.

'All right,' said Lukas when Jarek remained silent, 'one point five. But that's my final offer.'

Jarek spread his hands. 'I really wish I could take this job, but at the moment I simply can't accept anything that long-haul. I'm sorry.'

Lukas looked as though Jarek had mortally insulted him. 'It's your choice, of course. You know, you really aren't acting yourself, Sirrah Reen. Is there something you're not telling me?'

Jarek experienced a sudden moment of paranoia. Of course Lukas' name wasn't on his list of possible Sidhe contacts, but it wasn't a complete list, and those doing their bidding didn't always know who they were really working for.

Hell, if he started thinking like that he might as well sell his ship, find a nice quiet world and spend the rest of his life hiding under a rock.

He responded as casually as he could, 'Being totally honest? Yes and no. As you probably know, I've been out of the loop for a while. I'm currently investigating various avenues and options, as a result of which I can't commit to a job that far outside the hub network. I'm sure you understand that I can't say more than that without compromising another party's trust.'

Jarek could see by the agent's eyes that he wasn't buying it. But he just said, 'Of course. What you do outside of our busi-ness arrangements is your own concern.' He leaned back. 'And I imagine that unexplained absence was just a well-earned rest with some pleasant company.'

'Something like that,' said Jarek, forcing a grin meant to be both sheepish and knowing. No one was fooled, but the immediate awkwardness had been defused. 'If you have anything more local, I would definitely be interested. And I wouldn't expect preferential treatment, given the inconvenience I've caused you by not being able to take the Krishnan job.'

'I might have a few more local runs coming up soon,' said the agent, less sniffily. 'Low pay, but it's all credit.'

'I'm only a com-call away.'

'Well then, I'll try and keep you in mind.' Lukas stood up. 'Good day to you, Sirrah Reen.'

Taro wasn't sure about skim-boats. When they first left Stonetown, the craft glided over the surface of the sea, but then it sped up, rising up out of the water at a scary angle. According to Mo the vehicle had grav compensation, but it wasn't allowed to actually fly, because aircars were strictly regulated outside Stonetown. Apparently they spoilt the view. As a result the skim-boat travelled close enough to the water for Taro to see just how fast they were going, throwing up twin plumes of spray in their wake. Occasionally a high wave would make the whole craft shudder, causing an outbreak of nervous smiles among the passengers. Of course, it was very unlikely anything would go wrong – you need to keep the punters safe if you want to keep them coming – and if it did, well, he and Nual could just fly free. But that didn't mean he was enjoying the ride. He took Mo's advice and fixed his eyes on the horizon, where a small green dot, the only thing in sight besides the blue sky and bluer sea, was rapidly growing in size.

Nual sat beside him in silence. They'd had another minor row about this job the evening after Mo told them about it. They were needed for two days' work, with bed and board provided. The additional payment was a choice: money, or the opportunity to stay on the island for free for a further ten days. Taro had argued that they should go for the second option, because they'd found out all they were going to in Stonetown. He didn't admit that he also fancied seeing some of the natural wonders he'd heard about, and if Nual had picked up his ulterior motive she hadn't said anything. In the end, she'd backed down without a fight.

The island they were heading for, Ipitomi, was close enough to make out details now. A low spine of land rose from the sea, the slopes covered in pale green vegetation. Taller, darker plants – palm trees – crowded into the space between the hill and the sea. They were inside the lagoon that surrounded the island before Taro spotted the landing stages and low well-camouflaged buildings under the trees. Further back he glimpsed more houses, small and square and apparently made of dried bits of plant.

He was glad to be back on land again, though their journey wasn't over yet. They piled into a waiting groundbus which drove them round the bumpy coastal road to the far side of the island. Taro made sure he got a seat on the outside and he watched the scenery unroll past the window: wide bays of sparkling white sand and tree-covered outcrops, and beyond it all the sea, bright as a jewel. They saw a few locals walking in the road, but no other vehicles. Most of them stopped to wave as they passed.

The bus pulled over next to a pair of single-storey blockhouses and the visitors here to work – about half those on the bus – got off. Each block had four twin rooms, with a shared kitchen and bathroom. The whitewashed walls, bare floors and scuffed furniture almost made the hostel in Stonetown look luxurious, but Taro'd slept in worse places. They dropped their gear off, then walked down to the beach on a well-worn path through dense, untamed bush. The damp air felt heavier than in Stonetown, making movement more of an effort, and Taro's nose was full of the rich scents of growth and rot. The plants around them came in every shape and every shade of green. Taro kept stopping to peer into the undergrowth where flowers – scarlet, violet, blue – made brighter splashes of colour in the gloom. When one of the flowers darted towards him he cried out, at first in shock, then in delight – it wasn't a flower, it was some sort of animal, with a jewel-like purple-and-green body half the size of his clenched fist and wings that beat so fast they were a blur as it thrummed through the air.

The beach, when they reached it, was an expanse of perfect pale sand that made him want to kick off his shoes and run down to the sea. Unfortunately, that wasn't an option. The workers boarded their final transport, a half-boat-half-bus that took them across a shallow channel to the small private island where the wedding was being held. This place looked like one big garden, shaded by high palms and with stands of flowering plants arranged according to some grand scheme which included every colour in the world: all the natural wonders of Ipitomi, only distilled and tamed. Two bars, a restaurant and a complex of different-sized pools were reached by flower-edged paths across neat lawns.

The workers reported to a rather less glamorous set of buildings hidden by tall bushes where the housekeeping staff put them to work on preparations for the wedding the next day. The main organiser, a stern-faced man the other staff referred to as the *tuari* asked his temporary staff about their previous experience. On the basis of their answers Nual was put to work in the kitchen while Taro was sent round the back to sort fruit to be made up into baskets for the guests. The shade wasn't complete, and though the work wasn't hard Taro found himself getting overheated. He quickly gave up on his shades, which kept sliding off his sweat-covered nose whenever he looked down. He was tempted to lose the gloves too, until a bug crawled out of the pile of yellow fruits he was working on. It was an amazing-looking beast, with eight long-jointed red legs and a tiny green body. He used a gloved finger to flick it into the undergrowth. By the time he'd gone through all the fruit, he'd encountered and redistributed a wide variety of the island's creeping, crawling and scuttling inhabitants.

Though the sun was sinking, work wasn't over yet. He and one of the permanent staff members went out with a grav-trolley loaded with the completed fruit baskets, some of which were so big they needed two people to carry them into the guests' rooms. The rooms were actually self-contained huts, like upmarket versions of the houses they'd seen when they first arrived on Ipitomi, decorated with wooden carvings painted in red, white and black.

Inside, they were pure luxury, with beds that were wide expanses of white linen and washing areas that included miniature pools and cascades. Some of them were in the gardens, while others were reached by bleached wooden walkways that extended out over the lagoon. These huts had partially transparent floors and Taro found himself entranced by the evening light dappling the complex underwater world below his feet. As darkness fell the light-globes strung through the trees and bushes began to glow in soft pastel colours. When the day's work was finished they returned to the kitchen for a spicy fry-up of rice and flaked fish.

On the bus-boat back to Ipitomi it rained, a sudden shower that hissed into the sea and soaked them in seconds. The fat, warm drops were nothing like Khathryn's thin drizzles. He felt tired, dazzled by beauty, and faintly resentful that he was only here to make things perfect for other people. The rain passed as quickly as it had arrived, leaving the air feeling fresher. When they landed they were greeted by the chirrups and rasps of unseen creatures calling in the night. Above them, the sky was already clearing.

The path back to their accommodation was picked out by light-globes, though he was still glad of his good night-sight. Two of the three moons were just rising through the last of the clouds, and Taro kept stopping to look up at the sky.

Mo said he was going to brew up some caf in the kitchen and invited them to join him. Nual declined. Taro said he might come along later.

They pulled the screens on the windows closed before he turned the lights on: unlike the luxury bungalows, their sleeping block didn't have sonic bug-shields to deter the wildlife. Several small lizards had already found their way in and now waited, silent and watchful, around the walls. Nual said, 'I think they hunt insects.' They watched one that was loitering at eye level raise one tiny foot, wait, then dart forward, almost too fast to follow, jaws snapping. They both laughed at once and Taro felt a slight lessening of tension. They were finally alone, in their own space. If she would just apologise, tell him she'd never again do anything like what she'd done …

The moment passed and she didn't say anything. Finally he said, 'Reckon I'll take Mo up on that caf after all.'

When he got back Nual was asleep. Looking at her, he couldn't make the link between this beautiful, peaceful woman and the Angel, the Sidhe, the killer who'd taken dozens of lives, and irrevocably fucked up his.

He raised a hand, wanting to reach out to her, just once more. Then he made himself turn away. He wondered if he ever would touch her again.

CHAPTER SIXTEEN

Nual understood Taro's revulsion, even as she remembered her experience with the pilot with guilty pleasure. Guilt: such a very human emotion, though one she had discovered for herself even before she met Jarek. She still shied away from that memory, the part of the story Jarek didn't know. As she'd said to Taro: we can never go back.

She had apologised to Taro, but of course that was not sufficient for him. Even if she told him what he so desperately wanted to hear it would not change what she had done, nor alter the fact that she would do it again if there were a good enough reason.

Jarek had been concerned about the possibility of conception when he told her about the close relationship between Sidhe and humans – a revelation, which, now she had had time to digest it, reassured her somewhat, caught as she was between the two races. His fears had been unfounded: when she'd tested herself in the *Judas Kiss*'s med-bay, the test had come up negative; she'd also found and used a one-shot treatment that would act as contraceptive and inoculation against most sexual diseases for the next year. But there had been other, unexpected, consequences of her congress with the pilot. She had been in minds at the moment of death before, when she had acted as the Minister's executioner back in Khesh, and she had relished the sensation because it was a moment with no barriers, no illusions. The pilot had been different: that contact was much deeper, more lasting than any she had experienced with her previous victims.

She had, in more than one sense, taken his life.

For several days afterwards she had found memories surfacing that were not hers, her choices infected by reactions she had never experienced and opinions she had never held. She had to stop for a moment to recall where she ended and where the life she had absorbed began. It helped that the pilot had left his name and human identity behind some years ago, though in the end she had taken even that. She wondered if she would one day come to think of this knowledge as her own, rather than information ripped from a dying mind.

The act she had committed had changed her in other ways. Since leaving the Sidhe she had repressed her powers in order to fit in with humans. What had happened with the pilot had been her first attempt to develop and stretch her abilities, and her success had surprised her.

Which brought her back to Taro. He was, in many ways, a victim of those abilities. If she wanted reconciliation, she would have to lead the way. She didn't blame him for sleeping with Jarek to spite her, but his pain and anger remained undiminished, and that, combined with his jealous streak and his stubborn nature, ensured that the first move had to be hers. After their argument in the hostel she had thought long and hard about whether reconciliation was truly what she wanted, and if she did, whether she was wise to want it.

The day working in the kitchen at the resort had left her with a satisfying physical tiredness that had freed her mind to think clearly, and as she lay there she reached her conclusion.

The next morning she awoke before Taro to the sound of a raucous dawn chorus from the local birds. Today concerns that went beyond her emotional life would come to the fore and she could not afford the distraction of having to block out Taro's projected pain whenever he was near her.

She waited until he was up and dressed, then said, 'Taro, this cannot go on any longer.'

He looked startled, then nodded.

She said, 'I have to know whether you can forgive me, and accept what I am.'

The harsh early light made him look older than his seventeen years. 'I can forgive you, if you're truly sorry.'

'For hurting you? I am. I have said that, and I meant it. For doing what I did? No, because it was necessary, and because it was in my nature.'

'To fuck him or to kill him?'

'Both.'

He flinched at her admission. 'And could you've chosen not to kill him?'

'I believe so.'

'Then why the fuck did you?' His anger was rising again.

'Because that was our deal.'

Taro threw his hands up. 'But if you can control yourself like that, then why the fuck did you refuse to sleep with me? Why lie to me over that, and then screw that smoky arsehole? Or were you just waiting for someone who was used to doing it with a Sidhe to come along?'

She forced herself to ignore the insult. 'I wasn't lying to you, Taro. I did not know what would happen when I had sex.'

'And now you do?'

She hesitated. 'I know what I am capable of.'

'What the fuck's that's s'posed to mean?' He was shouting now, and for a moment Nual worried that they would be overheard. She briefly considered dealing with that potential crisis, but solving one problem like that would lead to many more.

Pitching her voice low she said, 'I know what I can do, when I am in control.'

'And with me you wouldn't be? Is that what you're saying?'

'That is precisely what I am saying.'

'So what's the big difference?'

'I think you know.'

His voice dropped and he ground each word out slowly. 'I want you to tell me.'

She did, without hesitation. 'Because I love you.'

He closed his eyes, and tears spilled out of them.

She watched him until he opened his eyes again, then carried on, 'But that doesn't change what I said. So, I ask again: can you forgive me, and accept what I am?'

His voice small, he said, 'I don't know.'

She continued, before her emotions got the better of her, 'If you cannot, then I will end this.'

He looked at her. 'What d'you mean, *end this*?'

'Taro, you know that our feelings are the result of the contact we had in Khesh, firstly when I healed you, and then the unity we shared in the Heart of the City.'

'So what if they are? It's still the way I feel.'

'But it doesn't *have* to be. I made this love. I can break it.'

'You can stop me loving you?'

She nodded. 'I believe so. I am finding out more about what I can do all the time.'

'I … I need to think about it.'

'Of course.' Part of her demanded that she influence his thoughts, dispense with giving him the choice: make his love unconditional, giving them both what they wanted. She quashed that urge.

Mo called them to breakfast soon after. Taro was quiet throughout the meal and on the journey over to the resort.

When they reached the island they were split up. Taro's unusual looks meant he would be working behind the scenes, whilst Nual and the other more presentable labourers were given smart green and white uniforms and instructed by the *tuari* on how to ensure the guests never wanted for anything. As he was explaining which beverages would be served for each section of the day's festivities, a large aircar came in to land on the pad at the edge of the gardens and disgorged dancers and musicians, men and women garlanded with flowers and wearing skirts woven from multi-coloured grasses. They had anklets of shells which rattled as they moved, and their chins and eyelids were stained in dark patterns. The musicians carried small drums and even smaller stringed instruments. Some of the men formed up in a line facing the landing pad, while the women and the musicians joined Nual and the other servers in the clearing where the ceremony was to take place. This was an open space shaded by palms, with chairs

117

ranked in a half-circle around a small dais on the seaward side. The dais was shaded by a cupola of live blossoms. The serving staff had been told to wait in front of another impressive floral display at the back, which hid the drinks and food they would be dispensing. The display picked out the symbols of the two *ngai* participating in today's ceremony: a leaping fish in green on blue and a breaking wave in dark blue and white. The scent the flowers exuded was so sweet as to be cloying.

The guests began to arrive. Most of them came by aircar, which, given the restrictions on flying vehicles, indicated how important they must be. They were greeted by the costumed men, who performed what looked like a cross between a dance and a ritual challenge, with lots of whooping, stamping and exaggerated gestures. When the new arrivals reached the main area they were entertained by softer music and the delicate, sensuous movements of the female performers. The servers moved up with trays laden with iced drinks and delicate nibbles served on shaped leaves or seashells.

Nual's job required her to pay attention to what was going on around her, but it also gave her the opportunity to read some of the new arrivals. She picked up nothing unexpected: most looked forward to the sumptuous celebration, though she also registered some mild and unfocused misgivings, generally from the more formally dressed guests, many of whom wore subtle brooches, pins or hair decorations displaying the logo of their *ngai*. This was apparently not a union that had universal approval. Many of these individuals also had the chin and eye patterns she had noticed on the dancers, intricate and abstract tattoos that looked odd to her outsider's eye, as did the use of bright, highly patterned fabrics in the executives' smartly cut suits.

She saw no weapons, nor any overt security. She had no idea whether their employer had checked deeply enough to find out that she and Taro were registered assassins; if they had then they were obviously not overly concerned by this fact. Politics here was not the extravagant and deadly game she was used to, though that didn't mean that there were no hidden agendas and dark secrets.

After a while people began to take their seats. Finally a woman in an impressive headdress of blood-red flowers and iridescent green feathers came forward to stand on the dais. She welcomed the guests in the name of the Lord of the Sea, and wished them joy and good fortune. Her speech was peppered with words in the native language.

She fell silent, and a few moments later the bride and groom approached the dais from opposite sides. They wore masks of green leaves and heavy cloaks. When they met under the cupola and turned their backs for a moment Nual realised the cloaks were made of feathers, with geometric patterns picked out in black, green and gold, each subtly different. The priestess took their hands and led them round to face the congregation. Attendants came forward and lifted off their masks. As she saw them clearly for the first time Nual picked up their emotions: nervousness from both of them, and a deep love from the man. The woman's feelings were more complex, tinged with regret, apprehension and guilt.

Guilt because of her lover. Someone here was the true object of this girl's affection. She made this match only to please her family. It would not work out. Nual sensed the future course of this union as a wrongness, a certainty of pain – no details, just a feeling as sure as knowing that a dropped glass would fall, a plucked flower die. The realisation came with a strange physical sensation, hot as ginger in the back of her throat.

This was not knowledge she had read in the usual way. At this distance she could only pick up a stranger's overall mood and immediate intentions; to uncover such a deep deception as a secret lover from someone she did not know she would normally have to go deep into their mind and tease out the knowledge. This information had arrived in Nual's consciousness fully formed, a flash of certainty about what had been, was now – *and would be*.

This was prescience, the rarest Sidhe talent, which manifested in only a few revered elements amongst the unity.

Nual watched the ceremony without seeing it. The bright colours and piercing light combined to give the scene an air of unreality and she felt a faint and disturbing echo of the wrenching dislocation from the universe that was shiftspace.

When one of the other servers asked if she was all right she realised she was grasping the edge of the table for support. She nodded, and let go.

With the formal ceremony over the servers dispensed coco-nut shells of *kava* to the guests so they could drink the health of the newlyweds. Nual used the task to ground herself, and she managed it without mishap.

After that people drifted down to the beach where some of the men were holding races in sleek wooden outrigger canoes. Nual found herself focusing on the guests as they wandered past, both hungry for and fearful of another flash of unprompted insight. She got no more than the usual sense of their emotions and the occasional more coherent strong surface thought.

The next hour or so left little time for introspection, as she and the others worked to clear the chairs away, then to set up tables for the wedding feast, and finally to help carry great platters of meat, fish and root vegetables from the earth-ovens where they had been cooking all day. The servers were given their own portions behind the screens once the guests had their meals; the food was smoky-sweet and deliciously tender.

After the meal, with the light-globes glowing in the trees, some of the tables were moved back to make space for the dancing. The servers had an easier time of it now, required only to make occasional forays out amongst the guests with jugs of fruity cocktails or bottles of imported wines.

Following a couple of show-pieces by the professional dancers, the guests formed two lines, men and women opposite each other, with the bride and groom each heading a line. Nual focused on the bride, but could pick up only her current emotions: she was more relaxed than she had been, quite tired, still a little apprehensive. Nual scanned the men, trying to discover which one was the bride's lover.

She was so intent on the dancers that she almost missed the figure getting up from the top table. The woman had been sitting between an older man and a girl of about twelve, both of whom she spoke to briefly before she left. Nual switched her full attention to the woman as she headed down the path back to the aircar pad. The woman was agitated, her mind reeling from having received unwelcome news. Nual tried to dig deeper, but at this distance she could not read much detail, though she did deduce that whatever had prompted her to leave now was unrelated to the wedding and not an entirely unexpected development, though the timing had taken her by surprise.

Then the woman moved out of sight up the path, and someone was pressing a tray into her hands and telling her to go and top up the guests' glasses.

CHAPTER SEVENTEEN

There was no easy way out. Though Taro was kept busy all day fetching and carrying plates and glasses, and loading and unloading the dish-washing machines, he still had plenty of time to consider what Nual had said. He couldn't see a way to avoid getting hurt. She was the most amazing person he'd ever met, but she was capable of terrible things. To not love her was unthinkable – but she'd admitted she was likely to hurt him again if he stayed with her. Since he'd met her he'd defined himself by her, based most of his adult decisions around her – but was that really the smartest thing to do?

Would he be better off without her?

He had no way of knowing, nothing to compare against. He'd never felt his own ignorance so keenly.

The only thing he knew for sure was that she'd caused the feelings he had for her, replacing one addiction with another. She'd done it with his consent, but this love was still Sidhe magic, not a real, genuine, normal, *human* emotion. Jarek's view of how far Nual had influenced Jarek's own feelings was smart and practical: he didn't know, and he believed she wouldn't mess with him on purpose, so he'd saved himself a lot of trouble by not worrying about it, just going with the flow. But Jarek was just her friend.

By the time they were back on the boat, he'd made his choice, and he needed to act quickly, before he changed his mind. *Before he came to his senses?* As soon as they reached their room in the blockhouse he said, 'I want you to cure me.'

She didn't question or argue, but said only, 'Sit on the bed.'

He did as she asked, his heart pounding. A small voice in his head was telling him not to do this. He wondered if it was his voice, or hers.

She sat down opposite him and took both his hands in hers. 'When I tell you, look up,' she said. She sounded nervous.

'What happens if this goes wrong?' he asked.

'Nothing, I hope.'

'You *hope*?'

'This is not something I have ever done before. All I can promise is that I will be careful, and gentle.' She hesitated. 'We do not have to continue if you do not truly want to.'

He wasn't sure he did – but he never would be sure, not while he was under her spell. 'What's the worst that could happen?'

'You may lose some of the memories associated with … what I did back in Khesh. In some ways that might make it easier on you, but it is still wrong.'

'But you can't … damage me?'

'I will not enter the areas that define your personality, just those that hold the memories that bind us.'

The memories that bind us. When he heard her say that he almost changed his mind— *No*. He had to know how much of what he was feeling was really him. 'All right,' he said. 'Let's do it.'

He looked up, and fell into her eyes at once. He was instantly back in Khesh City, or maybe it was a dream of the City. He remembered meeting Nual, and how she'd rescued him from himself. He remembered the choice she'd given him: she would cure his dependence on the drug his enemy had forced on him and dull the pain of the torture he'd undergone, but the healing would link them. She hadn't known then about the deeper union they'd share later, and how that would strengthen their love.

The love that was a lie – *is* a lie. The love that is no love because it's not about choice.

That's not love at all: that's adulation, obsession.

Violation.

'*Get out!*' He didn't realise he'd shouted out loud until he opened his eyes.

Nual was instantly gone from his mind. She drew back physically, but he was already scrambling off the bed. He ran from the room without looking back.

That night, he slept outside, on the beach – or rather, he lay on the warm sand, sobbing, drifting in and out of uneasy sleep. He wasn't sure what he was crying over – lost chances, his own stupidity, or simple self-pity, maybe – but whatever the reason, he didn't stop until he was sure he'd washed everything away. When he came back to the blockhouse in the morning he felt as though something had been ripped from deep inside him, leaving a great, gaping hole.

He met Nual in the kitchen. She was a stranger, a beautiful stranger, no more and no less. The way the space in his chest contracted and threatened to stop his breath would pass soon, he knew it.

They weren't alone, so neither of them said anything, but she followed him out and whispered, 'Are you all right?'

How odd, that this beautiful stranger cared about him. 'I will be,' he said, and turned away.

The only way to get over this was to live his life, live it hard and full. And he was in the perfect place to do just that.

Mo and the others who'd stayed on were full of suggestions as to how to have the most fun for the least credit. The beach was free, of course, and most days started and ended with a dip in the blood-warm sea. One day they walked inland to a low waterfall with a deep, frothing plunge-pool. The next day they went foraging for coco-nuts; no one had the skill or nerve to climb the tall palms, and Taro wasn't going to let on that he had his own method of getting up there, so they just took the fallen ones.

A pair of buses – there were just the two – drove around the coastal road all day, providing free rides for both the tourists and the workers who served them. The one road had just the one town on it: Anau, the settlement Taro'd glimpsed when they first arrived, but the road also passed through five other resorts on the far side of the island. They weren't as smart as the offshore resort, being for normal families or honeymooners, but the nearest was happy to welcome day-visitors, and Taro had a go at kayaking, body-surfing and diving in the lagoon, all pastimes he'd never known existed a few months before.

Diving required goggles and fins, and a contraption rather like the mask Jarek had been wearing when they first met him at Elarn's house. These masks had a tube at the side: flick it up when you swam on the surface; flick it down and you could breathe underwater for up to ten minutes. There was an earpiece too, so the leader of the group could talk to you, and it buzzed to tell you when you needed to surface for more air. The sea was a whole new world to Taro: he'd thought the bush was prime, but this was pure blade. There were swaying plants of green and gold and red, and fans and towers and walls of coral in every colour from pale flesh-pink to a blue so deep it was almost black. And it was alive, all tiny mouths flicking and thin streamers trailing, home to thousands of animals, from tiny translucent critters that bounced round on puffs of water to violet-and-black sea-snakes with bodies thicker than his arm. Some of the plants looked like animals, with false eyes and fins that turned out to be leaves moving in the current; some of the animals looked like plants, like the painfully bright flat patches that draped themselves over the coral, only to jet off at a touch, revealing an underside peppered with star-shaped mouths.

Taro's personal favourites were the carpet-worms: a pair of half-metre long blue-green snakes lying side-by-side on the sand – unless you stirred up the water around them, when they instantly snapped straight while levering themselves up and out, and a living, sparkling mesh fanned out between them, ready to snare any passing small creatures. Once they'd caught their prey, the worms toppled over and slammed the net back down into the sand. He'd been tempted to try and touch one of the nets, until the dive leader warned him it could deliver a painful shock.

Life on the reef was simple: the world was divided into things you ate and things that ate you. If you were lucky enough to be the thing that nothing ate, then your life was perfect, and you didn't have to worry about having a hole where your heart had been, or waking up crying sometimes.

Once he'd got used to the water, his implants gave him an advantage, though he avoided using them where anyone else could see.

Mo was impressed at how well he'd taken to diving, and suggested, 'Sure you don't want to try deep-diving?'

Deep-diving was what you did outside the lagoon. It needed expensive equipment, was potentially dangerous, and you didn't get to see so much pretty stuff. 'Not really,' said Taro.

'I'll see if I can sort something else for your special day, then,' Mo said with a grin.

It took Taro a moment to work out that Mo meant his eighteenth birthday, which would also be their last day on the island. Birthdays hadn't been much of a cause for celebration in his life up till now – he wasn't even sure of the exact date; when the Minister had issued his ID, Taro had just picked a likely day. He'd been ignoring the upcoming birthday; it reminded him that he wasn't in some bubble of paradise that would last for ever, that soon he'd have to leave this beautiful place and work out what to do with his life.

Though he'd like to think he hadn't been pondering the future, he knew he was kidding himself. When it came down to it he'd probably carry on Jarek's mission, even if that meant staying with Nual. She might not rule his choices any more, but that didn't change the fact that there was nothing for him in Khesh – and, more importantly, he hated the Sidhe. Shit and blood, he hated them more than ever now. Sometimes he thought he hated Nual, because she'd fucked him good, and hurt him bad, and she was pure Sidhe, then he'd catch a glimpse of her, or hear her voice, and realise he could never in a thousand years hate her, no matter what she'd done, or did do, to him.

They'd reached a strange unspoken agreement where neither of them said anything to criticise or hurt the other one. For the first few days after he let her break their link, they were tender and careful around each other, like distant relatives brought together by loss. After a while Taro felt the numbness start to lift. There was still pain, but he was sure it would fade in time. He took to testing his ability to survive without Nual; not exactly avoiding her, but not going out of his way to find her either, and focusing on other people whenever she was around. Clearing up alone in the kitchen one night he looked up at the same time as she walked in. She stopped dead in the doorway, then turned on her heel. He started to call out to her before realising that he had no idea what he'd say. After all, if he was staying clear of her, he could hardly blame her for doing the same to him.

Sharing a room was hard, so they altered their sleep patterns, he coming to bed after she was already asleep; she rising before he awakened. When, despite all their efforts, they did find themselves alone they talked business, never anything personal.

For the moment, they were getting by. Taro was looking forward to the day when they'd be over the whole love thing and ready to restart their friendship.

All the while Taro was getting his head straight, Nual was actively pursuing their mission, spending time in Anau, getting to know the locals. Her cover story, that she was studying their culture, combined with her own innate abilities to ensure doors quickly opened to her. Nual befriended the old and the young, who were around during the day when most people were working at the resorts. She soon discovered that there were islands that weren't marked on the tourist maps, though not even her unnatural powers of persuasion could find the locations, for the locals themselves didn't know. She did get close to an old lady whose grandson was a security guard on one of the islands owned by Tawhira-*ngai*; if he knew what went on there he had never told her, but he had let slip that whilst some of the hidden islands were for the *ngai* execs and their families, others, like the one where he was based, had research facilities – built underground, to avoid aerial surveillance. He was due back on leave in a couple of weeks, and after Nual had planted the idea in his grandmother's head that there might be a good match to be made here, she agreed to introduce Nual when he came home.

Taro listened to her findings and tried to ask useful questions, though two weeks felt like an improbably long time in his current state. When he asked if there was anything he could do to help, she shook her head.

'Enjoy yourself while you can,' she said. She sounded like she meant it.

He said, with a grin only slightly forced, that he'd got that covered.

The evening before his birthday he went with the others to the bar in the nearest resort, where they met a girl, on holiday with her sister and her sister's boyfriend. She was out for fun, and she wanted Taro to be part of that fun. So when the others left to catch the last bus, he stayed, thinking that if he didn't get lucky, he'd have a long journey back – though he could always fly home. In fact, the idea of flitting across the darkened sea was quite appealing.

When it came to it, he didn't need to worry. She didn't plan on letting him go before dawn.

CHAPTER EIGHTEEN

The first databreaker Jarek hired had told him that the encryption on the files was like nothing he'd ever seen before, and there was no chance he could break it. Another, more expensive, operator gave him the same response, leaving Jarek with only one alternative, though he was wary of it. He'd initiated contact, but given his previous dealings with the individual in question he expected to be waiting a while for a result.

Meanwhile, he might as well see what he could unearth in the Alliance archives. Sifting data wasn't his idea of fun, and he wasn't entirely sure what he was looking for, but he didn't have anything better to do right now. He'd delved into the Freetraders' records before, following up leads to current Sidhe activity, but this time he focused on the past. Unfortunately, so much had been lost when the Protectorate fell that the past was a real mess. Human-space was like the shadow of a greater empire; an empire that had not, contrary to popular belief, been dead and gone for a thousand years.

Some of the information he needed was stored at Freetrader offices in other hubs, and getting those records took time, and there was a charge for files that had to be beeveed in. His other main resource – which was also eating up time and credit – was the Salvatine Archive. The church prided itself on being the force that had saved humanity from descending into chaos after the Protectorate fell, though Jarek suspected they'd spun their own place in history to suit their needs.

He checked up on the contacts used by the *Setting Sun,* as

extracted from the pilot by Nual. They were a mixed bag of traders, minor functionaries and – by far the largest group – corporates, which supported a long-held suspicion. It made sense for the Sidhe to use corporations rather than civil administrations: commercial ventures were likely to be more efficient than any planetary government, not to mention more susceptible to greed and paranoia – and hence easier to manipulate. He also discovered an unexpected bias away from hubs towards planet-based groups and individuals.

He found himself briefly distracted by references to something called zepgen, a term he'd come across once or twice, but never before followed up. Zepgen – zero-expenditure-generator – was a legendary power source, both compact and limitless, allegedly created by the male Sidhe. It was thought to draw its energy from shiftspace – or possibly even another universe. Some of the companies he came across had invested in – apparently fruitless – research into this area. From the look of it, if zepgen had ever existed then the secret had been lost with the fall of the Protectorate.

Talking of lost ...

He turned his attention to Serenein. There were plenty of legends about uncharted systems, but concrete information was predictably lacking. Certainly no world of that name appeared in any records he could access. He was pretty sure that Serenein was outside human-space, because their unusual night-sky didn't match anything in the *Judas Kiss*'s comp. Not that its location mattered greatly; the mapping between realspace and shiftspace was highly illogical: systems only one transit apart were sometimes many hundreds of light-years distant from each other, and others in relatively close physical proximity might be at the opposite ends of transit-path chains.

If he accepted that there had never been a beacon at Serenein then the next step was to find out if there was any way to transit into a beacon-less system without slipstreaming another ship. Although the Sidhe could obviously do it, he could find no record of any ship travelling between two systems that way.

He remembered a story from the Book. He'd been forced to

study the Salvatine holy text at school on Khathryn, and had promptly forgotten most of what he'd learnt, but this one story had stayed with him because it was about space, which had fascinated him even then. The beacons that allowed humanity to navigate around the stars had been seeded by angels, according to the Holy Book: not the flying assassin kind, the religious messenger kind. The more devout Salvatines who believed in the literal truth of the Book claimed that the Almighty, appalled at the blasphemy of the Sidhe in setting themselves up as divine, had actually created the beacons for humanity's use. The more rational saw these 'angels' as the freedom-fighters who overthrew the Protectorate – under God's direction, of course. The general consensus was that these heroic, divinely blessed individuals had subverted the Sidhe beacons for humanity's use, transporting some of them to unexplored ember-star systems where they set up the hubpoints, which then became the focus for human resistance.

But he now knew that the Sidhe didn't need beacons to get around. So if there hadn't *been* any beacons before the fall of the Protectorate, perhaps they weren't Sidhe artefacts at all – but if the Sidhe hadn't made them, who had?

Taro caught the first bus back in the morning and found the others waiting outside the blockhouse. Nual was with them. He felt a sudden stab of emotion, which he quickly suppressed. He had nothing to feel guilty about.

Mo leapt onto the bus and threw Taro's swimming gear into his lap. 'Almost thought you were going to miss your own party there! Good excuse though, eh?'

'The best there is,' said Taro, who could actually have used some sleep before they got going.

Mo sat next to him; Nual sat by herself two seats forward. She'd told the others at the blockhouse that she was interested in studying native customs and they'd accepted this as her reason for not joining in with them. As the bus rattled off Mo nodded towards her and said, 'I reckon she's been working too hard, so I got her a ticket too.'

'Thanks,' Taro said. He was glad Nual was here; she deserved some fun. 'How much do we owe you?'

'You don't. It's a birthday present.'

'Thanks, Mo!'

'No problem.' They found themselves looking at the back of Nual's head. She'd cut her hair in Stonetown, and the long plait was gone, replaced with a short bob. 'Is she all right?' asked Mo. 'Last night when we got back from the bar she looked like she'd been crying.'

Taro felt his jaw tense for a moment. He'd thought she was doing fine; she certainly acted like she was around him. 'Like you said, she's all work and no play,' he said. 'This'll do her good.'

They got off the bus at Anau, where a smartly turned-out boat waited by the landing stage. The native couple who owned it greeted the visitors with self-effacing warmth and the boat set off around the coast, keeping inside the lagoon. Once out on the water, Taro forgot how tired he was.

The morning started with a shallow-dive. The Captain ('You won't be able to pronounce my real name, friends; and you can call my wife the boss-lady!') came down with them to point out underwater wonders they'd otherwise miss, and told them all about the history and legends of the reef. Taro recognised a practised guide working his audience, though in his experience – giving, rather than receiving, the tourist spiel – there would be a grain of truth in most of what was said.

For the second dive of the morning, slightly further out in the lagoon, the Captain issued them with spearguns. He apologetically got them to sign waivers before showing them how the weapons worked. Then he said, 'Time to catch lunch,' and plopped backwards over the side of the boat.

Catching lunch turned out to be fun, but far from easy. The 'boss-lady' came in with them this time, watching their backs to make sure no one pointed their speargun near anybody else. Her husband showed people how it was done. He seemed to concentrate on the female members of the group, and Taro suspected his wife was there partly to watch him. Predictably he started with

Nual; equally predictably he wasn't with her long before something persuaded him to leave her alone. At the end of an exhausting and exhilarating morning Taro had caught one small spiky beastie with an unappetising mass of tentacles around its mouth, while she had managed to land a fat rainbow-scaled fish.

They took their catch to one of the uninhabited islands that edged the lagoon. The Captain lit a fire and set up a grill over it, then left his wife to do the cooking. Lunch was delicious, washed down with cold beers and nips from an unlabelled bottle that the Captain produced 'for the birthday boy'. The sweet spirit evaporated straight from Taro's tongue into his brain, and for a while the sea sparkled brightly enough that even with his shades on he kept blinking.

Back on the boat, the Captain was all smiles. 'The news is good,' he said, 'we have a big group of *ahuatai* heading this way soon.' The *ahuatai* – spirit-rays – were huge, gentle beasts with their own personal light-show. When the tides were right they came in from the deep sea to skim along the outer edge of the reef. The tides were perfect, said the Captain, and the *ahuatai*, the oldest, wisest creatures in the sea, were happy for people to swim amongst them when they visited the shallows. Getting close was fine, but to touch was *tapu* – forbidden. Mo caught the Captain's eye and his grin widened. He pointed to Mo and said, 'You know the best part, then, my friend?' Mo nodded eagerly. The Captain continued, 'The *ahuatai* are the children of the Lord of the Sea. They are thinking creatures, like us, and they know when other thinking creatures are among them. Their love will enfold you.'

The Captain's wife, monitoring the screens, started the engine and steered them out of a gap in the reef. Taro suffered a moment of queasy panic as the little vessel, which didn't have a skim-boat's gravitics, surged up and down, fighting the waves rolling through the worryingly narrow passage, but the boss-lady brought them to a stop a safe distance off the reef, in water several shades darker than that of the lagoon. The Captain went over to have a quick word with her.

Nual looked uneasy.

Taro was about to ask if she felt all right when the Captain called over, 'In now! They're coming!'

People jumped, slid or fell off the boat according to their skill and preference. The water was a lot colder out here, and Taro could feel the current pulling at him. In his earpiece the Captain said, 'Follow me!' and swam past them. People formed up behind, keeping close. The sea out here was very different to the warm, still waters of the lagoon. The reef was a colour-splotched wall on their left; to the right the land dropped away sharply into a blue-black abyss.

The captain dived, and at the same time Taro heard his voice in the earpiece. 'Everyone down now! Down and turn!'

Taro obeyed, though the open sea was making him feel vulnerable and he wasn't sure he wanted to leave the sunlit surface. For a moment he hung in the blue void. He made out Nual, waiting nearby, and Mo further off, turning on the spot in an attempt to be the first one to see the spirit-rays.

Suddenly the light was blotted out by a great triangle of darkness overhead – no, not darkness: the underside of the creature was covered in twinkling blue lights, glowing patterns extending down the long, translucent streamers trailing behind it.

Taro felt a deep sense of peace. His earlier concerns about the depth of the sea, about Nual, about ... anything: all gone. He knew that the animal above him knew he was there and – as the Captain had said – wanted him around.

The Captain, his voice a whisper of wonder, said, 'Swim with them. For as long as they stay near the reef, they wish our company.'

Taro flipped over and did just that. He could make out more spirit-rays now, perhaps a dozen of them. He knew they'd slowed down to allow the swimmers to keep up, and he swam along with them on his back, watching the light-show, aware that he was in the presence of an ancient creature of great wisdom.

All too soon, he sensed a change. The spirit-rays wanted to leave. In his ear the Captain said, 'Let them go on their way now.' A moment later the *ahuatai* above him turned, heading slowly off into the deeper water.

Taro watched it leave, feeling a sweet mixture of regret and fulfilment. He wouldn't have missed this for the world.

The spirit-rays sped up, flapping gently like great graceful birds, angling down towards the depths.

One of the divers was still with them.

Taro knew instantly what had happened. His cry was both mental and physical: *NUAL! NO!*

He felt a soft echo return: she'd heard him, but he mustn't worry. He should let her go now.

She'd found the unity she'd lost. And it was going to kill her.

Taro hesitated. This was what she wanted. And if he granted her wish then he'd truly be free.

The Captain was shouting in his earpiece, 'Turn around, lady, please, come back now!' He swam past Taro, kicking hard, but the rays were already far ahead, moving faster than any human could.

Any ordinary human.

Taro turned, put his arms by his sides and flexed his feet. His implants cut in at once and before he could even think he was flying diagonally down. The water pushed against the top of his head, making his neck ache. His ears popped. He pointed his toes until his feet threatened to cramp, driving the implants harder. He hoped he was still heading the right way. Around him the water was getting colder by the moment. Pressure began to build in his head and chest.

He broadcast a mental shout, over and over: *<Nual! Come back! Please! Come back!>*

No response. He slowed, just enough to look around. Shit and blood but it was dark down here! He glimpsed vague shapes in the gloom off to his left, and caught a brief blue flash. He changed course. Though he could hear and feel himself breathing hard, he couldn't get any air into his chest. His heart beat slow and heavy, and a piercing headache was building behind his eyes.

He made out a smaller shape, closer than the rays. Nual had fallen behind. He kept calling, kept flying, though dark spots speckled his vision and his breath had been reduced to quick, painful gasps.

A faint buzz sounded over the near-constant popping in his ears. A moment later he realised what the sound meant: he was running out of air. Adrenalin flooded his system. He strained harder against the building water-pressure.

The spirit-rays were gone, swallowed by darkness, leaving Nual behind. She hung limp in the water, sinking slowly.

Taro, his body disobedient under the stress, ran into her, then rebounded. Her head swayed, rippling her dark halo of hair. Her eyes were closed and what he could see of her face above the mask was relaxed and serene. If he left her, she would happily die down here.

As if.

Taro turned and wrapped his arms around her, pointing his toes down.

All too slowly, they began to rise.

Taro tried to take a breath, but nothing happened. A tight band was squeezing his head and his chest felt like it was about to implode.

No way was he going to die now, not when he'd come this far! That would be unfair, and he wouldn't put up with the universe giving him that sort of shit any more.

He stared up at the glittering surface above them, heading towards it with all his remaining strength.

CHAPTER NINETEEN

The answer came to Jarek while he was eating a solitary supper on board the *Judas Kiss* after another tedious day in the archives. As he shovelled gloop into his mouth he found his mind wandering, half-consciously linking the idea of beacons with that of transit-kernels. There were plenty of parallels: both beacons and transit-kernels interacted with shiftspace, both were powerful artefacts necessary for human culture that didn't take well to being tampered with, and both came from an unknown source.

Unknown – until he'd stumbled on Serenein. So now he knew where transit-kernels originated – or rather, he knew what made them what they were: the living mind of a Sidhe boy. But genetic tampering by the female Sidhe had left these minds damaged, apparently simple, even before they were subjected to whatever unholy process transformed them into shift-kernels.

Suddenly it hit him: if transit-kernels came from male Sidhe, then maybe beacons did too. Shiftspace beacons could have been a vital secret weapon in the rebellion against the Protectorate, breaking the female Sidhe's monopoly on interstellar travel and allowing human rebels in different systems to communicate. Male Sidhe must have provided this weapon to the downtrodden humans. That also explained why beacons had no built-in failsafes: in a war situation all that tedious messing around at safe distances that was required today would be a liability; quick and dirty would have been the only way to operate in a guerrilla war against the Sidhe.

Whether beacons were, like transit-kernels, actually built around the mind of a male Sidhe was another question. Would the free males have been willing to make such an enormous sacrifice for their human allies?

Jarek really needed to talk to one of the old Sidhe males. Unfortunately they'd all been dead for a thousand years.

His com chirped. The number was unlisted, but he hit receive anyway. The line went dead.

It chirped again. The same thing happened.

Normally that kind of weirdness would worry him, but Jarek had been expecting this.

The third time he received a single-word text message: *Tarset*.

Time to get moving.

As soon as Taro broke through to the thin, warm air, he tried to take a huge breath, but the mask was covering his nose and mouth – and he was still going up. When he shot free of the sea, gravity pulled at Nual, tugging her out of his arms, and he grabbed for her with one hand while ripping the mask off with the other. Even as the welcome air rushed into his lungs he felt her slip from his grasp. The bright light began to fade and new points of pain broke out all over his body. He flexed his toes and fell back into the sea.

He felt himself being hauled face-down over something hard, then a pinprick of cold in his arm that quickly spread. He had a growing urge to throw up, and gave into it, spewing hot darkness and cold water, until the two combined to swallow him up—

His next clear memory was of being in an aircar – apparently emergencies let you spoil the view – with someone bending over him. 'Wh—? Nual?' he croaked.

The woman said, 'Try to relax. Your sister will be fine.' Then she eased something over his mouth and nose. The cold was back, but at least it was dry now.

He decided it was all right to pass out again, and did.

Taro woke up in hospital in Stonetown. He was feeling a lot better. The mask had stopped him getting water in his lungs, but he'd fallen back in and been fished out by the Captain's wife, who'd given him some sort of shot to offset the worst effects of going down so deep. As a result he had only minor damage: some burst blood vessels, a lingering headache and a ringing in his ears. The doctor said he was lucky he'd been using shallow-dive equipment: apparently anyone coming straight up from that depth using the full deep-dive gear would have been seriously fucked. He started to explain, but it was beyond Taro. He was just glad to have survived.

They let him check out the next day, but Nual, who was in a different ward, was kept in. Her heart had stopped while she was in the water, but the Captain and his redoubtable wife, used to crises like this, had got it restarted themselves. Taro sent silent thanks in their direction.

He was allowed to see Nual, but she was still groggy, her bloodshot eyes unfocused, and she didn't seem to know he was there. He felt cold all over again, but resisted the urge to try and contact her mentally. 'Will she be all right?' he whispered to the doctor. 'Is there ... lasting damage?'

The doctor looked at Taro. 'I'll be honest: there is a risk, though the tests look positive so far. We'll keep you informed, don't worry.'

Mo was at the hostel. He'd brought their stuff back with him from the island, but he was a bit strange when Taro thanked him – as if he felt uncomfortable around him. Kise, on the other hand, had just got an interview with one of the *ngai*, and it was making her unexpectedly sociable. 'You want to know what's up with Mo?' she asked. 'Just check the chatnets. You're today's news, Taro!'

Mo had sold the story of the dive-gone-wrong and Nual's dramatic rescue to the local media. He'd told the journos he'd never seen anyone move like Taro – and now the hostel's messaging service had three offers of well-paid interviews, if Taro was interested. He wondered if anyone had worked out he had implants, and what that meant. If not, he sure as shit wasn't going to tell them.

When he visited Nual the next day she was awake, propped up on her pillows. She looked at him as he came in. 'Thank you,' she said quietly.

After his initial surge of relief at seeing her alive and well had passed, Taro wasn't sure how to respond, but she saved him from having to by continuing, 'I'm sorry. What I did was ... unjustified.'

An odd way of putting it, Taro thought. 'It's all right,' he said, more because it seemed like the right thing to say than because it was.

If they'd been lovers he'd have rushed over and held her close. Instead they talked about small stuff while he perched on the end of the bed. When he told her about Mo selling the story she grimaced and said, 'Nothing we can do about that now.'

'Could this tip them off about us?'

She knew who he meant, of course. 'I don't think so. They may have my ID after what happened on Khathryn, but they have no reason to look for me here. You are not known to them at all.'

The next day the hospital commed to say they were releasing Nual, and when Taro arrived to collect her he found her talking to a heavyset man dressed in a garishly patterned shirt and shorts. She turned to Taro and said, 'This gentleman has kindly paid my bill.' In his head, she added: <*I am not picking up any ill intent, so we'll go along with this for now.*>

The gentleman in question beamed a smile. 'You must be Taro,' he said. 'Would you two care to join me for a short drive?'

'Where to?' Taro noted that the man hadn't offered his name.

'Oh, just around,' he said with a disarming shrug.

Nual said, 'I think we could do that, although we would like to know with whom we will be riding.'

'Of course.' The man didn't appear to take offence. 'You can call me Patai.'

Patai's ride turned out to be one of the locals' distinctive ground-cars, a high-topped vehicle with an open pen for stashing luggage in the back. It was wide enough for the three of them to sit side by side in the front.

As they got in Patai said, 'That was quite an adventure you two had out on Ipitomi.'

Taro gave a noncommittal grunt.

Nual said, 'I suspect you are not here to talk about the diving incident.'

'No, you're right. I'm not with the holonets.' He pulled away from the hospital, driving slowly and carefully. 'I represent a third party. One who would be interested in hiring you for a job.'

'What sort of job?' asked Nual.

Taro kept silent; best let her handle this.

'The sort that needs the advantage of your unique talents.'

Taro thought, *<He knows we're Angels, then.>*

Nual responded, *<It wasn't as though we could hide that from anyone who made the effort to check.>* Out loud she said, 'I see. Precisely which aspect of our unique talents would your third party be interested in?'

'Your ability to fly, mainly.'

'What is the nature of the job?'

'We would like you to get someone out of a secure facility.'

<That sounds well smoky!>

<Perhaps. I believe that jobs like this often use outside professionals here. Let's hear him out.> 'Can you be more specific?' she asked.

'At this stage, not really. I can tell you that the person you will be removing wishes to leave the facility, and that the security there, whilst normally very tight, will have been compromised by the time you arrive on the scene. Oh, and I am authorised to offer a generous remuneration.' He named a sum that was nearly as much as the Minister had given them when they left Khesh. 'It would be ten per cent up front, the remainder on completion.' Patai turned down a minor road. 'I imagine you'd like to discuss this in private. I thought I might drop you at the east gate of the park. I will drive round to meet you on the far side. Normally I'd allow longer, but time is of the essence in this case. Will that be acceptable?'

'I believe so,' said Nual.

They carried on in silence. Taro resisted the urge to chat mentally with Nual. He was enjoying being let into her head again, now the whole love/addiction problem was sorted. But they needed to stay focused on business.

The park was the largest green space in Stonetown, with neat lawns shaded beneath palm trees. Flowers spilled from planters next to carved wooden seats. After Patai dropped them off they strolled in the dappled shade.

'I think we should take him up on this offer,' said Nual.

'The pay's top prime for sure,' said Taro, 'though it ain't exactly Angel work.'

'The money would be useful, but that's not why we should do it. This involves two of the three hi-tech *ngai*.'

'Really? Which ones?'

'I do not know yet. Patai is merely a broker, so he works for whichever *ngai* pays at the time, but the sense he has of this job is that it is connected with the conflict between those three. To find names and specifics I would have needed to go deeper into his head, which would be unwise at this stage.'

'So, you gonna read him fully once we've agreed to take the job, then make him forget he ever met us?'

'That would be a mistake, given the organisations he works for. And though he may have useful information, I doubt it is what we are after. But by doing this job we may get access to just the kind of hidden hi-tech facility being used to create the transit-kernels; perhaps while we are there we might take a look around. By making ourselves useful to the *ngai* that hires us, we may additionally gain a way into their confidence.'

'Right. It's just ... I've never done anything like this before.'

'Do you wish me to carry out the job alone?'

'No, of course not.' He wasn't going to leave her without back-up.

'Are you sure? Taro, I know that you have killed only in self-defence, and you are not used to combat. If you do not want to come on this mission, you do not have to.'

'I got the implants, and the conditioning,' he said. Then, with more confidence than he felt, he added, 'And who said anything about combat? All we gotta do is lift some cove who wants to leave anyway.'

'Then we had better give Patai his answer.'

CHAPTER TWENTY

It was a good job Taro was up for it, because the mission needed both of them. They had to infiltrate the island facility where the mark lived, find their man, then fly him out to a modified aircar which would be submerged just offshore. Once he was safely on board, they'd earned the rest of their pay.

Patai'd said time was of the essence because a massive storm was due to hit the island in two days' time. Another team would be going in under cover of the storm to do some smoky stuff of their own. 'You don't need to worry about Team Beta,' Patai told them. 'The only thing you need to know is that they'll be acting as your diversion.'

The job didn't sound so hard, Taro thought – and it got better: Patai's employer wanted Taro and Nual on top form for the mission, so they'd been installed in a suite in a downtown hotel.

The only less-than-prime thing was the weaponry, or rather, the lack of it. Nual, asking if there was any chance of getting their gun out of customs, was told that wasn't 'appropriate'. Patai'd issue them with tranq-pistols, and they were to stick to non-lethal force. Apparently the *ngai* had some sort of honour code against taking lives. The man had a point, Taro admitted: an x-laser wasn't exactly designed to subdue opponents.

The suite had a large living room, and two double bedrooms off it. Taro had previously only seen the like in the company of well-heeled punters able to pay for the room – and for him; he'd not had much opportunity then to admire the luxurious surroundings. He sat on the bed and bounced up and down experimentally.

'I could get used to this,' he called through the open door to Nual. 'Did Patai say we could use room service?'

Nual stuck her head in and smiled. 'He said, "Whatever you need, within reason." I assume the *ngai* is paying for these rooms so we do not have to plan our mission in the hostel.' Her smile faded. 'But they have given us little information to plan with.'

'I s'pose not. What d'you think they'd have done if a pair of Angels hadn't happened to show up?'

'Hire others – I imagine there are always those who can make themselves useful in the conflicts between the *ngai*. No doubt they have access to stealth air vehicles, perhaps even personal grav-harnesses. However, we come already equipped with the ability to fly – plus, being offworlders, we are deniable.'

'Yeah, that's true. You sure this ain't some sort of set-up?'

'Yes,' she said, looking a little doubtful, then qualified her statement. 'At least as sure as I can be without using my abilities so explicitly that I would give myself away.'

'That's good enough for me.'

Another smile, warmer this time, and suddenly Taro saw what a bastard he'd been, how badly he'd hurt Nual by making this all about his own pain. He'd been acting like what she felt didn't matter.

'What is it, Taro?' she asked gently. 'Are you all right?'

She could find out easily as snapping her fingers; she just had to read him to know what he was thinking. But he'd told her to stay out of his head, and she had, other than to share the stuff they needed for the mission. She was giving him respect and distance and consideration. All he'd given her was anger and blame.

'Yeah— No—' He tried again. 'Listen, Nual, when you— When you *undid* what you did to my head, did it work both ways?'

'You mean, when I broke your love for me, did I also break mine for you?'

'Yeah, that.'

'No. I did try but—' She stopped, then continued softly, 'It appears I can influence the emotions of others far more easily than I can control my own.'

'Shit and blood, so you still feel—? Shit! I've been a total fuck-wit, haven't I?'

She raised an eyebrow. 'That would be one way of putting it.'

'Is that why you went off with the spirit-rays? Because you wanted …' He couldn't say it, couldn't say out loud: *did you want to kill yourself*?

'Perhaps – I was befuddled by the *ahuatai*, it is true, but I would not have allowed them to affect me so deeply had I not been trying to run away from my pain. Letting myself be drawn into their simple unity was stupid and cowardly. Though I told myself it was for the best, I was taking the easy way out. I will always be grateful to you for risking your life to save me.'

'No worries, that's what friends're for.' He stood up. 'Can I—? Would you like a hug? Just a hug – for friendship?'

Nual looked surprised at Taro's offer, but she smiled wanly. 'I would, yes. Very much.'

He held her close, and it felt right. Just a hug, like he'd said, between friends.

Their coms chirped simultaneously.

Nual stiffened, and Taro let her go.

He glanced at his hand to see a message telling him his credit balance had just shot up. Patai had sent the down-payment; they were committed to the mission now.

He looked up as Nual swayed on her feet. Her eyes were glazed and her face looked drained.

'What is it?' he asked. 'Are you all right?'

She put a hand out and staggered backwards. Her throat worked and for a moment he thought she was going to throw up. He reached for her, offering his support and she let him catch her hand.

She dipped her head, swallowed hard, then said, in a voice as quiet and still as death, 'I think we may have made a terrible mistake.'

'What d'you mean?' Taro steered her to the bed and she sat down heavily. He kept hold of her hand.

'This mission …' She swallowed again and shuddered. 'I think something bad will happen.'

'I don't understand. I thought you said Patai ain't setting us up?'

'He isn't. At least he doesn't think he is. But …' She raised her head, but wouldn't meet Taro's worried gaze. 'Do you know what prescience is?' she asked softly.

'Nope. Sorry.'

'It's the ability to see the future.'

'Is that something Sidhe can do?' Though he knew of shysters back on Vellern who'd claimed to read tourists' fortunes, it hadn't occurred to him that anyone – not even the obscenely powerful Sidhe – could genuinely know about stuff that hadn't happened yet.

'To an extent, yes: because I'm sensitive to the minds around me I sometimes know what someone is going to do an instant before they act. It can make me more dangerous in combat, but any skilled human fighter can develop their own version of this ability. There is something else though, a very rare talent. It's like a vision— no, that's not the word. It's more like – let's say, a *certainty*. Like sudden and overwhelming intuition.'

'And you can do this prescience thing?' He'd had no idea.

'Not exactly. Remember I thought my powers changed after I used them with the pilot?'

'Yeah, I remember.'

'I think I might have unlocked something inside myself. I believe I may be developing this ability. During the wedding on the island I saw, just for a moment, that the marriage would end badly.'

'Badly, how?'

She shook her head. 'It wasn't specific, just a feeling. A really strong feeling. What I experienced just now wasn't specific either, just a premonition of something bad – at the moment the deal was clinched. When that future course was set, it felt like a web of possibilities closing, and I felt positive that pain and suffering would result. *Will* result.'

'Whose pain and suffering?' Taro was worried. Nual was

normally so assured, and the way she was acting now was down-right freaky. He tried to make a joke of it. "Cos I'm thinking it might be them poor coves who try'n get in our way.'

She looked sideways at him. 'Sometimes I really need your sense of perspective, Taro.'

'Thanks.' He felt a glow at her words. 'So does this mean we ain't taking the job after all?' he asked carefully. Her odd feeling sounded like a pretty gappy reason to pull out, but he trusted her, so if she said the deal was too smoky, they were out. 'I guess we'd have to give back the money ... and this Patai cove won't be too pleased with us.'

'You're right, of course.' She drew a deep breath. 'I could just be imagining it – I have no way of knowing if this is real. Until something I foresee actually happens ... And if we let Patai down, he will be unlikely to consider hiring us again.' She got up. 'I'm just being foolish. We need this job.'

Nual was still preoccupied the next day so Taro tried not to let his own nerves at the upcoming mission show. She needed him to be strong for her.

When he suggested they go for a walk to distract themselves she shook her head. 'I'm not sure ...'

'What is it? Have you seen something? A future something?'

'No, I just—' She turned to him and he felt the change. She'd been holding herself tightly wound, but now, just for a moment, she released the tension. It was like a wave washing over him, a crazy mix of fear, pain, shame ... and *desire*.

'What is it?' he breathed.

'You,' she said. 'I— I want you. I have never felt such need. It is almost as though loving you now is the only remedy for the dark future I glimpsed.'

'You do know how gappy that sounds?' asked Taro gently.

'Yes! Of course I do – but I can think of nothing else. And I cannot decide whether I should send you away, or give in to my need.'

'If you did give in,' said Taro carefully, 'would I end up like the pilot?'

'Dead? No, I have more control than that now. But ... enthralled, possibly, yes. It might undo all that work we put in, curing you of me.'

'Nual, I'm willing to take that risk,' said Taro. He still wanted her; of course he did. And he could be careful, make it just about the sex. 'Remember what I am – what I *was*. I know what I'm doing. And I'm your friend; of course I'll help you. So if the help you need is me, then you've got it.'

She stood hunched in on herself, everything locked down again, not influencing him in any way. 'Are you sure?'

'Aye, lady, I am.'

'Then ...' She straightened, and the barriers came down.

Her beauty made him want to cry, it shone so bright. He gasped as lust thrummed through him and his body came up with a better plan. Three steps to close the distance, then they were kissing, his head bent over hers. Every part of him that touched her was on fire.

The kiss ended, and it was like the world ending.

They staggered to the nearest bed, ungainly in their desperation. They pulled the clothes off each other, then Nual paused and put a finger over his lips. 'We have to be careful,' she breathed. 'Try and keep control.'

'I'll do my best,' Taro said. He *knew* sex. He understood how it could be many things, how every time was different. He got the give and take of pleasure, knowing when to lead and when to let himself kick back and enjoy his partner. He used what he knew.

She helped him, keeping it purely physical, staying out of his head, but still it took all his concentration to act like she was just another punter, and not the centre of the universe.

Inevitably, the time came when he wasn't going to be able to hold on much longer. Nual, sensing how close he was, murmured, 'I can block it,' out loud; the safe way, the human way. 'But I don't want to.'

He just about managed to speak. 'Don't want you to either.'

'When you let go,' she whispered, her voice barely audible, 'it won't just be physical. Do you understand?'

'I ... No— Yes. I don't know!' Nual's words brought him back from the brink of orgasm. His mind felt strangely clear. 'I can't understand: I'm only human. But I know one thing: whatever I've been telling myself these past few days, I still love you.'

She smiled. <*And I love you, Taro.*>

And even before he began to move in her again he felt that welcome presence in his mind, and as he opened himself to her he felt her do the same to him. Her sensations began to overlay his: he was still himself, but now he could feel every surge of pleasure he caused in her, the smallest sensation magnified and returned. He knew all she was, saw into her heart, her soul. There was darkness there, and destruction, but he embraced it because it was part of her, part of his love.

Their bodies were moving with increasing urgency, spiralling towards ecstasy. She – *they* – held off, their combined energy feeding each other, each enhancing the other ...

... until they were one, in a place of utter peace with no boundaries, no past and no future, only the divine moment.

Finally, because even souls in perfect harmony have to return to their bodies eventually, they let go.

CHAPTER TWENTY-ONE

The sign used to say, *Welcome to Tarset*. Since Jarek had last visited, ten months ago, some wag had shorted out the display on the two Ts.

Hubpoints sometimes gave themselves airs. Most people lived out their lives on the planet of their birth, so hubbers generally considered themselves superior to the dirtborn. The constant throughput of travellers did give some hub stations a distinctive, cosmopolitan style. Tarset, built from a cluster of gutted colony ships dating from the original expansion and located off the main tourist-routes, had no such pretensions. It was pure utility, just a point where transit-paths could be accessed, ships serviced and business done. There were always people on Tarset in need of raw materials to maintain infrastructure and industry, and though his chosen cargo of mixed semi-refined ores wasn't going to make him an enormous profit, it was something Jarek could pick up at short notice and always be sure of shifting. And the cargo provided the perfect cover for the run; freetraders moving around without registered cargo attracted awkward questions from customs officials, who tended to assume, often correctly, that they were carrying something dubious.

Tarset as a location wasn't ideal – it was seven transits from Kama Nui – but it was a suitably anonymous place to meet someone who remained a mystery to Jarek despite the fact they'd been in contact for the last four years.

When Jarek had first embarked on his search for the hidden empire, he'd had little success. After three years without turning up any firm leads, he decided on a different approach: he started to look for those who had contact with the Sidhe instead, specifically freetraders who might be supplying them. He'd encountered Orzabet first while looking for patterns in trade routes.

He'd taken a couple of weeks off from trading to search the archives, before reluctantly concluding that this new approach wasn't working either. Then a text message arrived, sent direct to the *Judas Kiss*: 'Are you looking for who I think you are?' It was signed 'Orzabet'.

He'd replied, in text, asking if 'Orzabet' could be more specific.

He'd heard nothing for five weeks. Then he received a data-spike containing some of his own research data – and more, listing odd routes and unexpected absences of certain tradebirds, with records stretching back over a century, all correlated and indexed – but with key data apparently corrupted. The hardcopy message with the 'spike consisted of a remote data-drop address and the following text: *If this was complete, how would you use it? Tell the truth and maybe you can have the key.* Caught between exasperation and fascination, he'd replied, *I'd use it to find those who don't want to be found and shouldn't still be around.* Two could play at being obtuse. 'Orzabet' replied the next day: *I believe we're looking for the same thing.* The message had a decryption key appended which unscrambled the data, and so gave Jarek his original list of suspicious ships. This was how he'd found out about and followed the *Setting Sun* on its regular run to Serenein.

Since then he'd built up a cautious relationship with Orzabet – although, four years later, he was still none the wiser as to whether Orzabet was a man or a woman, or even a group of individuals operating under that name. Whoever it was, they occasionally provided Jarek with information that helped him spot possible Sidhe influence; in return he reported anything of interest he came across, and from time to time transported small packages – he suspected they contained dataspikes, but he'd never opened them – between hubs. Orzabet used text or comp-generated voice, and messages could come from anywhere. Any physical contact was through third-party logistics services. Either Orzabet moved around a lot, or he/she/they were able to spoof message-tags somehow. Or possibly both.

When Orzabet finally got in contact this time, he'd used the most secure of the messaging services they were currently employing to send a text that took their combined keys to access. It said: 'I have the complete memory-core from the *Setting Sun*. Interested?'

The reply, received within two hours, was a single character '!' followed by a new contact procedure, this time routed via a hubpoint in a different sector. This led to a terse, time-delayed conversation. The memory-core wasn't something Jarek was willing to trust to a courier; he needed to give it to Orzabet in person – not that he intended to just hand over something so potentially valuable – and incriminating – to someone he'd never met. He requested an initial face-to-face meeting – without the item in question – and was deeply relieved when Orzabet agreed.

As soon as he reached Tarset, he commed the latest number Orzabet had provided. It connected, then promptly went dead. A minute later his own com displayed an address and a time, two hours from now.

Registered weapons were legal on Tarset, so Jarek went armed. A pistol, even loaded solely with tranq, felt reassuring.

The address was an office in a commercial section that was sublet to various small businesses. He hadn't imagined Orzabet operating out of anything so mundane as an office, and he wasn't surprised when his com listed this particular suite as currently unoccupied.

When he rang the chime a woman's voice issued from the wall-com, asking, 'Who am I?'

For a moment Jarek was confused, until he realised that since that first communication they'd never used names. 'Orzabet,' he said.

The door opened onto a small office, empty save for a desk and a chair behind it, on which sat a nondescript woman in her late twenties or early thirties. The only item on the desk was a large hardcopy book propped up in front of her, which Jarek thought an odd affectation for someone who dealt in virtual data. She watched

Jarek enter in silence. He kept his hands in view as he walked towards her. The door hissed shut behind him.

'No closer please,' she said, her voice toneless.

Jarek stopped. He saw Orzabet's gaze go to his belt. 'I probably shouldn't have brought the gun,' he said, trying to sound casual.

'Of course you should,' she said flatly. Her own hands remained hidden.

When she didn't say anything else he opened his mouth to speak, but she cut across him. 'Are they all dead? The crew, I mean.'

'I'm sorry?' The woman was creeping him out. He was tempted to just turn around and leave; maybe that would improve her attitude. But he was pretty sure she had a gun of her own, perhaps hidden behind that book, which appeared to be a technical manual for a vintage groundbike.

'The crew of the Sidhe ship, the *Setting Sun*. Are they all dead?'

'The Sidhe in charge are, yes. They had mutes; I let them go.'

'So they still use mutes? Interesting.' For the first time her voice showed a trace of emotion.

Jarek decided he was dealing with someone for whom data mattered far more than people.

After another pause she said, 'And you're sure no one knows you have this data?'

He didn't like the implications of that question. 'I'm not certain what you're getting at,' he said carefully.

'Ah, I see,' she said. Her expression softened. 'You're right: if we're to trust each other then perhaps that wasn't the best way to put it. What I'm after is an assurance that the Sidhe don't know what happened to their memory-core.'

'The Sidhe have no idea what happened, and they won't be coming after me.'

'Good. I needed to hear that from you before I agreed to take this job on. We can discuss payment for my services now.'

Jarek decided not to take offence at the implication that he might've traipsed halfway across the sector only to fail a character-judgement from someone exhibiting all the warmth and empathy of a landing strut. 'Actually, payment might be a bit tricky at the moment.'

'Quite. You're broke.' She paused and watched as he processed her meaning. 'I know that because I'm the best databreaker alive, Sirrah Reen. Which is one of the reasons you need my help.'

'And the other reason is?' he said, a little coldly.

'Because you and I are probably the only two humans alive who know the Sidhe are not dead.'

Though that wasn't entirely true, he couldn't argue with her logic. 'Fair enough. I was going to offer you a down-payment and a contract to repay the rest, once we'd settled on your fee. Assuming you're willing to trust me.'

'If I were not willing to trust you we would not be having this conversation. But I don't want your money. I want a full copy of the data from the memory-core, once I've decrypted it.'

'Ah.' He should have expected that she'd want information for her services. If she was as good as she claimed then she wouldn't lack for funds. The information Nual had got from the pilot would probably be worth a lot to her, but she'd want to know how he'd got hold of such valuable data and he could hardly admit that his Sidhe ally had killed a human man to get it. The *Setting Sun*'s files were all he had to trade, and once he handed them over she could easily rip a copy for herself anyway.

He realised she was watching him, waiting for his answer. Rather than endure her appraising scrutiny, he said, 'I need to think about this.'

She looked momentarily disappointed, then nodded curtly. 'I understand. Will fifteen hours be long enough for you to reach a decision? My contact protocols change again after that.'

'Fifteen hours will be more than long enough. I'll be in touch.'

As he turned to go she called out, 'We're on the same side, Sirrah Reen.'

Jarek wasn't entirely convinced.

CHAPTER TWENTY-TWO

Taro wondered whether it would be unprofessional to hold Nual's hand. The driver of the bus-sized aircar wasn't paying the two of them much attention. He exuded an air of slightly menacing professionalism, ignoring his passengers unless or until they decided to brighten his day by posing a threat.

Taro decided not to risk it. It wasn't like he needed to touch her to get close. Not any more.

Despite himself, he yawned. The mission was taking place in the early hours of the morning, but though they'd spent the afternoon in bed, there hadn't been much sleeping, until Nual had insisted, as evening fell, that they got some rest. Taro had fallen asleep pretty quickly once he realised she meant it.

Waking up a few hours later was a new and wonderful experience for him; before, sex had been business or pleasure, and once it was over, he was gone. To wake up with your lover in your arms was the best way to start the day; no, the *only* way to start the day, and it was how he planned to start every day from now on.

Or maybe not exactly like this: they'd been awakened by the peeping of an alarm after less than four hours' sleep. When Nual leaned across to silence it, he thought to her, *<Can't we just stay here for ever?>*

<No. I'm sorry.>

<What's the worst that'll happen if we don't turn up for the mission? Someone coming in and shooting us? Right now I don't care what happens to me, as long as I'm with you!>

He sensed tension and knew she was recalling the moment, as

they were building to their fifth or sixth shared climax, when he'd nearly lost himself entirely. He'd begun to tire, but her energy seemed boundless, and he'd wondered if he should just give her the last of himself and be done with it. His life was complete; whatever came after this would be a disappointment. He made the offer wordlessly, willing her to accept him, to take him utterly and completely. For a moment he thought she would, but she'd drawn back, and he became aware of their surroundings. They lay on their sides, face-to-face. She reached up and brushed away a sweat-soaked strand of hair from his forehead. Speaking out loud for the first time in some while, she'd whispered, 'That is the one desire of yours I would never grant.'

And now here they were, only a few hours after waking up together, on the way to a secret island where their target was waiting to be rescued. For the first two hours of the journey they'd flown through bursts of rain, arriving at the aircar's registered destination, where they'd gone into stealth mode, slowing down and taking a dive underwater. Now, half an hour later, the driver brought them up to just below the surface, where the storm-mixed waters would hide their approach.

Nual hadn't had any more bad feelings – he'd probably've known if she had, the way things were between them now – but that didn't stop Taro worrying. It didn't help that yesterday's exertions had taken a lot out of him. His body ached with exhaustion. He knew a few substances that could've helped his condition, at least for a while, but they weren't going to be available on room service. Perhaps their hard-nut driver had something. Then again, he couldn't risk anything that might mess with his judgement. He'd have to ask the driver one favour though, thanks to the gut-churning effect of the buffeted aircar.

'Excuse me, friend,' he called forward.

The driver looked over his shoulder, his face impassive. 'Yeah?'

'I don't s'pose this vehicle's got a—?' He struggled for the right word.

'A head?' The driver jerked a thumb back. 'Door next to the weapons locker.'

As he got up he sensed Nual's mixture of amusement and sympathy.

The head turned out to be about the same size as the weapons locker. While trying to fit into it and close the door Taro knocked the paper-holder out of its niche. As he picked it up he saw a small logo on the rim of the dispenser: a gold-edged cream circle, and inside it a gold-brown shape which he identified after a moment as a stylised *vaka*, one of the islanders' long wooden boats.

He waited until he got back to communicate his findings to Nual, adding, *<Ain't that the symbol for Makoare-ngai?>*

<It is, and I thought I glimpsed something like it on the inside of our armour too. So it would appear they are our employers.> They'd been issued vests of hardened material that covered vital body organs, and lightweight helmets with pull-down visors, precautions that did nothing to calm Taro's nerves.

The dark froth washing over the screen began to brighten as a silver glow grew in the distance. The driver said, 'This is as close to the shield as it's safe to get. We've got a few minutes before the man inside's due to disable it.' He stood up and went to the weapons locker, pulling out a pair of lightweight pistols and a piece of paper that he also offered to them. Stuck on the paper were two light brown strips the size and shape of Taro's little finger. 'Have you used com-strips before?' he asked. His tone was neutral; when Nual had read him she said she'd picked up a mixture of respect and unease: he knew they were trained assassins, but they weren't the kind of people he usually worked with.

'Sorry, no,' said Nual.

The driver said, 'Before you go in, stick them on the side of your throat, just here.' He pointed to his own neck. 'You only need to sub-vocalise and everything you say will be relayed to any attuned com-strips within range. Remember that range is short, no more than 500 metres, even less once you're underground. I'll be wearing one too, so as soon as you've got the target outside, call me and I'll bring the car back up to the surface.'

'Can we call you in if we get into trouble?' asked Taro.

'Depends on the nature of the trouble. If it's safe, I'll do my best to provide back-up, but this is a deniable mission, so I can't take any risks.' Taro decided not to mention the giveaway logos inside their armour; if the opposition got to see them then things would've gone to shit anyway.

A minute later the silvery light ahead faded. 'We're on,' said the driver.

Nual stuck the com-strip just below her jaw. Taro followed suit. 'Can you hear me?' she whispered. He heard her voice twice: out loud, then with an echo in his ear via the com-strip. 'Yeah, I can,' he replied at the same pitch.

A faint light-source became visible, coming from above. As the aircar broke the surface water foamed across the screen and the background shaking and bucking increased as they came up into the full fury of the storm.

Taro eased the visor down over his eyes. The cabin became a blur of bright greens and blues, quickly fading as the helmet's tech adjusted to the light-level. He tried pulling the hood of his shimmer-cloak over the helmet, but it wouldn't fit. It would've looked pretty stupid anyway.

'Good luck,' said the driver, and opened the roof-hatch.

Nual took his hand and they leapt out. The roar of the storm was muffled by the helmet's pick-ups as they rose from the aircar. The rain hit them like a thrown pail of water and the wind tried to snatch them from each other. He had a moment of panic; he'd never flown in conditions like these, though his implants came with the knowledge of how to use them.

Nual tightened her grip on his hand, pulling him up, saying, <*We need to fly high enough to not get hit by the waves, but low enough to avoid detection.*>

He did his best. Between the driving rain and the spray from the heaving sea, Taro's arms and legs were already soaked and he could feel water trickling down inside his armour, cold and ticklish.

The visor showed the rain as a faint blue mist overlaying a

green-blue seascape. Numbers flickered at the edge of his vision, telling him all about the types and ranges of nearby objects. The island showed as a low hump of thrashing greenery a hundred metres ahead and they arrowed towards it.

Suddenly everything went white, and a heartbeat later a great boom sounded around them.

Taro froze in terror, but Nual tugged at him. *<Don't worry, Taro! It's only thunder and lightning – perfectly natural, and highly unlikely to harm us.>*

Her silent words reassured him. The quicker he got moving, the sooner he'd be under cover again, he told himself. There was another flash as they approached the island; this time Taro managed not to jump. The storm was lashing the palm trees so hard they looked like great angry beasts nailed to the ground. When they reached land they slowed to fly carefully between the creaking trunks. No way would an aircar fit under here. Occasional scraps of foliage fell on them, though there was nothing big enough to injure them.

A new image appeared in their visors as they picked their way through the trees, and a few seconds later they landed behind a cube just over a metre square with a round grille across the front. Nual, a red outline in his enhanced eyesight, took a small cylinder from a pocket in her armour and reached over to stick it to the top of the cube: some sort of scrambler, provided by their employer to mess with the local surveillance. She came round the front, took out a small blade and prised off the grille. An indicator on the anti-surveillance gizmo flashed once: it had intercepted the tamper warning. She clamped the rappelling gear they'd need to get their man out to the side of the cube. *<I'll go first, so you'll need to unwind the line when you come,>* she said, then grabbed the edge of the opening and slid in. Taro attached the rappelling line to his belt and followed, hovering briefly as soon as he was inside until he was sure he sensed her waiting below him. She floated downwards; he followed.

The screech of the wind died away as they descended. The shaft ended in a smooth-sided passage carved into the rock. Taro heard a faint rising-and-falling tone in the distance, possibly an alarm. As he was unclipping and securing the rappelling line a gold blip appeared at the edge of his vision <*Is that him?*> he thought to Nual.

<*It must be.*> The target had swallowed a tracer which was activated by stomach juices – Taro had no idea how that worked; all he knew was that while it was in their man's belly, their visors would give them distance and direction to him. All they had to do was home in on it.

A moment later Nual said out loud, 'I think we should use the com-strips from now on.'

Taro knew what she meant. Her presence in his head kept stirring up delicious but distracting echoes; right now they needed to share information, not emotions. 'I guess you're right,' he said wryly.

Flying along the passage was harder than dropping down the shaft. After the third time he banged his head on the low ceiling he gave up and crawled. At junctions they would pause to confer, and for Nual to stick a marker on the wall to show which way they'd come – not that they'd really need them, given the wide, wet trail left by their sodden clothes. Occasionally they passed over grilles in the floor, some of which housed recessed fans turning slowly over brightly lit corridors. The target was straight ahead now, but the passage was narrowing. Taro was crawling on his elbows, and even with the helmet's pick-ups on full he couldn't hear the alarm any more; he hoped that was a good sign.

Ahead of him Nual was also having trouble with the cramped conditions. 'I think we'll have to come down soon,' she said.

'Reckon you're right.'

They stopped on either side of the next large grille. Before she levered it off Nual flipped up her visor. 'If we do meet anyone I'll be able to neutralise them more easily if I can make eye contact. Can you keep monitoring the target?'

'Sure thing.' The further in they went the more confident Taro felt. The mission was beginning to feel like one of the virtual adventure games he'd played on Jarek's ship. When and if the bad guys turned up he knew they could deal with them. Nual and him were Angels, flying killers. The opposition didn't stand a chance.

They floated down into the corridor, relieved to find it was deserted. He looked around until his virtual vision picked up the gold dot. 'This way,' he said, then wrapped his cloak around himself and set off on foot. Walking would be safer than flying, and just as quick, and the ability to unexpectedly take to the air might give the opposition a nasty surprise.

The corridor ended in a T-junction. Irritatingly, the visor put the target dead ahead. 'We could go either way here,' said Taro. 'Might be a good time for a little of that prescience.'

He sensed how unfunny she found the joke, though all she said was, 'Your guess is as good as mine.'

He guessed left. After ten metres the corridor turned and ended at a locked door.

They turned and retraced their steps, then took the other option, which led into a corridor with several turnings and doors off it. This was more like it.

They started down the corridor, then Nual grabbed him. <*In here! Quick!*> She pulled him into a side turning. <*People heading this way.*> He pressed himself against the wall next to her. Sometimes mind-speech was the best option after all.

Four figures jogged past the end of their corridor, coming from the direction they'd been heading. The combination of the bulky shapes and the weapons data scrolling down the side of the visor display told him these were guards, armed and armoured, probably on their way to deal with the other team.

He waited until Nual said they were clear. The next corner led them to another long corridor. According to the helmet display their man was about halfway along, off to the left. Taro was relieved to find that the door the signal came from didn't have a lock on it. Though they'd been given a basic bypass kit, neither of them were experts. The target had been told to try and make sure he wasn't behind a locked door.

Taro got out his gun and clicked the safety off, just in case, while Nual closed her eyes for a moment. 'One person inside, awake and expecting someone, presumably us. I can't read more than that from out here,' she said.

Taro opened the door and strode in. On his first step into the room he saw the golden signature. On the second, Nual's voice exploded into his head <*Taro, that's not him!*>

Before he could react something thudded into the floor behind him. He whirled round to find the doorway blocked by dark lines. A red shape reached out to touch the lines, and was thrown back. Someone shrieked, more in surprise than pain.

He raised his visor to see Nual stagger back against the wall on the far side of the corridor. She recovered at once and bounced forward again, though she was careful not to touch the lines. With normal sight he saw what they were: thick vertical bars. Nual was looking past him, her expression grim. Taro turned to see a man on the far side of the otherwise empty room, standing behind some sort of floor-to-ceiling clear barrier. He wore loose sleeping-clothes and he looked pretty pleased with himself. His arms were crossed and there was a small smile on his face.

Taro reckoned he wouldn't look so smug if there was any chance they could get to him. He raised his hand and extended a finger in what he hoped was a universally recognised gesture. The man's smile deepened.

Suddenly the man clutched his head, his mouth opening in a silent scream. He collapsed to the floor and began to thrash. After a short while he stopped moving.

Taro turned back to Nual. She wore an expression of fierce delight and was almost glowing, though it was more like some sort of anti-glow, a compulsive air of darkness. For a moment he was terrified of her. Then the effect faded and he felt her combined emotions: panic, fear, shame and overwhelming concern. 'We have to get you out of there!' she said. Taro reckoned she was speaking out loud because right now her head wasn't a nice place to be.

'I'm open to suggestions,' he said, then swallowed to moisten his mouth. He had to stay calm.

Nual started examining the doorframe and surrounding wall.

He did the same on his side. The bars fitted snugly into holes in the floor and ceiling. Even if there hadn't been some sort of repelling effect on them he doubted they could cut them, even with their blades. The walls, floor and ceiling were all solid rock.

Suddenly Nual stiffened and looked up.

<What is it?> he asked.

<Guards coming.>

<How many?>

<A lot.>

<Then you have to go!>

<I can't abandon you! I got you into this.>

<If you stay then they'll have us both. That's stupid.>

She hesitated.

<Please, you have to leave me!> The idea he might die was bad; the idea she might die was unbearable. *<Just go!>*

She came up to the bars. He reached through carefully to grasp her fingers for a moment. *<I will get you out of this!>* she said. *<And if I can't then I'm going to find and kill those responsible.>*

<Tell you what: I'll help.>

She smiled. He felt the full force of her emotion as she both thought and spoke to him, *<I love you.>* Then she turned and left.

He waited until he could no longer sense her presence, then he ripped off his com-strip and watched as it dissolved into sticky fibres on his fingers. He was just wiping his hand on his armour when the guards arrived. If he'd been smart he'd have moved to the side so they had to come in to get him, but it was too late now. He fired his pistol at the lead guard anyway, but the puny dart just stuck in the man's armour.

He stood his ground when the guard drew a rather larger gun, raised it, and shot him.

CHAPTER TWENTY-THREE

Given what she was, Jarek should've expected Orzabet to be well-informed, but she'd still managed to wrongfoot him. He had hoped to use their initial one-to-one conversation to find out a bit more about her, but it was like trying to analyse a machine. She certainly wasn't a people person.

In some ways, with her unmemorable looks, cautious demeanour and lack of social skills, she was the opposite of a Sidhe. And that, if he was as paranoid as *she* appeared to be, could indicate he was in a lot more trouble than he'd thought. The pilot had known there were Sidhe abroad in human-space who'd undergone surgery to tone down their beauty, and who repressed their aura of majesty to avoid drawing attention to themselves. Perhaps that was what Orzabet was: a Sidhe in disguise. Maybe she was playing the long game to ensnare potential investigators who got too close to the truth. Up until now she'd just been monitoring him, but when she'd heard about the memory-core she'd realised she would have to get her hands on it before he managed to get it decrypted. And even if she wasn't actually Sidhe, she could be one of their agents, knowing or otherwise …

In which case he was fucked. He should run like hell, right now. Except it was probably too late: maybe he should just blow the last of his credit on the best night out this shithole had to offer, then wait for them to come for him.

In fact, it was odd that they hadn't come for him yet.

He stared at the flatscreen view of the dock outside the *Judas Kiss*, waiting for someone official to stride into view, and listened for the incoming com-call telling him he was under arrest, or otherwise detained.

After a few minutes during which his body went through all the usual fear reactions but nothing else happened, he decided that beyond a certain level he really couldn't be doing with paranoia. Orzabet had helped him over the years, and he'd come a long way to meet her. Trust had to start somewhere.

And it was worth remembering that she hadn't tried to get anything out of him other than a copy of the data – which she could take anyway, leaving him none the wiser.

If she was a Sidhe agent, he was already damned. And if she was trying to con him, she wasn't doing a very good job of it.

He reached for his com.

The address Orzabet provided this time was a mid-range apartment in a poor but respectable accommodation section, the kind of place where a couple of hardworking dockhands might make a modest family home. He knew better than to think Orzabet actually lived there.

The door opened before he could press the com, revealing a small lounge, untidy and lived-in. The couch looked comfortably saggy and toys spilled from a box in one corner. Orzabet sat facing him across the dining table at the far end; now the book that hid her hands was a children's storybook.

He took a few steps into the room, stopping a safe distance away.

She looked at the heavy holdall slung over his shoulder. 'Is the core in there?'

He eased the bag onto the floor. 'It is.'

'Could you bring it over here?'

'I could. And could you maybe show me your hands?'

She started. 'Ah yes. Of course. My apologies.' She brought her hands out from behind the book. One of them held a heavy-duty needle-pistol. Jarek tensed, but she just laid the gun on the table. It still pointed at the door, so he walked around the back of the couch, out of the direct line of fire.

165

'You can sit, if you like,' she said, pointing to a chair at the end of the table.

As he moved towards it he saw that behind the storybook the gun had been resting in a frame, and it looked like she'd rigged some sort of dead-man's switch: the pistol would've taken her head off instantly if she'd released the pressure on the switch. She obviously knew that pointing a gun at a Sidhe – or oneself – was futile; you'd be throwing your weapon away before you'd even realised you'd moved. Something like this set-up would be the only way to outwit them.

He nodded at the contraption. 'I see you weren't taking any chances,' he said, trying to keep his voice even.

'I never do.'

'Can I ask how you got involved with all this?' The ingenuous suicide rig showed a disconcerting level of commitment.

Given her earlier reticence he was surprised when she answered at once, 'They took away my only chance at happiness.' She looked over at him. 'And you?'

'Idealism, originally. Then vengeance.' For torturing him at Serenein. For destroying his sister.

She nodded, satisfied with his answer. It appeared they'd passed each other's tests.

He pulled out the chair. As he sat down he asked, 'Do you know how long it'll take to decrypt the data?'

She frowned. 'I have no idea until I get to work.' She turned to face him. 'I'd be very interested to know where the *Setting Sun* was going … if you'd be willing to tell me.'

Was he? There was plenty he didn't want to divulge – particularly regarding his allies – but she was right: they were on the same side. 'A world called Serenein.'

'Serenein?' Orzabet blinked, then said, 'There's no such place.'

Jarek was surprised at her certainty. He'd visited a fair proportion of the 933 human-settled systems, but he couldn't remember all their names off the top of his head. 'Not on record, no. It's a human colony, but it was set up by the Sidhe. They keep it hidden.'

For the first time her lips edged towards a smile. 'A lost world? That's fascinating. It's logical to assume there are still viable lost colonies out there, and it's likely that the Sidhe would have contact with them, but this is the first actual evidence. Do you have any more data on it?'

'Not a lot. It's very lo-tech, and I'm not sure how to get back there.' Which was not a lie, technically speaking.

'That's a shame.'

He tried to work out from her tone whether she knew he wasn't telling her everything. If she did, she wasn't pushing him, so Jarek decided to risk raising the other matter he wanted to discuss. 'Listen, I was wondering whether there's any way I can change my ship ID.'

Her gaze sharpened. 'Do *they* know about the *Judas Kiss*?'

'I'm afraid so. They got my ID at Serenein. Given all the Sidhe there are dead I don't think they're actively looking for me yet, but if things start to hot up ...'

She looked sharply at him, then said, 'You're right, it might be wise. But ship IDs are complicated: if it's even possible, it would be potentially very expensive – your current credit-balance certainly wouldn't be sufficient.'

'I can owe you,' he said hopefully.

She thought for a moment then said, 'It's in my interest that they don't catch you so I'll see what I can do. In return, I'd like you to act as my courier, if I need one.'

Assuming she just wanted him to transport small packages, then he'd already done that. 'No problem,' he said. He got the impression it was some time since she'd trusted anyone; he decided to return the favour. 'Listen, there's something you need to know. The way I got onto the *Setting Sun* originally ... the Sidhe captured me, and they read me. They went pretty deep. Obviously I don't know how much they got, but there's a risk they know about you.'

He had expected her to react badly to the news, but she remained sanguine. 'So they may know the name Orzabet. By itself, that is very little use to them. I've had no unexpected contacts or protocol violations, nor alerts from other quarters, which implies they didn't get any important data. No, I don't think this changes anything.'

Jarek suddenly realised what it was that made Orzabet different, besides her distant manner. Whilst she was more paranoid than most people he'd met, she wasn't afraid: she had no fear of dying, only of failing.

CHAPTER TWENTY-FOUR

'Just go!' Nual found herself repeating Taro's words to her; the aircar driver didn't need to be told twice.

'We're out of here,' he said, and the roof-hatch was barely closed before he had taken them down again.

Nual collapsed onto the bench-seat, her legs shaking.

Part of her was desperate to force the pilot to fly in and land, to make him go back with her and attempt a rescue. That same part had been screaming at her to turn around as she fled from the room where Taro was trapped. She had felt his presence in her mind suddenly disappear, and she had realised with a pang that he must be unconscious. *But not dead.* She would have known if he were dead ...

As she pulled off the armour she found her eyes were full of tears. She ignored them.

Without turning round, the driver said, 'What happened?' He sounded disappointed – after all, a failed mission meant less pay – but he also sounded concerned.

Nual suspected this was not the first time he'd lost people on jobs. 'It was a trap,' she spat.

'Shit,' he said. But professional that he was, he didn't ask for details, nor did he make unnecessary conversation during the journey back to Stonetown.

The original plan had been for the two of them to accompany the successfully extracted target to a safe house, where they would be contacted later that morning. Instead, the driver called in the code to indicate that the mission had failed and was instructed to drop Nual off at the harbour. As she got out he said, 'Sorry about your brother.'

Nual nodded an acknowledgement and walked away, through streets already warming in the morning sun. She passed early shoppers and locals on their way to work. When she reached the hotel she half expected her key to have been invalidated, but it still worked. The room had been made up, the bed where they had made love for hours on end was now pristine and impersonal.

She gathered their possessions, barely enough to fill a small holdall. The only items in the drawer next to Taro's bed were his bone flute and his com, the latter left behind to avoid any chance of identification. Nual sat on the bed, cradling the flute in her hands, and finally permitted herself the indulgence of tears. If she could not keep her promise to rescue him, this would be all that was left of Taro, his only mark on the world.

Had she done what her nature demanded and treated Taro as a willing slave, then she would not now be feeling his loss so sharply. Love, that most difficult of human emotions, was a weakness unbecoming in a Sidhe.

As Taro would say, *Fuck that*.

But it did appear that her new-found talent – or curse – had been entirely accurate. Something awful *had* happened. She had felt no details, just this awful presentiment of disaster, yet even as she'd gulped back against that strange sensation of burnt spice she'd believed – *hoped* – that Taro was the remedy. That belief had grown; she had become certain that sleeping with Taro was the right thing to do to avert the future disaster she had sensed.

But she had been deluding herself … after so long in denial, she had finally let lust and loneliness get the better of her, rationalising sex as a solution to a problem whose nature she didn't understand. Or worse: what if she had *caused* him to be captured? Would he have been caught so easily if they hadn't both been tired and distracted?

She knew this feeling: guilt and despair combining to freeze the will into dark, self-consuming pity. But no. She had nothing to feel guilty about. They loved each other, and by mutual consent they had done something that was long overdue. He was captured, not dead. And she was still free, and far from powerless.

She went downstairs and checked out. The hotel receptionist told her that the bill had been paid and asked if her stay had been satisfactory. Nual asked to see the manager in private.

The manager, a very correct-looking offworlder, emanated concern. 'Was there a problem, Medame?' she asked with an earnestness that bordered on fawning.

'Not at all,' said Nual. 'I just wanted to know who paid our bill.'

The manager was eager to please. 'Let me check – ah yes, it was Ruanuku-*ngai*, Medame,' she said. Afterwards she might wonder why she had so freely given away the answer to such a sensitive question, but now, she felt unexpectedly happy when Nual thanked her. It was the least Nual could do.

Nual checked into a more downmarket, anonymous hotel. She paid for a week in advance, and dumped their stuff in the room.

She wasn't surprised that Makoare-*ngai* were not the real backers. The incriminating logos had been just a little too easy to find, especially given how tightly run every other aspect of the mission had been. She considered questioning Patai, but he'd been using a data-drop contact number, valid only for the duration of this one mission; finding him would be complicated, especially so early in the day. Perhaps later, when the sun went down and the shadier characters came out to play. In the meantime, rather than walk the streets or sit alone and mope, she decided to visit the hostel.

Mo was in the kitchen, eating breakfast. He was surprised but pleased to see her. 'Let me guess,' he said around a mouthful of cereal. 'Taro's still in bed ... somewhere.'

Nual made herself smile and responded normally, 'Oh, I imagine so.'

'So, what's up?' Mo asked. 'I thought you two had moved out.'

'We did, but it's ... complicated.' Nual was already regretting her decision to come back; all she had achieved so far was to remind herself of her time here with Taro.

'Fair enough. While you're here you may as well say goodbye to Kise. She's off to her new job today.'

And Kise's interview had been with Ruanuku-*ngai* ... if Nual had believed in a deity she might have dropped to her knees and given thanks then and there.

She found Kise in the women's dormitory, packing her case. She looked up and smiled as Nual came in; Nual had left an echo of friendship in the girl's head when she first read her. 'I'm sure I didn't have this much stuff when I arrived,' she said in exasperation.

Nual smiled in return. 'Here, let me help.'

Though they were alone, Nual would have preferred to take her somewhere more discreet, but Kise was expecting her ride soon, so she'd have to resort to overt coercion to get her to leave right now, and even if she wiped Kise's memory afterwards, the girl would still know something highly unusual had happened to her. She'd have to manage.

As she held the case shut so Kise could seal it, Nual said, 'Well done on the job. Do you think it will be everything you hoped for?'

'Oh yes – their facilities are amazing!'

Nual picked up the image of sterile, clean spaces with equipment Kise had always dreamt of using. 'So where is this perfect job of yours?' she asked.

Kise grinned, a little smugly. 'Off the map. I didn't realise, but there are islands out there that aren't shown in the normal com downloads.'

'Really?' said Nual. Excellent: Kise probably still had the location in her com, and the co-ordinates of Ruanuku-*ngai*'s private island were just what she needed, but Nual decided she might as well try for additional detail. Keeping her tone light she said, 'Given how luxurious the public islands I've visited with my brother are, these hidden company islands must be very special.'

'You're not wrong! They gave me the full tour and—'

Using the trigger of Kise's recollections to launch her, Nual was in, deep and fast. She ran through Kise's day with the *ngai*, replaying the memories at dazzling speed: overflying an island that was one huge extinct volcano ... being greeted by executives and scientists ... questions from a panel in an underground room ... a tour of the facilities (here Nual slowed the images a little, in case she could spot something of use, but none of the tech looked related to their original mission) ... Kise's lunch with her guides in an open-sided café ... then a chance to look over the spacious wooden house that would be hers if she got the job, set in lush jungle on the inner slope of the caldera ... finally a walk up a tree-shaded path to a far larger house, a chance to meet the head of the *ngai* she might be working for, fresh juice and conversation on the balcony—

Nual knew her, the head of Ruanuku-*ngai* – it was the same woman who had run from the wedding on the resort island. Nual froze the memory and examined the details, focusing on the woman's demeanour and conversation. Before she dropped the memory she took a while to examine the view from the balcony.

That would have to be enough; she had already been in contact for too long. As she withdrew, Kise fell back onto her bed, eyes glazed. Nual touched her com to the girl's, and once she had what she needed she shook Kise gently.

Kise twitched and looked up with an expression of near-comical surprise.

'Are you all right?' asked Nual.

'Wh—? What happened?' Kise shook her head.

'I think you fainted.' According to Nual's com, she'd taken nearly four minutes. Hopefully Kise wouldn't realise how long she'd been out. 'It must be the heat. Can I get you some water?'

'Water? Y-yes. Please.'

As she got up to fetch Kise a drink, Nual permitted herself a small grin of triumph.

Jarek had a choice: wait here on Tarset for Orzabet to finish the job, or return to Xantier, where he was closer to Kama Nui and more likely to pick up some form of lucrative cargo. The second option was the most logical, but that meant leaving the memory-core with Orzabet. Not that he thought she'd run off with it; he was pretty sure once she'd decoded the files she would want to get them to him as quickly as possible, because he was an ally in her great fight. The problem he foresaw was that she'd insist on bringing them in person, and that would mean her usual high level of security, which was likely to make things complicated. In that case, the closer he was, the better. He'd sleep on it ...

But the next morning he awoke to find a message from Nual waiting for him:

No definite progress on the mission, and we have fallen foul of a local company in matters unrelated to our reason for being here. My companion has been captured by this organisation. I intend to do my best to rescue him. I will update you on my progress every twelve hours. If you do not hear from me for a full day, assume we are both lost.

Oh shit. It would take him the best part of three days to get to Kama Nui from here, though he realised Nual hadn't actually asked for his help. But if he left now, he'd be leaving the files behind. He needed to contact Orzabet to see if she'd made any progress on the decryption.

Her full-text response came back twenty minutes later: an address, still on Tarset but in a part of the station currently being refurbished, and a time, three hours from now.

The door opened as he approached to reveal a dimly lit room, empty save for a bored-looking man sitting on a paint-spattered chair. He wore station overalls and ear-defenders, but the large gun on his lap implied he wasn't here to fix the lights. He was unsurprised to see Jarek, and simply pointed through a curtain of builders' netting into another equally bare room where Jarek found Orzabet sitting on the floor. Her face had the blank stare of someone deeply interfaced with technology; Jarek recognised that look from his old partner, a hubber who used to fly the *Judas Kiss* on neural interface rather than what he called 'the old-fashioned way'. He briefly experienced the theocracy-born's unease at being in the presence of a heavily enhanced human; the Angels were odd enough, but at least their brains were their own. As he came in she blinked once, slowly, and focused on him.

Jarek nodded back at the curtain. 'Who's your friend?'

Her expression impassive, Orzabet said, 'A man I hired to kill us both if we're disturbed.'

Jarek barely suppressed his shudder. 'You're nothing if not thorough. So I take it we have a result?'

'Not exactly. There're two levels of security here. First, the management software on the memory-core was designed to interface only with the system that originally wrote the data – the files should be readable only on the computer you took it from. I've managed to set up a virtual reader that fools the encryption so it doesn't just turn the data into unsalvageable gibberish when I try to access it. But then we're onto the second level: I haven't yet managed to work out the code-key to unlock the high-security files and turn everything back into plaintext. The good news is that the encryption isn't QE or one-time' – seeing Jarek's expression she shook her head – 'sorry, being technical. The short answer is, I'm sure I *can* unscramble the contents of the memory-core, but it's going to take me another thirty to thirty-five hours – say two to three days' elapsed time. Even then, all we'll have is raw data. A *lot* of raw data. I don't suppose you have any idea what you've actually got here?'

Jarek sighed. 'Sorry, no.'

'Well then, we might have a problem.' Her tone and expression belied her words. Jarek had the distinct impression she was enjoying the challenge.

'I realise it'll take as long as it takes, but I might have to leave in a hurry.'

'Oh, that won't be an issue,' she said.

'Really?'

'No. I've also been looking into your other little problem, and I think I have a solution that I can be ready to implement within a couple of hours. The only problem is that you'll need to take me with you the next time you make a transit.'

CHAPTER TWENTY-FIVE

'Hush now, there are no demons here.'

Marua Ruanuku smiled down at her daughter. For the second time this week Taimi had woken up from a nightmare of creatures from ancient islander legend chasing her through the dark. Taimi was at that difficult age, soon to become a young woman, though for a girl in her position there were additional worries beyond the usual ones of approaching adulthood. Her oldest daughter and heir was just coming to the same realisation Marua had reached at her age: that the luxurious life she lived came at a price.

No demons here.

What she'd told her daughter was not entirely true – but then again, what are demons except names for that which we fear and do not understand? She grasped Taimi's hand, a quick reassurance, nothing so smothering as a hug. 'Will you be all right? Shall I leave the light on?'

'I don't need the light,' said Taimi defiantly. 'I'm not a baby.'

'Indeed you're not. Sleep well, my sweet.'

Marua paused on the landing outside her daughter's room. Taimi was as clever as she'd been designed to be, with as much empathy as could be reliably coded into a normal human child. She was probably picking up Marua's own troubled state of mind.

Although she had suspected for some time that Doctor Grigan was hiding the full extent of his illness, his sudden death two weeks ago had been a shock. The news had introduced a sour note into the long-awaited wedding day of one of her second cousins to a scion of Tawhira-*ngai*. Though Marua had never been comfortable with

176

her chief neuroscientist's Ascensionist views, he'd given her *ngai* many years' loyal service in areas both highly complex and, to her softly Salvatine upbringing, morally grey. He had almost finished the final encoding when he died, and Marua suspected that his final push to complete the process may have hastened his end. His assistant was attempting to carry on his work but Grigan's talent had been a rare one, and even though the job was almost complete, Marua was not convinced Tikao would be able to finish it.

She'd started looking for a replacement for Grigan as soon as he'd admitted he was ill. Her spies in Tawhira-*ngai* had found a scientist in that *ngai*'s employ with compatible skills and, more importantly, the expensive interface implants and the one-in-a-million ability to fully utilise them. Professional and personal reasons had combined to put Doctor Pershalek in a position where he wanted to leave his *ngai*, but he'd come too far up the ladder for Tawhira to just let him go. Right now his loyalty was for sale, the price being a route out of his luxurious prison – straight to another one, of course, but such was life at the top. She had not been surprised to find that Makoare-*ngai* were also interested in Dr Pershalek, for projects of their own. She'd been foolish to let apprehension over their interest combine with her anxiety about the upcoming visit to panic her into acting hastily. The truth was she was afraid: nothing mattered more than convincing her visitors that she could continue to deliver the essential service her family had provided for longer than the *ngai*s had been in existence.

Sometimes Marua could almost feel her foremothers looking over her shoulder, depending on her to keep promises made millennia ago. As long as she fulfilled her obligation, then her family, her employees and her *ngai* would remain in a position of strength. Her very existence, like that of her mother's before her and her daughter's after her was tailored to serve her *ngai*: a bright if slightly curtailed life balanced by the promise of an eternal reward. Marua was not certain she believed in Heaven, but she believed in her own value and in her responsibilities. If she faltered now they could lose everything.

Had she been superstitious, she might have blamed the failure of the mission to extract Pershalek on her own actions: making a move against a *ngai* she had just sealed a blood alliance with was a dishonourable act. But she had recently discovered the real reason for the disaster, and she was still coming to terms with it.

She sighed. Her husband was out playing backgammon, so she might as well return to her office; there was never any shortage of work in her position. She was sat at her desk, going through the endless polite, meaningless exchanges that kept the relationships between the *ngai*s essentially cordial, when a faint rustle of cloth, barely audible over the night-sounds from the forest below, made her stiffen. When it came again, Marua raised her head, expecting to see Taimi standing in the doorway, but there was no one there.

She turned to the other door, open to the balcony, as a cloaked figure stepped into the room, carrying with it the shadows of night. Even as she was shocked at the intrusion, Marua knew she was seeing some sort of stealth technology in action. She felt a flash of anger: a family home was *tapu*, and for a rival *ngai* to break that tradition was a grave mistake. But as she raised a hand to call security the figure lifted its own hands and lowered the hood.

A dark-haired, pale-skinned young woman stood there. Her delicate, immaculate face looked drawn but Marua barely had time to register her appearance before she met the woman's eyes and was overcome with a sudden desire to trust and co-operate. She dropped her hand to the desk. There was nothing to be concerned about. This person did not mean her any harm.

'I need information,' said the visitor in a gentle, compelling voice, 'and then I will leave you in peace.'

Now her visitor was in the light, Marua felt sure she had seen that face before, and recently. 'What do you need to know?'

'I want to know about the mission against Tawhira-*ngai* last night. I need to know what went wrong.'

A complicated request. As Marua considered the best way to fulfil it, she recalled where she'd seen this woman before – and realised how she had been able to enter Marua's home, set on a near-vertical slope. 'Are you—? You're one of the Angels, from Vellern, aren't you? Your brother—'

'—was captured, yes.' The woman's melodious voice was tinged with tension. 'And I wish to get him back.'

Marua was fighting the desire to tell the Angel everything she could about the disastrous job. She said instead, 'Why do you think I'll be able to help you? Missions like this ... they go wrong. You're a professional, surely you know that.'

The Angel advanced on her and Marua felt the strangest sensation, as though someone else's anger was about to eat her up and spit her out. Then it was gone, and the Angel said quietly, 'If you are the leader you make yourself out to be, then you must know the reasons for the failure.'

'I ... Of course I do,' Marua felt as though she'd been at the *kava*; her thought processes were heavy, vague. 'There was a traitor, a man called Olias Kahani. It's ... it's his fault.' Marua was desperate that it not be her fault, because if she incurred the Angel's wrath then something terrible would happen. She realised the other woman was still looking at her, expecting more. 'He was a facilitator, a close advisor of mine. He was the one who talked me into attempting the extraction, and he's the one who suggested I use you and your brother. Now I know what sort of man he really was, I suspect he must have been working for Tawhira-*ngai* for some time.'

'Where is he?'

'I don't know. He disappeared, cleaning his bank account out – which was the final evidence of his guilt. He may try to leave Kama Nui, though I think he would find that quite difficult.'

'Have you tried to find him?'

'We have made some effort, though we will not exert ourselves overmuch in pursuit of a traitor. He no longer has the means to harm my *ngai*. To pursue him purely in the cause of vengeance would be both dishonourable and indicative of weakness.'

'I need you to give me everything you have on Olias Kahani, including the results of the enquiries you have made so far.'

Marua found herself turning back to her computer and searching out the relevant files. As she set the download running she looked up and asked, 'What will you do if you find him?'

The Angel just smiled.

When the download was complete Marua picked up the data-spike and held it out. The whole encounter felt surreal, but something about it was beginning to nag at her, as though she should recognise what was going on here.

As she took the dataspike, the Angel gave her a long, hard look. Marua's sense of dislocation grew—

A door slammed, somewhere below. The pressure in Marua's head intensified, and for a moment she thought she would pass out.

'Still working hard, my sweet— Marua, are you all right?' She looked up to see her husband standing in the doorway, looking concerned.

'I'm fine,' Marua heard herself say. A glance towards the balcony showed that the two of them were alone. Had someone been here?

'Are you sure? You look tense.'

'No, no. Everything's fine.' And it was, she thought. Just fine.

The next morning she wasn't so sure.

In the bright light of day Marua thought at first that she had dreamt the strange night-time visitation. But the more she thought about it the more she suspected it hadn't been a dream at all. The Angel had come to her and—

—and what?

After breakfast, she rescheduled a couple of non-urgent meetings and walked around the caldera to another house, a little smaller than the one she shared with her husband and children, but equally well-appointed. She found her mother in the garden, tending her orchids. Marua wondered what her own focus would dwindle to when her time to retire came. She knew that in twenty or thirty years her mother would be dead and she'd be living here, burnt out by the stress of running one of the most powerful organisations on the planet. It wasn't a bad fate, provided the succession was assured, the future guaranteed. Family mattered more than any one individual.

'Hullo, Mother,' she said.

Her mother turned and smiled, a vague but genuinely happy expression, very different to the astute, careful smiles Marua remembered from her own childhood. 'Ah, it's you! What a lovely surprise! Can you stay to take tea?'

Marua smiled in response. 'I'm sure I can find time to share a cup with you this morning, Mother. But I also need to talk to you.'

'Of course, sweet. What about?'

'The *hine-maku*.'

Her mother frowned. Marua knew that frown: not one of annoyance, but of mild confusion. Her mother's memory was not what it had once been. But perhaps Marua had not been as clear as she could have been; she had used the islander term to avoid the name that every human, in any culture, knew, a superstitious touch she felt vaguely ashamed of.

Then her mother's gaze sharpened. 'Ah,' she said gently, 'you mean the Sidhe.'

CHAPTER TWENTY-SIX

When the water splashed up over her knees, Nual decided that she needed to find somewhere to stop and rest. It had been twenty-four hours or more since she'd last slept – those few snatched hours with Taro, before the disastrous extraction. Getting out to Ruanuku-*ngai*'s island headquarters had involved a seven-hour skim-boat trip to a tourist island in the rough vicinity, then a six-hour flight over open water. Her implants were designed to return her gently to the ground if she passed out, but out here there was no ground to return her to, so if sleep did overcome her, she'd end up in the sea. She pointed her toes and rose above the water again, up into the warm, moonlit night.

She had programmed her com to navigate back to the tourist island, but she would never make it that far, so instead she set a search for the nearest scrap of land, however small. She tried not to weep in relief when the tiny glowing screen showed a chain of uninhabited islets about ten klicks south-west of her current position. They would do nicely.

Paradoxically, knowing that she would be able to rest soon woke her up a little and as she made her way towards her new destination she considered her encounter with Marua Ruanuku. After years stifling her powers in order to get by amongst humans it had felt good to exercise them fully. She was pleased and surprised at how quickly her abilities were developing. But she was not entirely sure she had acted wisely ... her plan had been to go in, get what she needed, then edit the woman's memories to remove any recollection of what had happened, leaving her peacefully asleep at her desk. She had considered the more drastic option of killing her, but to murder the head of an *ngai* was asking for trouble. Besides, when she'd read the house she had picked up the sleeping minds of three children; she preferred to avoid killing their mother unnecessarily.

If her probing had revealed that Medame Ruanuku was to blame for what had happened to Taro, she might have changed her mind. She was tempted for a moment, when her scan revealed that her *ngai* was the one she and Taro had been looking for all along. But to kill her as punishment for having dealings with the Sidhe would have been petty, and pointless.

How very un-Sidhe her reactions had become, Nual thought. She was developing an almost human conscience. A true Sidhe would not have hesitated to commit murder rather than risk being interrupted ... but a true Sidhe would not feel this all-consuming need to rescue her human lover either.

The islets came into sight: five dark shapes gilded in moonlight. She chose one of the two with trees on and landed on the beach. The sea whooshed and rushed gently all around her, and insects made a surprisingly loud racket for such a tiny patch of vegetation. She sat down on the sand, above the high-tide mark. It still retained some of the day's warmth. She pulled her cloak around her and curled up. Despite the hard surface and a vague concern over whether the islet was home to anything that might bite or sting, she soon dozed off.

She had hoped to dream – and she did ...

The process of dreaming was more ordered for the Sidhe than for humans, though in essence the same thing was happening: the subconscious exercised itself while the body rested. But when a Sidhe dreamed, she could decide to watch the dreaming process, observing the images and sensations as they unfolded, or ignore it and return to true unconsciousness; she might even choose to join in, participating in the dream, directing its course. A Sidhe who lived in unity was most alone in her dreams; dreams were contained purely in the dreamer's head.

Usually.

Nual knew that the seers, those amongst her people blessed – or cursed – with prescience, sometimes used dreaming as a tool to trigger their abilities. She had no idea how to do this, and no one to guide her, but now she tried to bend her will to this end, to direct her dreaming mind to show her the course of action she needed to take in order to rescue Taro.

The result was not what she expected.

No images or insights came; instead, she was aware of a familiar presence in her mind. Even as she recognised Taro, the pain broke through.

This wasn't a dream. This was happening to Taro, *now*. She was sharing his experience.

The pain was low-key, a disturbing background constant. His thought processes were muddled by it, or perhaps by something he'd been given. She tried to work past the distracting physical sensations and into his heart.

She sensed his query as a wordless, distant cry of hope. She responded, and after a moment felt her own name forming in her head: <*Nual?*>

<*I'm here, Taro.*>

<*Hurt!*>

<*I know. I feel it too.*>

<*Save me!*>

<*I will. Where are you?*>

<*Where … ?*>

<*Do you know where you are, right now?*>

<*No … they keep hurting me.*>

<*Who is hurting you?*>

<*Not sure. Shadows …*>

<*But they're not in your head?*> Though it was highly unlikely the Sidhe had him, she had to be sure.

<*No. Men are outside. Just you in my head. Coming to save me.*>

Nual felt a surge of relief: she was only facing humans. <*I will. I will save you. You have to hang on until I can get to you. Do you understand?*>

<*Hang on for you … aye.*>

The contact was fading. She reached out to him <*Taro?*>

<*Making me sleep now ...*>

The sense of him receded into darkness. Rather than follow it, she opened her eyes to the star-dusted night sky. The world's primary moon was just setting. She lay there for a while, wondering if the shadowy men who had Taro had any idea what a big mistake they were making.

It was a good job he'd tidied up the living quarters on the *Judas Kiss* when Nual and Taro came aboard. Jarek didn't think Orzabet was someone who'd put up with a mess.

She'd already insisted on taking a shower, though that was fair enough; she must've got pretty hot and sweaty in that crate. Though Jarek had occasionally transported paying passengers this was the first time he'd taken on someone who'd had themselves delivered to his ship as freight. Still, if it was what she needed to do ...

It would take them four and a half hours to reach the beacon radius. Hubpoints were located at low-temperature dwarf stars, so the orbit shared by a hub station and its beacon was tighter than in most planetary systems, and the distance between them consequently smaller. Orzabet announced that she would use the time to get some rest, though from the sound of it she was pottering around in the rec-room. She was obviously nervous about going into transit awake and unsedated, but her plan relied on her being fully conscious at the moment they entered shiftspace. Jarek was apprehensive too. Orzabet's scheme was an elegant one, but it unsettled him.

He found himself thinking about his life on the *Judas Kiss*, his home for the last fifteen years. It was the longest time he'd lived in one place, even if that place did move around. He'd been happy with his lifestyle, though he'd always been on the look-out for causes to support. And now he'd committed himself irrevocably to the one he'd been dabbling in for seven years. He'd managed to buy a couple of dozen reels of nanoweave cable from Tarset, hoping to sell it on Kama Nui – it could be used for shipping and adventure sports – but he'd bought the cargo as much to keep customs happy as because he expected to make much of a profit on it. Trade was no longer his priority.

'Sirrah Reen?' Orzabet had stuck her head through the hatch onto the bridge.

'Come in. Listen, given we'll be travelling together for a while, why don't you call me Jarek?'

'All right. Jarek.' She hesitated. 'And you can call me Bez if you like.' She looked away, and Jarek wondered when she'd last let anyone use that name. Her discomfort lasted a moment, then she said, 'I need to patch into your main comp now, assuming we're still on schedule to go into transit in twenty minutes?'

'We are.' He carried on with the pre-transit checks and initiated a modified version of the system shutdown routine while she settled herself on the floor and spread her tech out around her. Giving a relative stranger access to the systems on his ship's bridge made Jarek uneasy, but he squashed his fears: he'd decided to trust Orzabet – *Bez* – and that was that. He preferred the diminutive; it sounded more human.

Her plan required split-second timing, allied with her unique expertise: she intended to use a mirror-worm, a message impersonating another, which would, she told him earnestly, set off a data-cascade at the receiving system. Jarek nodded intelligently, although he had only a vague idea what she was talking about.

All that mattered was the end result: the Sidhe would no longer be able to track his ship.

There was a downside: if their ruse was successful it would become a lot harder for Nual to contact him. Her last message, received just over five hours ago, hadn't updated him on her status, just that she was still all right. Her next one was highly unlikely to reach him, though he'd warned her of that, adding that just as soon as they were home and dry he'd find a way to get back in contact.

But now he had business. 'Thirty seconds to transit,' he called out.

Bez nodded tersely. 'I know.' Her hands hovered over her

keyboard – she couldn't risk using a neural interface, as she would still be connected when they entered the shift. As it was, the flat-comp she was using – the most complex piece of technology still active on the ship at this point – would most likely come out of the transit irrevocably fried.

Jarek tried not to fret. He was putting the fate of his beloved ship into the hands – literally – of a paranoid sociopath, someone who tended to see the real world as an inconvenience getting in the way of nice, ordered data. In some ways she reminded him of a certain priest he'd met recently – and that wasn't a relationship that had ended well.

Bez's fingers flew over the keys in a flurry of activity.

Her hands froze.

Then they were in the shift.

There wasn't much of a criminal underworld on Kama Nui – rather a contrast to Khesh City, where criminality in its various forms was almost the default career choice – and the only useful contact Nual found in Medame Ruanuku's files was someone she had already met. The files had plenty on Olias Kahani's past, but no clues as to where he was now. It did, however, list a certain Miku Tuan as one of his associates. Tuan also went by the name of Patai.

Given the limited scope of the criminal community, Nual had to proceed carefully. She started by requesting a meeting with Patai – in a public place; as he had hired them for the failed mission she doubted he would agree to meet her alone. She made it quite clear her business with him was unrelated to any past associations, and emphasised the potential profitability for them both. If that didn't hook him, nothing would.

When they met in the square in Stonetown, she claimed that she had been hired directly to track down a certain individual. At this stage she would not divulge the hiring party.

'And who would that individual be?' asked Patai carefully. She was scanning his surface thoughts: he was wondering, reasonably enough, how she had got hold of his number and become involved in the kind of work he usually dealt in.

'Olias Kahani.'

Patai's face gave nothing away. His mind however—

'I don't know the name,' he lied.

Nual smiled. 'I think you do. In fact I *know* you do.' Adding just a feathering of coercion she added, 'Have you seen him recently?'

'No.' Then he thought better of it. 'Maybe.'

'Either you have or you haven't,' said Nual equably.

Patai's gaze flitted towards the heavily built man lurking by a nearby tree, no doubt a bodyguard hired in case the encounter with the Angel went badly. 'No offence but, if I had, why would I tell you?' he asked.

In public and under the minder's watchful eye, she would have to be subtle. She let her shoulders sag and projected a faint whiff of despair. 'You're right. I don't have much to bargain with, do I?'

'Perhaps if you told me who your employer is?'

She sensed Patai's genuine concern that business like this could occur without him hearing about it: this was the only reason he'd agreed to meet her. Time to change tack. Looking out over the square, she said, 'There isn't one. I lied to you.' She turned back to him, letting him feel her desperation. 'I want Kahani for myself, because he betrayed us and I have lost my brother as a result.'

Patai's silence was a pause for thought rather than an attempt to make Nual uncomfortable. However, she maintained her air of unease, giving the – not entirely inaccurate – impression that she was near her wits' end. The combination of his honour code and the natural empathy that made him good at his job inclined him to be sympathetic to her, and she built on this, subtly enhancing and encouraging it.

Finally he said, 'Family is important.' He nodded slowly. 'And Olias Kahani has acted in a shameful manner. I'll tell you what I know.'

CHAPTER TWENTY-SEVEN

'You don't have to stay, *ariki*.'

Marua thought she detected a note of embarrassment, perhaps even resentment, in Tikao's voice, though as she was hearing it through speakers she couldn't be sure. 'Of course I do,' she said reassuringly.

Technically Tikao was right: the machines in the laboratory and in the sea outside would be recording every aspect of the test and if anything did go wrong there was very little a human observer could do. She had volunteered to come down to the lab to witness the final live transit-kernel test to show her support for Tikao; though he'd monitored the interface readouts on previous tests, Grigan had always been the one strapped into the two-metre diameter sphere that floated outside the lab's observation window. Tikao should not be alone when he tried this, and there were few others in her *ngai* permitted to observe what was about to happen. Fewer than fifty of her employees even knew this lab existed, and only a dozen were aware of what really went on here. Even her husband did not know the complete truth: he believed that the subjects who arrived in stasis were already dead. He had no idea of the exquisite torture involved in creating a transit-kernel. For her part, Marua tried not to think too closely about the details and instead kept focused on the bigger picture.

'I'll start the countdown,' said Tikao.

Tikao had been eager to fill his late boss's shoes – he'd first asked about completing the final encoding the day after Grigan's funeral – but Marua remained unconvinced of his suitability. It took a certain type of personality to repeatedly interface with insane alien minds that were able to leave the universe at will. Tikao had been fully trained, and had demonstrated a limited ability to interact with the transit-kernels, but Grigan had never involved him directly in the delicate, time-consuming discorporation/transference process; the integration of flesh into technology took many painstaking months for each subject.

Fortunately the kernel at the heart of the sphere floating before her was fully integrated, and Grigan had started the programming. But though the hard work was done, failure at this stage was by no means unknown; the failure rate was over ten per cent. Grigan had had good results in the shift-and-return tests, but a transit-kernel had to do more than just transport itself through shiftspace: it had to create a bubble of reality and extend it around its vessel and any other beings contained within. To do this, the vessel needed to be a discrete item in a low-density medium. When the kernel was finally wired into a shiftship, ready to transit between beacons, the medium would be as low-density as it got – the vacuum of space – but the initial tests took place in the more forgiving environment of Kama Nui's ocean. The test was being carried out in shallow water and Tikao wore a pressure suit, but there were still risks. The kernel must be convinced to take the entire vessel, and only the vessel, into the shift; it must return all the vessel – and only the vessel – to the same relative point, which meant successfully compensating for the planet's movement through space during the fraction of a second the vessel was outside the universe. Marua wished there was some way of carrying out initial unmanned tests, or using animals, but the kernel's first encumbered shift required the mind that was programming it to be part of the test.

If only she hadn't made that foolish promise two months ago. For as long as she had been aware of the family secret Marua had borne in mind her mother's advice regarding the Sidhe: *never give them a reason to doubt us.* Her mother had delivered thirty-three transit-kernels when her time had come. Now Marua was determined to prove her own worth to her associates, and, ultimately, to humanity. That was why, when Grigan had assured her that the final subject would successfully encode, Marua had sent the Sidhe a message telling them she would have twenty-eight transit-kernels ready for collection on their arrival. To only pass on twenty-seven now would reflect badly on her.

She had hoped to have Grigan's replacement here to finish the job by now, but Kahani's treachery had put paid to that, at least for the moment, so she was relying on Tikao to keep her promise for her.

'May the Lord of the Sea go with you,' said Marua.

If Tikao made a response it was lost in the countdown. Though he was fiercely proud of his islander heritage – he'd hated that Grigan and his proposed replacement had both been born off-world – Tikao paid only lip service to his culture's faith. His god was ambition.

As the numbers ticked down, Marua watched the sun-dappled sphere, her mind blank.

On zero, the sphere disappeared. Turbulence washed the observation window.

Marua held her breath, straining to see through the bubbles and rushing water, before remembering the readouts on the console in front of her. Green: the sphere had successfully transited and returned. She gave an explosive sigh. 'Well done!' she said warmly. 'You did it!'

There was no response. The water had cleared enough for her to make out the sphere now, hanging exactly where it had been.

She checked the monitors more closely. Though she lacked the technical knowledge to fully interpret Tikao's readouts it looked like he was in there, and alive. She commed again, 'Tikao, are you all right?'

No answer.

Then she saw the brainwave monitor.

Olias Kahani had not attempted to leave Kama Nui yet, but Nual suspected he might try once he had a new ID. He had asked Patai, and though Patai was unhappy dealing with someone so dishonoured and dishonourable, Kahani obviously had some sort of hold over him – Nual got the distinct whiff of blackmail – so Patai had put him onto a man named Roake, who dealt with such matters, and who would have no such qualms about his customer.

Nual commed Roake herself, and mentioned that a mutual acquaintance called Patai had suggested he could help with ID-related problems. He told her to come to a certain bar later that afternoon.

The address was beyond the area of Stonetown tourists normally saw, further up the coast and away from the pleasure-boat harbour. Desalination plants and hydroponics farms were interspersed with neighbourhoods of neat but basic shacks clustered along unsurfaced roads. The bar was one of the few two-storey private buildings. When she arrived the place was deserted save for a pair of ancient, *kava*-dazed locals and a shaven-headed barman who pointed wordlessly to an unmarked door as soon as Nual walked in. This led straight into a poky back room made even smaller by the various crates and boxes stacked around the walls. Roake himself sat behind a wood-effect desk like any legitimate businessman; a well-muscled minder with a dartgun sat on an overstuffed chair next to the door. As knowing who was really who was Roake's business, Nual guessed he already knew she was an Angel. As he gestured for her to take the seat opposite she had another thought.

'Would I be right in assuming this conversation will be recorded?' she asked. Her original plan had been to read Roake for information on Kahani, then implant plausible false memories of the meeting, but a later review of his surveillance could tip him off that something odd had occurred – as would the extra human observer.

'Of course.' Roake thought she was being unprofessional, but it was too late to back out now.

She glanced around the room; its small size might work to her advantage. As she went to sit she contrived to kick her seat, tripping and apparently falling towards the minder. The man reached for her, half to catch her, half to fend her off, and as she let him touch her she made eye contact, doubling her chances. She darted into his mind, instructing him to let her go, then to sit back down, be relaxed, think of nothing, do nothing: just wait calmly until touched or spoken to. He had a gratifyingly simple mind and complied almost at once.

'Medame sanMalia?' said Roake. 'Are you all right?'

'I'm sorry, I tripped. I'm fine now.' Nual blocked the fixer's view of his man as best she could as she sat down, then turned her full attention on Roake. As she began to talk to him about the pretext for her visit she skimmed his mind, using natural pauses in the conversation to dive deeper whilst cutting his consciousness free so he would not recall the extra time passing. She was aware of the bouncer sitting quietly behind her, but still subject to only the softest of compulsions, and of the recording being made, and of how suspicious any long silent gaps would look if Roake chose to review this meeting.

As apprehension made her heart speed up and her hands sweat Nual found herself having to block her own responses and she was relieved when she finally had what she needed and was able to bring the conversation to a close. Hopefully Roake would recall only that he had agreed to look into her request for a new ID, but had decided it wasn't a priority, because she'd inadvertently let slip that she did not currently have the means to pay his asking price.

She said a hurried farewell to both men, rousing the bouncer from his torpor with an insignificant word. As she left she was barely able to resist the temptation to run or fly from the bar as fast as she could.

No one followed her, and she calmed down as she walked the dusty lanes back to the main road. She was angry at herself as much as anything, for assuming all her problems could be solved with Sidhe talent.

She commed for a cab and got it to drop her round the corner from a certain back-street brothel. The place was about as seedy as Stonetown got, furnished in shabby red and faded gold, with a pervasive odour of sweat and sex. She asked for 'Peach Blossom', and after paying the appropriate introduction fee was led to a room decked out in dark colours probably chosen because they didn't stain. The incense burning on the dresser almost hid the smell of previous clients. 'Peach Blossom' was about Nual's own age, with a heavily made up face and obviously enhanced breasts. She was a little disconcerted to find a female client waiting for her, but at Nual's gesture sat on the bed next to her. As they chatted lightly, Nual dived into the girl's mind, looking for her tie to Kahani – and was surprised to discover that 'Peach Blossom' – real name Lori – was his half-sister.

That Kahani had let Lori languish in this flesh-market while he was riding high in the favour of the *ngai*s did nothing to enhance Nual's opinion of the man.

The memory Nual created in Lori's mind was probably less convincing than the one she had left in Roake's head, but it should be enough to cover her tracks. Nual already knew from Taro that the best way to survive in the trade was not to dwell too closely on time spent with clients. She transferred a generous tip to the girl's account and left her sleeping peacefully in the large, tawdry bed.

She unfolded her cloak from her bag and once covered sneaked down the back stairs to the building's dank basement. The half-dozen doors off the dingy corridor looked identical, but she knew which one she needed. She gave three short knocks, paused, then knocked twice more.

'Who is it?' called a male voice from inside.

Trying to keep her intonation the same as Lori's she said, 'It's our father's littler one.' A stupid code phrase, which he'd insisted on.

'Is there a problem?'

'No,' she said, 'but I have a package for you, from Roake.'

'Why the hell didn't he call me to let me know it was ready?'

'He didn't say.'

'What's wrong? You sound a bit odd.'

Nual cursed the limitations on her powers imposed by the physical barrier of the door. 'Just a client … I'm fine now. Shall I leave the package outside?'

'No, wait there. Hang on.' She heard the sound of a bolt being drawn. She stepped to one side and drew the cloak around her, dropping her head to hide her face. The door opened a crack and she looked up carefully to see Kahani peering into the corridor, a small pistol in his hand. His wary expression grew more confused at finding no one there. He pulled the door wider.

Nual stepped into his field of view and threw back her cloak. She stifled his cry with a thought, grabbed him and charged into the room, kicking the door shut behind her.

The room was tiny, a store cupboard with a makeshift bed and a rickety table. She pinned Kahani to the wall with one arm, raised her other arm in front of his face and very slowly extended one of her blades. For this it would be worth paying the fine.

He began to gibber excuses, his eyes round with terror.

She didn't bother to reply, just went straight in, riding on his fear. Olias Kahani had a very interesting mind – unpleasant, but interesting. He was only half islander, and the behavioural constraints imposed by the *ngai*'s honour system both annoyed and bored him. He genuinely believed himself above such concerns as compassion and morality, seeing them only as signs of weakness. He would have been far more at home somewhere like Khesh City. He particularly delighted in betrayal; the chance to screw over those around him was the highest excitement, particularly when – as often happened – he could arrange for someone else to take the blame.

Nual found such cunning detachment almost admirable, in a detestable way. It was certainly a reminder of how great the range of human worldviews could be, locked as they were in their individual heads with little or no idea what those around them were thinking. Sidhe experienced no such divisive variety in their outlook and motivations ... except for her, of course.

Once she had full access to Kahani's mind she took her time extracting the information she needed, and she did not worry about breaking any mental constructs to get it.

Despite his skill, Kahani's mistakes were starting to come home to roost now the extent of his perfidy was coming to light. His wife, finally tiring of his lies, had left him a few months before, though he had turned the marriage break-up to his advantage when questions were being asked at work, claiming he'd been under a lot of pressure due to his wife's unreasonable behaviour ...

He'd started setting up their mission soon after, playing the *ngai*s off against each other as he loved to do. He told Ruanuku-*ngai* one of Tawhira-*ngai*'s top researchers wanted to defect, a rumour they'd already heard from another source; when Ruanuku set up the mission to extract him, he also tipped off Tawhira-*ngai*. As part of Kahani's manoeuvrings he had got hold of the floor-plans for the island research base, provided by an agent within Tawhira-*ngai*. Rather than pass these on to Ruanuku-*ngai* he had withheld them, a bargaining chip in case things went wrong. Now the big players were wanting nothing to do with him, he was in negotiation with several smaller *ngai*s to sell the plans. The plans alone made the effort of finding Kahani worthwhile.

Delving further into his acutely twisted mind, Nual discovered Tawhira-*ngai* had wanted the extraction brought forward because of her and Taro – the *ngai* wanted the Angels involved and captured – but Kahani had no idea why Tawhira-*ngai* had such an interest in Angels.

Finally Nual decided there was nothing more to be gleaned from Kahani's mind. She withdrew until some awareness of her physical surroundings returned. She could hear his breathing, harsh and uneven, and smell the stench of urine where he had lost control of his bladder.

She had no doubt that the world would be a better place without this man. She released her hold on his neck at the same time as she stopped his heart.

CHAPTER TWENTY-EIGHT

'You're not dead!'

Jarek felt Bez's cry like a physical blow, the vibrations in the air assaulting his eardrums. He looked over at her, carefully ignoring the way her skin fluoresced and shimmered. 'No ...' he began, the word oozing out between his lips, 'I'm— I'm not dead ...'

'Oh, Tand,' she continued more quietly, 'I thought I'd lost you.' She reached out towards Jarek's face.

Ah – she thought he was someone else. An easy mistake to make in shiftspace; he'd made it himself, sometimes when he was alone.

He caught her hand and she looked at it, alarmed. 'Bez, listen to me. You're hulloci—halla— Bez, this isn't real. We're in transit. The shift is playing tricks with my – *your* – mind.'

'My ... mind?'

'Yes, that's right. Weird shit is going to happen. You just have to let it. Try to ... go with the flow.' Talking his passengers down during transit was getting to be a habit.

If anything her expression was growing more glazed. Suddenly she blinked rapidly, then looked dismayed. 'Gone ... Nothing there.'

'No, everything's still here, only ... it's a bit fucked-up right now. This will pass. Honestly, it will.'

'We're in transit?' Finally she looked directly at him.

'Yes!'

'I didn't think that had happened yet ... but it must have.' She stiffened. 'You're touching me. Please don't.' Jarek let go of her hand. 'I want ... leave me alone now.'

Jarek hesitated. She sounded in control again, but he knew from experience that when someone as tightly wound as Bez went off, they *really* went off.

'I mean it,' she said, sounding almost normal. 'It's better if I … I'll deal with this. Alone. Please.' Jarek let her go and pulled himself up onto his couch. Unless she fell down the hatch into the rec-room – and he'd hardly be able to do anything to stop that happening – there was not much she could do to hurt herself on the bridge.

He kept an eye on Bez for the rest of the transit, looking away whenever she looked towards him. She occupied herself by watching her hands, flexing and curling the fingers, all the time muttering under her breath. She sounded like she was reciting strings of numbers.

At one point she froze, hands held out in front of her, palm-up, fingers clawed so hard that the tendons stood out. Distinctly, she said, 'What those bitches made you do—' then started to cry. Jarek began to get up, ready to comfort her, but she shook her head and shrank away. 'Don't—' she said.

He didn't. Eventually she stopped crying and went back to muttering.

When reality finally returned he called over, 'Bez? Are you all right?'

'I will be,' she whispered. 'Just give me some time.'

He suspected sympathy would probably only embarrass her further; he'd let whatever darkness drove her remain her own affair for now while he got to work restarting the ship's systems. Everything came up without a hitch. He sent a transponder burst to local traffic control; a couple of minutes later he received an incoming com.

'Gerault TC to incoming ship: we show a transponder mismatch. Your code is not on record. Hold off until we have queried your transit entry-point. Repeat, do not approach until your ID has been verified.'

Jarek replied in what he hoped was a tone conveying mild confusion and willing co-operation, 'Not sure what's happened there, but you go right ahead. We're in no hurry.' He waited, counting the seconds needed for the message to travel between the beacon and the hub station and for any reply to return, but there was nothing further. He allowed himself a relieved sigh. The man's threat to send a message back to Tarset wasn't a problem. In fact, they were counting on it.

Changing the *Judas Kiss*'s transponder signature had been relatively easy. The surface content of a ship's broadcast ID was largely up to the captain; what mattered was the embedded quantum key, which had to match ConTraD's records ... or not. Bez had created a brand new key and spliced it into his ship's transponder message, something Jarek hadn't even realised was possible. Naturally the ID he was using now wouldn't match the local system records for the *Judas Kiss*. In fact, it wouldn't match any ship local traffic control currently had on record.

He levered himself out of his couch and wobbled over to Bez, who was still sitting on the floor. When he reached out to help her up she gave him a slightly panicked stare, then took his hand.

'Let's get ourselves a drink while we wait,' he said as he helped her stand.

'I need to get clean,' she whispered.

'Sure. I guess things'll all happen by themselves now, anyway. Either your mirror-worm did the business or it didn't.'

'It did,' she said with a self-assurance he didn't feel up to questioning.

While Bez showered, Jarek drank caf and tried not to fret. At the precise moment the *Judas Kiss* had made its transit from Tarset, Bez's worm had been racing back at the speed of light, piggybacking the beevee message that was registering the transit with ConTraD and using this unique opening to insinuate itself into the usually inviolate records of the Consolidated Traffic Database. The timing had to be perfect, hence the need for her to be on the bridge as they entered shiftspace. Once her worm got access to ConTraD it would insert new registration data for a nonexistent ship with the quantum key that Jarek was now using; a fraction of a second later her update would overwrite the record that showed the *Judas Kiss* had just made a transit, replacing it with the now-valid ID of the new ship.

She'd already set off other updates lying dormant in Tarset's network. As a result, the local records would now show that the *Judas Kiss* had been sold to an independent dealer after tests revealed a fault in its grav-drive that would require a complete refit. The modified records would show that Jarek Reen had used the credit from the sale to buy himself into a newly initiated freetrader partnership. Bez had inserted the fictitious partnership's ship registration details, along with a comprehensive history that would stand up to all but the closest scrutiny, into the Freetrader archive before they left. The ship in question would be a perfect match for the records her mirror-worm inserted into ConTraD.

The really clever bit should be occurring about now—

Jarek planned to hang around here for only as long as it took his transit-kernel to recharge (he still felt faintly nauseous whenever he thought about what that actually meant); meanwhile, Gerault Traffic Control would send back the ship's new transponder ID to Tarset Traffic Control, who would match it against ConTraD. ConTraD should confirm that the ID did contain a valid key for a ship, but that the ship it belonged to had been inactive, listed as under repair, for some years; for some reason the update to put it back on the active ships' list hadn't been caught up in the regular synchronisation sweeps. Everyone knew how tardy freetraders could be in registering their dealings, and the update routines that propagated shared data throughout human-space weren't entirely reliable outside the core systems. These things happened occasionally. They'd flag it up manually to keep the records in synch and avoid a similar problem at the next system. After all, it had to be a mistake: the ship's quantum key was present on ConTraD, and no one could hack the Consolidated Traffic Database.

Bez had referred to this kind of update as an ourobourus; it was not logically possible, yet it held together on the assumption that it was.

It did rely on a human being deciding to intervene to keep their data nice and tidy. Fortunately traffic controllers did generally like their data to be tidy.

Jarek finished his caf. Bez was still in the shower. He resisted the urge to get up and pace.

Finally his com chirped. '*Heart of Glass*, this is Gerault Traffic Control. The issue with your ship's records has now been resolved. You are cleared for approach or onward transit.'

Jarek expelled a relieved sigh. It had worked.

Goodbye, *Judas Kiss*. Hello, *Heart of Glass*.

That night Nual didn't dream of Taro. Despite her attempts to reach out to him, her dreams remained the usual uninformative mish-mash of subconscious churnings. She hoped her failure reflected the fickle nature of dream communication and not Taro's worsening condition.

She slept late, but awoke with a clear head for perhaps the first time since Taro had been taken. She sat on the lumpy bed and thought through her options.

Olias Kahani had believed Tawhira-*ngai* would keep Taro alive and on the island where he'd been captured, so any rescue mission would mean returning there. Possession of the floor-plans for the island facility gave her an advantage, but she still needed to solve two major problems.

The first was how to get there. The island was pretty remote. In theory she could catch a skim-boat out to the nearest tourist island, but when she checked her com she could find no direct service from Stonetown, so the journey would take a while. After that she would have to fly for several hours. Once she got there, she would need some way of getting Taro out, as he was unlikely to be in any state to fly himself.

She concluded that she needed to hire her own transport and driver, ideally something as stealthy and discreet as the aircar they'd originally used.

Kahani's com provided her with plenty of interesting contacts, but she was cautious about using them; her naïveté with the shell game when they'd first arrived had shown how little she knew about the wheelings and dealings of the human underworld. Even with her Sidhe edge she could easily come unstuck ...

If only Jarek was here, Nual thought. She needed his experience, not to mention his driving skills – they could even use his ship for the rescue, though she hated to think how many traffic regulations that would break. His last message had said he was heading her way, but he would be a few days, and in the meantime he might not be able to pick up her messages. She had already informed him that Ruanuku was the *ngai* responsible for turning the boys from Serenein into transit-kernels, and now she sent him a file, with as much encryption as she could afford, containing a download of the juiciest data taken from the late Sirrah Kahani's com. Until he got back in contact she had to assume she was on her own.

She would have to contact Patai again.

She had left a positive association in his mind, though nothing strong enough to overcome his common sense, and she was relieved when he agreed to meet her later that day. If he could help with transport, that just left her with the second problem: the forceshield protecting the island. Kahani had set up the original run, which meant he must have known the arrangements for turning it off. Nual went back through the information she'd gleaned from Ruanuku's traitor. It wasn't like the pilot's knowledge; that had become part of her when he surrendered himself to her. The information she had got from Kahani was incomplete, a snapshot of stolen facts, images and emotions that would most likely start to fade if she did not access them.

But there was still a lot there, and Nual was determined. After a while she found what she needed: the shield had been deactivated by a low-level Tawhira employee Kahani had been blackmailing with certain recordings made at the brothel where his sister worked. Kahani did not think the blackmail victim – who was apparently otherwise loyal to his *ngai* – had been caught, so in theory she could pretend to be Kahani and get him to turn the shield off a second time. She used Kahani's com to send him a text message, stating he might be required to repeat the favour he had recently done for his 'uncle'. If the man had been compromised, then the message would tip off Tawhira-*ngai*, but it was a risk worth taking.

She got to the meeting with Patai early. He had chosen a harbour-side café at sunset and Nual was shown to a table in a corner with no view and a faint subliminal hum in the air that suggested the presence of anti-surveillance tech.

Patai arrived slightly late, and was followed by a waiter who carried a pair of cold beers. Nual sipped hers to be polite. Patai initially ignored his, saying, 'I'm afraid this will have to be brief. I have another appointment shortly.'

'I understand. It was good of you to see me under the circumstances.'

'Which circumstances would those be?' asked Patai carefully, toying with his glass. He was thinking of this morning's news reports of the body discovered in a backstreet refuse-hopper. It was found minus its com, eyeballs and fingertips. The media said that the only thing the authorities knew for sure was that the man was not a registered criminal, because criminals had a full DNA profile on record in addition to the usual biometrics. Patai strongly suspected the dead man was Olias Kahani, and that Nual had killed him, a possibility that made him wary, though not necessarily frightened ... not yet.

'I leave that for you to consider,' she said. 'When we last met I was ... not acting entirely rationally.'

'Understandable enough, given your recent loss. And now?'

'Now I wish to organise a rescue mission.'

'For your brother? He's alive then?'

'Yes. At the moment. And I need your help to get him back.'

'What form would this help take?'

'Transport to the location where he was captured. And someone to accompany me inside when we get there. Nothing you haven't organised before, in fact.'

'No, but without meaning to be rude, I don't generally do work like this for outsiders. There is a code governing conduct between the *ngais* which you may not be aware of.'

'I realise that. I would only be going in to get him back. I would endeavour to avoid committing any acts that might be considered *tapu*.'

He looked grave. 'I'm glad to hear it. To take a life is a far more serious affair here than where you come from ... even the life of a worthless traitor who has made himself *tapu* by his own actions.'

'I wish only to get my brother back. I regret any collateral damage I might have already caused.'

'I'm not entirely comfortable with this, but as it is a family matter ... I could procure transport, a driver and a couple of individuals to assist you.'

Nual remembered the state Taro had been in when she'd contacted him. She also recalled how much a job like this paid – or in her case now, would cost. 'Just one person to come in with me will suffice. But ideally I'd like someone with medical training.'

'As you wish.' Now Patai took a long drink of his beer. 'To the sordid matter of money ...'

Nual managed not to react to the price, though she wondered, in passing, what had made the original target so important that Marua Ruanuku would spend so much credit, and risk *tapu*, to get her hands on him. If they had not been interrupted she might have found that out from the Ruanuku-*ngai* leader's mind; as it was she'd only picked up on the Sidhe connection because it had been so near the surface of Medame Ruanuku's thoughts.

She engaged in a small amount of haggling, as Patai expected. His final offer was lower than usual, because he felt sorry for her, but the sum was still breathtakingly large. Rather apologetically, Patai said that he would not be able to start work without the standard ten per cent down-payment.

When Nual admitted that even this was beyond her means at present, Patai's parting thought was how unlikely he thought it was that she would find the credit – but if she did, he would do his best for her.

Back at the hotel she checked Kahani's com and found a reply from his victim in Tawhira-*ngai*. The man was, reluctantly, willing to turn off the forceshield when requested.

A check of the newsnets showed that Kahani's body still hadn't been identified; when it was, the man was likely to have second thoughts, meaning she had to hurry – as if the thought of what might be happening to Taro was not enough!

Nual needed money, lots of it, and fast.

CHAPTER TWENTY-NINE

Apart from a slight change to the onboard entropy level – a result of Bez's obsessive cleanliness – the ship was still the same old *Judas Kiss*. Jarek would have liked a new identity for himself as well, but that wasn't practical. His business relied too much on contacts who already knew him, and he couldn't afford to give up freetrading altogether: travelling the stars for pleasure was only an option for the super-rich tourists who lived on the starliners. Bez had provided a compromise: the *Heart of Glass* was actually registered to one Amad Kelsor, and Jarek was named as a secondary partner only deep in the paperwork. Kelsor's name would be the one leaving a trace as they passed through human-space. Unfortunately, Sirrah Kelsor currently only existed as a handful of records in the Alliance's database. It was entirely possible to create a convincing identity out of nothing – he'd paid for someone on Khathryn to do it for Nual when he first found her – but until he or Bez managed to flesh out Jarek's fictitious partner, anyone who took the time to check would spot the ruse.

His immediate priority was to find a safe way to get back into contact with Nual. In theory her messages would automatically be routed to his 'new' ship once Bez's updates had percolated throughout the beevee network. However, because Nual's messages were text-only – both cheaper and more discreet than voice or visual – he had no way of being sure they actually came from her. If she were captured, or her com fell into the wrong hands, sending a reply to one of her messages could provide their enemies with his new ship ID.

Before they'd left Tarset, Bez had put a stop on any messages arriving there for the *Judas Kiss*, routing them to a data-drop. Now they needed to pick up those messages, and find a way to reply safely. Well, not 'they', for Jarek had no idea how to go about it. He hoped Bez did.

When they grabbed a meal before the next transit he took the opportunity to ask her. She said, 'Is this more important than the *Setting Sun*'s memory-core?'

'Yes – my allies might be in trouble.'

'These allies of yours are on Kama Nui, aren't they?'

'That's right.'

'Doing what?'

'Investigating Sidhe influence. It's complicated …' He explained about Serenein's strange harvest, and admitted that they got the link to Kama Nui and its location from the *Setting Sun*'s pilot, who was now dead, though he didn't give details. Bez would definitely be happier not knowing that one of the allies he was rushing to help was actually a Sidhe.

She listened intently and asked pertinent questions. Finally she said, 'I'll see what I can do to re-establish secure communication.'

As she stood up, Jarek held out a hand. 'Wait. I was wondering where you wanted me to drop you off. We didn't really discuss it before.'

'I thought I might come with you,' Bez said.

'To Kama Nui?'

'Yes. It makes sense for me to stay with you until I crack the memory-core. Besides, it's meant to be very beautiful.' She made one of her strained attempts at a smile. 'Perhaps I should take the opportunity for a holiday.'

Jarek wondered if she was being ironic, but had no idea how he'd tell. He needed to put her off, in case she was serious. 'On a world where the Sidhe might have influence? Are you sure that's a good idea?'

She looked chastened. 'If they are active there … then you're right. But we don't know that.'

'No, we don't.'

Jarek left Bez to work and went up to the bridge. He'd just set the initial pre-transit checks going when he got an incoming message light, showing Nual's com-tag.

He called down to Bez, 'That was quick!'

'The message? It arrived at Tarset just as we left.' Bez's voice sounded a bit odd.

The single line of text gave the name of the company on Kama Nui that was processing the transit-kernels, and said: 'They might well have direct contact with our enemies.' He looked up from his console as Bez came up onto the bridge.

'I'm guessing you read this when you collected it.'

'It was in plaintext.'

'And do you still want to come to Kama Nui?' asked Jarek.

Bez dropped her gaze. 'I'm not ready to face them directly yet,' she said, 'so no, I won't take the risk.'

Jarek tried not to let his relief show. 'Where would you like me to drop you off?'

'Xantier's on our route; that's as good a place as any – unless you want me to come as far as Mercanth.' Mercanth was the hubpoint nearest Kama Nui.

If she did stay around that long then she might find time to crack the *Setting Sun*'s memory-core while she was still with him. On the other hand, the more the back-to-back transits took their toll, the less capable she'd be of getting any useful work done, and the more likely he was to strangle her for obsessively clearing away his half-finished drinks. 'Xantier sounds good,' he said. 'Will that give you time to set up a way for me to respond to the incoming messages?'

'I'm not sure whether it's possible to do that without giving away your new ID,' she admitted, 'but I'll spend the recharge period between the next two shifts looking into it.' She glanced at the drive-column, no doubt thinking about what was actually in there 'recharging'. Jarek had almost managed to forget.

Bez spent the next transit in the comabox, so she would be fresh to continue work on the problem. Jarek woke from a long overdue nap to find that she'd retrieved another message, this one encrypted and zipped; it contained a selection of sensitive data on two of Kama Nui's corporations, including the compromised one.

Bez said, 'You should get all incoming messages automatically from now on, though there may be a delay of several hours. If you answer them, you'll get through, but with a similar delay, and with the new ship ID appended to the message.'

'Then it's not worth the risk. Thanks for trying.'

She wished him luck when they parted company at Xantier. Jarek suspected she was happy to be on her own again, and eager to get back to her beloved data.

Nual devoted the early evening to working out how to get the sort of credit she needed. The best way for someone like her to make big money was to be employed by someone like Patai on behalf of the *ngais*, but that assumed someone needed her services; her skills as an assassin would be of limited use in a culture where lethal force was forbidden. And even if there were other jobs in the offing, they probably wouldn't pay enough to fund her own mission.

Theft was an option, but she had no idea how to go about that. She briefly considered coercing a stranger to transfer credit to her com, but that was hardly subtle, certainly traceable, and very unlikely to give her sufficient funds.

As she lay on her bed she thought of the shell game again. She had managed to avoid being duped by reading the boy rigging the game, so perhaps her abilities might give her an advantage in other games of chance. She had almost no experience of gambling, though she understood it was a popular tourist pastime. She sat up, energised, and commed for guidance on the subject. Unlike Khesh, which had a whole street devoted to such activity, here gambling was merely tolerated as something that had to be provided for the visitors. Unlicensed gambling was illegal, and though some of the larger resorts had casinos, there were only three listed gambling establishments in Stonetown.

She decided to start with Sea Breezes, which claimed to be the most upmarket of the casinos, with no house limits. That should make it the best place to win the kind of money she needed. The hotel was large and tastefully appointed, and when she approached the casino entrance, she found a heavily built but well-dressed gentleman politely barring her way. 'I'm afraid that we have a dress-code, Medame,' he said.

Nual looked down at her sun-bleached once-green top and yellow-and-orange wrap and felt her cheeks redden. 'Of course, I'm so sorry,' she said, cursing herself for her thoughtless mistake, and left.

She watched the clientele coming and going for a while to establish the kind of look she'd need. Some of her old outfits from Khesh might have cut it, but she'd abandoned her luggage back on Khathryn. Since then she'd dressed purely for comfort. She checked her com for shops that might sell appropriate clothes, but Kama Nui's laid-back culture didn't lend itself to all-night fashion boutiques. Reluctantly she returned to her own hotel.

She tried to contact Taro again as she slept, and felt sure she got through at some deep and wordless level. But then, that was what she *wanted* to believe. She had no objective evidence that such tenuous contact was real.

The next morning she went shopping. The dress she chose was mauve and deep red, cut to go up and down in all the right places. She was amazed that something that used so little fabric could cost so much, and of course she needed shoes and jewellery to go with it. But it certainly did the trick, even if it also showed up what a mess her hair and face were. Given the casinos didn't open until dusk she decided she might as well go all the way, and spent the afternoon at a beautician's. She tried to quell her unease at being pampered while Taro was imprisoned, perhaps being tortured, distracting herself by scanning the minds of the vapid men and women who were making such a careful if superficial effort to make her feel special.

Though the same bouncer was on duty at the door of Sea Breezes, he didn't recognise her. Inside, beautiful people glided between tables and wheels offering dozens of variations on games of chance. Nual bought herself some tokens and began to work her way around the room, deflecting the inevitable attention from the men, and a few women, who misinterpreted her reasons for being here.

She quickly realised that she wasn't going to be able to cheat her way to a fortune: the shell game had employed sleight of hand and she could pick up the sly moves from the operator's mind; the games in Sea Breezes operated on random chance, not human interaction. If they were rigged, then the process was strictly mechanical. Some of the card and dice games used skills which she could learn, but other than that, there was no human element for her to take advantage of. Even her superior intuition provided no help; if anything it was counter-productive, for her reliance on her instincts often made her overconfident when placing bets. When she'd lost half her initial stake she decided to give up.

The second listed gambling establishment billed itself as a total entertainment venue and boasted a restaurant, live music and scantily dressed acrobats performing on wires above the gamblers. She stayed long enough to ascertain that the games were all of the same sort as those at Sea Breezes, then left.

As it was still relatively early, she decided she might as well try the last address. The Flotsam and Jetsam also promised additional entertainment, including a personal escort service. The guides claimed the club was for those with more adventurous tastes – hopefully that meant fewer spinning wheels and flashing lights, and more direct interaction with the other gamblers.

The establishment was in a basement, down metal stairs threaded with red and gold lights; Nual suspected these colours were some sort of code for prostitution here. Seductive bass beats throbbed up from below. The bouncer at the top, another large man with a big smile, looked at her a little oddly, but let her pass. As there was another couple standing behind her she didn't linger long enough to read the reason for his reaction.

She came down into a room full of people obviously having fun. The bar, which took up most of one wall, was a crescent sculpted to look like a huge shell, with the staff serving patrons from inside the scalloped pink interior. The level of intoxication and emotion in the room was higher than in the other two casinos, and she had to strengthen her shields to avoid being battered by the wash of mental froth. There were shadowy booths around the walls and various doorways off to the sides. The largest exit led into a room where the beat was loudest and the lights brightest, presumably the dance floor. She wasn't sure which exit led to the casino itself, so she decided to work her way to the bar and ask.

As she wove through the press of partygoers, a woman who had been sitting alone in one of the booths stood up and came towards her. She was tall and thin, with perfectly coiffed black hair that belied a face wrinkled with laughter-lines. She was the only person in the room wearing traditional islander dress. Nual read no ill-intent, and she turned to the woman, who beamed a smile and said, 'You want some company?' She had to shout to be heard over the music.

Unsure whether she had heard correctly, Nual dropped her shields enough to skim the woman's mind. The woman was the club's proprietor; she wanted to know if Nual wished to purchase the services of one of her escorts. Nual saw that she'd misjudged the situation again; to be here alone and dressed like this implied she was rich but naïve, probably looking for what Taro might describe as *a bit of rough*. It was easy to forget that humans judged solely on appearances.

She shook her head. 'I'm here for the games.'

The woman pointed through one of the archways. 'In there. Good fortune to you.'

Nual nodded and headed into a room about the same size as the bar, but far quieter. There were a couple of wheel-based games of chance to the side, but the main activity was betting on some sort of race which was being held on a table with high sides. Nual went up to the table and saw large multi-legged bugs, their backs daubed with colour, skittering along wooden runs. She made a brief attempt to reach out to the creatures' minds, but was unsurprised to find that she was unable to influence them: the Sidhe dealt in sentience.

As she turned to go she heard the phrase, *Doesn't compare to six-stud*. She paused, looking for the speaker. A man on the opposite side of the bug-run was talking to his friend; like most of the customers they were offworlders, but a little younger than the average, and dressed with a conspicuous lack of care; neither of them were particularly handsome. She made eye-contact with the man who had spoken, just long enough to catch his attention. He stared at her, mouth open, while his companion stared at him, then followed his gaze until he too was looking at Nual.

She smiled.

The first man patted his companion's arm and started to make his way around the table to her. Nual tried not to show her amusement at the effect she was having; he simply couldn't believe his luck, to have attracted the attention of such a – and he actually thought the phrase – *heavenly creature*.

When he reached her side, mildly surprised that she hadn't bolted, he cleared his throat and asked, 'Are you enjoying the races?'

'I prefer games with bigger risks and a little more interaction,' she said, looking at him.

She wanted to kick herself at his predictable reaction to her comment. He wasn't thinking of the same game as her; in fact he was so clogged up with hope and lust that he was barely thinking at all. Damn these human mating rituals.

'Like six-stud,' she added, trying to clarify the situation. Some tourists on the liner had played six-stud: it was a game of bluff, and the ability to read one's opponents was a massive advantage.

'Oh,' he said, predictably confused. 'Right.'

'I overheard you mention it, but I've not found anywhere to play. Is it legal here?'

'Not exactly.' He hesitated, and she waited for him to reach the inevitable decision. 'But … it does go on. In fact' – he cleared his throat – 'in fact we were just discussing a game that'll be happening later tonight.'

She leaned a little closer to him. 'Really?'

'It's quite high stakes.'

'That's not a problem.

'And legally it is a bit of a grey area—'

'Also not an issue for me.'

'Great. Wow. Well' – he drew himself up – 'I might just be able to get you in.'

She smiled again. 'That would be wonderful.'

'I'm, um, I'm not sure about the dress.'

'I'm sorry?' she said, though she'd already sensed his meaning.

'It's … Well it's a great dress – a *really* great dress – but where we're going it would be a bit too … well, conspicuous.'

'Of course. When does the game start?'

'The game—? Oh, I see. Midnight.'

'Then if I were to get changed and come back you'd still be here?'

'Oh yes.'

'And you'd be willing to escort me to the game?'

'Absolutely.'

'Then I won't be long.'

She picked up a taxi outside the club and went back to her hotel. After she'd changed she took a few minutes to brush up on the rules of six-stud, then headed out again. She paused on the threshold of the hotel. No cabs in sight, and a wait of six to eight minutes if she ordered one now, but the local map also showed a cut-through just up the road that would get her back to the Flotsam in five minutes. She extended her senses to check there was no one down the alley and registered the faint trace of a couple of animals; rats, probably.

Perhaps a dozen steps in, she felt something sting the back of her neck. She slapped at what she assumed to be an insect, but an instant later a chill began to spread from that point. She whirled round, at the same time reaching out mentally, trying to locate possible enemies.

Nothing. No presences anywhere nearby.

The numbness was spreading fast. She stepped forward, her blades half-extended, her mind reaching out in panic: was she under attack? How could that be when there was no one there?

She tried to kick off to activate her implants, but suddenly her body wasn't working properly. She stumbled, barely saving herself from a fall.

A shadow moved, and her heart skipped. She could hear nothing above her own sharp, hard breaths. She strained to see into the darkness, but the harder she looked, the more her vision began to blur.

A second dart hit her cheek.

The alleyway started to tilt to the side.

Panicking now, she put all her strength into a mental compulsion, commanding whoever was out there – *Stop this! Help me!*

Her mind briefly lit upon a pair of presences, before sliding off them like oil off polished metal.

Before she could try again, her body gave out.

CHAPTER THIRTY

Jarek felt like shit. Every transit left him more strung-out; in his waking moments he was lethargic and unfocused, while his sleep was filled with nightmarish recollections of his time as the Sidhe's prisoner or vivid reruns of his experiences on Serenein. His mind circled impotently, fretting over the unknown fates of those he cared about. If the consorts hadn't turned up at Kama Nui yet then Kerin must have managed to defend her world against the Sidhe who'd gone to investigate the disappearance of the *Setting Sun*. But the Sidhe wouldn't give up: Serenein's fate in the long term was in his hands.

One problem at a time: first he needed to meet up with Nual and get Taro out of trouble.

As soon as he was in range of Kama Nui's comnet, Jarek called Nual's number. He wasn't surprised when he got voicemail – it was, after all, the middle of the night in Stonetown. He scanned the local news: this morning's breaking story was the identification by a local prostitute of a body found a few days earlier under mysterious circumstances. The man had been mentioned in one of Nual's messages as the likely cause of Taro's capture, so Jarek had a good idea who'd killed him.

He flew into Stonetown at dawn. The contrast between the shining blue-green sea and the dull yellow-brown of the land was almost unreal in the brittle early light, and the rising sun turned the saltpans edging the settlement into lakes of tarnished silver. Back when his obsession had been more a sideline he'd always told himself he'd come to Kama Nui for a proper holiday some time, maybe spend a while on one of the less expensive islands. It had never occurred to him that the Sidhe might have any influence here, yet Nual was certain one of the most powerful organisations on the planet was in league with them.

After he'd completed the formalities and registered his cargo with a local brokerage firm he visited the last address he had for Nual, a cut-price hotel where a small bribe revealed that she'd been out all night. A larger bribe gave access to her room.

'Perhaps she got lucky,' said the greasy-looking offworlder youth on the desk as he handed over the key.

Jarek doubted it. He found a spectacular dress discarded on the bed, and Taro's com and bone flute amongst the minimal possessions in the drawers.

Nual had no way of knowing he was on Kama Nui, so until she came back to her room – or got in contact via the torturous beevee route set up to forward to the *Heart of Glass* – there wasn't much Jarek could do. He decided he might as well wait here for a while, and make use of the bed to catch up on some much-needed sleep ...

He was lost in one of his recurring dreams, faceless enemies chasing him through corridors that got darker the faster he ran, when someone shook him awake. He blinked up at an acne-cratered face, taking several seconds to remember who he was looking at and where he was. 'What is it?' he mumbled at last.

'You wanna sleep here, you pay,' said the boy aggressively.

'God's sakes!' He sat up. 'All right, I'm going. If Medame san-Malia comes back, I need you to com me.'

'Now why should I do that?' the boy sneered.

Jarek sighed. 'The usual reason.' He held out his com.

He considered trying to find some of the people Nual had named in her messages, but she'd left only a sketchy overview of her activities and he had neither the credit nor the local knowledge to go deep; he could easily get into trouble in Stonetown's insular criminal underworld.

However, he was used to schmoozing with spacers and port personnel – he'd chatted with a couple of the spaceport staff already. As was often the case, those working in the port considered themselves a breed apart from the locals, being made up of a mix of adventurous natives, who saw the job as the first step out of their gravity-well, and offworlders, who liked the fringe benefits of working in a place like this. Given they usually dealt with rich tourists who saw anyone in a uniform as a lower form of life, a freetrader was a welcome visitor.

It was coming up to midday, so he made his way to the bar one of the immigration officers had mentioned. He bought lunch for himself and drinks for various port staffers, then spent a couple of hours passing on spacer gossip and asking a few questions of his own.

One of the customs officers mentioned that his cargo was hardly worth the effort, and asked if he was actually here for a holiday. That got a few laughs, but he heard the interest behind the question, and so he admitted to an ulterior motive straight up: a pair of Angels who wanted discreet transport offworld. The ship that had brought them here hadn't been called the *Heart of Glass*, and he hadn't stayed long enough to meet anyone on the ground last time, so he was reasonably sure no one would work out he'd brought them here in the first place – and even if they did, he'd just explain that he'd changed ships recently. But no one said anything. Jarek told his new acquaintances that the Angels had offered to pay well, but neither of them was answering their coms; did anyone know anything about them?

One of his drinking buddies mentioned a recent incident with the local wildlife: apparently two tourists had got into trouble on a sightseeing trip, but it turned out they were Angels, and they'd used their implants to avert disaster. The dramatic rescue had made the news a week or so ago. But no one knew where the pair were now.

Stepping back out into the bright afternoon sun, he commed Nual's hotel again, but the venal youth had no news. Jarek said he could earn himself more credit by making sure whoever came on shift next also kept a look out for their missing guest.

He had only one course of action left, though it wasn't something he was happy doing. Up until recently his conflict with the Sidhe had been entirely one-sided: they pursued their mysterious schemes, and he tried to glean what he could while remaining beneath their notice. Serenein had changed that, but he'd just gone to considerable effort to ensure that his cover wasn't entirely blown as a result of what had happened there. Actually admitting some of what he knew to someone who had contact with the Sidhe went against all his instincts. But it was looking like he was the only one who could get Taro, and probably Nual, out of whatever trouble they were in.

He picked up Nual's latest message, but it didn't tell him anything to make him change his plans. Then he paid a visit to a backstreet demi-tech dealer he'd overheard a customs officer talking about in less than affectionate terms. The woman who served him had a roly-poly figure but sly eyes, and she was careful not to ask any questions.

Next he checked into a cheap hotel nowhere near Nual's but close to the road out to the starport. He'd have liked to get some more sleep, but he didn't have time; instead he made a com-call.

The face that projected over his new com was that of a local man somewhat older than Jarek, with intricate geometric tattoos on his chin and brow-line. He looked predictably confused.

Before he could say anything, Jarek said, 'I need to speak to Marua Ruanuku. Please tell her that it is a matter both urgent and delicate.'

'This is a private number: how did you get it?' asked the man.

'That's not relevant right now. I think Medame Ruanuku will want to speak to me.' Actually he had no idea how Nual had got hold of a direct line to the head of one of this world's most powerful companies.

'Your com ID is unregistered and your image appears to be scrambled. Who are you? What do you want?'

'You can call me Sais,' he said. The name came unprompted; he'd spent three months answering to it recently and it felt ...

comfortable. 'And as for what I want … actually it's the other way round: I have something you need.'

'I doubt that—'

'I understand your reaction, so I'll come straight to the point: I have full plans and schematics for Tawhira-*ngai*'s primary research facility, and I am willing to pass them on to you.' Thank you, Nual, he thought, deeply relieved she'd thought to send the data to him.

The man's eyes widened. 'Ah, I see. I think— Leave your number, and someone will call you right back.'

'Sorry, but no. I'll call you back in five minutes. And when I do I'd like to speak to the head of your *ngai*, please.' He cut the connection.

Jarek's heart was pounding. Before Serenein he'd played games of bluff and bravado only with agents and traders. Now he was starting to make a habit of doing it with planetary leaders. He hoped he hadn't overstepped the mark this time.

He called back five minutes later to the second and was relieved when the com image showed a middle-aged woman in a brightly coloured blouse. She had the broad, friendly face that was the common local phenotype, but she wasn't smiling. She had similar tattoos to the man who had first answered; Jarek suspected he might be her husband.

'I don't generally talk to strangers who refuse to give a full name and then use a scrambler on their com-image,' she said at once. 'So you might as well just tell me straight up how much you want for the plans.'

Cutting to the chase was fine by him; despite the assurances of the woman he'd bought it from, this com could probably be traced if the call went on for too long. 'I don't want money. I want two favours. The first is for you to rescue Taro sanMalia.'

Her expression gave nothing away. 'And what would you say if I said I had no idea who you are talking about?'

Jarek wondered briefly if there was a way to answer without accusing her of lying, before deciding there wasn't. 'I'd say that I have it on good authority that you do.' And now it was his turn to lie, or rather to guess, and hope his guess was a lucky one. 'I also have it on good authority that you plan to return to the location where he's being held – something you'd find a lot easier if you had full plans and security data for said location.'

'Well, Sirrah "Sais", you certainly believe yourself to be well-informed.'

'You'd be amazed what I know.'

'Really?' She looked hard at him – or rather, at his fuzzy com-image. 'You mentioned two favours? What was the other one?'

'Information, in return for which I will withhold certain information myself.'

'That doesn't sound like a particularly attractive deal.'

'I understand you might see it that way. However, the information I'm holding back from release to every media source on this planet regards your business associates. The – what's the local word for them? – the *hine-maku*, that's it.'

Medame Ruanuku said nothing, and her face gave nothing away. Jarek breathed deep slow breaths and tried not to dwell on the possibility that by admitting he knew about Ruanuku-*ngai*'s association with the Sidhe he might have just made himself the most wanted man on the planet.

Finally she said, 'Even if what you claim is true, what makes you think anyone would believe such a bizarre accusation?'

Jarek said, 'Are you willing to take the risk?'

Again, she was silent. Then, speaking with exaggerated care, she said, 'I can think of only one person on this world who might have been in a position to claim such a thing.'

'And who would that be?' Jarek suspected, even as he spoke, that it was a pointless question.

Her smile confirmed his suspicions. He found himself torn between fear, admiration and irritation. But he didn't have time for games. 'All right,' he said. 'The person who told me what your company is up to is the one I want information about.'

'What makes you think I am in possession of such information?'

Putting more assurance than he felt into his voice he said, 'I am quite positive you are.'

She paused for a moment then said, 'What if I were to tell you that this person may well be in the same location as the other individual you referred to?'

'I'd say that's unlikely.' Nual's last message had said she was trying to raise credit in order to fund a mission to Tawhira-*ngai*'s facility; she didn't expect to be in a position to try and make the run until tonight at the earliest.

'Then I fear we may have reached an impasse.'

Was that a hint of smugness? Had she decided it was no longer worth continuing the call because she'd traced it? Were men with stun-batons and heavy boots about to kick his door down? As evenly as he could, Jarek said, 'Not regarding Taro sanMalia we haven't. Get him out when you go in on your other business, and I'll provide the plans of Tawhira-*ngai*'s base to make your little mission go more smoothly. That way we both get what we want.'

'Agreed,' said Medame Ruanuku. While Jarek was still mastering his surprise she added, 'But on one condition: you accompany my team into the complex.'

Jarek had every intention of going in himself; it was the only way to ensure they would also rescue Taro when they went back. However, he understood her own motivation for asking him along too. 'Yes,' he said 'and if I do, I expect your hirelings would be on hand to witness any nasty accident I might have during the mission. So now might be a good time for me to explain about the "insurance" I've organised. If I don't regularly check in with a certain independent party, then the information I have about you and your business associates will go out to everyone I can think of who might be even remotely interested. Getting me killed would be a sure way to find out just what your fellow corporations think about you trading with humanity's old enemies.'

'I see,' said Medame Ruanuku tightly. 'Then perhaps it might be safer if you didn't accompany my team.'

'I think I will come in, if it's all the same to you. I'm sure your people can keep me safe,' Jarek said cheerfully.

'What if I said that having you along would be an unacceptable risk?'

'Then I'd say the deal's off. If we don't do this my way, then I will have no choice but to take my offer elsewhere – and then to release everything I've got on you. After which I will simply disappear.'

CHAPTER THIRTY-ONE

Though he'd been relieved when Medame Ruanuku accepted his terms, ten hours later Jarek was having second thoughts. He'd got nothing like enough rest, and fatigue still gnawed at him. Some of the others in the aircar – all hard-looking mercenary types – were giving him looks that made it clear they weren't sure what he was doing on their mission. They had a point.

They looked pretty tough, but the local honour system meant they were armed only with heavy-duty dartguns. This *tapu* thing managed to be both anachronistic and adaptable; the locals harked back to a bloody warrior culture back on Old Earth, but attitudes and practices that would've resulted in brutal battles between villagers armed with stone axes made for mayhem and genocide once you brought corporate politics and hi-tech weaponry into the equation.

When the aircar picked him up at the harbour, he'd been introduced to the mission leader, a heavily built woman of mixed blood called Quin, and to Yenemer, a lithe, dark-skinned young man heading the team of three who'd been detailed to search for Taro – and Nual, if she really was in there. He'd heard nothing from her since the last rerouted message. It was possible she was dead. He wasn't sure how streetwise her years in Khesh had left her, but she'd been pretty naïve when he'd met her. Her unnatural advantages could also make her arrogant, and she might easily have fucked up without even realising it.

The aircar was uncomfortably crowded with twenty mercenaries plus him and the driver packed into a space designed for a dozen people. The mercs were professionals, and most of them passed the time napping or in silent contemplation. A couple of the younger ones were chatting to each other, from which Jarek gleaned that though there had been rumours of a mission like this for a few days, in the end it'd come together in a rush. Jarek suspected his delivery of the plans to Ruanuku-*ngai* was responsible for that. There was also a feeling that the gloves were off now, despite the lack of obvious lethal weaponry. One of the youngsters said whichever *ngai* was funding the run must be pretty desperate to go in mob-handed like this, a comment which got him a stern look from Quin.

Shortly after that she stood up. 'Listen up. Those of you who were on the original mission know how that went down; the rest of you will have read your briefing notes. This time, there's no storm to give us cover, so they'll know we're coming. More importantly, there's no one inside to turn off the shield, so we'll have to trash it to get through. Fortunately our transport has had a few non-standard mods, so it'll be up to the task.' She nodded at the driver, who flashed her a tight grin. 'However, remember that we are still subject to the rules of *tapu*. Fatalities must be avoided if at all possible. I hope those of you who follow the Lord of the Sea have prayed for understanding from Tongaroa.' This last comment was delivered with the same serious expression as her short briefing, and afterwards she sat down again.

Silence fell until the driver called out that they'd been detected. After that, a few of the mercs bowed their heads and muttered under their breaths. Ahead, the island's shield was a pale dome glowing in the darkness.

The growing tension made Jarek want to fidget. He looked at his hands and practised the simple breathing exercise he sometimes used to calm himself during transits. *Count in, two, three ... wait ... count out, two, three.*

'Everyone brace!' called the driver. 'Shield impact in five ...'

Jarek looked up. 'Four ...' The view ahead, filled with silver light, suddenly dimmed as a shade slammed down over the screen.

'Three …' The mercs hunkered down in their seats, and Jarek followed suit.

'Two …'

'One …'

Even through the shade, the screen flared brightly. The air-car veered, then shook. The internal lights went out, and Jarek instantly went from apprehensive to terrified. Without power they'd *crash* – were they still over the sea or were they going to hit the island? It was pitch-dark in here, and it felt like they were falling—

The internal lights came on and his stomach bounced back up to hit his diaphragm. Relieved sighs came from all around.

'Right, people,' barked Quin, 'helmets sealed and active.'

Jarek pulled his visor down and the chin-guard up, locking them together. The cabin was reduced to readouts and heat-signatures. People sub-vocalised call-signs to each other to check their coms. Jarek himself had trouble speaking around the control unit that slotted under his tongue; the thing tasted cold and metallic and he kept having to swallow to avoid triggering his gag reflex.

'First surface team ready to roll.'

Two men unbuckled and headed for the door. The aircar touched down and the pair of mercs jumped out as soon as the door opened; the aircar took off at once. The fast put-down was repeated a few seconds later. These teams would rig up gas canisters to pump sleep-gas into the surface air intakes; after that they'd make their way inside as a rearguard.

Those left in the aircar formed up, with Jarek near the back. He glanced across at the screen to see a rough mass that his helmet didn't register as a target – trees, maybe? – and a blocky structure, a building of some sort – that did. Then they were down and the door opened.

Sealed tightly in his suit, Jarek's only impression of the world outside was darkness overlaid by readouts. He was carried forward in the wave of jogging troops, heading for the building.

After about a dozen steps he felt like he'd suddenly run into mud. His body grew unbearably heavy, and an excruciating vibration sang through his gut and jaw. His ears began to ring. He tried to keep moving, but whatever it was, it was affecting everyone. Then, abruptly, the sensation went from unbearable to merely uncomfortable.

Quin's voice came over the com. 'Hold your positions, team.'

He'd just worked out that his suit must be counteracting the effect when Quin added more urgently, 'Damp visual!'

Unfamiliar with the suit's controls, he was almost too late: at the same moment as his view went dark, something thin and bright shot overhead. A fraction of a second later a muted light burst into life ahead of him, followed by the rough brush of a concussion wave.

'Everyone all right?' asked Quin. Presumably everyone was, as shortly afterwards she added, 'Carry on!'

They set off again, and this time, as there were no more nasty surprises, they reached the building and the forward team went to work on the heavy main doors.

Jarek used the brief pause to com Yenemer. 'What just happened back there?' he asked.

'Sonic cannon. They must've installed it since the first run. Good job we brought missiles, though we've definitely broken *tapu* now.' Yenemer sounded quite excited at the prospect.

Jarek was beginning to think he'd made a serious mistake coming along. Just because the rules forbade lethal combat, it didn't mean he couldn't get killed.

A small explosion marked the end of the doors. The two advance teams ducked inside, Jarek's unit following behind. His helmet overlaid the dark enclosed space of the building with the internal layout, no doubt taken from the files he'd provided. He saw two heat signatures lying on the ground; others, tagged as friendlies in his helmet display, were heading for a stairwell. Shortly after they disappeared down the stairs Yenemer called a halt. 'Guards with netguns have set up an ambush below. We'll need to wait for the men on point to clear the way.'

'What about the gas?' Jarek's helmet indicated that the air outside was no longer breathable.

'They must've managed to suit up before it hit.'

'Oh.'

Now they weren't in immediate danger Jarek found that his breath sounded surprisingly loud in his ears. As he dialled down the audio damping he heard a two-tone alarm from outside. It felt both absurd and fucking terrifying, the four of them waiting poised at the top of the stairwell in their ridiculous suits. At least he was too wired to feel tired.

Yenemer's voice came over the com. 'We're clear. Move out.'

At the bottom of the stairs one of the mercs was freeing another from what looked like a giant ball of string, hacking the threads with a definitely lethal-looking knife. Another team member was down, with a liquid heat source – blood – seeping out from under the body. The defenders must be using something heavier than tranq ammo. Further up the corridor three more unconscious bodies lay sprawled, two armoured, one displaying the absurd sartorial combination of sleeping clothes and a rebreather.

They picked their way past, heading for the research labs. The other teams moved off to the accommodation section, where their target was most likely to be found at this time of night. There was a good chance Tawhira-*ngai* had already worked out this was a repeat of the original, failed, mission and now they would be concentrating their resistance there. Jarek briefly wondered what made the man they were after so important that Ruanuku-*ngai* were willing to go to such extreme lengths to get their hands on him. He'd probably never know.

His team advanced by the numbers, checking corners, taking turns on point, moving as a tight unit. Jarek made sure he kept up and didn't get in the way. He checked doors as they went: the locked ones still showed red; though there was a chance that the mercs might be able to disable the central security, it wasn't their priority.

They came across two dead or comatose guards who had succumbed to the gas, then, round the next corner a civilian, a woman in a suit who'd passed out with her hand on her wrist-com. According to the plans, a lot of the security was com-activated and as Yenemer removed the com, prising the woman's limp fingers off it, Jarek was quietly relieved that they hadn't had to hack out someone's implant.

Two more junctions and at last they were in the right area. They used the appropriated com to open locked doors and started checking rooms, most of which were laboratories or workrooms. One lab held a couple of scientists who'd been working late and now lay sprawled on the floor. Other than that, everywhere was deserted. Two of the doors had DNA scanners; they'd come back to those if they had to.

Yenemer's voice came over Jarek's com. 'Quin says they've got the primary target. We need to get a move on here; there's a good chance Tawhira-*ngai* is flying in reinforcements.'

Now they tell him. 'Right.' His team's orders were to keep him safe and ensure he got the individual he was after. It had to be his call if they bugged out.

'We do have an alternative for the doors that won't open,' said Yenemer carefully.

'As in, something that's a little against the rules, like that missile earlier?' asked Jarek equally carefully.

'Correct.' Yenemer wasn't a local, and apparently he was less concerned about the whole *ngai* honour thing.

'Then at this stage, I'd say "Fuck the rules".'

'I hear you.'

They split into two teams to speed up the search and checked the last few remaining com-locked rooms first. When that proved fruitless, they met outside the first of the DNA-locked rooms and Yenemer produced a mesh bag of eyeball-sized silver globes. He pressed one into the centre of the door and it stuck there.

'Everyone back,' he cried, and once they were safely round the corner, he made a complex cutting gesture with one hand.

There was a muffled bang, and Jarek felt a faint tremor. They returned to find the doorframe blackened, the door a buckled rectangle burning on the floor. The room beyond was another lab, with nothing of interest in it.

The second door they blew led into a short passage with another door at the end, this one a pressure-door not dissimilar to the ones on Jarek's ship. He didn't much like the look of that, but they were out of options.

The small room beyond contained a couple of workstations and what appeared to be a silver-grey coffin, wired up to more machinery. Jarek approached the coffin cautiously. It had a clear lid. Inside, lying on white padding and clad in a blue hospital gown, was Taro. His eyes were closed and his skin was as pale as the cushioning around him.

Jarek called the team's medic over. 'Is he dead?' he asked her, careful to keep all emotion out of his voice.

The medic examined the machines carefully. 'No, just in deep sedation.'

'Can we move him?'

'I should be able to unhook him safely, though this is rather an odd set-up.'

'Odd how?'

'Well, it's an auto-surgery and isolation unit – battlefield tech.'

'Just do your best,' Jarek said, and left her to it. The mercs were standing around awkwardly. 'Any of you good with comps?' he asked.

When one of them raised a hand Jarek pointed to the main workstation and said, 'How about we download everything we can from that while we wait.'

'If you like; we'll have to pass on a copy to the patron.'

'Fine by me, as long as I get one too.'

The man nodded.

After a few minutes, the medic called over, 'I'm opening the box now. I'll put a rebreather on him, but he'll be out of it for a while. We'll have to carry him.'

'I'll do that,' said Jarek. He hoisted Taro over his shoulder. The boy weighed even less than he expected.

Getting out was easier than getting in, and the rest of the mercs were already waiting nervously in the aircar. They were barely on board before the driver took off.

The other team had succeeded too: the aircar's med-bay was

already occupied by an unconscious man. Jarek lowered Taro to the floor and removed the rebreather. The medic came over and checked him out.

'Is it safe to bring him round?' asked Jarek.

'Should be. Might take a while.' She gave Taro a shot.

After what felt like an hour but was probably only a few minutes the boy's eyelids fluttered, then opened.

'It's all right!' said Jarek. 'You're safe now.'

For a moment Taro looked distraught. Then his gaze cleared and he began to shiver. Jarek grabbed a thermal blanket from the medic and wrapped it around him.

'You c-came ...' he whispered. 'Thank you.'

Jarek was about to say that was what friends were for when Taro tensed again. 'N-nual,' he stuttered.

'Was she in there, Taro? Have you seen her?' If they'd somehow missed her then they were screwed – there was no way the mercs would go back in now.

'N-no— N-not here. But ... I dreamed her.'

If he'd been talking about anyone else Jarek would have assumed the boy was delirious or deluded. 'Do you know where she is?'

'Yeah,' Taro whispered miserably. 'Somewhere very bad.'

CHAPTER THIRTY-TWO

Nual opened her eyes. Her throat was dry, implying she had been unconscious for a while. She was naked. She appeared to be in the cabin of a shiftship, though she couldn't sense the near-subliminal hum she generally associated with space-travel. She got up shakily and walked over to the cabin door. There was no obvious lock, but she was unsurprised when it remained closed. The only other openings were air vents above the door and bed, both far too small to be of any use.

She extended her other senses, reaching out to locate any presences beyond the door—

—and ran up against a mental wall. Everything outside the physical confines of her cabin – her cell – was off-limits to her mind.

Whoever had sneaked up on her in the alley had been able to hide their presence. Discovering she was now under a mental blockade confirmed her suspicions: she had been captured by the Sidhe.

She tested the unseen wall, looking for a weakness, but there was none; the construct was built and maintained in unity: several Sidhe were devoting themselves to making her imprisonment mental as well as physical.

She'd been in this situation before. This time, however, she had no intention of accepting her fate. She extended her mind again, pushing harder.

The wall pushed back.

She realised her mistake just in time and withdrew.

In the brief moment before she disengaged from the other minds she sensed an unexpected emotion:

Disappointment.

She had been blessed amongst her people, yet she had turned against them. They were sad for her, she who should have been a source of hope but had become a source of shame. If she would only repent, then perhaps in time she might be forgiven.

Part of her yearned to do as they suggested. Compared to the communion of unity, human speech was little more than noise, vague and inaccurate. She was being given the chance to return to a state of grace no ordinary human could comprehend, and she had missed that so much.

But the unity was not welcoming her, it was chastising her. Before she could be accepted back into its all-consuming embrace, she must make amends.

It was too late for that. She had made her choice seven years ago.

'You realise he's undergone surgery?'

Jarek jerked fully awake. After the adrenalin rush of the mission had faded, his abused body had given in. It needed rest. He looked over at the medic who was examining Taro where he lay on the floor of the aircar. The boy had lapsed back into unconsciousness after a brief and not entirely coherent conversation: he claimed he'd somehow been in mental contact with Nual when Jarek rescued him, and that she'd been abducted by the Sidhe. Jarek was half-hoping Taro was drugged or hallucinating, for that news was about as bad as it got.

'Surgery?' he asked the medic. 'What sort?'

'That unit we found him in is designed to perform complex medical procedures without the need for a human expert. Someone programmed it to operate on him several times over the last few days, at various points in his abdomen and lower thoracic area.'

'Will he be all right?' Jarek hadn't thought to check Taro over before he'd carried him out.

'It's all keyhole surgery, so the wounds aren't major. I'll redress them. The only problem would be if there's much internal work been done. From the location and shape of the wounds I don't think they were attempting anything serious, but you'll need to get him checked out.'

'So what the hell were they doing?'

'I'm not sure,' said the medic, 'but this appears to be exploratory work. If I had to guess, I'd say they were looking for something that doesn't show up on normal scanning equipment.'

Something like Angel implants.

She wondered if they had attempted to probe her before she regained consciousness. Probably not: Sidhe shields were at their strongest when the mind was turned in on itself in sleep or unconsciousness. Even if a Sidhe had the strength to enter a shielded and unconscious mind, she made herself vulnerable to the psyche she was invading, and might find the tables turned on her.

Perhaps her best bet would be to stay asleep, locking herself away from her captors just as they had locked her away from the world. It was not a long-term solution, but it was worth a try. And there was a chance she might be able to contact Taro.

However, though reason said sleep was a wise course, it felt like cowardice to return to it at once. Though she wasn't afraid, it aggravated her to be kept in such ignorance and isolation. So she waited for a while, hoping for some change in her circumstances or environment. Finally, thirst and boredom combined to convince her to give up on consciousness. She put herself into a deep sleep and was unaware of anything until her sleep cycle took her closer to the surface, into the dream-world of her own subconscious.

For a while she observed her mind undergoing its daily internal routine of cleansing and filing via her dreams. She retained a peripheral awareness of her connection to the waking world – if her captors were persistent enough to try and break down her defences while she slept, it would be now, when she was nearest consciousness – but nothing impinged on her shields, so when the time felt right, she focused her thoughts and reached out.

She felt Taro's presence almost at once, and experienced a giddy surge of relief. While he was alive and they could communicate, all was not lost. But he was barely coherent, his thoughts fuzzy with pain and drugs.

Initially she concentrated on supporting him with her unseen presence. In his confusion, he assumed she was on her way to save him, and it hurt to have to kill his hope. She tried to pass on her own situation as far as she understood it, despite the pain his answering despair caused her; then, without warning, he was gone.

She was alone in her head.

Nual braced herself for an attack, and when none came she realised that the link must have been broken from his end. It looked like her contact with Taro did not compromise her mental defences, perhaps because it was a different kind of unity to the one she had been brought up in. It was possible that the Sidhe keeping her imprisoned could not even sense her connection to her lover; certainly they had made no attempt to use it.

After a while she slipped back into true unconsciousness ... until she became aware of a strange physical sensation: shaking, coming from deep inside, and a chill blowing across her entire body. Her mind began to build a dream around it – flying through freezing clouds while thunder rattled around her – even as she recognised that the cause was something external.

She woke herself up. When she opened her eyes she was in darkness, shivering violently, her teeth clenched against the urge to chatter.

What was happening?

She reached out wildly. Her left hand hit a wall; she snatched it back. She must still be in the cell, but they had turned off the light and heat. She edged across the bed to put her back against the wall, then drew her legs in and curled up to conserve body-heat, channelling warmth into her core. This might be a precursor to an attack, so she tried to keep her mind sharp and focused, ready to defend herself.

She wondered how long it would take for unconsciousness to become a necessity rather than an act of defiance. This time, though, she might not have the option of waking up. Her entire body was spasming now, and her jaw ached from trying to control her chattering teeth. She curled tighter, fighting the impending hypothermia ...

She dismissed the first touch of warm air on her face as hallucination, then, slowly, the lights began to come up again. By the time they were back to their normal level the room was warm enough that her shivers had subsided into the occasional twitch. That just left the raging thirst and the cramps in her empty belly.

Her captors had just been reminding her who was in control. They wanted her to know that she couldn't hide in her head for ever.

'Can you walk?'

Taro wasn't sure he could, but he nodded anyway. After what Jarek had just done for him, he wasn't going to give him any trouble.

He'd come to with a rush that just had to be chemical. As he helped him to his feet, Jarek told him to avoid driving or operating heavy machinery; from his tone he guessed Jarek was making a joke. When the door of the aircar opened, the walls of Stonetown jiggled and throbbed in his vision, confirming that his current sharp-and-ready state came courtesy of some serious drugs.

The aircar dropped them off on the harbour wall and promptly swung away. 'Who were those coves, anyway?' asked Taro shakily.

'Local muscle, hired to finish the job you got shafted over.'

'Nice of them to get me out too.'

'Nice doesn't come into it. They did it because they were paid to.'

'Like I said ... I owe you.'

'Don't worry about it. Let's get ourselves a cab.' He put an arm round Taro's shoulders and Taro leaned into the support gratefully. It was still early, but already too hot for sensible people to be out and about.

When they limped into the harbour-side market they got some predictably odd looks. Taro glanced down at himself and saw how he was dressed. 'I tell you, lady, it was a top prime party!' he called out to a woman who'd stopped examining the produce on a nearby stall to stare at him. She looked away hurriedly.

They found a cab on the far side of the market. Its interior was wonderfully cool, and Taro leaned back into the soft seat with a sigh.

'I'm sorry to ask, but I need to know: how much can you remember?'

He opened his eyes to see Jarek watching him. He thought for a moment, feeling a chill beyond that of the aircon as he recalled glimpses of the stone ceiling, the uncaring, unfamiliar faces, the muffled voices, the sense of constriction. 'Not much, just flashes. Nightmare stuff. They kept me drugged up' – spikes of distant agony, deep inside him – 'oh fuck, I think they cut me!' He'd been trying to place what else was wrong besides generally feeling like shit: underneath the drugs that were masking the pain he felt like he'd been kicked in the guts. He put a hand on his belly and touched what he realised must be dressings. Jarek caught his wrist.

'Yes, they did. And we're going to make sure there's no serious damage. I think they might have been after your implants.'

'My implants?'

'Yes. Can you still fly?'

'Not sure.' He flexed his feet, which felt further away than usual. A moment later he lifted free of the seat. He stopped the motion. 'No worries. The bastards didn't get them.'

'That's good. Very good.' He sounded relieved.

Taro looked out the window. He realised they were heading out of Stonetown. 'Where're we going?'

'To the starport.'

'We're leaving?'

'Not immediately, but my ship's med-bay is a lot less conspicuous than a trip to hospital. And after that ... well, I've stirred things up a bit around here. We might have to take off at short notice.'

'We can't leave! Not without Nual.'

'So you meant what you said, about dreaming her.'

'Yes! We have to rescue her!'

'From the Sidhe?' Jarek's voice didn't give anything away.

'Yeah, from the Sidhe. And before you say it, I know that I'll probably end up dead, but I have to try.'

'I'm guessing you two made up,' said Jarek drily.

Despite everything, Taro grinned. 'You could say that. Listen,' he said more soberly. 'I know you got your mission, and I'm sorry we didn't do nothing to help you—'

'—actually Nual did. She found out which *ngai* produces the transit-kernels. I'll tell you all about it later.'

'She did? I knew she could. The thing is ... you gotta carry on your fight against the Sidhe, but what I gotta do is find Nual.'

'I don't suppose you have any idea where she is?'

'No, but when we were dreaming together I got this sense she's in a ship's cabin.'

'Well, that would narrow things down. I'm guessing she must be somewhere in this system for you two to share dreams. Any idea where this ship is?'

'No, sorry.' Taro decided not to mention the other sensation from the dream; the feeling that there were a lot of Sidhe near her.

'Hang on a moment, I need to make a com-call.' He had a brief chat with someone official, someone he obviously knew. At the end he thanked the person and hung up. He turned to Taro with a sigh. 'I was just checking for recent arrivals – going back to the ship if a Sidhe ship's in port would be unwise. But there's just me parked up, and the only other traffic in the last day was a tourist shuttle.'

'So, are you gonna help me find her?'

'I'm going to make a few enquiries later today. If there's come-back from your rescue or a whiff of any other trouble, we're out of here. We should probably prep to go anyway, given this ship

Nual's on is presumably either in orbit or hanging around some-where nearby.'

'So that's a yes, then?'

'That's a yes.'

CHAPTER THIRTY-THREE

Although living in the caldera had many advantages, it did mean that neither sunset nor sunrise was visible from Marua's house, so once a week she took the steep walk up to the rim to watch the dawn. The path wound around the inner slope through barely tamed bush alive with birds and insects. It was a popular route, yet she never met anyone on it. She suspected her security and housekeeping staff ensured she was not disturbed, a move she found mildly annoying for she didn't like inconveniencing her people unnecessarily. On the other hand she was flattered they cared enough to ensure she got this time alone.

When she'd last come up here, the day after the Angel's visit, she'd been at her nadir: her first attempt to recruit a replacement for Grigan had failed; she'd just uncovered the treachery of a trusted aide; she had unexpectedly met someone who might be Sidhe; and the next day she had let Tikao attempt the extension test on the last transit-kernel, with disastrous results – both he and the kernel had returned from the shift brain-dead.

A couple of days after that, the Sidhe had turned up.

Their representative, a surprisingly ordinary-looking woman calling herself Lyrian, had listened to Marua's explanation of why there was one less transit-kernel than promised. Then she said simply, 'And do you have the means in place to start processing the new intake as soon as they arrive?'

Marua, feeling like a naughty child, had admitted that she was still working on it.

Lyrian had nodded curtly, as though Marua were fulfilling her low expectations.

So, as if to win herself back into the Sidhe's good graces, she'd told Lyrian about the Angel – not that 'Ela sanMalia' (or whoever she really was) was necessarily Sidhe; how could a Sidhe end up as a registered assassin anyway? But Marua had no intention of holding back anything the *hine-maku* might want to know. She felt no enmity towards the Angel – quite the contrary, given that Olias Kahani's subsequent death had almost certainly been her work – but she felt compelled to please her dangerous allies.

Now she allowed herself a smile as the sun pulled itself free of the shining water and full daylight burst over the world. Thanks be to Tongaroa, things had finally started to improve.

The buyers had what they came for, and though they hadn't yet left the system, she wouldn't have to deal with another visit from the *hine-maku* until the suppliers arrived, whenever that might be. More importantly, she'd finally secured the replacement for Grigan. Dr Pershalek was due to arrive some time in the next hour; she would give him time to recover from the trauma of his midnight relocation, then go and meet him in person.

Which just left the new problem.

If this man Sais had contacted her before the visit from Lyrian and her associates, Marua would have felt obliged to tell them about him too. She was glad he hadn't: his actions reflected badly on Marua's *ngai*, implying she was not operating with the discretion the Sidhe required. And Sais was obviously an honourable man: so far he'd kept his promise and not released the information he held on her *ngai,* even though he now had what he wanted. His threat to expose her had brought Marua near to panic; hence her desperate lie that Tawhira-*ngai* might have both the Angels, and her eagerness to let him join the mission while hoping he might die during it. She was not proud of that response.

She wondered how much the man actually knew. Had he even realised that the main target of the mission was as integral to the Sidhe's plans as Marua herself? Possibly not, given his information had been instrumental to Dr Pershalek's extraction, and he'd made no attempt to interfere once he had his Angel back.

But he knew enough to be very dangerous. Though his allegations might not be believed, the very act of publicly linking her *ngai* to a Sidhe conspiracy could damage her already shaky status with the other *ngai*, and, worse still, damn her in the eyes of the Sidhe.

She needed to deal with this last loose end, quickly and discreetly.

By the time Nual next tried to sleep, her physical condition was becoming a serious distraction. Nothing had changed in the day – or however long it was – since she had been awakened by the induced cold. She had divided her time between brooding about her situation and fantasising about the imminent arrival of something to eat and drink. Periodically she made cautious tests of her mental prison, and found it as secure as ever. She experienced a growing urge to shout out loud, demanding that her captors get on with whatever they planned to do to her … Unless they were just going to leave her to die.

Though the hunger was uncomfortable, it was the dehydration that would kill her. Already her head throbbed monotonously, and every breath she took was like swallowing knives. Her tongue felt like a bloated sack of sand. Though she tried to get up and move around every now and again, standing up was becoming too much effort.

She was torn between the desire to block the ever-increasing physical discomfort and the need to monitor her deterioration. Not that there was anything she could do to stop it. In the end, she did not so much drift into slumber as fall into merciful unconsciousness.

She swam back towards awareness when she reached the state of light dream-ridden sleep necessary to contact Taro. She made a vague attempt to find him, without success. She tried not to read anything into her failure. He might not be in a receptive sleep-state, and even if he was, her concentration was blown to hell. She fell back into predictably unpleasant dreams of dark despair and gnawing hunger.

When she awoke, a woman was sitting on the chair next to her bed.

The pain and exhaustion were blown away in an instant. She braced herself for the mental attack.

When nothing happened, Nual was confused: why send someone in now, when she was weak and feverish, unless she was there to spearhead a unified assault on her shields?

Then she saw what the woman had in her hand.

The water came almost to the top of the beaker. Nual couldn't look away from it. She had to have it.

She blinked, feeling her eyelids scrape across her gritty eyes, and forced herself to look at the person holding the beaker. The woman, who was watching her with a faint smile on her face, wore practical, comfortable clothes and was somewhat older than Nual. She looked friendly, trustworthy; Nual clenched her fist, digging her nails into her palm until the skin broke, using the pain to focus. Her visitor was Sidhe, and the air of trustworthiness was just glamour. She must not let herself be taken in.

'It's not drugged, you know.' The woman's voice was loud after so long in silence. It had a mellow, almost amused, tone. 'If we wished to drug you then gas would be a far simpler option.'

Nual said nothing.

'You don't want it?' The woman moved the beaker away.

'Didn't ... say ... that.' Nual had to force the words out round her swollen tongue.

'Good. Well, here you are then, my dear.'

Despite herself, Nual snatched the beaker, slopping water over her shaking hands. She took a great, greedy gulp, nearly gagging when her stomach went into spasm. She stifled the reflex and continued to drink, ignoring the liquid spilling down her chin. Nausea stirred in her guts, but she didn't care. She kept the beaker pressed to her lips even after it was empty, waiting with eyes closed for her body to adjust to the sudden arrival of the longed-for liquid.

She briefly considered trying to physically attack her visitor, before deciding that even if she were physically capable of such action it would be foolish. The cell might be fitted with protection; her unnamed visitor had already mentioned gas. And even if she did succeed, all she would do was aggravate her captors, who would probably just choose a new mouthpiece. She lowered the beaker and let the Sidhe take it from her.

'I—' She coughed hoarsely, then tried again. 'I don't suppose there's any point in asking where I am?'

'None whatsoever,' said the other curtly.

'How about why I'm here?' She had already run through a number of scenarios, none of them pleasant.

'Now that I *can* tell you. We'd like you to answer a few questions.'

Nual decided she might as well play along for now. Though they had softened her up by deprivation, actual torture seemed unlikely; such extreme measures were more often than not counterproductive, only driving the victim deeper inside herself. And there was relatively little risk to her mental integrity while they were using speech: for all their potential for misunderstanding, spoken words provided no foothold into a shielded mind. 'What questions would those be?' she asked.

'We'll get to that in due course,' said the other Sidhe pleasantly. 'However, since we're doing this the human way, why don't we start with introductions? Your current ID claims you call yourself Ela sanMalia, but the one before that was for Lia Reen. Do you have a preference?'

Nual said nothing.

The other Sidhe sighed. 'Fine, as you wish. I'll use Ela. The name I use when dealing with humans is Lyrian.'

Nual decided to ask a question she hoped she already knew the answer to. 'Are you a member of the Court?'

'No, I'm not. If I were, I doubt we would have to resort to this slow and frankly inconvenient method of exchanging information. I am, however, the most appropriate person to speak with you.'

By which she probably meant she was the most powerful Sidhe aboard. But still not powerful enough. Stifling a smile Nual asked,

'Because you can't get me to co-operate any other way?'

With just a touch of exasperation in her voice Lyrian said, 'Yes, because you are too strong for us.' Then she added, 'Actually, that's not entirely true. Acting in unity, I'm sure we could breach your defences, but we are ... *wary* of you. However, before you get elevated ideas of your own importance, I should say that our reasons for caution have less to do with your unusual heritage and above-average abilities than with certain events, seven years ago. Which brings me onto my first question: what happened on the mothership?'

Nual stayed silent and concentrated on keeping her shields strong and her expression neutral. But one of her fears had been confirmed. They were keeping her isolated not only to sap her will, but because they were worried she was tainted. *Was she?* How would she know? No, she must do as Jarek did: when she couldn't know the answer, assume the best for the sake of her sanity.

'I can see this might take a while,' said Lyrian. 'Well, we have a couple of days.'

'Before what?'

Lyrian smiled nastily, 'Now Ela, you can't honesty expect me to just tell you that, can you?'

If Tawhira-*ngai* had done anything more than have a look round inside Taro, the ship's med-bay couldn't spot it. The drugs the medic had given the boy ran out while Jarek was completing the final scan, and he left Taro sleeping naturally on the med-bay couch before crawling off to his own bed for a few hours' sleep.

Taro was still out of it when Jarek woke up. He fixed some caf, then checked out the data he'd lifted from the lab where he'd found Taro. It was password protected, so he turned the package over to the decryption suite Bez had set up while she'd been a guest on the ship. After that he spent a while checking the public com for news and traffic updates. As he'd hoped, scheduled arrivals and departures at the port were openly listed. None of the ship names meant anything to him; there were no matches against Bez's list of possible Sidhe ships.

He went back down to the rec-room to find Taro sitting up on the med-bay couch, trying to work out how to get the monitors off him.

'Here, I'll do that,' said Jarek, going over to him.

Taro stopped fiddling. 'So, what's the plan now?'

'I'll get us some food, then I'm going to go back into Stonetown to get your stuff; it's at the hotel where Nual was staying. I'll spend the rest of the evening talking to some of my spacer contacts, see what I can find out from them.'

'Can I come?'

'You're in no state to go anywhere right now, not to mention being a bit conspicuous.'

'Guess you're right. Can we at least get the gun out of customs?'

'We'll do that in the morning.'

Jarek went out, leaving Taro with a supply of unhealthy snacks and the run of the ship's games library.

When Jarek reached the bar he was welcomed warmly. Word had got round about his generosity, and he found himself buying drinks all evening in return for very little in the way of useful information.

He did manage to confirm something he'd suspected. He bonded with one of the junior cargo handlers who'd been eyeing him up in a somewhat predatory fashion. Turned out they supported the same terceball team in the All-Worlds' League, and though in Jarek's case it was fairly muted support, he played it up. Lali was also an offworlder, and had a bit of a chip on her shoulder about the best jobs going to locals. After a few beers she was happy to admit that not every ship that came into Kama Nui airspace landed at the spaceport. The most powerful *ngai*s had their own facilities: 'One rule for most of us, one for them,' as she put it sourly. Obviously all comings and goings were still monitored by traffic control, but she didn't have access to their data. He let her chat him up for the rest of the evening, before making an excuse of having to work and a vague promise that he'd see her the following night. He felt a bit guilty that his personal tastes didn't lie that way, but she was his most useful contact so far and if it helped to let her think she was in with a chance, so be it.

In some ways her information made the situation worse: the Sidhe ship might still be dirt-side, presumably at one of Ruanuku-*ngai*'s landing facilities, or it could have already left. Either way, there was no way of tracing it.

Back on the ship Taro had fallen asleep on the couch, curled up in a nest of food-wrappers with the gaming headset discarded on the floor next to him. He looked peaceful enough, so Jarek let him be. He frowned when he noticed the three empty bulbs of extra-strength black beer amongst the discarded wrappings before relenting and clearing up the mess. The boy certainly had sorrows to drown.

CHAPTER THIRTY-FOUR

'This isn't what I was led to expect.'

Marua made herself smile. 'Is the accommodation not suitable? We have other houses.' Dr Pershalek was used to living in cramped underground quarters; she couldn't imagine how having his own house in a lush caldera could be a disappointment to him.

'No, no, this place is fine.' The scientist waved vaguely at the wood-panelled room where the two of them sat on comfortable couches in the warm afternoon light. 'I mean the work you're expecting me to do. I was told that I would be given the freedom to complete my research into areas that my last employer wouldn't allow me to pursue.'

By Olias Kahani, no doubt. From his tone, Pershalek considered Tawhira-*ngai*'s refusal to indulge him to be their loss. Kahani would have played on that sense of injustice. Marua decided to continue to indulge the scientist's ego for the moment. 'I assume you mean your theories regarding the effects of shiftspace transits on neural interface technology? Groundbreaking stuff, insofar as I can understand it.'

'Yes, yes.' He nodded as though his genius was a given. 'But strictly theoretical – it's not like they could give me access to shift-space—'

'But we can,' said Marua.

He looked annoyed at being interrupted, then said dubiously, 'So one of your people told me.'

Marua remained silent. She did not have to be his friend, she merely had to persuade him to do his job.

When he realised she was waiting for him to continue he added, 'The fact is, I came here believing I would be continuing my own research with whatever facilities I required and a full team reporting to me.'

I'm sure you were, but that was a promise made by an inveterate liar. 'You will be given adequate chances to pursue your work when not employed on the main project, and our facilities are the best of any *ngai*. However, given the sensitive nature of your work, I'm afraid we can allow you only one assistant.' When they managed to find a replacement for Tikao.

'If you don't value me enough to assign me a team, then frankly I'm surprised you bothered to recruit me,' he said, sitting back.

Marua wondered if the real problem was his discovery that his leftfield theories had already been explored and applied by someone else. 'I'm sorry you feel that way,' she conceded. 'But you have to understand that the work you will be doing for us has to be carried out in the utmost secrecy. The fact that you will be working alone is a result of this constraint, and not a reflection of how important your unique skills are to us.'

'Whilst obviously I *can* do the work, I must say I find what you are doing here to be ... *ethically dubious*.' He spoke the words as though trying them out. Which he probably was, if his profile was anything to go by. He obviously valued cold science over human concerns. 'I hadn't initially realised that the procedures you carry out use adolescent boys. Little more than children!' The man was trying to work himself up into a state of moral indignation, but, not having well-developed morals, it was taking some effort.

'The subjects are not exactly normal human boys: they do not perceive the world in the same way we do. However, I do understand that you might still be uncomfortable with the process.' Actually she doubted it. Marua herself probably had more qualms, and she had long since accepted the price as worth paying. 'But you need to understand *why* we are doing this. This facility is the *only* place transit-kernels are created. Without the work we do here, human interstellar culture is doomed.'

'I have to say, that did surprise me when I read the briefing this morning,' said Pershalek. 'In fact, I find it a little hard to believe. Why here? Why *only* here?'

'That is something I'll explain later, once you've accepted the job.'

He seized on her refusal. 'No, I need to know now. You can't expect me to co-operate unless you tell me everything.'

Grigan's Ascensionist views had provided her mother with a lever when she recruited him; Pershalek, amoral and egotistical, was turning out to be far harder work. Rather than acknowledge his defiance she said, 'You do know that you can never leave this island.'

'Is that a threat?'

'No, merely a statement.'

'Then put me on a different project. I'm sure I could be useful in other areas.'

'I'm quite sure you could, but this is something that only you can do.' *Much as I wish otherwise.* It was somewhat ironic, given the trouble she'd been to, that the suppliers still hadn't turned up. She wondered if they had ever been this late before. As had happened when her mother dealt with them twenty-five years ago, the buyers were still lurking in-system. Presumably they intended to liaise with the suppliers before the incoming Sidhe dropped off the stasis-units containing the next batch of boys. That was what had happened last time, according to Marua's mother. Marua would have liked to know what was going on, but Lyrian hadn't been in contact since she'd picked up the completed transit-kernels.

'And if I refuse, what then? Will you kill me?' Pershalek was scared, but he knew his worth; he was testing her.

'Absolutely not. You are too useful to us.'

'And to kill me when I'm your guest would be *tapu*, wouldn't it?' For the first time, Pershalek smiled. He obviously didn't think highly of the world's honour-code.

'You're right, it would,' she said tightly. 'However, depriving you of your freedom and the privileges that would otherwise be yours would not.'

'I'm not exactly free now,' complained Pershalek.

Marua looked round the pleasantly appointed room with its vases of flowers and colourful hangings. 'Trust me, your situation could be a lot worse.'

He raised his chin in an almost childish gesture of defiance. 'Then maybe we can discuss this again when and if it becomes so.'

Alone again, Nual considered Lyrian's offer. It sounded almost reasonable: tell us everything we ask and you will be forgiven, your past wiped clean. You will be allowed to take your rightful place amongst your people.

Nual knew Lyrian had not coerced her – if she could do that, then she would be free to read her, rather than having to resort to the clumsy human method of communication. No, the attraction of Lyrian's offer came down to simple logic, combined with Nual's own feelings about her flight from her people. 'We're not looking for blame,' Lyrian had said, 'just explanations. We know the events on the mothership must have been traumatic for you.'

Lyrian was right about that. The memory of those few days, when her life changed for ever, still haunted her in her dreams, quite possibly influencing her decisions in ways she was not always able to identify. Nual wondered how much Lyrian already knew. When Jarek rescued her, the mothership had been dead in space, its transit-kernel burnt out. The Sidhe must have found it, presumably as a result of information extracted from Jarek's mind. If the mothership's comp had survived – and there was no reason to suspect it hadn't – Lyrian would know of Nual's rebellion and subsequent imprisonment. She wondered what else they'd found when they boarded the wreck. When Nual left, most of the others on board were already dead and she herself had barely escaped the influence of that strange, appalling contagion that had driven them to turn on each other. Even now she shied away from that memory.

Part of her wanted to tell Lyrian what little she knew, even though admitting her role in the downfall of the mothership might damn her in her sisters' eyes. At least then she could start to deal with her terrible mistake.

It was Lyrian's other questions that she was not willing to answer: what Nual had done since leaving her people, who she had had dealings with – by which Lyrian meant: who knew the Sidhe were still abroad and wielding power? Nual had no doubt that her people would hunt down and eliminate any threats to their secret hold over humanity. The Sidhe already knew about Jarek, and poor Elarn was dead now, thanks to her.

But Taro ...

In some ways love complicated everything. But it made certain decisions effortlessly simple. She would die before she betrayed Taro.

She had tried to avoid thinking of her lover because to do so caused an almost physical pain. But now she wondered if her failure to communicate with him was down to nothing more sinister than simple timing. She had designated the current time 'about midday' in her head because she had been awake for several hours, but she had no idea what the true time was back on Kama Nui. Taro might well be in a receptive state again now; she should have another go at contacting him.

She lay on the bed and prepared to put herself into a trance. First she shut off the distracting signals from her raw throat and sour, shrunken stomach. Then she slowed her breathing and heart-rate. Though she was familiar with the use of trance she had never done anything quite like this: trying to enter an active dream-state whilst awake, and at the same time attempting to establish a link whose nature she barely understood.

She found her remaining physical sensations falling away.

This was a riskier proposition than true sleep. She sensed the unity, waiting on the edge of consciousness.

She braced herself, ready to withdraw, or fight.

The waiting presences did nothing. Perhaps they could not exploit this state after all. Either that or, for fear of her taint, they did not want to risk direct confrontation.

Because this was not a true dream, the contact would have to take a different form. She focused directly on Taro, homing in on him through the paths of her memory. She recalled his voice, his touch, the smell of him. The experience was sensual, almost erotic, and she was half tempted to lose herself in it, to escape her current situation in a happy daydream ... but no, that would be no more than a temporary respite.

She honed her recollections, moving away from the physical to the less quantifiable: the feel of his mind, the flavour of his soul.

At first she thought she was merely slipping into a true, deep – and fruitless – sleep. Then she sensed him.

And she felt him sense her.

CHAPTER THIRTY-FIVE

Jarek's body-clock was still messed up after his transit marathon, and despite his late night he woke early.

He wondered how Bez was doing. No news was probably good news. She'd tell him when she'd cracked the core.

Thinking of her reminded him that he'd forgotten to check the decryption routine last night. The quietly pinging comp on the bridge indicated that Tawhira-*ngai*'s data had been unlocked, as he had hoped.

Jarek sat down and started to read. The files weren't big, but there was a fair bit of corporate crap and scientific jargon to wade through, so it took him a while to work out why the *ngai* had wanted an Angel. When he did, he reread the relevant section to be sure, then breathed, 'Holy shit,' and jumped up.

Taro was still asleep, sprawled across the couch in wanton in-elegance. As Jarek approached he saw the boy's eyes moving under their lids. He reached out and shook him, gently but firmly, at the same time calling his name.

For a moment Jarek thought Taro wasn't going to wake up. Then he gasped, opened his eyes wide and tried to thrust Jarek away.

'Easy!' said Jarek, grabbing one of Taro's hands. 'It's all right, you're safe now.'

'No!' Taro blinked rapidly, batting at Jarek. 'No, I have to—'

'Have to what?' Jarek realised Taro wasn't properly conscious; his movements were jerky, his eyes unfocused.

'Have to ... gotta go back. She's here.' He looked at Jarek and his expression fell. 'She's gone,' he said, his voice devastated.

'"She" as in Nual?'

Taro nodded miserably. 'I felt her, reaching out,' he said woozily. 'We were close, so close. But ... gone now.'

'Shit,' said Jarek. 'Sorry. I had no idea.'

For a moment neither of them said anything, then in a sad, mildly accusatory voice, Taro said, 'Why'd you wake me anyway?'

'I've decrypted the files we stole from Tawhira-*ngai*. I know what they wanted with you.'

Taro sat up groggily. 'That's more than I do,' he said.

'So you don't know what zepgen is, then?'

Taro shook his head. 'Never heard of it. Or them. Sounds a bit like one of them topside alt-metal bands back in Khesh.'

Jarek knew the boy was trying to lighten the mood – which made the conversation they needed to have even more difficult. 'Listen, why don't you get cleaned up and I'll get the caf on. We can talk about it after you've had a chance to wake up properly.'

'All right.' Taro's voice had some of that old sulkiness Jarek recalled from when they first met, but this time he couldn't entirely blame the boy.

After his morning ablutions, Taro accepted a mug of caf and sat down opposite Jarek. He still looked half-asleep. 'So,' he said, 'what's this zepgen stuff then?'

'It's a very unusual, very potent power source. Zepgen is a lost technology; if it existed at all it was probably created by the male Sidhe.'

'And what's that gotta do with me?'

Jarek thought he detected a note of uneasiness under Taro's apparent indifference. 'According to the files we lifted, you've got a zepgen system inside you.'

'What?'

'Something must be powering your implants, and there isn't anywhere in that skinny body of yours to hide a fusion plant. I'd wondered about it myself, though the topic never came up. But apparently your gravitics are powered by zepgen. The system was implanted in your body along with the grav-tech, and that's what Tawhira-*ngai* were after.'

Taro leaned back, as though worried about catching such a bizarre idea. 'You sure you got the right file?' he said, his voice somewhere between uneasiness and mockery.

'Well, Tawhira-*ngai* believed it enough to kidnap you and cut you open.'

'And what'd they find?' He looked down at himself, as though he expected to be able to see the alien tech.

'They used both scans and surgery and in the end they discovered several extremely small implants inserted into your ribs and lower spine.'

'But they didn't ... they didn't get them out, did they? I mean, I can still fly.' Taro's hand was fluttering over his stomach. With some effort he looked up and put both hands on the table, trying to steady himself.

'No, they didn't remove the zepgen generator.'

'I guess I'd have died if they had.'

'Actually,' said Jarek softly, 'that wasn't what they were worried about. They decided there was a high likelihood the system was designed to work in concert with your body. When you die, it goes inert, making it useless. But any serious interference with the zepgen implants while you're alive can cause the system to overload and self-destruct. Violently.' Taro went a shade paler, but said nothing, so Jarek continued, 'Tawhira-*ngai*'s scientists were keeping you isolated; they obviously took the risk pretty seriously. When I rescued you they'd decided to put you on ice while they tried further tests, but they were reasonably sure the zepgen implants couldn't be removed.'

'Shit,' whispered Taro.

'And you really had no idea there was something like this inside you?'

Jarek realised how dumb that question was even before Taro snapped a reply. 'Of course I fucking didn't!'

Jarek considered leaving it there, but he still hadn't brought up the issue that had made him wake Taro in the first place. 'Taro, I'm sorry. I know you don't need any more shit—'

Taro snorted, but Jarek pressed on '—but there's something I need to ask you.'

'What's that?' said Taro warily.

'I told you I needed to try and get hold of a beacon so I can bring Serenein back into human-space. For that, I need to find a male Sidhe: I'm pretty sure they're the ones who made the beacons in the first place. Now, in order to have ... what you have ... inside you, you must have encountered one.'

For a while Taro said nothing. Jarek gave him time to compose himself.

'Yeah,' he said finally, 'you could say that.'

It was another beautiful day: early sunlight patterned the hardwood floor of Marua's study and birdsong drifted through the open shutters. She loved the way the world smelled in the morning after rain; so rich and full of life. She would like nothing more than to take her cup of tea out onto the balcony and forget her troubles for a while. When she heard the knock on the door she sighed to herself then called out, 'Come in, please.'

The island had no facilities for detaining people; there was no need. Marua had improvised, moving Pershalek from his house to a lab that had been stripped down prior to refurbishment, providing only the basic amenities of a bed and bucket, and putting a pair of guards outside the door. Those same guards had marched him here in silence. They were waiting downstairs.

She glanced up from her desk. 'Feel free to sit down,' she said, nodding at the seat opposite.

Dr Pershalek looked tired, but not cowed. 'I'm fine standing, thank you.' He crossed his arms. 'Actually I'm surprised you wanted to see me so soon. My previous employers had me in solitary confinement for the best part of two weeks before your people got me out. I was beginning to wonder if they were interested in renegotiating our relationship at all. Or if they were even willing to break with tradition.'

'Break with tradition in what way?' Marua affected a tone of disinterest to cover her irritation. He was right, of course: this game of negotiation he wished to draw her into meant he would expect to be left to stew for more than one night. Unfortunately, she didn't have the time to make her point that way. The situation had to be resolved quickly, one way or another.

'By killing me.' His mocking tone indicated how unlikely he thought that possibility was. He was an irreplaceable asset, and he knew it: if the *ngai* he'd betrayed would not kill him, then the rival *ngai* who'd risked so much to get their hands on him surely wouldn't.

Marua tapped the file she'd been viewing closed and gave him her full attention. 'Don't tempt me, Dr Pershalek.'

He looked understandably taken aback at her blunt answer. 'But *tapu*—'

'Is a very complicated matter, difficult for outsiders to fully understand. And each *ngai* is different.'

'Ah.' He eyed up the chair. 'You said I could sit ...'

'Please do.'

She waited for him to break the silence. 'Perhaps I was being a little hasty yesterday,' he said carefully. 'I'm sure we can come to an arrangement that suits us both. However, I meant what I said about how I wish my skills to be utilised. Building transit-kernels alone in a lab is not—'

'—what you expected to be doing. I realise that. However, it is the job I wanted you for. It is the job you will be doing. And you will give it your full and enthusiastic support, and you will never dream of betraying my trust in any way.'

'Just what makes you think—?'

Marua's upraised hand silenced him. She leaned forward and said, 'Allow me to answer the question you asked yesterday.'

He radiated growing unease; the rules he was used to obviously didn't apply here. 'Which one?' he said nervously.

'You asked why this is the only location where transit-kernels are manufactured. There are two answers to that. One is that only a very few suitable subjects are made available; there is little point in setting up a second facility for such a tiny number. The second reason is the need for utmost secrecy, given the uproar that would ensue if people realised what really powers their shiftships – though that would be nothing compared to the uproar should they discover who provides those shift-minds.'

'What are you talking about?'

'I work with the Sidhe.'

His reaction was predictable: confusion, then incredulity. 'I'm sorry, I thought you said the Sidhe.'

Keeping her expression carefully composed Marua said, 'I did. And if you do not cooperate fully I will simply hand you over to my Sidhe associates. They can ensure your obedience, from now until the day you die.' But only while they were still around. Which was why she needed to be sure of him before Lyrian left the system.

'This is ... ridiculous. Laughable.' He wanted to dismiss it as a joke, because that was what the Sidhe had made themselves; legendary monsters to frighten children. No one believed those foolish tales about them not being dead after all. But he could see she was deadly serious.

'I'm not laughing, Dr Pershalek. If you would like to speak to their representative now, I can introduce you.'

He looked over his shoulder, as though expecting a monster to materialise in her office. 'They're here?'

'Not currently. But they're only a com-call away. Would you like me to make that call?'

'No.' He swallowed, then mastered himself. 'How do I know you're telling the truth?'

'Without calling them, you mean? You don't. As I say, secrecy is essential, and that is why, now you know the full truth, your options have narrowed. Either you willingly take on the task we recruited you for, or I give you to my associates and they ensure that you *become* willing.' She paused to let him take this in. According to family legend that had happened a few times, but it was not the preferred option, because the process often damaged the very areas of the brain that were needed to interface with the transit-kernel technology. And to ask the Sidhe to intervene would reflect badly on Marua when she had already lost face with them.

'You can have a few minutes to consider, if you like,' she said magnanimously.

Pershalek had been staring at her desk, eyes defocused. He looked up. 'I … you really mean this, don't you?'

She leaned forward and said forcefully, but without anger, 'Yes, I really mean this.'

By her desk clock, he considered for just over a minute. Then he said, 'All right, you win. I'll do it. But I want the chance to do my own work too.'

'You'll have it, provided the transit-kernels are always your priority.'

When he didn't make any move to go Marua cleared her throat and said, 'Was there something else?'

'Uh, no.' He began to get up, then paused. A hungry look came over his face. 'Actually, yes, I was wondering … do you have zepgen?'

'I'm sorry?' For the first time, he had surprised her.

'Zepgen. It's—'

'I know what it is, Dr Pershalek. I'm just not sure why you're bringing it up now.'

'It's Sidhe technology; does that mean they've given it to you? Because it's a fascinating area, and if my other duties permit then I'd be very interested in—'

'Not every legend about the Sidhe is true,' said Marua shortly. 'There's no such thing as zepgen.'

'Ah, now that's where you're wrong.' He sounded delighted to have caught her out.

'Am I?'

Puffing his chest out, he said, 'Despite my problems with my late employer I still had my ear to the ground. When Tawhira-*ngai* caught that Angel it was so they could investigate his power source – which is zepgen.' When Marua said nothing he couldn't resist planting a last barb. 'Odd that they'd give it to assassins and not to their supposed friends.'

'You'll be wanting to see your new laboratory now,' said Marua tightly.

He half-bowed and left without another word.

Once she heard the door downstairs close, Marua called her security chief. 'Any progress on decrypting the files from the island run?' she asked.

'Not yet. I'll let you know as soon as we have anything.'

Pershalek could be lying, but she doubted it. He had nothing to gain by such a lie. Of course she should not expect the Sidhe to share everything; this was a business arrangement, after all, quite aside from their essentially secretive nature. But she could do so much with zepgen, even if the Sidhe forbade her from making the knowledge public! If they did have this technology then it would be in their interests to share it with her, given the massive power requirements of the transit-kernel encoding process.

Pershalek's dig reminded her that even if she liked to think of them as her associates, the Sidhe were actually her mistresses.

CHAPTER THIRTY-SIX

Though Nual tried to contact Taro again, she had no success. He'd woken up at exactly the wrong moment. But at least she knew he was still alive, and, from the momentary touch she had felt, no longer in serious trouble – the wisp of his consciousness she had connected with had been unclouded, and not in any pain or distress.

She experimented with the trance state in an attempt to force another prescient incident, but she was not surprised when she failed; foresight was apparently less an ability that could be honed than an unexpected visitation of knowledge.

The next morning – she had decided to designate the time she woke up as morning until proven otherwise – Lyrian was there again. This time she'd brought food as well as water. It was the recycled paste that had been a staple aboard the mothership where Nual had grown up: tasteless, pappy stuff, yet redolent of her past. Not that Nual savoured it; she was too hungry.

'Don't eat so fast, you'll be sick!' advised Lyrian.

Nual looked up, her lips smeared with paste. Lyrian was smiling, and for a moment Nual almost smiled back. The other Sidhe really was very good.

When Nual had finished eating Lyrian said, 'So, what shall we talk about?'

While Lyrian was giving her the chance to ask questions, she might as well take it. 'How about what the Sidhe were up to on Khathryn?' she asked. 'I assume you got to Elarn's lawyer there.'

'No, not him, we knew you'd read him. We had a word with

one of his aides after we visited Elarn. When you turned up, the young woman sent us your new ID and, as instructed, hired a team to capture you – or failing that, to kill you. Then she went and had a nice long lie-down, poor thing.'

So it looked like the ship that had spooked them into leaving the Khathryn system early *had* been Sidhe, coming to pick her up if the thugs had succeeded. 'Whereas on Vellern you just wanted to kill me,' she said with forced levity. She had a good idea why that had been, but she wanted confirmation.

'Ah yes, Vellern. How long did it take for you to make contact?'

Nual decided she might as well answer that one, as it was hardly relevant to her current situation. 'I discovered the truth about Khesh City within two hours of arriving. One of the City avatars found me and we had a little talk. Didn't you feel it was overkill, attempting to bring down the whole City just in case I passed on my "taint" to him?'

'"*It*",' said Lyrian coldly, 'would be a more suitable pronoun. And no: we didn't wish to take any chances.' She smiled. 'Thank you for that.'

'For what?' asked Nual uneasily.

'You've just put one of our fears to rest.'

Nual said nothing, though behind her shields, her mind was racing.

Lyrian said, 'We were wondering if the males were up to their old tricks, and had somehow recruited you to their cause and then offered you sanctuary. However, it now appears you had no idea they were even still around until you met one by accident. From that I would conclude that whatever happened seven years ago might not have been their doing after all.'

Nual cursed her carelessness. Given how little they knew about the attack on the mothership, of course her sisters would suspect their old enemies first. Rather than give anything else away, she decided to go on the offensive.

'Just as a matter of interest,' she asked, 'why *are* we still in the Kama Nui system?'

Just as Nual had hoped, Lyrian was thrown by the question – she would have no idea how Nual could know they hadn't left yet. Not that Nual was sure of it; all she knew for certain was that she was in the same system as Taro.

Lyrian sat up straighter. 'My, my, your powers have certainly come along since you left us,' she said, her voice like poisoned honey. 'I don't suppose you'd care to tell me how you know that?'

'No,' said Nual, 'I wouldn't.'

'Hmm. Then I don't see why I should tell you what we're doing here.' Lyrian waved a hand dismissively. 'It wouldn't mean much to you anyway.'

'Try me.'

Lyrian was silent for a while. 'All right,' she said finally, 'we're waiting for the consorts.'

Of course! The boys from Serenein. That made sense, now she thought about it.

'You know,' said Lyrian, 'your mind might be impenetrable but your face betrays you sometimes. You know who I mean, don't you?'

Damn! Nual had been caught out again.

When Nual didn't respond to her initial question, Lyrian asked, 'Did you know you were sired by a consort?'

Nual tried to think of something to say that would put her back in control of the conversation. She failed.

Lyrian, confident she had the upper hand again, was beginning to enjoy herself. 'Well, you always knew you were special, didn't you? Your sort often question and probe before you settle down.'

'My sort?' she said. 'You mean naturals? I assumed you were natural-born too.'

'I am. Like you I was conceived in the act of love. Well, love of a sort. No, I'm talking about those whose genetics are the very best, the most likely to breed true.' Though Lyrian was as tightly shielded as ever her voice betrayed envy, even contempt.

The consorts were Sidhe, of course, albeit mentally constrained ones; these days they were the only full-blooded males around – on the motherships, any boy-child showing Sidhe abilities was put down before he could become the enemy. It was logical that before the consorts went to their final fate powering shiftships they would contribute their potent genes to the Sidhe bloodlines. That Nual came from such a union made sense: she had always felt different from her sisters, even other naturals. But Lyrian's comment raised further questions. 'You say "conceived in the act of love". That implies it isn't just a case of using male genetic material.'

'Quite so. We've found that using males as, aha, nature intended gives the best results.'

'I see. No wonder you're so tetchy.'

'What do you mean?'

'I'm guessing the consorts must be late, if we're still here.' Nual knew this was indeed the case, thanks to Jarek's actions on Serenein.

'They'll be here soon enough.' Lyrian's tone was confident, but Nual imagined she must be getting worried.

Despite herself, Nual grinned. 'But until then, we have a ship full of eager Sidhe getting more and more frustrated.'

Lyrian's face showed brief irritation at the jibe. Then she pursed her lips and said, 'Of whom you would most likely have been one, had you not turned your back on your heritage.'

Which also made sense. They would want to strengthen already strong bloodlines. Lyrian was waiting for her to speak, so Nual asked, 'And my mother, was she of the Court?'

Lyrian smiled nastily. 'The concept of *mother* is such a human one. The unity was your mother, the true parent that nurtured and protected you.'

'She was, wasn't she?'

Again that fleeting gesture of irritation: Lyrian expressed the emotion with a tiny asymmetrical straightening of her lips, no more than a quick twitch. Then she was back in control. 'It isn't relevant. Though it's interesting that you mention the Court. None of those august personages are currently on board. Which is why we've had to request their presence.'

Nual felt a chill creep up the nape of her neck.

Lyrian continued, 'When I passed news of your capture on to

our wise and powerful sisters, they were eager to send in someone to interrogate you. A specialist. She'll be arriving within a day or so.' Lyrian sat back, her body-language all comfort and control. 'We've found no taint in you so far, but even if we've missed it, I'm sure she'll be able to deal with anything unexpected that still lurks within you.' She leaned forward again. 'With one of the Court leading our probe, those secrets you are guarding so closely will soon be exposed.'

Nual remained silent, working hard not to let her dismay show.

Lyrian added, 'I strongly suspect the questions she'll ask you will be the same ones I've already put to you, so perhaps you might want to reconsider while you still can? Truthful answers now may save you considerable pain later.'

And anything she revealed would reflect well on Lyrian, who would want to be able to please her powerful visitor by having made headway with their prisoner. Nual said nothing.

Lyrian stood up. 'As you wish. I have a lot to attend to before our guest arrives. I'll return later today, when you've had time to think over your options.' She swept out.

For the first time despair began to gnaw at Nual's spirit. She already felt ground down by her incarceration and to find the Court had taken an interest in her was the worst possible news.

It took her a while to calm herself enough to evoke the dreaming trance. At first she got no inkling of contact, then she felt the echo of Taro's mind: he was asleep, but too deeply for her to impinge on his consciousness. She wondered if she could somehow bring his mind into a receptive state, but she was concerned that she might risk damaging him if she failed, so instead she waited, enforcing patience and concentrating on maintaining their tenuous contact until he began to dream.

He was in the Exquisite Corpse. The detail was perfect, right down to the smells of burnt mash, roasting meat and the odd mustiness of the place's alien barkeep. It was dark, so he was spared the ball-shrivelling view through the clear floor to Vellern's surface far below. The place was empty. That was bad, because he was here to find someone. Even as he thought that, Taro realised he was dreaming. And as soon as he did, he was no longer alone.

Nual sat at the table where they'd once shared a meal.

He took a careful step, knowing the floor would be slippery under his rag-bound feet. 'Is it really you?' he asked.

Nual stood up. 'It is. I am in your dream.'

He felt himself smile. 'I knew it had to be you before, but that were just your voice, and the sense of you. This is ... so real. It's amazing.'

They'd closed the distance now, though he wasn't sure how. He reached for her. She returned the embrace. Suddenly the dream went off in a whole new direction; he was desperate to kiss her, to feel her touch on him.

'We can't—' she breathed.

He made himself pull back. 'We've been here before, ain't we?' he said wryly.

'Not exactly. But— Listen, I don't know how long I have, and I must keep control.' Nual stroked his shoulders lightly where she held him. 'But it is so good to see you, and know you are safe! Are you hurt?'

'I'm fine now. Jarek rescued me. But where're you?' An odd question, when all his senses told him she was here with him.

'I'm not sure. Still in-system, on a Sidhe ship; I think it might be parked up somewhere. The ship is waiting for the consorts; as they haven't arrived I think it's safe to assume that Serenein has not fallen.'

'I'll let Jarek know that. We're still in—'

'No!' Nual grasped him hard. 'Please, you must not tell me anything!'

'Why not?'

She looked away for a moment. 'Because although I have managed to keep myself safe so far, my captors have summoned a member of the Court – a very powerful Sidhe. She might be here within a day, and she will almost certainly be strong enough to find out everything I know. Please, tell me nothing about where you are, or what your plans are!'

The true horror of the situation began to dawn on Taro. 'Shit, Nual, that's— We gotta get you out of there before she arrives! There must be some way—'

'You'll die. There are dozens of Sidhe here, maybe more.'

'I can't just leave you!'

'I'll prolong this contact for as long as possible. And I will try to find you again, if I can. Our sleep-cycles are different – for me it is late morning now. I can try for contact any time I am alone and not in deep sleep, but I do not think I can access your waking mind – while your consciousness is processing the real world it leaves me no opening. Ideally you need to be somewhere between sleep and waking – in a waking dream.'

'There's drugs in the med-bay, we used them for the transit; when I wake up I'll take some of those. That way I'll be ready for you. But we've got a while now, ain't we? A while together—'

'I'm not sure we do.' Her expression was becoming oddly vacant.

'What is it? What's wrong?'

He could feel her growing insubstantial in his embrace. Her voice suddenly seemed to come from far away. 'Something is happening, back at the ship. I have to—'

'Don't go—!' he cried.

His arms closed on mist. She was gone.

CHAPTER THIRTY-SEVEN

Marua's databreakers finished decrypting Tawhira-*ngai*'s files a couple of hours after Pershalek had gone down to the encoding lab. The data confirmed his claim that the Angel had been kidnapped because they believed that Angel implants included zepgen generators. Their tests had supported this hypothesis, even if there was no way to get the valuable technology out without destroying it.

And Marua, friend to the Sidhe, hadn't even known that zepgen really existed.

This afternoon the *Ariki-Marae* had issued a motion of censure against her *ngai,* formally reprimanding them for their actions against Tawhira-*ngai*. She had stretched the rules of honourable engagement to their limits, and the combined representatives of the other *ngais* had declared her actions *tapu*. Considerable fines were levied, and less tangible gestures of reconciliation would be required in order for honour to be restored. She would be paying the price for recruiting Pershalek for months, if not years. The consensus amongst *ngai*-watchers – and, she suspected, some of her own people – was that she'd made an uncharacteristically bad judgement call.

Finally, as she was sitting down to the evening meal, a time of the day she made an effort to share with her family whenever she could, good news arrived, from an aide in Stonetown who managed her less formal contacts there. It was nearly midnight in the city, but she'd impressed upon her man the importance of getting full and accurate information on 'Sais' as quickly as possible. All they'd had to go on was a picture taken by a hidden camera in the aircar on the run against Tawhira-*ngai* and the high-level trace on his original com-call which confirmed that it had originated from Stonetown, but the aide had done well, following all relevant leads before bringing what he had to her. He had discovered 'Sais' was actually a freetrader called Jarek Reen, and he was still in Stonetown, on his ship in the starport. Given he was an offworlder and not a frequent visitor to Kama Nui, he would likely have only a few options for the dissemination of his blackmail material, and that meant the 'certain independent party' allegedly in possession of the incriminating data-package had to be one of the standard data-services.

With her *ngai*'s power and influence, it should not take long to find out which one.

The cobbled streets of the City of Light were hot and foetid. Overhead, the perfection of the summer sky was marred by a twist of dark smoke from the pyres. Trash and sewerage clogged the open drains, and somewhere nearby a street-seller was crying his wares, fresh incense to honour the Mothers. He knew he shouldn't be here – he was an impostor – but he'd decided to take the easy way out and try to fit in. He'd be fine, provided he never looked up. When he saw the boy standing with the painted strumpets at the side of the street he knew it was Taro, and that this was someone from his other life, the one he'd left behind. As though reminding him of that, he heard an artificial-sounding chirp. He ignored it. It'd been too long since he'd got laid, and now the opportunity presented itself, he wasn't going to be distracted. His wife understood him, she wouldn't mind if he just—

Jarek opened his eyes. The chirping continued. It was his com. The dream fled and he fumbled for the device. He blinked until the caller-ID and time came into focus. The time was 01:33. The caller's name meant nothing, and the message-tag said the call came from cargo management. *What the hell?*

But he could hardly pretend not to be at home to a member of spaceport staff. He and Taro had been on the ship all day, fees and duties all paid, prepped and ready to leave. On Taro's insistence they were waiting until the next morning, in case there was any more news on Nual's whereabouts. Taro had been in a right state all day, and though Jarek understood how love made you crazy at that age, he had begun to lose patience with him. He was still digesting the fact that Taro and Nual had been working for an old Sidhe male on Vellern.

He accepted the call and rasped, 'Yes? What is it?'

A vaguely familiar face appeared on the screen. 'Hey there – sorry to disturb you so late,' said the woman, 'but I thought you ought to know that someone's been asking about you.'

He recognised her now, though the last time he'd seen her she'd been wearing a flower in her hair, not a smart uniform cap on her head, and the name she'd been using had been a shortened version of her full ID. 'Oh, hi, Lali – er, what was that you said?' Despite his feigned confusion, he was wide awake now.

'Someone was asking after you. *Ngai* security I think, though they weren't wearing uniforms. They had a picture, but no name. They wanted to know if anyone had seen you.'

'What did you tell them?'

She looked faintly offended. 'Nothing – what d'you think?'

'Thank you, Lali, I really appreciate that. Um, when was this?'

She looked embarrassed. 'Actually it was earlier this evening. Sorry, I had to wait until I had a break before I called you.'

'No, no, that's fine – it was good of you to call.' It wasn't fine, but presumably Ruanuku-*ngai* – he assumed it was them – either hadn't managed to ID him yet, or else they weren't in a hurry to apprehend him. 'I don't suppose you know if they spoke to anyone else?'

'They spoke to everyone, so the chances are someone talked.' She looked sheepish. 'I told you as soon as I could.'

'I understand. And I'm really grateful. I owe you dinner for this,' he added, feeling a twinge of guilt at the incredibly high odds that he'd ever be in a position to buy it.

'Great,' she said, 'it's a date.'

Jarek's guilt deepened; even if they did meet up again he was going to end up disappointing her. 'Yeah, absolutely. Listen, better go – speak to you later, right? And thanks for the heads-up.'

Jarek ran through the rec-room and up to the bridge. He could use a caf, but that would have to wait. He threw himself onto the couch and commed traffic control to request clearance to depart.

With everything in order and ready to go, he'd been hoping for an automated response and he stifled a curse when an unfamiliar image appeared over the holo-plate. The uniformed young man wasn't one of his drinking buddies. 'I'm afraid that we are unable to grant departure permission to you at this time,' he said, a little nervously.

Jarek's heart started to beat faster. 'Why not? I've already registered my state of readiness. Is there a problem I don't know about out there?' His external cameras showed nothing amiss outside.

'Oh, there's nothing to worry about,' continued the official, his tone carefully light. 'Just a few minor irregularities that customs might need to discuss.'

'What sort of irregularities?' asked Jarek, equally carefully.

The man shrugged, looking uncomfortable. 'You'd have to ask them,' he said.

'All right, put me through please.'

'They're— Uh, the office is closed until oh-six-hundred. Sorry.'

Jarek leaned forward. 'I'm on a schedule here. Now, either there's a problem – in which case I'll do everything in my power to help the authorities so I can be on my way – or there isn't, in which case I'd like to leave now please.' Though the cause was different this time, the situation wasn't unfamiliar. He'd had to call officials' bluffs before; sometimes because they were operating in a legal grey area, more often because he was. He knew how it went. He hoped this wasn't a problem that would require financial lubrication. The docking fees had eaten up the last of his funds.

'I have instructions …' started the official.

'From?' asked Jarek, though he had a very good idea whom. 'Because, as I say, I'm happy to comply with local laws, but I'm within my rights to know what's going on.' Jarek thought it unlikely that customs really did want to check him over: he'd sold two-thirds of his cargo through a respectable broker and though leaving without trying to offload the rest was irregular, it certainly wasn't against any law. 'Detaining me without due cause would be an illegal act under pan-human law – I can't quote the exact Treaty and Clause offhand, but we could always look it up – and would make you extremely unpopular with the Freetraders' Alliance.'

'I'll … I just need to check with my supervisor,' said the young man, looking harassed.

Jarek forced himself to breathe evenly as he prepped the ship. A port like this was unlikely to have any offensive capabilities, so they couldn't physically stop him leaving. The question was: did they want him enough to send someone after him? Though the *Judas Kiss* – now the *Heart of Glass* – was fast as tradebirds went, it was unlikely to be able to outrun an in-system interceptor.

Before he committed himself to anything drastic, he'd wait for the official to call him back.

It took six minutes and fifteen seconds. Jarek knew, because he watched the digits tick over on his com. It stopped him thinking too closely about what he was doing. *Running away. Abandoning his friend to her fate.* Taro would be devastated when he found out. But if Ruanuku-*ngai* were onto them, what choice did they have?

The chirp of the com made him jump.

The young man reappeared, looking slightly flushed. 'There appears to have been a slight mix-up,' he said. 'You're free to go, but make sure you keep a channel open in case we need to contact you again.'

Jarek tried not to let his relief show. 'I always do.'

It was a rush as intense as any she had felt before – at least, until the day she and Taro had made love – but it was far from pleasant. Afterwards Nual likened it to being dragged screaming through the void at the speed of light – which in some ways was exactly what it was.

She was being attacked. *No doubt of that*, she thought as Taro's

273

dream dissolved into formless speed and panic. Someone was trying to enter her mind while she was in trance.

The initial thrust met her shields …

Pain!

The probe was sharp and focused, a needle piercing down through her consciousness, seeking the answers she had so far withheld. And it had the power of the unity behind it.

She deflected the probe – but barely.

She became vaguely aware of her surroundings: she was lying on her back and there was an unpleasant pressure on her shoulders. She shut off all physical sensation and concentrated on fighting the invading presences.

They changed tack, spreading and diversifying their assault to batter at her shields.

Even as she bent all her strength to repelling the assault she realised they would not be trying this unless they truly believed she was free of any taint. What a small mercy that would be, if they broke her now.

What if she were to let them in? The pain would stop, and they might still forgive her, let her back into their world—

She recognised this second, more insidious attack for what it was. They were working on two levels now, trying to undermine her deepest barriers while infecting her surface thoughts with a creeping empathic malaise. Whoever was spearheading the more subtle attack had already got some way into her head.

Clearly, and without letting her deep shields waver, she thought back at them: <*Go fuck yourselves.*>

The surface presence withdrew, but the main assault continued. She had lost all bodily awareness now, all sense of time, almost all sense of self. She was living defiance and keeping them out was all that mattered.

It became a test of endurance. She was just one individual. They were the unity. In the end, her shields would crumble, and they would win.

And when they did, it wouldn't be just her who was doomed.

She had to fight back, for Taro's sake. If they broke through they would find out about him; perhaps they could even exploit her link with him and she couldn't risk that. It would be better to emerge from behind her defences and go out fighting. She might even do some damage herself before they destroyed her. But she was exhausted, drained both mentally and physically, and she had nothing left to fight back with.

Except she did. She had something they lacked. Her bond with Taro was a type of unity they could never know, built on complete trust, and the willingness to put the life of another above the self. She had been afraid that love would make her weak. Perhaps it'd had the opposite effect.

With some effort, she reconnected with her body. The sensation in her shoulders was agonising, a weight grinding her bones into the bed, and as she began to block the worst of the pain she started to realise what must have happened. Lyrian had come in and, seeing her in a trance, she had decided to take advantage of Nual's vulnerable state.

Time to turn the tables – and if she failed, then better to end it quickly and cleanly than wait to die and risk betraying her friends. She drew on the strength that her secret gave her. Then she opened her eyes, focusing all her remaining willpower into a counter-attack.

Lyrian had been crouched over her. Nual felt her strike connect with the other Sidhe. Lyrian shrieked and fell back. The pressure in Nual's head was released at the same time as that on her shoulders: as she'd thought, Lyrian had been the focus for the assault and without her making the connection, the unity lost their hold.

Nual drew a deep, ragged breath. She had defeated them – for now.

From across the room Lyrian growled, 'You couldn't blame us for trying, could you?'

Actually, she could. Nual struggled into a sitting position, but said nothing. Any illusion of trust or friendship was gone. There was no more use for words between them.

Lyrian had composed herself again, though she stayed on the far side of the room. 'I guess that's that then. Well, no matter.

What I originally came to tell you was that our visitor is ahead of schedule: she'll be here in a few hours.' She walked to the door, then turned and added, 'I may have failed. She won't.'

CHAPTER THIRTY-EIGHT

Marua stood on her balcony, staring out into the dark. She wished she could see the view: the verdant slopes of the caldera, the occasional glimpses of her people walking on the leafy paths and tracks between home and work and meetings with friends. She needed the perspective brought by overseeing such quiet order, the certainty and comfort of knowing that this was her kingdom, these her people, and that all was well with the world.

Self-doubt was not in Marua's nature, but thanks to her recent experiences, she was having some trouble believing she was entirely mistress of her own destiny.

She did not hate the Sidhe. They were expedient, ruthless and capricious, but she truly believed that their control of humanity's destiny – however far it extended – was motivated by the same desires that had led them to elevate humans to the stars in the first place. They knew how selfish and short-sighted people were, how close humanity had come to wiping itself out in the past. Marua's part in the Sidhe's schemes helped ensure that humans had continued access to interstellar travel, a birthright the Sidhe themselves had bought for everyone.

No, to hate them was unfair, pointless, and, in her position, extremely dangerous.

She was, however, angry with them, a deep seething resentment that had come together over the last few days. The power Marua exercised over her people was tempered with understanding, but the Sidhe cared only for results, not reasons. Lyrian had treated her like an incompetent child, as though such patronising disdain would actually solve the complex problems Marua was trying to deal with in order to please her associates – and she had been trying to please the Sidhe.

Not giving them reason to doubt her was one thing, but she strongly suspected that whilst in their presence she had been subject to their manipulation. Looking back on her almost fawning eagerness to impress her visitors, Marua was increasingly convinced she had been a victim of their persuasive powers, a far subtler coercion than that exerted by the renegade Angel, but there all the same.

And then there was the matter of zepgen. If the technology was available, why not give it to her? Some believed that zepgen had been developed by the old Sidhe males, who were thought to be long dead. But then, most people assumed the same was true of the females.

The more she considered it, the more one-sided her relationship with the *hine-maku* appeared.

She had to give them everything they demanded … But if they didn't know about something, they could hardly ask her for it, could they?

Which was why she had no intention of telling them about Jarek Reen.

She had considered arranging a fatal but untraceable accident to remove the threat posed by Sirrah Reen once his blackmail material was safely neutralised. In the end, she had decided that the logistical difficulties and risk of possible comeback were too great.

She hadn't counted on him trying to leave before she'd got her hands on the incriminating data. The call from her contact in traffic control forced her hand: should they let him go, or did she have a valid reason to detain him? Her *ngai*'s influence allowed her to request that arrivals be reported and departures delayed, but she was already sailing close to the wind after the public censure for the débâcle with Tawhira-*ngai*. She had thought for a moment, then told the starport to let the freetrader take off.

She had reluctantly despatched an interceptor to shadow his ship at a distance, waiting for word that the blackmail threat had been dealt with. The destruction of a ship out near the beacon might not immediately be attributed to her *ngai*, but when it was, further condemnation would follow. She dreaded the inevitable lengthy enquiry and eventual allocation of blame.

She told herself that to let him live was careless and unwise. That didn't make killing him a course of action she was comfortable with.

Half an hour after Reen's ship took off, her Stonetown agent commed to tell her he'd tracked down the data-agency the free-trader had used, but there was no need for further action: Jarek Reen had already cancelled his contract and the agency had wiped the data.

He had acted with an honour her so-called allies never displayed.

Marua gave silent thanks to the Lord of the Sea that she had continued to prevaricate. Sirrah Reen's choice to delete the data vindicated her decision to follow her heart, not her head.

She recalled the interceptor.

Of course, honourable though he was, the danger posed by what he knew had not diminished. Leaning on the railing, breathing the sweet-scented night air, she suddenly saw that there was another way to deal with this problem, one which kept her honour intact and paid back Jarek Reen for his actions – both the good and the bad. It was risky: if the Sidhe read Reen's mind they'd know that Marua hadn't been entirely honest with them – but she got the impression that if it came to it, he was not the sort of man to let himself get taken alive.

She would give him what he'd said he wanted. And if it got him killed, then so be it.

Nual decided there was just one option left open to her. It was not something Sidhe did, though she had already come close to it once. That time, she had been confused, acting foolishly. Now it was the only logical choice.

Before reaching her conclusion she considered whether the bond with Taro that had given her the power to break Lyrian's hold could also save her from the Court. But Lyrian had managed to wrench her away from Taro; a member of the Court could easily do the same.

What if she went in deeper? The area of Taro's psyche where they had shared the dream was comparatively shallow – subconscious, but not primal. She had entered the depths of his soul, both back in the Heart of the City on Vellern and more recently, when they made love. Could she do so again? Could she hide herself there?

But if the Court interrogator was strong enough to follow that link, she would get access not just to Nual's mind, but to Taro's too, and she couldn't risk that deepest of betrayals. And now she knew the visitor was arriving ahead of schedule, she dared not attempt any further contact with Taro, in case the Court representative found her in a trance. She could not even risk a final goodbye.

She had already lost her lover and her freedom. A mental reset would be the best she could hope for once the Sidhe had what they wanted from her, leaving her reprogrammed and restrained, little more than a mute. Given the risk of after-effects from her brush with darkness, not to mention the crimes she had committed against her people, they were far more likely to kill her once they had no more use for her. Taking her own life would give her more control. It would make the inevitable end less painful – and it was the only way to guarantee the safety of those she cared for.

She sat back against the wall, breathing hard.

Slowly, deliberately, she shut off her body's reactions to the realisation of what she was about to do.

Even so, when she put her palm on her solar plexus she could feel the banging of her heart. She turned her wrist, so the heel of her right hand was pressed against her left breast. She would only get one chance; she needed to make sure that when the blade emerged from her forearm, it would pierce her heart cleanly, killing her at once.

The sweat on her palms threatened to make her hand slip on her bare skin. She wiped her hand on the bed. Somewhere deep inside a small voice was screaming, demanding to know how she could even consider this insane act.

She placed her hand back in what she hoped was the correct position and closed her eyes. She let herself think of Taro: a snapshot of his face, laughing. It was only right that the last image in her mind should be of him.

Then she flexed her hand.

Someone with a more finely honed sense of paranoia might've been convinced that the sensor blip was a pursuing ship. Jarek had to allow for that possibility, but unless and until it tried to close in on him he'd do his best not to fret about it.

He still wished he'd spotted the ship before he'd trashed his blackmail file. He'd been in two minds about deleting it, but once he left the local comnet he wouldn't be transmitting the regular signal that stopped the data going public; if he didn't get rid of it now, he'd be leaving a ticking time-bomb behind him. He'd been tempted: let the *ngai* dealing with the Sidhe pay the price for that collaboration … But if he allowed the dirt on Ruanuku to go public, he'd be risking planet-wide corporate chaos in order to punish a few execs. More importantly, he'd be tipping his hand to the Sidhe.

He found himself watching the other ship almost obsessively. When it changed course and headed back to Kama Nui he sat back in his couch and let out a long, slow breath.

With his own ship safely underway and no immediate threats to enliven the dull journey out to the beacon, what he should really do now was wake up Taro. The boy'd been dreaming earlier, but the last time Jarek checked he was deeply asleep. If he left him, he was only putting off the inevitable. Taro wasn't going to be open to reason, regardless of when Jarek woke him, but as it was currently the middle of the night, hopefully he'd be dazed enough that he wouldn't try to disembowel Jarek when he found out they'd left Nual behind. He might as well get it over with.

He still found a good ten minutes of not-entirely-necessary duties on the bridge, but finally he sighed and headed for the ladder.

He'd just stepped off the bottom rung when his com chirped. The message was from the Stonetown data-agents who had been sent their final payment and had, as far as he knew, done what he'd asked and destroyed the packet. He'd never expected to hear from them again.

And they, he suddenly remembered, only had the number of the locally bought com he'd used in his dealings with Ruanuku-*ngai*, which was useless now he was outside the local comnet. This message had been sent direct to his ship.

He tapped the screen. A single line of capitalised text appeared:

LOOK FOR HER ON THE DARK SIDE OF RANGUI-ITI

Rangui-iti: Kama Nui's smallest moon. As for who they meant by 'her' ... it had to be Nual.

Who the hell would send him such a message?

Someone who claimed to know where she was and who had his ship ID. Could it be the Sidhe? He sat down at the base of the ladder, simultaneously hot and cold.

But if they were onto him surely they'd have made their move back in Stonetown, most likely drawn him out of his ship with the promise of a lead, then quietly nabbed him ... unless they hadn't traced him until after he'd taken off. In which case they'd either blow him out of the sky or trail him until they could lure him somewhere quiet and carry on where they left off reaming his brain. Somewhere like the dark side of a moon ...

He wasn't going to be caught out again, not like at Serenein. But this wasn't their style. If they weren't just going to trash him outright, they'd want to encounter him face-to-face, not out in space, when he was safely ensconced on his ship and immune to their powers.

But if the Sidhe hadn't sent the message, then who had?

He checked the full message-tag on the file and was unsurprised to find nothing beyond the agency's ID. Whoever sent this had the power to bypass normal procedures. And that left only one possibility.

But why would Marua Ruanuku give him this information?

Whoever the message came from, he needed to decide what to do about it quickly. He scooted back up the bridge ladder and called up data on the relative positions of Kama Nui's three moons. If he was going to act on the tip-off he needed to cut his speed and turn around. His hand hovered over the controls.

If he didn't follow up this lead, he'd always wonder what had happened to Nual. And Taro would never forgive him.

And if he did do this, then there was a strong possibility he'd end up encountering *them* again, and the nightmares that haunted his sleep would take over his waking world once more.

CHAPTER THIRTY-NINE

Nual felt the wave of tension go through her, an unconscious reaction to the command she was giving.

A command her body was refusing to obey. Her blade remained sheathed inside her arm.

She moved her hand away from her breast and tried again, in case the implants would not work when they might harm their owner.

Still nothing.

So the impulses that activated her implanted weapons were being blocked. Some sort of nullifying field? She shook her head, trying to clear it. It was getting very stuffy in here. She needed to lie down to consider this further.

She was unconscious for no more than a couple of minutes – the sweat that filmed her body had only just begun to dry and chill – but she came to feeling relaxed and lethargic. After a while she managed to think clearly enough to work out that she had been sedated. Something must have been pumped into the room when those watching realised what she was trying to do. She stayed where she was until her head cleared. Then she pointed her toes, a motion that should have caused her to float off the bed. Nothing happened.

None of her implants were working. And any attempt to harm herself resulted in sedation. Her less physical weapons would be no use either; though she could kill humans with a thought her unconscious defences would block any attempts to stop her own heart.

Her choices had not just narrowed: they had disappeared. Even the option of taking her own life was no longer available to her. Her vision blurred with sudden tears. She blinked them back and sat up. She would not give her captors the satisfaction of knowing how close to breaking she was.

She pulled her legs up to her chin and hugged her knees, concentrating on the immediate physical reality of her body, the small, hopeless bundle of misery she had been reduced to. Forcing herself to remain outwardly calm, she sat motionless on the bed and fought the rising tide of despair.

Taro's attempt to hold onto his dream after Nual disappeared quickly descended into absurdity. Mo came into the bar, chatting up Kise, who was juggling coco-nuts with a manic grin on her face. The room was suddenly full, only it wasn't the Corpse any more, it was one of those open-sided Kama Nui bars, bustling and loud. Taro looked up, trying to focus, to somehow get back to Nual. His gaze was returned by the jewel-like eyes of hundreds of tiny lizards sitting in the rafters. He looked down again as a local girl, dressed in a shimmer-cloak that kept swinging open to reveal naked brown flesh, sashayed up to him. He wanted to refuse her, to keep trying to contact Nual. Instead he heard himself agreeing to go outside with her.

Even as they fell together onto the soft, yielding sand and lust drove everything else from his mind, he cursed himself for his inability to control his own dreams.

His mental frustration only increased after the inevitable yet unsatisfying conclusion of his imaginary grind with the dream-girl as his sleeping imagination took him on through more weird situations and strange half-memories. He was enduring a normal night of dreams, watching them unfold from a distance, unable to act.

Eventually he slept too deeply to dream.

He felt himself twitch, and someone spoke, telling him not to panic. He wasn't panicking, he was— Where was he? He opened his eyes. He was in the spare cabin on Jarek's ship. His body felt heavy, his mind slow. Jarek was sitting on the bed next to him. Though Taro had dimmed the lights before he slept, they were on full now. Something else had changed too, though he couldn't quite work out what it was.

'I'm sorry,' said Jarek. 'It's still early, but you didn't look like you were dreaming any more, so I thought it was safe to wake you.'

'Aye … she's gone.' Suddenly he realised what had changed. The cabin was filled with a gentle hum, felt as much as heard. He struggled to sit up. 'Wait, are we—? Where are we?'

'Just over two hours out from Kama Nui; the actual co-ordinates wouldn't mean much t—'

'No! You said we could wait longer, in case you found any more leads!'

'Actually,' said Jarek, 'one might have found us.'

'What d'you mean?' Taro was wide awake now, though his head ached and his guts felt loose.

Jarek told him about the message he'd received, and after a moment Taro said, 'So that's where we're going? Rangui-iti?'

'I've stopped accelerating, but I haven't programmed the course change yet. For a start we don't have any way of knowing for sure the message refers to Nual—'

'Yes, we do! She said the ship she's on ain't moving; that fits with it being parked up on this moon, don't it? That's where she is, I'm sure of it.'

'You may be right. I wonder what they're doing there.'

Taro struggled to remember the other details of the shared dream. 'She said … she said the ship she's on is waiting for the consorts.'

'Aha! And they haven't arrived. Thank God for that.' Jarek ran a hand through his hair, looking relieved.

'I guess your friends at Serenein held the Sidhe off.'

'Yes – at least for now. Did she tell you anything else?'

'She …' Crap. If he told Jarek about the visitor from the Sidhe Court it might scare him off.

'She what, Taro?'

'She ...' Lying had always been easy in the past, the safest option. But not to his friends, not now. 'She ain't given anything away so far, but she – she thinks there's a more powerful Sidhe on her way, someone from the Court. She's due to arrive in the next day. We gotta get Nual out before she gets there.'

'In principle I agree, but I'm not sure what we can do.'

'We have to go to Rangui-iti, to see what's there!'

'You make it sound so simple. This might be a trap.'

'If they know we're here we're fucked anyway. Jarek, we gotta look!'

'You're right. I just wanted you to insist we followed up the tip-off so I could say I told you so when it goes wrong!' He grinned wryly.

'I knew you wouldn't leave her behind.' Taro tried to smile back.

'Your faith is heartening. But if anything takes off from that moon, or if I spot any other ships heading our way, then we bug out.' He stood up. 'Okay, I need to get back to the bridge. I've got some course changes to programme.'

'Before you go ... Nual reckons she might be able to make contact with me again later. Only she can't do it when I'm awake. I need to be sort-of half-asleep.' He grinned. 'A bit stoned would be perfect.'

Jarek raised an eyebrow, then nodded. 'If that's what you reckon you need to do, I can sort something.'

Taro decided against telling Jarek that Nual had told them not to come after her. That wasn't lying – after all, he hadn't actually asked.

Leaving aside the more obvious impossible wishes, like her freedom, or a last kiss with Taro, the thing Nual wanted more than anything else was a way to tell the time.

After a while the hopelessness had settled into numb acceptance and now she just wanted it over with. Unconsciousness was still an option, for it would pass the time and temporarily impede her interrogation, but she wanted to be awake to look her enemy in the eye.

When the door finally opened, she was beginning to doze off. She jerked upright to see a Sidhe she had never met before.

Except …

Except this was not a Sidhe – in appearance, yes, but every unseen signal was screaming that the figure standing in the doorway was something else: a wrongness, an abomination. Despite the terrible dissonance between sight and sense, Nual recognised what she was seeing. She knew this all too well.

A member of the Court might violate her mind. This thing could violate her soul.

It used the possessed Sidhe's body to step into the room, and spoke: 'Sister, come to us, join us …'

She tried a brief mental stab, knowing the act futile even before the attack was deflected.

It looked offended.

Fighting back would be futile; no amount of Sidhe talent would prevail against this adversary; on the contrary: the more powerful the mind, the more this *thing*, this creature would desire it. She would resist, but in the end, she would fail, as her sisters had failed, one by one, seven years ago. She had to get away, to hide her soul while she still could.

Her limp body fell back on the bed while her panicking consciousness fled, seeking for refuge in the only place left.

Taro was seeing the funny side. Who'd have thought that their master plan relied on him being stoned? He was a little hazy on exactly what the actual plan was, but that was probably because he was stoned.

He'd fired up a mindlessly pretty game and now he lounged on the couch, occasionally waving his hands to encourage the visuals along. He had an idea he'd been here for some time. Not that the stuff he'd taken was wearing off. In fact, he was just getting to the bit where everything was funny. He started to giggle, and it felt good, so he did it some more—

And stopped as something slammed into his mind: a pure wave of mental energy; and riding it like someone riding a wave – Nual. His eyes rolled up and he was in his head, with her, sober and alert.

He began to express love, relief, a desire to help. She was distracted, and terrified.

He asked why. He could sense her barely checked terror.

<*The thing that infected my people when Jarek found me: it's here!*>

<*Here?*> Taro was instantly scared, though fear was an oddly distant sensation without a body.

<*On the Sidhe ship. Hide me, please!*>

Of course he would. As their joint awareness intensified into an unbearable brightness he just had time for one thought of his own – Ah yes, *this* feeling – before he was – *they were* – beyond thought.

CHAPTER FORTY

They were in luck: Rangui-iti was currently on the beaconwards side of Kama Nui, so Jarek wouldn't have to go back past the homeworld in order to reach its moon. He still decided on a wide-angle turnaround; slower than a straight brake-and-turn manoeuvre but if he widened the arc enough he could come at Rangui-iti from sunwards, hiding their approach from anything on the moon's dark side.

Though Jarek could've trusted the comp to plot their course, he used enough manual input to stop himself thinking too closely about what they were doing. Even with the bulk of the moon acting as cover, he took care on the final approach, braking slow and steady, deploying the ship's minimal countermeasures and cutting active sensors. Grav-sensors were passive and relatively long-range – watchers rather than bouncers, as his old partner used to say – but they weren't picking up anything odd as he closed on the barren chunk of rock. Neither did the high-level passive EM-sweep he initiated when he got a little closer. He might be drawing a blank because the ship really was on the dark side of the moon, or because it was on the light side but powered down and using the sun's glare to mask its signature, or because there was no ship.

If the target was on the far side and actively scanning, it would probably pick him up as soon as his trajectory brought him round, but he wasn't doing anything wrong, even if his stealthy approach might be considered suspicious. Assuming the Sidhe didn't have his new ship ID, he was confident of his ability to bluff it out if they decided to hail him. And if they did have his ID, he was probably fucked anyway.

He crossed the terminator, and the empty landscape far below him went from burning light to the true darkness of space. If a ship down there had its grav-drives primed for a fast getaway, he'd soon pick it up ... but he wasn't getting anything yet.

He'd just decided to ramp up the thermal imaging for a more detailed scan when the comp pinged. It'd spotted a heat-emitting anomaly in the otherwise freezing landscape, a faint point-source tucked under the rim of a shallow crater.

He changed course to come in a little lower over the anomaly and cut his speed again. Then he focused his full EM suite on the area, dialled up to maximum sensitivity. Yes, that was definitely a ship. It looked like a mid-sized starliner: a bigger vessel than he'd expected. It was unlikely to be armed, unless of course it had been modified. There was not a light showing and, according to its thermal signature, it was running on minimal. That was fine: if it was powered-down then it wouldn't be coming after them in a hurry.

His sensors hadn't picked up any active scans, so he decided to risk a closer look. Though he had no idea whether he needed to, he tried to keep his mind focused on his own ship's systems and project only a faint curiosity about the ship below him. He'd already come up with a cover story: if questioned, he'd say he was out here teaching his new partner how to fly around gravitational masses away from large, inhabited ones like Kama Nui itself. Traffic control might ask why he'd decided to fly partway to the beacon before coming back to the moon, but so far they hadn't. And it wasn't traffic control he was worried about.

The ship remained unchanged, and the com remained silent.

Then he spotted the smaller ship docked at the aft airlock, the sleek arrow-like shape of a corvette, the smallest class of shiftship. It could just be an expensive lifeboat ... or it could be the ship that had transported the Court representative. But she wasn't due for hours yet ... Then again, he couldn't be sure how accurate that estimate was, given it had been conveyed through a dream from someone being held captive by practised deceivers.

He'd already set up a programme of easy and non-threatening manoeuvres for his ship to execute in the moon's vicinity, the kind of stuff a new pilot would use for practise. He initiated the auto-pilot and went to check on Taro.

He found the boy lying on the couch, completely out of it. Jarek bent down for a closer look. He'd assumed Taro would be either dozing under the influence of the euphoric/sedative mix he'd given him, or else in dream contact with Nual, but instead, he appeared to be totally comatose. Jarek, a little frightened, put a hand to his neck to check for a pulse. He was deeply relieved to feel it there, weak but unmistakable. Something about the way he was lying there implied a stillness that went beyond sleep.

Though he wasn't sure what *was* meant to happen, he suspected something wasn't right.

He called out, 'Taro?' and when there was no response he shook him gently.

Taro's body lolled like a corpse, threatening to roll off the couch. Jarek was certain this was wrong. He shook harder.

Taro's eyes sprang open and he drew a sudden, startled breath.

Rushing through the void—

This time Nual knew what she was likely to face when she returned to her body. She was aware that the presence had tried to broach her shields, but despite her initial fears, it had not penetrated far. Most likely it had been looking for a part of her that hadn't been there. Something which, because her unity with Taro had been disrupted, now was.

She opened her eyes.

Everything was skewed; she had fallen onto her side. It was also darker in here than she remembered. Hurriedly she pushed herself upright. The not-Sidhe was standing just as it had been, with its head tilted to look at her. As it adjusted its stance Nual thought how its body-language spoke of concentration, of power held in check, and at the same time of a certain inability to interact normally. It was like some monstrous yet frighteningly potent child. She did not recognise this individual; if she was one of the Sidhe who had originally been infected on the mothership Nual would have expected to know her by sight, even if the mind inhabiting the body was alien.

'What is puzzling you?' asked the creature, sounding genuinely curious. 'Ask, please. Or let down your shields a little, if you prefer.'

'I do not prefer,' said Nual with a shudder. 'Can you ... you could read me if I let you, then?' Despite her revulsion, she knew she must try for whatever information this thing was willing to provide.

The being nodded rapidly. 'Yes, indeed. We retain some of the abilities we had before we became as we are now, though they are ... imperfect. Hard to balance and deploy. But we do remember who we were.' Again, the smile, this time cold and emphatic. 'Only now we are – I am – so much more. The unity is a mere murmur in the dark compared to this!'

Nual felt as though she was staring into an abyss. Now she knew how humans must feel when faced with Sidhe.

When she said nothing the other continued, 'Let me show you our true potential. Watch.' It reached a splayed hand towards the chair. At first nothing happened. Then the back of the chair began to change. Nual's initial impression was that it was disappearing, being eaten away by the illusion of invisibility. But she knew in her soul that this was no illusion. Matter was being *unmade*.

She tried not to react. Though males could move matter into and out of shiftspace, this was something else, something no Sidhe could do.

'We are ... everything,' whispered the creature. 'We see, we interact, we understand ... in ways you cannot comprehend – unless you join us.'

'No!' she said. 'You are ... wrongness incarnate. You should not be.' Simply being in the thing's presence was making her nauseous.

'But we are! And we can only get stronger. Most Sidhe are too weak to survive the change. Those that do become avatars of a power greater than anything we have dreamed of before. You are strong enough to wield that power.'

'I would rather die.'

The avatar looked disappointed; its face was at once open and wooden, the expression almost a caricature. 'That would be a great shame. We particularly wish for *you* to join us.' Now the cold smile again. 'After all, you brought us into existence.'

Bile rose in Nual's throat. *It knew her.* Somehow – perhaps from reading the mind of Lyrian, or maybe another Sidhe here, perhaps because it shared information between the physical bodies it used – it knew her. It knew what she had done.

'Yes!' it hissed. 'You remember now, don't you?'

And she did, though she tried not to. She remembered how she had been expelled from the unity during transit, left alone in the dark to face the insane mind at the heart of the mothership. But instead she had dared to reach out and away, into the void. And there she had made contact with a presence unlike any other she had sensed before.

'You were our conduit, our catalyst – our key,' whispered the presence.

Its initial touch had paralysed her; even as she felt the unknown energy flow through her, she had been left passive and yielding, unable to do more than observe.

'You …' Nual swallowed, then continued, 'You let me be once you had used me.' When it was gone and she was alone she had barricaded herself in her cell and hid in the dark. She had no idea how long she had waited there to die, or to be subsumed. 'Why did you not try to … infect … me then?'

'Because we wished you to be accessible for later use.'

And it *had* tried to use her again. After some indeterminate time, during which the other Sidhe were fighting and dying outside her cell, the ship had gone into the shift and she'd felt the vile touch return, forcing her to reach out in shiftspace again, trying to use her to bring more of itself through. But she'd wriggled free from the thing's grasp, and in doing so had made an unexpected contact: Jarek. Because he was a mere human, the entity had not registered his presence, either then or later on the mothership. 'It didn't work, did it?' she said shakily. 'And you ended up destroying the transit-kernel as we left shiftspace.'

'Yes, that was unfortunate.' The thing gave a rictus grin. 'And your unwillingness made you useless as a gateway after the initial contact. But we learn by our mistakes. We evolve.'

'You can evolve without me, then,' said Nual.

'We can, that is true. We came to this place because we knew there would be a large number of Sidhe here: more potential recruits. But now we have found you, and we wish to offer you the chance to—'

'You can't make me join you.' Nual had had enough. If it *could* force her, she was sure their conversation would have been a lot shorter.

'We can try, and eventually we will either succeed, or we will destroy you. We would rather you joined us freely. We do not wish to force you.' It spoke almost tenderly.

'You are highly unlikely to get your wish, then.'

It affected a sigh. 'So be it. It appears we will have to do this the hard way—'

Suddenly the avatar's head jerked sharply to the left. Nual wondered if this was some unorthodox attack. Then, as the figure crumpled to the floor, Nual saw Lyrian standing behind it, holding what looked like a length of pipe in both hands.

The fallen avatar lay still, its neck at an impossible angle. It appeared that without a functional host body the entity was powerless – how long for was another matter. 'We should get away from here,' said Nual.

As Lyrian looked at her Nual saw the beginning of madness in her eyes. Lyrian had been infected, but she was trying to resist the entity's influence. As Nual watched, her gaze cleared.

'You have to fight it!' hissed Nual. Whatever had been between her and Lyrian before was past; the rules had changed.

Lyrian blinked and drew a long, slow breath. She looked at Nual, and recognition dawned in her eyes. 'You,' she said distinctly, stepping over the body. '*You brought this upon us.*' She lunged for Nual, her impromptu weapon raised.

Nual dived off the bed, ducking under Lyrian's swing. She felt the swish of air as the pipe passed over her head. Already weak from her ordeal, she landed badly, coming down onto her hands and knees. She heard a curse and a thud: Lyrian, thrown off-balance, had tripped over the body.

Nual threw herself forward again, half-leaping, half-stumbling towards the open door ahead. As she lurched through it she expected to feel the pipe on the back of her head at any moment. She could hear Lyrian close behind.

The corridor was lit by the reddish glow of emergency lighting. For a fraction of a second Nual was back on the mothership, but she banished the memory and the attendant instinct to run. Instead she pointed her toes and kicked forward, and experienced a near-ecstatic relief when she felt the floor recede. Either the nullifying field was only effective in her cell or it had cut out when main power went off. Whatever the reason, her implants were back. She extended both blades and turned in the air.

Lyrian was right behind her, her eyes blank with hatred and the pipe extended; as she turned Lyrian swung at her and Nual parried the blow with her left blade. The jarring impact vibrated through the bones of her arm and twisted her off balance, sending her spinning backwards and upwards. Her head hit the ceiling. It hurt, but pain brought focus and she jammed her right arm against the ceiling, stalling the turn.

Lyrian swung again, grunting with effort, but the ceiling was relatively high, and the pipe heavy and short and she could only reach up as far as Nual's hips now. As the pipe came round Nual whipped her legs up and curled into a tight ball. The blow didn't connect, but Lyrian, unbalanced again, took a step forward and Nual uncoiled and swooped, her blades extended.

One blade caught Lyrian in the chest, entering just below the shoulder-bone. Nual felt the momentary resistance of flesh; there, then gone as she pierced Lyrian's lung. She withdrew the blade when she felt the tip jar on a rib, and the blade snicked back into her forearm in a brief spray of red.

Lyrian dropped her pipe, gave a wet gurgle, and fell to the floor.

CHAPTER FORTY-ONE

Beyond her cell, insanity had already taken hold. The first Sidhe Nual found, further along the corridor, was sitting against the wall, her knees drawn up to her chest as she stared intently into space. Her chin was filmed by a thin sheen of blood-threaded drool and her lips were moving.

Though Nual had withdrawn her senses to avoid detection – or risk of infection – she could not help but pick up the woman's sub-vocalised mumblings: <... *if the universe ... if ... if ... if ... we don't have to see it that way! ... layers, always layers ... the map is not the territory ... so vast, so vast and beautiful ... so terrible ... help me, I can't hear you any more ... too much, it's too much! ...*>

Nual locked down her mind more tightly and hurried past.

The infected Sidhe's mutterings reminded her of snatches she'd picked up when her mind had accidentally touched the sentiences at the heart of transit-kernels, experiences she'd considered at length during her recent imprisonment. Most of the time the shift-minds were beyond words – they'd been mad for years, even centuries. Whatever this was, it had only just arrived, and even if Lyrian had killed the original carrier, the infection was on the loose now. *Perhaps in the very air* ... no, that made no sense: she had suffered no ill effects on the mothership, where for several days she had breathed the same air as those who were infected. This contagion required contact.

Nual realised that her heartbeat was skipping, her breathing a fast pant; she must not let herself give in to such illogical fears. She paused for a moment to override her body's responses, going from the verge of panic to detached concern in a matter of seconds.

She considered what to do next.

The thing must have arrived in a shiftship. She had to find that ship, and use it to escape. In the meantime, she must avoid contact with those already infected. She obviously had some resistance to the contagion, but she wasn't immune, or at least the avatar had not believed she was, given the effort it had expended to recruit her. Quite aside from the risk of becoming tainted, she was also in danger of physical attack: her memories of the flight from the mothership included glimpses of the aftermath of carnage.

The corridor ended in a junction. Unwilling to extend her more arcane senses, Nual peered round the corner. She could make out few details in the gloom; as far as she could see both directions were empty, and identical. She had no idea of the layout of this ship. Perhaps if she found someone who wasn't infected, she could persuade her to guide her out ... No, that wouldn't work: she had no allies here.

As she turned left, someone screamed in the distance, a cry of pure animal anguish, suddenly cut off. She forced herself not to react, though the effort of overruling her instinctive terror was beginning to make her limbs quiver.

In some ways the layout and décor reminded her of the starliners in which she and Taro had travelled to Khathryn, and that gave her an idea. Before she could test her theory, she heard someone approaching; something about the movement sounded wrong, and the breathing was that of a woman engaged in a moderately athletic task. She flew up, pressing herself flat against the ceiling just in time to avoid a Sidhe who scuttled round the corner on all fours – no, not on all fours, on two arms and one leg. The other leg was obviously broken, with splinters of white bone sticking through blood-soaked cloth, and it swung from side to side as the Sidhe moved, a sickening *flop-and-wrench*, *flop-and-wrench* movement. The Sidhe did not appear to be in pain, just in a hurry. She did not look up, or give any sign of knowing Nual was there. When she'd gone, Nual shivered, then floated back down.

She found what she was looking for a couple of corridors

further on: a console set into the wall, provided for guests who were not linked into the ship's comnet. She waved a hand over the sensor. For a moment nothing happened and she began to wonder if this system was one of those that had gone down; then a menu appeared, overlaid with a flashing message: 'Please return to your cabin and await instructions from your steward.' Her suspicions were confirmed: it had been a starliner once; aside from the motherships, the Sidhe used human technology to travel the stars. Despite the warning message, the system was still functioning, so she called up a floor-plan: what had been the crew sections were marked as off-limits, with no details, but she could see enough to work out that had she turned the other way when she first came out of her cell she would have found herself only two corridors away from the smaller airlock at the front. However, she had already gone far enough through the ship to now be closer to the main lock at the back.

So much for relying on intuition.

Shortly after she set off again she heard someone else approaching, this time more cautiously. Again, she floated up, using the only place she had to hide. The Sidhe who came round the corner moved with purposeful sanity. She'd got hold of a gun from somewhere and looked as if she was advancing through the ship ready to take on whoever – *what*ever – she found. She was not being as careful as Nual, and had extended her senses. Nual hoped her own state of mental lock-down would stop her presence being registered.

Apparently not. The Sidhe looked up, her eyes widening at the sight of a naked woman floating at ceiling height. She raised her gun—

—and instinct took over. Nual looked her in the eyes, aiming to disable, deflect—

—and ran straight into the Sidhe's shields. She'd never tried these tricks on her own people, only on defenceless humans—

Something thumped Nual's arm, hard, slamming her up into the ceiling.

—the contact faltered. Sensations of shock and pain clamoured for Nual's attention and her vision swam. The Sidhe reasserted her will, pressing home her mental advantage.

Nual's attempt to fight back was hampered by physical distractions. She was losing this battle – how ironic, that they had finally found a way in. She retreated from the physical world, and for a time of indeterminate nothingness, they were locked in mental stalemate.

She felt the other Sidhe's barriers began to give and prepared to barge in, to enjoy the victory and take whatever she could – knowledge, energy – as her reward—

— and spotted, only just in time, the wrongness lurking like pus below the surface of the other woman's conscious mind, ready to draw her in. Nual withdrew, whipping her presence out and back into her own head.

Almost no time had passed. She found herself floating diagonally half way between floor and ceiling, her implants in the process of lowering her gently down.

The other Sidhe fell backwards and began to emit a high, inhuman shriek, beating at her temples with the flat of her hands.

Fighting Nual had given the infection a chance to overcome the Sidhe's defences. Thanks to her, it had claimed another victim, Nual thought with a shudder. She flew shakily past the screaming Sidhe to land a safe distance up the corridor, then permitted full physical sensation to return. She must have been shot with a stun weapon: her body was numb and heavy, and she couldn't feel her right arm.

Though she could stifle the shock and discomfort, she soon found that her malnourished, overstressed, and drugged leg muscles had become too uncoordinated to control her flight implants properly. Given the choice of bouncing off walls or staggering along the floor, she went for the latter option. She passed another couple of semiconscious Sidhe, and one, halfway out of a door, who was lying face-down in a pool of blood. She hurried past them all, careful to avoid any contact.

When she reached the airlock, all was quiet.

With her minimal knowledge of space-faring, Nual wasn't sure whether or not there was a ship on the other side. The panel had lights on it, but some of them were red. She crept closer to the door: two red lights, one green. And there was a reader, like the ones on the cabin doors on the starliner, attuned to coms or touch. She waved a hand over the sensor, but nothing happened. After a moment's hesitation, she pressed a finger to it. Still nothing.

Well, they would hardly leave the escape route unlocked, would they? She had been foolish to think otherwise.

One of the red lights blinked to green.

In her befuddled state it hadn't occurred to her that they would leave someone on board to keep watch.

She embraced her body's flight instinct, instantly dumping a spike of adrenalin into her system.

Then she ran.

'Everyone ignored you last time, right?' Taro knew the answer, but nerves were making him burble. He knew he had to do this, and he'd been relieved when Jarek agreed, but that didn't stop him being shit-scared. Jarek's request that Taro shoot him if it looked like the Sidhe were going to capture them didn't help. He wished Jarek hadn't entirely countered the drugs he'd been using to contact Nual. He could use a dose of chill right now.

'Like I said, most of the Sidhe on the mothership were already dead when I got there.' Jarek was checking the readouts in his ship's airlock. 'The infected Sidhe we met was interested in Nual, but she didn't even seem to notice me. That's how I managed to tranq her. Or it. Or whatever.'

Taro pointed to the weapon on Jarek's hip. 'That don't look like a tranq gun.'

'That's because it's a needle-pistol – considerably less of a problem than your own choice of weapon, Taro: a laser really isn't an ideal gun to use on a spaceship. The last thing we want is a hull-breach.'

'I've dialled it all the way down and I won't shoot any outside walls.' Taro'd already worked out what'd happen if he did, but even if Jarek'd had a v-suit that fitted him, Taro's gun wouldn't work with gloves on. So Jarek had said he'd go unsuited too, which Taro appreciated.

Jarek said, 'Right. Environmentals are all green, so we're good to go. Ready?'

'Let's do it.'

Jarek pressed the pad. The airlock door opened.

The other ship's airlock was empty and they walked in. Despite himself Taro jumped when the door closed behind them. Jarek checked the panel beside the far door. When he was satisfied, he opened the door.

The corridor beyond was lit by red light, but empty of threats.

'Smells a bit odd,' said Taro, more for something to say than because he thought there was a problem Jarek'd missed.

'Other people's ships usually do.'

'I guess so. So, where do we start?'

'Well, we're at the front of the ship, so we work our way back. Carefully.'

They found their first Sidhe in the next corridor.

She was sitting on the floor, legs bent to one side like she'd fallen. Though she was facing their way she wasn't looking at them. She was leaning forward on her hands, head down, face hidden behind a curtain of hair.

Taro and Jarek still stopped dead. She didn't move. They started to back off. She continued to ignore them. Taro glanced at Jarek; in the red light Jarek's face looked like a grim mask.

Back round the corner, Taro whispered, 'So, do we find another way, then?'

Jarek nodded, then as Taro turned, put an arm out. 'No, wait, the chances are we'll just meet another one round the next corner. Last time ... Last time the only live Sidhe I saw on the mothership were pretty distracted.' Taro got the impression he was getting up his nerve. 'I'm going to investigate. I'll need you to watch my back.'

'All right.' Taro wasn't entirely sure how; the knowledge that had come with his Angel mods didn't cover team tactics.

Jarek made his way down the passage, back against the wall, needle-pistol in hand. The Sidhe didn't move.

Halfway along he stopped, then in one quick movement held out the gun and fired.

From where Taro was standing he didn't hear the gun go off, but he saw the Sidhe collapse, her head jerking backwards in a shower of dark drops as she fell.

'Shit!'

Jarek looked over his shoulder at Taro's oath. His face was blank.

'What the fuck d'you do that for?' called Taro.

'Had to get in range.' Jarek's voice showed no emotion. 'We can carry on now.'

Taro joined him and they made their way past the body. Taro managed not to look too closely at the dead Sidhe. In this light the stain spreading out from under her looked more black than red.

Around the next corner, Jarek relaxed slightly and turned to Taro. 'I know that shocked you, but you've never met them, never fought them. I have. I know what they're like.'

'Yeah, but she ... I don't think she'd've attacked us. She looked pretty fucked-up.'

'Yes, and from what I saw on the mothership, I was probably doing her a favour.'

Taro had nothing to say to that.

The next one they saw, not long afterwards, was standing against a wall, staring vacantly into space. She was hugging herself and swaying slowly from side to side, dragging her head along the wall, sobbing and muttering. Taro let Jarek go past and deal with her. This time he kept quiet as they passed the body.

In the next corridor they found their first corpse – not a Sidhe, but a man in a short grey tunic. His head was caved in on one side. 'Is that a mute?' whispered Taro as they edged past.

'Yes,' said Jarek shortly.

'I thought this thing only attacked Sidhe.'

'Mutes are Sidhe. Besides, we don't know what happened here.'

Taro tried not to think about Jarek's comment about Sidhe and humans being almost the same. It wasn't like they were going to turn back now.

Jarek's com had a download of the basic layout – apparently the ship was a standard starliner design – so they shouldn't get lost. Finding Nual was another matter. Though they were back in range of Kama Nui's comnet here, there wasn't much likelihood that she still had her com, and a pretty high chance that someone bad did. Taro wondered if there was some way he could tune into Nual's mind, but he had no idea how to go about it. They'd just have to keep their eyes and ears open, and hope luck was with them.

The next Sidhe they found was lying across the corridor, staring sightlessly up at the ceiling. She looked dead, but Jarek shot her anyway.

As they picked their way round the body Taro heard a *swoosh* and looked round in panic. They'd triggered a door sensor. Beyond the door was someone's sleeping room. One Sidhe lay on the floor in front of the bed. Another straddled her chest. The upright one had empty, bloody sockets where her eyes should've been; she was banging the head of the other one against the floor, a wet rhythmic thudding that sent up little sprays of dark liquid from a pool of nasty wetness.

As Taro stared in horror, the upright Sidhe began to turn her eyeless gaze on him. Jarek stepped past him and shot her – *it*. The thing's face transformed into a mosaic of bloodied meat and it toppled over.

Jarek reloaded, then they carried on without a word or a backwards glance, though Jarek wore an expression of self-disgust and Taro kept having to swallow against the urge to puke. He'd just about got control of himself when Jarek stopped again. Taro halted too, though he couldn't hear or see anything odd.

'What is it?' he whispered.

'Not sure. I thought there was someone behind us.'

Taro looked back. The corridor was empty. 'Can't see anyone.'

Jarek shrugged. 'Probably just this place getting to me.'

'No shit,' muttered Taro.

'*Attention all passengers.*'

Taro jumped as the calm, sexless voice filled the corridor. '*We are experiencing some technical difficulties—*'

The voice sounded a lot like the com on the starliner from Vellern.

'*All passengers are advised to report to their steward. If he or she cannot be found please follow the indicators to your nearest assembly point and await further instructions. Kindly do not stop to collect personal belongings. Thank you.*'

Pale green arrows sprang to life on the walls, pointing back the way they'd come.

'What the fuck's going on?' asked Taro.

'That was an automated ship-wide warning message,' said Jarek. 'As for what triggered it … if I had to guess, I'd say someone's screwing with the ship's systems, and they've just managed to break something important.'

'How worried should we be?'

'Not sure. But it certainly isn't good news.'

CHAPTER FORTY-TWO

If the abomination found her now, she was lost. Nual had squeezed just about everything she could from her body, but after days with virtually no food or water, and with her system messed up by the shot from the stunner, she was going to have to stop soon. She wasn't sure if whoever – whatever – had opened the airlock had come after her, but by the time her flight had been reduced to a loping stagger, she decided to assume it hadn't. When she passed an open door to what must have once been a passenger lounge, she decided to risk going in. She would be trapped if she was being followed, but if so then at least she would meet her end somewhere comfortable. She collapsed onto a lounger, listening for sounds of pursuit over the rasp of her breaths.

When she neither heard nor saw any immediate threat, and had got her body back under control, she looked around.

The room boasted some of the amenities she'd used on her previous starliner trips, including a small bar area. She could see there was no stock behind the bar, but it might have water; worth a look. When she found a working spigot, she almost cried in relief. She cupped her hand under the flow and lapped up the water, stopping only when her stomach began to complain. She had just stood up again when a calm toneless voice filled the room:

'*Attention all passengers ...*'

As she listened to the less-than-reassuring announcement she looked for its source, and spotted the clear hood of a com-booth on the far wall. It looked like a proper com, not just an internal data-console like the one she had used earlier, which meant it might allow communication off the ship. When the voice fell silent she lurched over to the booth.

Inside, it came to life, and she selected touch control. With trembling fingers, she tried to call the *Judas Kiss*. The call went out, and she held her breath. The response came back a few seconds later: *No such vessel in system*. It looked like Taro had done the sensible thing and fled. At least he would be safe. For her, though, the last hope was gone. She sagged against the hood. Even if there had been someone else to call, she didn't remember any numbers; why would she? She always called com-to-com, and hers had been taken when she was captured.

Except ... she did know one number. She remembered the number of the com she'd bought for Taro back in Stonetown, because it was a cheap model, and she'd had to programme the number manually into her own com. Not that there was much point calling a short-range com when he probably wasn't even in the system any more ... but she decided to try anyway, for the unashamedly sentimental reason that if he still had his com registered with a local messaging service, then she might at least hear his voice one last time.

The call was picked up at once. 'Hello?'

It was him! 'I— Taro, is that really you?'

'Yes! Shit and blood, Nual, where are you?'

'On the Sidhe ship—'

'So're we. We've come to rescue you!'

Nual felt the crushing exhaustion and fear lift for a moment. 'That's crazy— That's *wonderful*.'

'Yes, yes it is. Wait ... Jarek asks, what colour are the corridor decals there?'

'What? Oh, I see. Blue, but I'm not in a corridor, I'm in a lounge.'

She heard Taro talking to Jarek, then he said, 'Is there a location ID anywhere on the booth you're calling from?'

'Ah – yes, on the screen.' Nual read it off.

'Jarek reckons he can find you! Stay where you are.'

'I'm not going anywhere.'

'Nual? Are you all right?'

'Yes, I—' She kept blinking, but the tears still came. 'I will be. Keep talking to me.'

''Course I will. Just try and stop me.' He sounded like he was simultaneously laughing and crying. 'What happened? I mean, you said, in the dream, about one of the Court coming for you. But this is something else, ain't it?'

'I think – I think the message to the Court must have been intercepted.'

'By this ... *thing*? What is it?' Taro sounded worried, as well he might.

For a moment Nual wanted to admit her part in bringing the entity into being. But now was not the time. 'I'm not sure,' she said. 'I think it might be some sort of hive mind. It wants to absorb Sidhe consciousnesses, but most of them aren't strong enough to handle it and they end up going mad, destroying themselves.'

'No shit. This place is gonna give me nightmares for weeks.'

You and me both. 'You should be safe. Infected Sidhe don't seem to notice humans.'

'That's what we're assuming.' Taro didn't sound entirely sure. 'So this is the same thing that invaded the ship you used to live on; I thought that ship got trashed, and left dead in space? How did the thing get here, pretending to be one of the Court?'

'I'm not s—'

'*Attention all passengers. We are experiencing multiple systems failures. Please remain calm but be prepared for the order to evacuate. Repeat: all passengers and crew are to prepare for evacuation.*'

'Taro? Did you hear that?'

'Yes! Shit. Nual, we're coming as fast as we can—'

'Good, good. Keep talking to me, please.' *Because I'm scared.*

'You bet. Ah, Jarek says this thing turning up might be his fault. The Sidhe who interrogated him at Serenein must've worked out where the mothership was and sent someone to investigate. When they got there, they found these whatever-they-ares waiting for them.'

'They call themselves avatars. Of what I'm not yet sure.'

Destruction. Chaos. Entropy. 'The one I met wasn't from my ship: the infection must have spread.'

'Can the infected Sidhe still do the scary mind-stuff?'

'I'm not sure. They can read surface emotions and strong thoughts, but they don't appear to have the finesse for anything subtle. As for control over others ... I don't think so, otherwise the one I met today would have tried it on me. But it did do something I've never seen before: they can affect nearby matter. She – it – managed to unmake a chair.'

'That don't sound good.'

'No, I—' Nual stopped and looked up. Her first thought when someone came into the room was relief, though Taro should have said he was that close.

But it wasn't Taro.

'Nual?' Taro looked at Jarek. 'Something's wrong!'

'We're nearly there – just round the next corner.'

Taro forced himself not to run ahead. When they reached the lounge the door was open, but they couldn't see inside without breaking cover. Taro listened as hard as he could, and thought he caught the rustle of cloth. He looked at Jarek who whispered, 'In after three, all right? One ... two ... three ... !'

The room looked like a stripped-down version of a starliner lounge. Two people stood next to one of the couches. One was Nual. She was naked and unconscious – or dead – and the other figure, clothed, had her by the shoulders and was shaking her like a ragdoll. That had to be a Sidhe. From the corner of his eye Taro saw Jarek raise his gun. Something went *pphhhssstt*, and a swarm of silver flashed through his vision.

Taro was instantly afraid for Nual in case he hit her, firing without aiming properly in bad light. Except ... Jarek hadn't hit anyone. How could he miss at this range?

The Sidhe turned to look at them. Something in the way she stared made Taro's bowels go watery. He'd met one alien in his life – two if you counted Nual – but this was totally *other*.

She said, 'We know you, little mind.'

She was talking to Jarek. And she wasn't a Sidhe. This was one of the avatars Nual had talked about. Taro wasn't sure if it'd deflected or actually *unmade* the fléchettes Jarek had just fired at it, but the result was the same: they were in deep shit. 'Fuck,' he breathed.

The avatar dropped Nual, who fell half on the couch, and Taro winced. It turned to face them. 'You have a link to this one, yes?' A momentary flick of its hand towards Nual. 'She is ours now. Leave us and live. Or stay and die. It is of little consequence.'

One good thing, thought Taro through the rising panic: it can't do the scary head stuff. At least, it hasn't yet.

'Attention please. An overload in the ship's power-plant has been detected. All personnel must board the evac-pods immediately. Crew members must follow full evacuation protocols. Passengers kindly remain calm and allow your crew to see you to safety.'

Without Angel conditioning Taro suspected he'd be having a hard time standing his ground right now.

The avatar cocked its head. 'They would destroy themselves to thwart us ...' It sounded amazed at this turn of events.

Jarek used the distraction to fire again. At the last moment, the avatar noticed the attack. A thin shower of silver rained at its feet. But some of the needles got through, though at reduced power. Pinpricks of red appeared all down its left leg.

It's gonna kill us now for sure. Taro was more angry than scared. They'd come so far, only to fail in the end!

The avatar glanced down at its wounds, then up at its attackers. Taro braced himself. But it just frowned and said, 'Are you so far in the Sidhe girl's thrall that you would die trying to save her? A shame time is short, for such displays of loyalty are intriguing. We would have liked to find out more before we dealt with you.'

The thing was in no hurry to take them out, presumably because it thought they weren't a threat. *Was it right?* It couldn't affect his thoughts – he was free to act. It *could* affect matter, so shooting it wouldn't work. His blades would probably be equally useless, assuming it didn't just unmake *him* when he got close enough.

But he had another weapon.

He'd entered the room with their assassin's rifle pointed down – waving it at the walls made Jarek nervous – but now he raised the gun and slipped a finger under the trigger-guard.

The avatar lifted a hand, reaching towards them.

As the firing pads warmed to Taro's touch the avatar-thing's gaze went to the gun. It hesitated, hand still outstretched, and said disdainfully, 'Do you not understand? *You cannot physically harm me.*'

'Wanna bet?' said Taro, and pulled the trigger.

The avatar's raised hand came off at the wrist. On the weakest setting the laser didn't cauterise the wound. The avatar's eyes widened in surprise as blood spurted from the stump.

Taro twitched the laser back.

The avatar shuddered …

… folded …

… and fell.

A grisly assortment of internal organs burst free from the massive wound in its side when the body hit the floor.

'Try some coherent fucking *light*, bitch!' Taro found himself shouting.

Beside him, Jarek muttered, 'Holy shit!' Then, a little louder, 'That seemed to work!'

Taro put the gun down and rushed over to Nual. He cradled her head, looking for signs of life. She was breathing, at least.

Jarek called over 'Is she—?'

'She's alive.'

'Thank fuck for that. Come on, we need to get out of here. Can you carry her?'

'Wait, I'll— I'm gonna try and wake her.' He wasn't sure he could, and given how they'd found her, he wasn't sure he *should*, but to finally see her, touch her – it was as though the world had come alive again. He held her close, trying to recapture the sensation of their mind-to-mind contact …

He felt her mind straining towards his, and then she blinked and looked up at him. And it *was* her, not something terrible looking out of her eyes.

'You know what?' he said, his voice near to breaking. 'If we'd gone to all this effort only to find you'd died on us, I'd never've fucking spoken to you again.'

She smiled, then frowned and rasped, 'Is it dead?'

Taro looked down at the mess by his feet. The only movement was a slow spilling of guts. He'd pretty much cut the thing in half. He swallowed hard and said, 'If it can survive that, then we're really fucked.'

'Which we will be anyway if we hang around much longer,' called Jarek.

Taro pulled Nual to her feet. 'C'mon, we gotta go.'

Jarek said, 'Right. Let's get the hell off this ship before it blows.'

CHAPTER FORTY-THREE

They'd just left the lounge when the ship's com announced:

'*Attention please. A power-plant overload is now imminent. Any remaining crew and passengers must evacuate the vessel with all possible haste. Repeat: power-plant overload imminent, abandon ship immediately*.'

Jarek cursed the infuriatingly calm voice. *How* imminent exactly? A minute? Twenty? At least a countdown would've told him how screwed they were. He glanced back at the others. Nual was in a bad way, but she'd activated her flight implants, and Taro had grabbed her arm and was towing her along. 'Ready to run?' Jarek asked.

Taro nodded.

And they ran, Taro dragging Nual behind him like some bizarre child's balloon. Jarek forced himself to slow down whenever they passed a junction and checked his com. Getting lost now could be fatal.

As they turned into the corridor where he'd killed the first Sidhe the lights went out. Though the guidance decals stayed illuminated, conveniently pointing to the airlock, they didn't give enough light to see obstacles and Jarek almost tripped over the dead Sidhe. He could feel by the way his feet slid around that he'd stepped in blood, but he slowed just enough not to lose his balance.

When they reached the airlock he punched it closed and carried on up to the bridge, leaving the other two to fend for themselves.

He powered up the engines – he'd had the wit to leave everything on standby, ready for a quick getaway – then undocked and shot off from the doomed ship at top speed.

When they were safely under way, the little moon receding rapidly behind them, he sat back in his couch. Nothing was happening to the Sidhe ship, and for a moment he felt oddly cheated. They'd gone balls-to-the-wall to escape, only to have the Sidhe ship not blow up after all.

Then it did.

He'd left the bridge shutters closed, and he hadn't bothered to select a projection to simulate the view, so the explosion registered as a simultaneous spike on all his sensors. He ran a quick diagnostic, letting out a relieved sigh when he confirmed that the *Heart of Glass* hadn't sustained any damage.

A few seconds later, traffic control hailed him.

Jarek's hand hovered over the ship's com. Of course they'd want a word with him. But if he answered, then things could get complicated, and they weren't home and dry yet. He ignored the incoming message, though he did moderate his speed so it didn't look quite so much like he was fleeing the scene of a crime.

With no further need for stealth, he fired up all his remaining sensors, focusing every instrument at his disposal on Kama Nui, watching for signs of a ship heading his way. It was a good job beacons operated independently of traffic control; if they'd had any way of blocking his transit, they might just have done so now. As it was they had about ten minutes to despatch pursuit, after which time he'd be out of range of even a fast interceptor. And once he was in the shift, he was safe; just being in the wrong place at the wrong time shouldn't be enough to invoke Treaty law against a freetrader, not unless the locals wanted the Alliance on their case.

He gave it fifteen minutes, just to be sure.

Once he was certain no one was coming after them, Jarek returned to the rec-room. Nual was lying on the couch, Taro sitting beside her. They helped her stand, and Jarek guided her to the med-bay. Its diagnosis was that she was experiencing the tail-end of a severe adrenalin come-down and had recently been shot with some sort of low-level neural disruptor, though the effects were already wearing off. Her main problem was lack of food and liquids. She refused Jarek's suggestion that he hook up a drip for her, but let him adapt a favourite hangover cure, adding a few extra ingredients suggested by the med-bay. Whilst she was physically better off than she had any right to be, it didn't take Sidhe intuition to work out that her recent experiences had left her severely shaken.

As his com hadn't relayed any further incoming messages, Jarek got himself a drink. Then the three of them sat in the *Heart of Glass*'s rec-room and swapped stories.

When they'd brought each other up to date Taro, who was sitting with one arm around Nual, asked Jarek, 'So, we found out what you wanted to know, even if we can't do much about it. What now?'

'We need to get back to Xantier and find out what Bez's got for us. What we do next depends partly on that: I'm hoping that with the data she can provide, plus what you've unearthed here, we can start to act against the Sidhe, and actually begin to undermine their power-base – though we'll have to be careful.'

'What about the avatar thing?' asked Taro.

'Hopefully the Sidhe themselves took care of that when they blew their ship up. And if not … well we need to avoid it, but we need to avoid direct confrontation with the Sidhe anyway.' Jarek had enough on his plate without worrying about where the infected Sidhe fitted in; the way he saw it anything that killed Sidhe had to be a good thing. 'My priority is to get hold of a shiftspace beacon, then try to get back to Serenein and open a new transit-path there.'

'I know you wanna help those people,' said Taro, 'but if the consorts didn't end up here, then don't that mean your friends managed to see off the Sidhe by themselves?'

'For the moment, yes they must have. But I doubt the Sidhe will give up. And there's something at Serenein that can help us fight the Sidhe.'

Nual spoke up for the first time since she'd finished recounting her adventures. 'What sort of thing?'

'Well, not a *thing* as such. People. The consorts themselves, actually. There's thirty-seven of them in stasis on the *Setting Sun*, which is parked up at the top of the planet's beanstalk. Those boys have powers the Sidhe can't counter. We can use that.'

Nual said softly, 'You are correct, of course. But have you thought through the full implications of cutting off the source of shift-minds?'

'I'm setting a world free. And I'm ending a lie.'

'True enough. But in the long run, you are also taking away humanity's ability to travel the stars. No more transit-kernels means no new shiftships.'

'Yeah ... I know. Believe me, I know. But I still have to do it.'

In the awkward silence that followed, Jarek's com chirped. He checked it. 'We're being hailed.'

'By traffic control?' asked Nual.

'No, I think they've realised I'm not going to answer. I need to get up to the bridge and find out who it is.' He stood up.

Taro and Nual followed him, waiting at the back of the bridge while he checked the sensor-logs. The unknown ship wasn't an in-system interceptor; it was a corvette, and it was heading their way. He called up a retroactive display of likely vectors, sending the bright little dots representing the two ships zipping backwards through the holo-cube. 'The ship was on its way in from the beacon – it must've arrived in-system earlier today. It looks like they spotted us heading away from Rangui-iti after the explosion, then braked and turned to follow. They're running silent, and they only hailed us when they were already on our tail. That's not friendly behaviour.'

'It's the Court,' said Nual in a small voice.

'What? I thought you said their ship got taken over by these infected Sidhe.'

'No, I— I wasn't thinking straight, was I? The avatar said it came to Kama Nui because the entity knew there would be a lot of Sidhe here, waiting for the consorts. I assumed it – they – must have intercepted the Court's ship, but it never actually said that. Jarek, I'm really sorry. I should have thought.'

'And I should have been keeping an eye on the beacon, not just the planet. We can do sorries later. Are you sure it's the Court?'

She nodded.

'Shit. And I thought today couldn't get any worse.' He ramped the drive back up to max. It was unlikely to make much difference, but it made him feel better. 'Shame we can't persuade them we're not worth bothering with ...' He'd been about to discard that option, but it wasn't an entirely stupid idea. Sidhe powers wouldn't work over a com, and they were close enough, and still going slow enough, for tight-beam messaging, so he wouldn't have to blow his new ship ID. Then again, at the rate the corvette was gaining, perhaps he should just prep for transit.

He realised the others were looking at him expectantly. 'I was wondering if it was worth trying to talk to them to throw them off the trail, but I think my time would be better spent getting us out of here.'

'Is that "out" as in an unscheduled transit?' asked Taro.

'This far from the beacon it'll have to be.'

'Ain't that a bit drastic?'

'That ship is way faster than us. They can't board us at this speed, but they might be armed, and even if they're not, once they've closed, they can tail us wherever we go – including into shiftspace. If it *is* the Court – and Nual's word is good enough for me – then we need to be gone before that happens.' He started the priming sequence on the transit-kernel and began to initiate fast shutdowns on the ship's other major systems.

'You're obviously a bit busy,' said Taro, 'but how about if I spoke to them?'

He turned to look at Taro. From the boy's expression, he was serious. Taro continued, 'The way I see it, if we don't answer them, they'll know something's up and keep coming after us. If I say we've got some sort of problem, so we can't stop and chat, maybe I can get them to back off.' He grimaced. 'But I guess that'd only work if there's some way of comming them without them recognising us. Forget it, it's a dumb idea—'.

'No, it isn't. Go to my cabin – there's a com in the cabinet beside the bed. Bring it up here.'

'Right. Back in a sec.' Taro kicked off down the steps.

The kernel-interface programme asked him to select an exit system. The most logical choice would be Mercanth, because it was a hubpoint ... but that was what their pursuers would expect, and if they had agents there they might alert them. After a moment's consideration he chose the least-used of the five transit-paths out of the Kama Nui system, an insular low-population democracy called Oril. Taking an indirect route to Xantier would delay getting to Bez, but right now all that mattered was losing the Court.

'Can you put me into stasis before we make the transit?' asked Nual.

'Sorry, no, there's no time. I'll try and sort out some drugs for us before we shift.'

'All right. Can I do anything to help?'

'No just ... stay out the way.'

Taro came back with the greymarket com from Kama Nui while Jarek was running a projection in the holo-cube, one eye on the readouts telling him how the initial shutdown was progressing. Even if all essential systems went offline without a hitch they'd be cutting it fine; the corvette would be only three minutes away from slipstreaming range when they shifted.

'Here, please.' Jarek held out a hand and Taro slapped the com into it. Jarek patched the com into the *Heart of Glass*'s tight-beam system with one hand at the same time as he shut down long-range sensors with the other. 'Right, I've activated the scrambler so they won't be able to see your face.'

'Good. Got it.' Taro took the com.

'I'm putting them through ... now.'

There was a small chirp, nearly lost amongst the other noises on the bridge. Taro spoke into the com. 'Make it quick, friend.'

Jarek put the reply through the bridge speakers. The woman who answered sounded understandably taken aback at Taro's terse greeting. 'Why didn't you respond to our earlier hails? And why is your signal so distorted?'

Taro replied, 'Because we've got problems! Now, we're in a bit of a hurry here, so if you don't mind—'

'What is the nature of your problem?'

'No offence, but what's it to you?' Jarek smiled at Taro's reply; the boy was enjoying being able to talk back to a Sidhe.

Jarek turned his attention back to his console; at times like this he wished he'd gone for the interface implants after all. The next choice was when to cut the in-system drive. The longer he left it, the more distance he'd put between them and the corvette ... and the greater the chance shutdown wouldn't complete cleanly before transit. Incomplete engine shutdown when they went into shiftspace was dangerous, and no working drive when they came out could be suicidal if they didn't shake off their pursuers. After a moment's thought, he killed the engines, then pounced on the expected array of error-indicators and started to override them. *I know, I know, taking the drive offline without completing preliminary shutdown is dangerous, invalidates the warranty and insurance, yadda yadda yadda.*

The next time he focused on Taro the boy was saying, '—haven't been to this Rangoo-eet place, sorry.'

'Really?' The Sidhe's voice was dubious. 'And what is the nature of this engine fault you referred to?'

'Like I said, the captain's working on it now. But we've already lost AG and the drive-to-reactor interface ain't looking so good.'

Jarek raised an eyebrow. The faults Taro described were unusual, but not impossible. And he was certainly conveying a convincing tone of panic.

The Sidhe said silkily, 'Can we be of any assistance?'

'Wish you could, but if I were you, I'd back off. If the drive does blow, it's likely to take the reactor with it. If that happens, you don't wanna be too close.'

The com went silent. Jarek's hands kept working on the shutdown of the remaining peripheral systems but he spared the energy to hope that Taro had convinced the other ship to leave them alone. He'd still make the transit as soon as he could but if the other ship slowed, even by a few per cent, then he wouldn't have to cut so many corners, and that would give him a far greater chance of coming out of shiftspace with his ship intact.

Finally the Sidhe said, 'Your caution is wise. However, you appear to be decelerating. Why is that?'

Jarek looked up to see Taro looking confused. 'Are we? I mean, so we are. Captain?'

Jarek shook his head. Taro shrugged, then flashed him a grin.

'Oh no!' screamed Taro into the com, 'It's gonna—'

He cut the connection with a flourish, then leant back against the bulkhead. 'Oh, bollocks,' he said.

'Actually,' said Jarek, 'that was pretty impressive bullshitting. You know more shiftship jargon than I'd expect for a boy born in a floating city.'

'Yeah, well, you got a good games library on board. I had a go at playing trader when you left me by myself.'

'Right.' He'd shut down the holo-plate but the numbers on his flatscreen showed the corvette still accelerating. Things were looking worse by the second. 'Thanks for trying, but our options are narrowing.'

Taro took the hint and shut up.

Most of the nominalisation subroutines had completed. A little manual intervention now might speed up shutdown on certain core processes—

'Are we going to make the transit in time?' asked Nual tersely.

'Don't know. Sorry, I need to concentrate now.'

'I must know: will you be able to initiate transit before they are too close?'

'Nual, for fuck's sake, I just said I don't know!'

The transit-kernel came fully online. Good. Now he just needed to get his ship ready to face the shift. Maybe he could shave off some more time by bypassing a few failsafes … but he needed to make sure they were the right ones. The moment the core systems were nominal, he'd force a shift.

His instinct, when the alarm chimed, was to override it. But when he saw what the problem was he snatched his hand back from the console. Reactor lockdown had failed. The containment system was already performing an automatic reset, thank Christos; another five seconds and Taro's lie to the Sidhe would've come true, and all that would be left of the *Heart of Glass* would be a rapidly expanding cloud of hot atoms.

But until the reactor was safely locked down, most of the other subroutines would just hang. They were going to run out of time.

He didn't realise he'd said anything until Nual called out cautiously, 'What is it?'

Perhaps he hadn't spoken out loud, perhaps she'd just picked up on the mental gurgle of the last shreds of hope disappearing down the pan.

'We're screwed,' he said. 'There was a problem with the reactor. If we're lucky then it should only take a few minutes to fix, but there's a shitload of other systems waiting on it. By the time those are offline the Court'll be on our arses.'

'Shit,' said Taro.

Nual said something Jarek didn't catch to Taro. Then she said distinctly, 'There may be another way.'

He spared a glance in their direction to see her disappearing down the hatch, Taro following close behind. Maybe they'd decided to get themselves dosed up for transit anyway ... It wasn't his problem any more.

For the moment, there was nothing he could do but wait for the reactor, hoping and praying for a fast, clean lockdown. He could feel sweat running down between his eyebrows and pooling in his armpits. He found himself mentally cajoling the numbers on the flatscreen in front of him, the only remaining active display on the bridge. *Come on, come on.*

The display changed: *Reactor stable and nominal.* 'Yes!' Lockdown had completed in record time. The other readouts sprang back into life as the remaining systems' shutdowns restarted.

The comp warned him that it would go into safe mode in one minute. He requested an estimate for shutdown completion on the last few systems. One minute fifteen. At which point he'd punch it and they'd be gone. He glanced at the other countdown, the one in red at the bottom on the screen.

Unless something happened to stop the Sidhe corvette, in fifty-three seconds it would be close enough to slipstream them when they went into the shift.

'Fuck it!' The oath escaped before he could stop it. It wasn't fair. He'd given it everything he had, and they weren't going to make—

CHAPTER FORTY-FOUR

'I'm not sure what you mean.' Taro had seen Nual like this before. She was considering something risky. He didn't want that, not when he'd only just got her back.

She looked around the rec-room, like she expected the answer to be there, then said quietly, 'Do you know why Jarek originally rescued me?'

Confused at the irrelevant question, Taro shook his head.

'Because I called to him. Through shiftspace.'

'Yeah, he said something about that. But don't you go crazy in the shift?'

'I did, yes. The initial contact I had with Jarek's ship was only momentary, and it was … painful. Afterwards, when we were running away' – she turned her head to look at the cylinder of the drive-column – 'in the shift all I could sense was the insane mind in there, forcing the ship through the shift. I could not help but be drawn into unity. Because that's how it works, for us …' her voice trailed away.

'Listen, if we're about to go into the shift, why aren't you preparing yourself? At least sort some drugs—'

'I am.'

'What?'

'I am preparing myself. I am explaining to you what must be done. Because I will need your help, your strength.'

'I don't understand.'

'Back then I was a child. I was uncertain and in pain. I did not have full control of my abilities. And I did not have you. With your help – if you will give it – I can influence what happens in shiftspace.'

'That's … heavy.'

'But necessary. We must act now, before it's too late. Will you help me?'

This was crazy: he wasn't even sure what she was asking, let alone whether he'd be able to do it. But he trusted her. 'What do I have to do?'

Before she could answer they heard Jarek's voice from above them, swearing loudly.

'Take my hands. Hurry.'

He did so. They felt small, warm, ordinary.

'Close your eyes.'

'Right.'

\<Now think of this\>

\<Of what?\>

\<Of—\>

Nothing.

Like nothing at all, like nowhere, like losing all ties.

For a moment, freedom. A release of sensation, of self.

He feels her as part of him, knowing he is part of her. They retain enough separation to remember who is who, but there is nothing left of *where* and *what* and *why*. Weirdly glorious. Unity.

Then, purpose:

They must reach out together (*been here before*) to find a third mind.

They do, and as they connect he recalls in a rush what they're doing, and is suddenly terrified. He tries to hold back. He can't.

His consciousness is swamped.

Pain, the bEauTiful Pain. Bring thE beaUtifuL pain!

i aM the pAth, tHe onE Who knOwS, the One wHo suFfeRs, whO muSt sUffer.

i aM—

\<Not alone.\>

\<Confused.\>

325

The impulse comes from the part of them that is her, the part that retains control, sanity:

<Open the way! Do it now! Take us ...There.>

ThEre=

sCenT of brUisEd LoVe+scReaMing iN tHe bEtwEen+SoUnds of

tOo-brIGhT LiGht+nEveRneSs oF loSs+FleSh ruBbeD rAw.

RubbEd Raw anD BleEdiNg uNtil tHere iS

NO FLeSH ...

The onslaught continues. It will overwhelm them. They're not strong enough.

He feels the familiar sensation: her in him. She needs his strength. He gives it, without thought. She takes.

The madness is lessening. No, fading. Everything is fading. He has given everything. She is taking it, using it. All he is, and more. He is becoming nothing, lost for ever. This is as it should be, as it was fated to be. The just end—

He feels her break the connection. *<No! I will not do this to you.>* He is jerked back from the edge. Awareness returns, and with it, the madness—

KeEp lOoking – keeP looKinG. hEre in The gApS tHe aNsweR liEs

CurlEd. ThePatternisWrongAnditMustBeMadeRight—

He tries to reassert himself, to rediscover what it is to be an individual who isn't part of the crazy nothing – and who isn't her, either. Not part of her, but *with* her. And not as slave, minion or worshipper. As partner. Lover.

He will give her his strength. But not himself. Not until she asks for it. When she does choose to do that he won't hesitate, because such sacrifice is the ultimate expression of love.

That is the only truth left now, this one incomprehensible emotion.

All else is agony and horror and the crushing void.

There was something stuck to his cheek. Something rough and hard and—

The floor. He was lying on the floor.

Jarek moved his head. Yes, lying on the floor, face pressed into carpet. It didn't smell too good down here, but he wasn't sure he could do anything about that, not if it involved moving. He remembered going into the shift, recalled the familiar hind-brain wallop and that sense of physical disassociation. It'd been a bad transit, bad enough that at some point his mind had given up trying to deal with the unreality and shut down. It didn't feel like he'd damaged anything when he passed out, but he wouldn't know for sure until he sat up. Which he really needed to do some time soon.

He got his arms under him and levered himself upright. His head swam and he felt queasy. He was on the bridge, which was good. But— *Oh shit*, now he remembered! They'd gone into the shift too soon!

He crawled over to the main console and heaved himself onto his couch. His hands went through the actions required to get his ship working again and almost at once the alarms started. He was getting system errors from environmentals, coms and main engines. Environmentals could wait: basic life-support was working, though they'd be a bit chilly until he got the heating back on full, and trying to take a shower at the moment would be a really bad idea. Coms just needed a manual reset. The reactor was coming up without a hitch but the grav-drive had already tried a cold-start, which would've done the AG unit no good at all. The journey through shiftspace had stripped the ship of its original momentum, and they'd been spat out at the beacon with a safe speed and heading relative to local spacetime. The nav-shields were working so they weren't about to get holed by passing space-debris, but until he got the engines back online they were effectively adrift.

As his fingers moved over the controls he realised that there was one alarm he wasn't hearing: the proximity warning. As soon as he had the immediate crises under control he fired up the sensors, to find there was nothing within several light-seconds. Thank fuck for that: the Court ship hadn't managed to follow them. He hoped Nual and Taro had got themselves buckled down before the transit—

Coms came back up with an *urgent incoming* message. He hit receive and got an annoyed male voice.

'Unknown vessel, unknown vessel, this Xantier TC. Kindly respond at once with your ID and intentions. Do you require assistance? Please acknowledge.'

The message repeated and he was about to compose a reply when he registered what he'd just heard.

This is Xantier TC ...

Xantier? What the fuck?!

Given what a screwed-up transit that'd been he could almost believe they'd ended up in a system other than Oril, but it still had to be a system on a direct transit-path from Kama Nui. Xantier was four transits away. Coming out there simply wasn't possible.

He opened the shutters and was relieved to find space looking the same as it always did: remote, beautiful and too big to comprehend. Nav systems were still offline, so he couldn't get a star-fix. He sent a text-only reply to traffic control, stating that they'd had a bad transit but were in no immediate danger. He said he'd be in touch again once he'd checked his ship over.

The remaining systems were coming back up by themselves, so he went to find Nual and Taro. He left the bridge, clinging shakily to the ladder as he descended.

He didn't spot them at first. Then he heard a small sound from behind him, and turned round. They were sitting, or rather huddled, against the drive-column, arms wrapped around each other. They were both conscious but dazed. Their faces were grey-white, save for a thin trickle of red under Nual's nose. They didn't notice him until he spoke.

'Are you two all right?' he asked. He was already recovering from the worst ravages of the transit and his body was demanding caf. It looked like they'd had a far worse time of it.

'We ... will be,' said Nual in a small, drained voice.

Jarek ducked under the ladder and helped them stand. They were trembling, the kind of constant unconscious shuddering that comes after great exertion. 'I think we should get you both to the med-bay. Nual, you've got blood on your face.'

She raised a hand to wipe her lip, then looked at the red smear with a mixture of confusion and irritation. 'I'm fine,' she murmured. 'Just need a drink. Please.'

'I could certainly use one myself,' Jarek agreed.

The three of them staggered over to the table and Jarek started making a pot of caf while the other two collapsed onto seats. He nodded to indicate the drive-column. 'How come you ended up sitting down there?'

He saw the look that passed between them – no doubt more than a look – then Nual said, 'Needed ... to get close.'

'I don't understand.'

Her eyes were still unfocused and despite her claim that she wasn't hurt, he wondered if she'd injured herself. Perhaps she'd fallen when the ship was in the shift, maybe banged her head. 'Close to the ... shift-mind,' she said.

Jarek put the pot down and turned to face her. 'I'd have thought that was the last thing you'd want to do.'

Nual started to shake her head, then winced, 'Not like that ... any more.'

For the first time, Taro spoke; though he looked even more exhausted than Nual, his voice was stronger than hers. 'Where are we?'

'Interesting question. Apparently we're at Xantier.' Jarek let his continuing disbelief colour his voice.

'That's ... where Bez, the hacker, is. Where you wanted to go, yes?' Taro glanced between Jarek and Nual as he spoke.

'Yes,' said Jarek, 'but that's not how transits work. You have to follow the paths—'

'I don't,' whispered Nual.

'What?' The question came out more harshly than he intended, but it had been a hell of a day and he'd just about reached the end of his endurance.

Nual's voice was stronger now. 'Xantier. That's where you wanted to go. So that's where I took us.'

'Holy fucking Christos!' Jarek's cry echoed through the ship.

CHAPTER FORTY-FIVE

Jarek would never get used to hollow-earth worlds. It came of being a planet-dweller for his first two decades; he'd managed to adjust to ships and stations where the horizon was cut off, but having the horizon wrapped around your head was just plain wrong. The residential and commercial areas of Xantier's 'ground' were edged by parkland, a green strip running around the wall at the level where the choice of views – up across the crop fields and into the 'sky' of blue-painted rock, or down onto civilisation – made for interesting conversation but uncomfortable living-space.

Most of the benches faced the habbed area, overlooking the pattern of apartments, manufactories and offices sweeping up the curve of the world below. Jarek found a seat that faced sideways, looking along a strip of green that receded into the mist obscuring the distant end-wall of the great cylindrical habitat. It wasn't a view he particularly relished, but he didn't want to appear to be paying too much attention to his immediate surroundings. He didn't want, for instance, to look like he was waiting for someone. As far as anyone watching was concerned – assuming anyone was, and he hoped they weren't – he'd just wandered out to the park for a bit of breathing space. Which was almost true: Nual and Taro were happily amusing themselves in their room, but he was glad to escape the less-than-luxurious hotel where they were staying while the repairs on the *Heart of Glass* were completed.

Thanks to the damaged grav-drive, it'd taken them three days to limp in from Xantier's beacon. Nual had spent a full day asleep and Taro hadn't been much better. They were both fine now, though Nual remained subdued. The med-bay said there was no lasting damage from their brush with raw shiftspace.

The ship hadn't fared so well. Jarek was putting himself deeper into debt than ever to get the *Heart of Glass* properly spaceworthy again. It was something of a cosmic joke to find his livelihood under threat and his business near bankruptcy at the same time as his view of the universe had been blown wide open.

He was used to thinking of space as a web of settled systems, the paths between them fixed. But that was only for humans, who used technology to travel through shiftspace. Sidhe weren't subject to the same restrictions. Nual reckoned she could transit his ship straight to any realspace point that the transit-kernel had experienced. Most of the time they'd stick to the normal method of transiting; quite aside from the considerable stress it caused Nual and Taro, bypassing beacons would attract attention from traffic control, and run the risk, however remote, of coming out of the shift too close to another ship.

But now he had a way back to Serenein.

'Mind if I sit here?'

He looked up and, though he knew the voice, for a moment he didn't recognise Bez. She'd changed her hairstyle and darkened her skin.

'Sure,' said Jarek casually.

As she sat Bez put the reader she'd been carrying down on the seat. Beneath the book Jarek glimpsed a second, smaller, box containing several dataspikes. Jarek looked over at her and said casually, 'Nice evening.'

Bez made a noncommittal noise, then said, 'Don't worry, we aren't being closely monitored, though we should still act as though this is just a random meeting between strangers.'

'Uh, right. So that's the data then?' He patted the bench, while staring out at the view.

'It is,' she sounded as excited as he'd ever heard her.

'Is it … good data?'

'It's better than good! It's fantastic.' She took a steadying breath. 'Look, the memory-core itself is in storage; you can pick it up when you leave, but it will never be readable on a normal comp. I've sorted and indexed everything for you, because otherwise you'd be lost. There's so much there! You've got three dataspikes of general info, two with details of corporations the Sidhe have got their claws into, and one 'spike of miscellaneous contacts with other groups: governments, underground Ascensionist sects, freetraders—'

'Freetraders?'

'Nothing to panic over. They just have a few people in the Alliance, which allows them to operate under freetrader cover, like the *Setting Sun* did. When you scan the files you'll find that most of those working for the Sidhe don't even realise it; they're being bullied, or blackmailed, or simply misled, and they only ever have contact with third parties. Those who do know who they're working for are either in thrall to them, or have a good reason not to want things to change.'

Jarek thought of the head of Ruanuku-*ngai* back on Kama Nui. An ally of the Sidhe, yet she'd helped him – well, sort of.

Bez continued, 'The data on contacts and operating methodologies are comprehensive – everything I could have wished for – but there is information missing.'

'Such as?'

'In order to co-ordinate as well as they do there must be a central control, rulers who stay aloof and keep an eye on the big picture. But all I found in the data was passing references to something called the Court. Does that name mean anything to you?'

'Ah, no, I've not come across it.' He was reasonably sure she wouldn't call him on his lie. He'd prefer not to withhold information from Bez, but if he admitted knowing about the Court she'd want to know how he'd found out.

'Fair enough. It's something to look out for. The other information I would've expected to find is some sort of location where the Sidhe can come together and plan. Not necessarily a planet, but perhaps a hidden station, with a beacon that's not on the charts.'

Or a mothership or six, which don't use beacons at all. 'That sounds plausible,' he said evenly.

'Well, I didn't see anything like that in the files. The info's focused towards interaction with humans, not Sidhe internal politics. But then, that's what we need to bring them down.'

'So, what are you planning to do with your copy?' asked Jarek.

'Initially, more research. I need to follow up the links, plot the patterns onto real-world situations.' She paused. 'This is big: it'll take more than the two of us. We'll have to bring in others, possibly begin to co-ordinate some sort of formal resistance.'

Jarek saw an opening. 'Yes, we'll need help. Which reminds me: I need you to sort some new IDs please.'

'You've changed your mind then? I thought you had to keep your current ID for your business.'

'I do, though a secondary one wouldn't go amiss. No, these are for the allies I mentioned before.'

Out of the corner of his eye he saw Bez nod. 'Of course. I'll need hair samples, holo-pix and full biometrics. Use the third local data-drop on the list I sent you. If you can get the necessary to me before midnight I'll get the IDs to you late tomorrow.'

'Great.' He was still uneasy at giving Bez a bio sample from a Sidhe, but Nual already had two IDs that claimed she was human, and Bez had no reason to suspect otherwise. 'Um, I can't actually pay you just now.'

'I know. We'll worry about that later.' Bez reached for her book, and made to stand. 'Anything else?'

Typically direct. Jarek wondered if she'd ever made small-talk in her life. But it was better this way: if he wasn't talking to her, he wasn't telling her any lies. 'That's it for now.'

'Then I'll leave you. Goodbye.'

He gave a friendly wave – just a casual farewell after a brief conversation with a stranger – but she didn't look back. He waited another minute or so, then scooped up the box of dataspikes and secreted them inside his jacket. He started back, choosing a different path from the one Bez had taken through the close-clipped grass and neat borders. The world's sun, actually a fusion tube running along the ceiling, was beginning to dim. He'd hate to live here in this manmade box, never able to see the stars.

He still had some misgivings about what he was taking on.

Quite aside from his justified terror of the Sidhe, this conflict had already taken him into morally grey areas. Marua was not evil, yet she colluded in something obscene ... and if she didn't, or if he stopped her, then humanity might lose its ability to travel the stars. It was complex, tricky, difficult – yes, all of that. But *things had to change*. Humanity must be free. He would do all he could to ensure that the reign of the Sidhe finally, truly, ended.

He realised he'd slipped his hand inside his jacket to touch the case containing the data from the *Setting Sun*. Finally he had a tangible weapon, a way to take the fight to his enemies. He felt a sudden elation. They might just win this war.

EPILOGUE:
A MIND OF TARNISHED GOLD

Dark now, and as silent as a shiftship ever gets.

Nual sits up against the bulkhead, Taro's head in her lap. Soon she will lie down and rest too. For now, she needs some time alone, and these days she is only truly alone when Taro is asleep.

They'll shift again tomorrow, on the latest leg of the three-week supply run that Jarek has taken on to meet the immediate demands from his debtors. He's sanguine about their financial troubles; he's been here before, and he has always managed to get through in the end. And he sees this job as a good chance for Taro to learn the ropes.

Nual glances down at her lover. Asleep, he looks so young, like the child that in many ways he still is. Yet now he is Jarek's business partner, replacing the virtual partner the databreaker created to avoid Jarek's name being associated with the new ship ID. It is a logical solution; the Sidhe know nothing of Taro.

Though it was founded in necessity, the change has delighted Taro, giving him a sense of purpose he has never had before. Nual finds she is glad for him; proud even. A strange feeling, to get pleasure from another's joy. Very un-Sidhe. Almost as alien as regret – or guilt.

She tells herself there is nothing to be gained by admitting she was the catalyst that brought the invading entity into this reality. She cannot change what she did, and telling those she trusts – and who trust her – that she caused this curse, however inadvertently, would only make them doubt her.

She has tried to look within herself, to see if she can find any taint left by the invader. Lyrian saw nothing. But since Lyrian last probed her, Nual has been unconscious in its presence, not once but twice. Did it reach inside her? And if so, what did it leave?

It appears that although her powers of foresight are growing, she remains unable to sense any hidden truths about herself.

Taro senses the pain she hides; even Jarek has an inkling of it. They assume her unease is a result of turning against her own people, but that is a human judge ment. She does not regret her choice to abandon her sisters – after all, they abandoned her. Yet she wishes with all her heart that she had not summoned what might yet turn out to be the agent of their destruction.

Jarek and Taro are assuming the contagion they encountered on Kama Nui's moon was destroyed with the Sidhe ship. They are wrong.

She is certain they have not seen the last of this agent of entropy; it has plans for the Sidhe.

And for humanity.

ACKNOWLEDGEMENTS

My thanks to the Tripod crit group for keeping me on track and to Milford class of '08 for feedback on how to start a third novel. Thanks also to my patient and thorough beta-readers, James Cooke, Emma O'Connell and Nick Moulton. Gratitude too to Dave Lermit for sexing up my brown dwarfs, to CB for the right book at the right time, to Nik Weston for detailed and invaluable advice on Islander culture and to the proper scientists who've let me pick their brains in my search for a good story, particularly Dr Dave Clements of Imperial College and Dr Mark Thompson of my old alma mater, the University of Hertford. A shout, of course, for Jo Fletcher, my editor at Gollancz, and for my agent, John Jarrold. The biggest thanks of all go, as ever, to Dave Weddell: avid reader, sensible advisor and long-suffering husband.

Jaine Fenn
December 2009

Turn the page for a sneak preview
of the new novel from Jaine Fenn

BRINGER
OF LIGHT

Coming soon from Gollancz

CHAPTER ONE

This was no way to save the universe. Taro fiddled with the sauce dispenser on the table and tried to look inconspicuous. Business like this should be going down in a dingy bar, with a scowling barkeep and shadowy booths where trigger-happy space-dogs were striking smoky deals. And here was he, in a family diner full of grizzling brats, wipe-clean surfaces and eye-searing ceiling lights. So much for the glamorous freetrader lifestyle.

His attempt to act casual was rewarded by a trickle of yellowish goo from the dispenser. He snatched his hand back, resisting the instinct to lick the sauce off his fingers. He'd made that mistake once already. Instead he wiped it on the edge of the table, warily eyeing the garish menu emblazoned across the tabletop. Now he'd finished his bowl of crunchy-deep-fried-whatever he expected he'd be asked to order more food or shove off. He probably shouldn't have eaten so fast, but even the local junk was a pleasant change from his usual diet. No matter how good a ship's reclamation unit was, shit was still shit.

When the menu display didn't light up and try to sell him more food he risked a glance at the nearest diner, who was tucking into a plate of orange rice-type-stuff using one of the oversized spoons that passed for cutlery around here. Nual had arrived a few minutes after Taro, because they didn't want anyone getting the idea she was with him – which, of course, she was, in every way.

She must have sensed him watching her because a warm spark blossomed briefly inside his head. He looked away reluctantly. Mustn't let himself get distracted.

Taro checked the door for what had to be the twentieth time. Still no sign of the contact.

The only reason they'd agreed to this meeting was credit – or rather, lack of it. Perhaps they should've refused the request from a local freight service asking if they could transport a box of 'biological samples' – but whilst they'd got themselves a paying passenger for the trip back to the shipping lanes, they had a half-empty cargo-hold, and half-empty cargo-holds made customs officers suspicious. Plus, the freight company had offered nearly as much as 'Apian Lamark' (almost certainly not his real name) was paying for his ride. Freetrading might be just what they did as cover for their *real* mission – the important, *secret* one – but if they didn't score some heavy credit soon, they wouldn't have a ship with which to carry out that mission. Jarek had still been sorting their ongoing cargo when Taro had commed him, but he'd agreed it was worth following up the request.

Rather than watch the animated woodland critters on happy drugs dancing around the walls, Taro looked out of the diner's picture window; the view was filled with flying people, locals and tourists alike in neon-bright wing-suits, swooping and gliding through whirling vortexes of multi-coloured petals against the pale mauve sky. The imaginatively named Star City sprawled up and along a ridge of pink-grey rock of the sort that was apparently common in this particular region of this particular continent on this particular world. (The world was called Hetarey, he remembered that much; he'd looked it up on the way here, but the details hadn't stuck. They didn't need to. It wasn't like they planned to be here more than a few hours.) The starport itself was on the flat top of the ridge; the other flat land, at the bottom, was for the rich coves who liked houses with flat floors and big rooms. In between, built into a slope that varied from inconvenient to impossible, were the houses of the average folks, plus all the diversions and entertainments that went with being the only place on this backwater planet where the universe came to call. The slope was extra-steep just here, and heavy-duty grav-units and massive fans had been installed at the bottom to give those without Nual and Taro's unnatural advantages a chance to fly.

When he saw movement out of the corner of his eye, Taro turned his head quickly enough to blow any pretence of being a casual customer. That *had* to be his contact. The locals had a thing about hair – everyone wore theirs long, and shaving was against their religion or something – and while that wasn't such a prime look on the men, especially combined with their preference for short trousers and stupid hats, on a good-looking woman waist-length red curls were pure blade. And this was a good-looking woman.

Even if he wasn't currently gawking at her, she'd have no trouble spotting him. Hetarey didn't see many offworlders – in a busy week, they might get two whole shiftships landing. Taro was unfeasibly tall and thin, and dressed the way he knew he looked good – big boots, tight leggings, vest top and black jacket – he had already attracted the attention of the other diners ('Eat your greens darling or you'll grow up *like that*' – not in this gravity you won't, kid). Nual had also drawn looks, though for a different reason: she was beautiful, probably the most beautiful woman they'd ever set eyes on – though Taro was biased. People looked at her like they wanted or admired her, and the same people looked at him like he was an alien who shouldn't be allowed. Which was funny, really, given he was the human one, and she was the alien.

The woman smiled and headed straight over. She had a sense of style most of the locals lacked, and she moved well. Her body wasn't bad, either, from what he could see of it under that flouncy top.

He felt a tickle of amusement in the back of his mind. He resisted the temptation to look in Nual's direction. Instead he smiled at the newcomer, and gestured to the chair opposite. She ignored the offer and instead took the seat at the end of the table, which put her immediately to Taro's right. More annoyingly, it meant she had her back to Nual.

'Thank you for coming, Medame Klirin,' he said. 'Did you, uh, want anything to drink? Or eat?'

'No. Thank you.' She tapped a dark spot on the table – so that was how you turned the damn thing off – then leant forward and gave him a sideways look. 'La, not meaning any offence, but why do we need to meet in person? Can you take the shipment? Or not?'

'We – *I* – just like to meet potential customers.' The gappy-sounding question thing was just how they spoke around here, so he added, 'Right?'

'Sirrah sanMalia, are you actually the captain of the *Heart of Glass*?'

Taro didn't need Nual to tell him what she was thinking: she was wondering why someone who'd yet to survive his second decade was making deals on interstellar cargo. 'No, I'm the junior partner. The captain is tied up elsewhere.' He spread his hands. 'If you'd got in contact sooner, I'm sure he could have met you, but at this short notice, I'm afraid you'll have to make do with me. All right?'

In the brief pause while she digested his apology he sent a silent query in Nual's direction. Her reply came through at once: *<She's doesn't mean you harm, but I can't pick up more than that from here. Try some leading questions ...>*

'Sorry,' Medame Klirin was saying, 'No offence taken, right?'

'Er, right. Really, we just wanna know more about this cargo you want us to ship. And why the sudden rush?'

She brushed back a stray strand of hair, and Taro tried not to be distracted. 'It's a matter of commercial confidentiality, see?' she said quietly. 'A delicate and perishable product which we need to get to a company in Perilat. All sealed and safe; and we'll provide the permits and specs to keep customs sweet, la. We've been watching the listings for a ship heading out to Perilat, haven't we? So when you registered that as your next destination we got in contact.'

Before Taro could query Nual her comment arrived in his head: *<I think she's lying.>*

<Can't you be sure? And which bit's a lie?> he sent back.

<No, I can't, not when I'm looking at the back of her head! I'm only getting this much because I'm in your *head when you hear her words.>*

Which was, Taro had to admit, somewhat freaky. Oops, Nual would pick that thought up too, of course.

'Are you all right?'

He realised Medame Klirin was staring at him. 'Yeah, I'm— Let's just say you were right to avoid the food here. Um, when you say "we", who d'you represent?'

'A corporate interest.'

<Definitely a lie.> This time Nual was sure.

'That's a bit vague,' said Taro. 'Can I have some details?'

'I can provide them, la.' She held up a hand to show her com; like his it was a slap-com on the back of her hand, not an implant. Jarek had advised them against getting implanted coms – not that he could afford one right now – because they could cause issues with their not-entirely-accurate-and-subject-to-future-change IDs; that she also hadn't got an implant was another point against Medame Klirin. Then again, what did he know? He was pretty new to this whole freetrading lark. Madam Klirin continued, 'Did you want details of the company at Perilat who'll eventually receive the goods? Given the confidential nature of our research, we'd rather you just dealt with their agents, you know?'

<All lies.>

Taro projected, *<You certain? She's coming over all confident and helpful.>*

<She's deceiving you. I just can't sense exactly how.>

<Fuck it, that's good enough for me.>

He realised Madame Klirin was frowning at him. 'Listen,' said Taro, with what he hoped was a sympathetic smile, 'I don't think we can take your cargo. Sorry.'

'What?' She looked understandably confused.

'It's just … maybe if the captain was here, he might think differently, but like I said, I'm the junior partner, and I really don't wanna make a bad call.'

'But he trusted you to meet me, surely he trusts your judgment … he does know you're here? Or are you acting alone?'

Taro had been in enough shit in his life to read the worst into that question. '*Yes*, Captain Reen knows I'm here; in fact, he's expecting me back at the ship soon. And he trusts my judgment, but I've decided to play it safe. Sorry to screw you around and all, but we've got a rep to maintain.'

'What are you implying here, la?' Medame Klirin said coldly.

Taro cursed his loose tongue. It wasn't like she'd actually said or done anything smoky. Then again, pissing her off – just a bit – might make her let down her guard. 'I ain't implying anything, and I ain't saying you and your people aren't prime and lovely. I've just decided not to take this job.' He made sure he had eye contact when he added, 'We can't risk potentially dangerous or dubious cargo.'

'Fine,' she said, and stood up. Her unspoken response was strong enough that he heard it in Medame Klirin's voice even though her words arrived via Nual: <*Too late for that, arsehole.*>

As she turned to go he began to stand, nerves thrumming. Nual's mental voice froze him in place: <*Stay there, but be ready in case this goes wrong!*>

He read what 'this' was and forced himself to sit back down. Even so, he felt the Angel reflexes kick in: body calm but ready for action, mind alert to danger without being impaired by fear.

Medame Klirin was making her way to the door. Nual, apparently oblivious, grabbed her tray, stood up and turned—

—and ran straight into the other woman. The tray went flying.

Taro heard Nual's embarrassed apology: 'So sorry!'

Medame Klirin tried to step back, and hit a table with her hip. Nual was fussing, trying to brush rice off the woman's top. Taro watched the woman's hands; one grasped the edge of the table she'd fallen against, the other was flailing; she wasn't going for a weapon. Around him, people were looking up, but no one was making a move.

Medame Klirin edged away from Nual slowly, like she was

slightly stunned. Finally Nual stepped back. 'I've got the worst off; are you sure you don't want a contribution towards your cleaning bill? That's such a lovely top, la, I'd hate to have ruined it.' She'd even managed to get the local speech patterns down pat, noted Taro admiringly.

'No ...' Klirin shook her head, then seemed to remember herself. 'I'm fine. Really. La, I— I should go now.'

Nual stepped aside, and at the same time projected to Taro: *<Stay here for three minutes, then meet me outside, by the upwards walkway.>*

<What are you going to do?>

<Nothing drastic: just call Jarek.>

<Why?>

<To tell him we need to get off this world as soon as possible.>